THE INHERITANCE

SHEENA KALAYIL was born in Zambia in 1970 where her parents were teachers seconded from Kerala, India. She arrived in the UK aged eighteen and, after graduating, worked all over the world. She has a doctorate in Linguistics and teaches at the University of Manchester. Her novel *The Bureau of Second Chances* won the Writers' Guild Award for Best First Novel, and was shortlisted in the Fiction category for the Edward Stanford Travel Writing Awards. She lives near Manchester with her husband and two daughters.

The Inheritance

Sheena Kalayil

Polygon

First published in Great Britain in 2018 by Polygon, an imprint of Birlinn Ltd.

Birlinn Ltd
West Newington House
10 Newington Road
Edinburgh
EH9 1QS

www.polygonbooks.co.uk

ISBN 978 1 84697 450 2
eBook ISBN 978 1 78885 041 4

British Library Cataloguing-in-Publication Data
A catalogue record for this book is available on
request from the British Library.

Typeset by Biblichor Ltd, Edinburgh
Printed in Great Britain by Clays Ltd, St Ives plc

Clouds come floating into my life,
no longer to carry rain or usher storm,
but to add colour to my sunset sky.

Stray Birds, Rabindranath Tagore

For my daughters

Part One

I

WHEN she tried to remember how it had all transpired, her memories always played out in front of her through a filter, as if viewing the past through raindrops, broken shards of glass, a thin gauze, so that, depending on why she was casting back, the two figures intersecting would be distorted, lucid or faded. There was always a beat in her head. Just as she told a tale through her feet when she danced, she could count the steps of each encounter from the beginning: rising, arcing, then falling to its end. Each memory unfolded with its own rhythm, its own tempo, distinct from the other. Later, she understood that it was her way of enclosing each moment in its own musical sheath, as one would wrap a precious jewel in cotton wool, to be unpacked and gazed at, before storing it away.

Those first days, before it all began, she took great big gulps of air, great big gulps of freedom. Once her family had taken leave of her, she knew not one person, there was not one familiar face. She devoured the newness: the clean sharpness of the air, the green against the grey of the stone buildings. Then, as the days slipped into weeks, she felt unsettled, struggling to mimic the sang-froid of her peers, pressing her books to her chest not in ease but rather so she could hold herself in, not betray her uncertainty. Did she really want to be here?

She had grown up in a house of elders. Her brother was ten years older; she was a belated surprise. Her parents were now in their sixties. She was suddenly now immersed in a world of youth, but she was determined to fit in. She was in halls, and the first month in she made dinner for the girls on her floor, which soon became a weekly tradition. And after the Christmas break she invited Julian, on whom she had had a crush since their first seminar. He was also studying anthropology, he clearly fancied himself and, if she had interpreted his signals correctly, her. The fact that he was interested in her was earth-shattering. She garnered a certain amount of respect from the other girls, but she adopted a blasé attitude which suited this new, more reckless self. Their first kiss, at the door to her bedroom, quickly became a frenzy of passion: his hands were inside her T-shirt when she drew away.

'Can't I come in?'

She pressed her face against his neck.

'It will be my first time,' she whispered. And then, 'Do you think that's weird?'

He had smiled, avuncular.

'Of course not. We can take our time.' But as he spoke she could see his mind whirring: how long would she take?

Years of yearning under the watchful eyes of her anxious parents, of terror at what her body could do, dissipated; she suddenly believed, more than anyone, in herself, and her right to make her choices. At a departmental cheese-and-wine gathering – where the more louche members of the faculty exchanged double-entendres with the more confident female students – Julian held her hand possessively, even protectively. At one point, he kissed her on the mouth, with intent, in front of the cluster of academics near the cheese board. She could feel their eyes on them – her personal tutor Ben Martin was among them – and she recoiled inwardly at Julian's bravado, while simultaneously recognising a pleasure in feeling owned, staked, desired. A validation. But only a week into their couple-hood he was sulky. He was busy, he said. He became unreasonably busy. Days passed when their schedules, once the same, could not intersect. She knew what that meant: he was waiting; she should not take too long.

The next time, he came into her room. There was the sour taste of beer on his tongue, which she found exciting in its unpleasantness. The expression in his eyes scared her slightly, but her body was alive as never before. She could only think of the moment, and when he tugged unsuccessfully at the waistband of her jeans, she drew her hands away from his neck and unbuttoned them herself, making him smile into her mouth. His voice was hoarse.

'I knew you wanted it.'

His words flicked a switch, and she took a step back in surprise, both at his tone, which had been triumphant, and her own sudden unwillingness. Perhaps it was the word 'it': harmless and frequent, but now ugly. She pushed him away, catching sight of herself in the small mirror above the washbasin in her room. Everything was now cold, and while she flinched at his assessment – that she was frigid, or a cock-tease – both epithets she was not sure she even understood, her eyes kept finding her own in the mirror, so that she was watching herself. Her pitiful performance in a disastrous ensemble.

Days later, she was returning from a seminar, down a now-familiar route: the small reading room to her left, Ben Martin's office at the end to her right. She looked out of the window down to the square below to see Julian, his arm linked through that of one of the other girls from their seminar group; as they walked, he leaned in and whispered. The girl laughed, throwing her head back, and he seized the opportunity to kiss her lips. A kiss when in motion, which the girl returned: practised, competent. The scene became blurry as her eyes filled with tears, which arrived suddenly in such copious amounts that they splashed off her chin onto her hand. Even then she knew they were tears over a job badly done rather than those of the thwarted. Even then she knew that she had found Julian's posturing unedifying but lacked the confidence to reject him. She might never get another chance, never turn another head.

She backed away from the window, bumped blindly against someone who was walking down the corridor. Two hands steadied her.

'Come in here for a bit.'

He opened the door to his office, led her inside, pulled a chair out, made her sit down. For a while he stood next to her; she could see his trousers in the corner of her eye. Then he moved away to sit at his desk, swivelling his chair slightly so that his back was not completely turned to her, and started tapping on his keyboard. She scrambled in her bag and found a used tissue crumpled into a ball at the bottom. It was quiet – there was no one else now in the corridor and the office was high enough so that there was little noise from the traffic on the street below. When she looked up, she saw that he was watching her.

'Feeling better?'

'Sorry,' she croaked, and her eyes swam with tears again.

'Anything I can help with?'

She shook her head.

'Something to do with your studies? An essay crisis?'

She shook her head again.

'I didn't think so,' he smiled. 'I only hear good things about you.'

She kept her eyes on her shoes.

'Is everyone all right back home?'

She cleared her throat.

'Yeah.'

'Where is home? Didn't you say London? Where exactly?'

'Tooting.'

'My parents live in Clapham,' he said. 'We're neighbours, relatively speaking.'

She attempted a smile.

'Just stay here until you're ready,' he said. 'To face the world.'

He turned away, started typing again. It was a small office with one wall completely lined from floor to ceiling with books, the other holding a collection of prints. There was a cream rug, shot through with crimson, thrown over the requisite blue carpeting of the department. His desk was large, extending across the width of the window. On the end, there was a photo in a frame. A woman, fair hair flying back in the wind, laughing into the lens.

She got up and said thank you, to which he mumbled not a problem, without turning round, and so she crept out, closing the door behind her.

It was a week later when she next saw him in one of the cafés around the square. He was sitting at a table with other members of the faculty, two other men and a woman. She was queuing for her coffee when she heard a voice behind her.

'Rita.'

He was smiling down at her. He had walked over, leaving his colleagues, and was standing beside her. 'How are you?'

'Fine,' she said, feeling her cheeks grow warm. 'Thank you again.'

She was unsure how to address him, shrinking from appearing over-familiar, and the sentence felt unfinished. As if reading her mind, he said, 'I think when you've been through what we've been through, we get to use first names. Call me Ben, and I'll keep calling you Rita.'

She tried to smile. 'OK.'

'Plus we've both got that London connection, right? Safety in numbers and all that.'

'Mm.'

'Good to see you on better form,' he said. He briefly touched her arm, before returning to his table. She had intended on sitting in the café, but she got a takeaway. She did not want him to think her solitude was a permanent feature. Why had he come over to her? A wave would have sufficed, or nothing even. Later, she would marvel at how much import she had given his decision to stand up and walk a few metres to where she stood.

Perhaps it was an indication of the isolation she must have been feeling at that time, the sense of not being where she should be.

And yet, there was never a moment when she did not know that he had a wife. Everyone knew that he was married. His wife was working on a thesis of some kind but had a condition that made her chronically tired. She could be seen walking around the library, but she was just as often seen in a wheelchair, being steered by Ben Martin. He was a devoted husband. The kindness he had shown her was only an extension of his nature, evidenced by the care he gave his wife. There was no call to interpret his actions in any other way. But his voice, commanding her attention, had set her heart thumping. What was more: it was nice to hear him say her name.

She felt as if she were starting again, post-Julian. She had wronged herself; her impatience to shrug off her sedate upbringing had only resulted in humiliation. Her friends at school had always teased her as prudish, berated her for not using her looks to further advantage. She had welcomed Julian's advances and so she could not blame him: he had only seen through her pretence. She decided to make up for the weeks, months actually, when her infatuation with Julian meant she had done only just enough to keep up with her studies. She returned to her books with determination to make up for her insipid attentions. She cooked dinner for a group of girlfriends she was afraid she had neglected but whom she found harboured no grudges: a reminder that Julian had taken less than a fortnight to disentangle himself from her. She joined two other girls from her floor on a Sunday trip to the beach, during which they arranged to leave halls in their second year and share a flat. And one Thursday evening she found herself waiting outside a dance studio, in the dark, in the chill wind on the other side of the city, responding to a nagging emptiness.

She had spent every Saturday over the last ten years at the Bhavan in West Kensington, where she was one of five girls who had been chosen to study Kathak. The teacher, Jayshri, had been in residence at the Kathak Kendra in Delhi and was an advocate of the Jaipur gharana – the most dramatic strand, with its intricate footwork, fast pace and swirling – until her husband uprooted her to Battersea. You will have to remember, Jayshri had said in the first lesson, to the small semicircle of awestruck little girls in front of her, that these stories we tell with our bodies are holy offerings to God. Never forget these movements take us closer to the universe and to the divine.

Kathak soon became all-consuming. Jayshri was temperamental and demanding. Extra classes sprang up. Last-minute performances were arranged, with the girls scrambling to rearrange swimming lessons, play dates and sleepovers. Rita had to forego a Saturday job and a social life, while her friends gathered boyfriends and escapades. The only males she met were the tabla and taal players: middle-aged men whom she called 'uncle'. There was no room for romance, which she could not deny she pined for. But it was because of her commitment to the Kathak training that her parents had folded at her choice of study. Their worry: what on earth did one do with a degree in anthropology? But by then they had seen how resolute she could be and had learned that even enlisting her older brother to put pressure on her, with his dark forecasts of employment difficulties, would not sway her.

The classes she now volunteered for were a twenty-minute bus ride from the university, and were led by a vivacious Colombian, Maria, who had spent a year in India training in Odissi, and who had marvelled when Rita presented herself. Maria was delighted to have the help on Saturdays – she might even offer a small stipend – but she was also organising an event. She immediately entreated Rita to commit to the next six weeks. Given her experience, Rita could choreograph her own performance: a fusion, perhaps, of Kathak and modern dance. It was not difficult to be convinced: both the classes with toddlers and children over the weekends and rehearsals for the performance lent a structure to her schedule that meant she need not worry about who she was spending time with and where.

It might have been only a few weeks after the episode in his office when, cutting through the park on the way to the library, she had seen them walking towards her. It was one of those magical spring days when the light fell through the budding green leaves of the trees. He was pushing the wheelchair, and his wife was talking. As they passed her, he had given her a quick smile and said hello, and at his words his wife had turned to her with a flash of electric-blue eyes. She was tall – even in a wheelchair it was easy to see that – with her white-blonde hair tied back in an elegant bun. But in the photograph on his desk, his wife had been bursting with vigour and energy; now she looked desiccated.

Then they were gone, past her, and she carried on, her bag bumping against her back, before she glanced back and then stepped off the path. She was out of their line of vision here, and she watched as he manoeuvred the wheelchair to a halt. And then his wife got up and walked ahead, while he remained bent under the wheelchair, probably setting a brake – she couldn't see. When he straightened up, he had a blanket in his hands. And she turned away, the next scenes playing out in her head: he would throw down the blanket, his wife would lower herself onto it, and he would fling himself down next to her.

As if fate was playing its hand more ebulliently, in one of the seminars the following week, while she was gathering her papers ready to leave, the lecturer had pronounced his name: 'Ben Martin is giving a paper on women's land rights tonight which I think you'll find interesting.' The reaction from the other students only proved to her that she did not have a monopoly on attention from Dr Martin: a few went to his office immediately to tell him they were coming that evening, showing a familiarity with him that was far from what she had acquired. If she was slightly deflated by the time she and a small group joined the sizeable gathering in a wood-panelled office overlooking the square, then she felt a delicious warmth flood through her when in the crowd he caught her eye and gave her a small wave. He clicked through his slides, spoke with no notes. She noticed several things: the dark hair on his forearms, the way his trousers fell long and straight over his legs, the set of his shoulders and his easy grace as he paced in front of his audience. How whenever his eyes rested on her they seemed to linger: this, surely her imagination. Of his topic she could remember little, even though she took notes assiduously.

The next time she saw him, he was in the library, with his wife; they had clearly had an argument. They were sitting side by side, but he was slightly turned away, browsing the pages of his book with studied nonchalance. His wife had two spots of colour on each cheek; her lips were pursed. He had raised his eyes from his book, given her a smile, as she passed them on her way to the mezzanine. When she had settled, she looked down and saw that he had been watching her, his hands folded in front of him as if in rest, as if he had decided to ignore his books and regard her at his leisure. When their eyes met, he did not break his gaze but smiled again. His wife had her head turned the other way so that the exchange of looks occurred unnoticed. She had flashed him a quick smile and then looked away. The library seemed empty, suddenly, except for the three of them.

2

A T their next scheduled meeting, his door was closed when she arrived. She could hear voices inside: his earlier meeting had overrun. She walked back a few paces and stood by the window looking down on the square. The same window from which she had spied Julian who was now, she had heard, ensconced with an American exchange student. The door opened, and he appeared alongside a professor from the faculty who continued talking even as they stood outside the office, before finally taking his leave.

'Sorry to keep you waiting.'

She waited as he cleared some piles of paper off a chair, looking around for somewhere to put them down. When he turned, his eyes swept over her briefly before he said, 'Actually, why don't we take this to a café? I could do with a coffee.'

He didn't wait for an answer but shrugged into a jacket, held the door open for her. There was only two minutes' worth of chat to be had, merely a checking-in, she knew, but did not say anything. On the street, he took her elbow briefly – no, no – directing her away from the café across the road, popular with students and faculty.

'Do you mind walking a bit? I know a nice place.'

He took long strides, and she matched them. He held the door open again. There was a wooden bar at the window where they sat and where he laid out the papers he had rolled up and stuffed into his pocket.

'What can I get you?'

She had ordered a hot chocolate, which she then regretted: it looked childish with its small mound of marshmallows spilling over the edge of the mug, arriving next to his elegant espresso. After he had ticked through some questions, made a few notes, he folded the pages, leaned back and smiled.

'So, well into your first year. How's it going?'

'Um. I think I'm doing OK.'

'You're taking a module with Marc Duplessis, aren't you? South African studies?'

She nodded.

'Are you enjoying it?'

'Yes, I am.'

There was a silence.

'What do your parents do?'

'My dad works at the hospital,' she said. 'My mum stays at home. Well, she works from home. She sews things for people.'

'Brothers and sisters?'

'One brother.'

When she didn't continue, he laughed.

'Not very chatty, are you?'

She flushed. 'I'm sorry, I don't mean to be—'

'No.' He laughed again, patting her arm briefly. 'That's not a criticism, just an observation. I've sort of put you on the spot, haven't I? I don't mean to be giving you the third degree.'

They fell silent, and he stirred his coffee before making a sweeping gesture to the streets outside.

'Is this all you wanted it to be?'

She paused, then answered honestly. 'I never thought I'd get in.'

He smiled. 'Well. You have.'

'Yes.' She tried to smile back. 'I guess I have.'

He didn't look away, but said, 'I felt the same way, you know. I felt like a fraud the first few years when I was at Oxford. It's a good feeling to have though. It shows that this means something to you.'

There was a pause.

'I enjoyed your talk,' she said.

'Oh yes, I saw you there. Thanks for coming. Although,' he leaned towards her so his shoulder momentarily bumped against hers, 'you made me slightly nervous.'

'Did I?' The question fell out of her mouth.

'Writing down everything I said so you could hold me to account later.'

'So I could try and make *sense* of it later,' she retorted without thinking, then bit her lip when he started laughing.

'Was I so opaque?'

She was mortified. 'Dr Martin—'

'Ben—'

'Please don't think—'

'Rita,' he was grinning, and he touched her hand lightly. 'Please. No need to explain.'

He returned his hand to his cup. 'It's actually good for me to hear. Next time I'll be more direct.'

She smiled weakly and cupped her hands around her mug as he sipped his coffee.

'Do you mind me asking? Were you born here?'

She shook her head. 'I was four when my parents moved over.'

He leaned back and folded his arms across his chest. 'We have that in common. Neither was I.'

A marshmallow bounced off her cup as if in reaction to his words, and she placed her teaspoon over it to hide it.

'Where were you born?' she asked.

'Harare, which was called Salisbury at the time. I came here, well, London, when I was sixteen. But you know, it makes us different people, that dislocation. I'd be a different person if I'd stayed on.'

He stopped there, but she found herself drawn into the conversation.

'How do you mean?'

He unfolded his arms, leaned against the counter, stirring his coffee.

'Well, there would be practical things. I'm sure I would have carried on playing cricket; I might even have made the national team, because I was a big fish in a small pond there. I might have married this girl I went out with who lived down the road.'

He turned and grinned, but she could see his eyes were serious.

'But it's more than that.' He tapped his spoon against his cup. 'There are subtleties. I've got used to a different type of rain. I listen to music I probably wouldn't have listened to. I would have stuck with listening to rock and punk and the like, but actually moving away meant that I started listening more to music from Africa. Do you like desert blues?' he asked suddenly.

'I don't know much about it,' she said after a pause.

'Well, I need to play you some songs sometime,' and then resuming as if he had not interrupted himself, 'I read different things, I connect with different things, laugh at different jokes.'

There was a pause as if he were about to continue, but then he straightened up.

'What about you? I know you were only little when you left, but how would you be different?'

She picked up her cup. It was empty, so she put it down again.

'Different clothes, I guess,' she started. 'Different language.' Her response was insipid and obvious in comparison to his reflections, and this only served to make her feel gauche and inept. 'I'd probably have a different hairstyle,' she heard herself saying, then seeing his eyes move in that direction she stopped, feeling self-conscious. She pushed some strands away from her eyes and cleared her throat. There was a smile playing on his lips, as if he were aware of how his attention unsettled her. Then he pushed his cup away.

'Are you enjoying yourself here?'

She nodded.

'Social life keeping you up at night?'

'Not too much.'

He narrowed his eyes. 'Don't be too serious, Rita.'

She felt her face burn as he continued. 'Come on,' he said. 'You must be batting them away.'

Then, when she remained quiet, not sure how to respond, certain that he was making fun, he said, easily, 'I'm just teasing', as if to confirm her thoughts.

'I've joined this dance group,' she blurted out.

'Really? Good for you.'

'There's an event actually,' she said. 'In a few weeks.'

She realised that she was telling him this because she wanted him to come. It was an overture – her way of modifying their acquaintance. It was clear that he was amused by her, she could see, and this made her feel safe in one way, as one does with a favourite uncle. But it also made her chafe against his interpretation of her shyness: there's more to me.

'Well, that's great,' he was saying.

She swallowed. 'It's a fundraiser actually, for a hospice . . .'

'How much are the tickets? I'll get two.' He was pulling out his wallet, slipping out some notes, which he handed to her.

'Just put them under my door if I'm not in.'

'OK,' she said.

'Good,' he said briskly. It felt like a dismissal, and so she slid off the stool.

'Well, thank you for the drink.'

'Sure.'

Now he appeared distracted, and he pulled out a newspaper she had not noticed before. She left the coffee shop with a strange sensation in her chest. She stepped out onto the street and noticed that it had been raining while they had been inside. Something made her turn her head. She glanced back hoping to meet his eyes but saw his head was bent, his hand to his ear now, speaking on the phone. If he had intended anything more than a friendly invitation, she had mistaken it. He was kind, and he needed a coffee.

That night, she searched his name. There were several Ben Martins in the world, few who had been born in Zimbabwe-then-Rhodesia. He had authored two books, was the keynote speaker at a conference in Copenhagen on Land Reform, he had studied at Corpus Christi Oxford. A few years ago, he had completed a half-marathon; a year ago, the Great North Run. Both times he had raised money for SOS Children's Villages, the first in Zimbabwe, the second in Mozambique. He had a full, complete life without any need for her.

She regretted telling him about the performance: he will have thought her a show-off, or worse, forward. And while she admitted that she wanted him to see her on the stage, that she was confident of how she appeared, she was less sure that she wanted his wife at his side to discern the schoolgirl crush on her husband. She could imagine them exchanging a knowing glance at her expense, laughing about it later that night. And while she ran through her head several times an imaginary dialogue when she would explain that there was a problem, that she had mixed up the dates/venue/charity – she even had a dream where she stood before him while she babbled on, as he shook his head with an amused smile, I don't believe you, Rita – she found herself, a few days later, slipping the tickets and loose change under his office door.

Her brother Joy, his wife Latha and their daughter Mira visited that weekend, staying in a hotel in the centre. Joy: so named because he brought joy to his beleaguered parents, baited and derided by their families for not producing a baby for several years. Joy: who seemed to have taken in the changes in his life – a new high-school, a new language and environment at age fourteen – in his stride, who now had a job in finance in the City. When he had decided to get married, he told his parents with customary self-assurance that he would arrange his own match, and within days settled on Latha, a pharmacist, whose parents owned a business in Bangalore, and who was keen to live in London. He was a perennial optimist, confident, slipping from Malayalam to English and back with an ease she never had.

That afternoon, she was their guide to the coast, where they climbed up the cliff from the beach, Mira on her father's shoulders. To her surprise, her brother had marched uphill, certain that Rita could keep pace with him, which she did, but leaving Latha puffing behind. It was as if he wanted to brandish the attributes he shared with his sister, as agile and nimble as he; to contrast his sibling with his more sedentary spouse. And when Latha, ever-confident, ever-critical, had finally appeared at the brow of the cliff, he had teased his wife, before holding out his hand to pull her up the last few steps, then pinching her cheek affectionately. It was with a frisson of Schadenfreude that Rita noticed Latha's hair in disarray, her flustered expression: a vision of times ahead, when she could be less daunted by her sister-in-law. Watching them, she remembered that before Joy had announced his intention to get married there had been a very pretty, fair-haired girl who had once come to the house and who Joy had, brazenly, in front of his parents, held around the waist. She remembered mutterings from her parents' bedroom that night, a few more visits from the girl, who then faded away, so that when Joy got married nobody mentioned his friend. A blip on his report card, just as she would be a blip on Julian's.

Aside from a tug at her heart when she felt her niece's small arms around her neck in a farewell embrace, she was glad when they left. She had spent the year before arriving at university explaining at length why she wanted to study anthropology, and there was still that incomprehension, that indulgence that belittled her decision to a whim rather than a seriously regarded selection. She would always be the youngest, she would always squirm under her sister-in-law's uncompromising scrutiny, her brother never let her finish a sentence. When they left, she waved them away and then decided to walk back from their hotel to her halls of residence.

The days were getting longer, and it was a beautiful evening. She felt the muscles in her legs stretch, and as the wind rustled through her hair she felt herself shaking off her family like cobwebs. When she walked past a bar with a group of drinkers clustered outside holding their beers, a man detached himself from the group and stepped in front of her, offering her his bottle. She hurried past, but the encounter evoked in her a strong sense of herself, her person: this body and these legs. She was alive; she held her face to the wind, feeling even the nerves in her fingertips. For some reason, as she laughed to herself at the man's predictable proposition, she imagined herself standing in front of Ben Martin, her face turned to his, his eyes looking down into hers.

3

O N the evening of the event, there was a confidence in the light, a longer dusk. When she saw him slip in, alone, to sit at the back of the hall, a hum began in her ears, so loud she feared she would not hear the music. The programme began with the youngest performers, followed by three adult-age groups. She would be giving the penultimate performance, Maria the finale. They had decided on a sequence that fused flamenco and Kathak, long regarded as cousins, and Maria had chosen a very flattering gypsy-like costume for her to wear. The rhythm was complex, so was her footwork, and there was great applause at the end. Backstage, Maria was ecstatic: Rita's contribution had helped to seal the evening's success. Afterwards, when some of the performers were gathering on the street, planning where to go for a drink, she saw that he was waiting for her outside, leaning against the wall.

She walked over to him. 'Thanks for coming.'

'My wife sends her apologies; she wasn't feeling too good.'

'I'm sorry you bought the ticket . . .'

'Don't worry about that . . .'

They had both executed the pleasantries and now fell silent. Then he squared himself in front of her.

'Rita,' he said. 'You were amazing.'

She gave a short laugh, trying to hide her delight.

'I mean,' he continued, 'I never expected you to be bad, but I never expected you to be . . .' He broke off. 'You took my breath away.'

His words were more than she had ever hoped for. A warm feeling slid into her, like molten metal.

'Rita!'

'You go,' he said, touching her arm briefly. 'Go and enjoy. You deserve it. I'll catch up with you later.'

Later that week, another departmental gathering: more cheese and wine and conversation. She was reluctant to go this time: if Julian were there, then there would be a sense of déjà-vu, only he would be proprietary with someone else. In the end she went, simply because she wondered if Ben Martin would be there, and if he were, what he would say to her. Julian was not there, Ben Martin was, sitting on the end of a table, holding a glass of wine between his knees, smiling and nodding while two other students, attractive girls with big fulsome smiles and long blonde hair, held forth. She munched on a handful of crisps, surprised at how miserable she felt. What did they talk about with him? How could they be so garrulous when he was so close, his eyes never leaving them? She could conjure a stage on which she could perform for him, but there were many others vying for his attention.

She dropped some crisps, bent to pick them up to avoid them being crushed into the carpet, when she saw a pair of shoes arrive in her vision. Straightening up, she saw it was him, having extricated himself from the two other girls, standing in front of her. He opened his mouth just as another lecturer came to stand next to him, so that his eyes held hers for a fraction of a second as if in apology before he turned to his colleague saying, 'Marc, I believe you teach Rita. She's one of my personal tutees.'

Marc Duplessis had come over to ask Rita whether she was considering taking his module the following year: she had made some very good contributions and he would be happy to see her again in his seminars. He was a warm, personable lecturer – from Durban he had told her when she first met him, before explaining that it was a city which had the largest Indian population outside of the subcontinent – but he was not Ben Martin, who now stood quietly, smiling and nodding, before he briefly touched her elbow and moved away. She was distracted for the next half hour, which she spent with Marc Duplessis and then with one of the other girls before she left, looking back to see him in serious conversation with another colleague – at least he was not being pigeonholed by another one of her peers. She was exhilarated: he had approached her, as he had done in the café. If she had not been clumsy, picking up morsels of crisps like the prig she knew she was, she might have managed a short conversation with him. He might have turned it to her performance; he might have wanted to know more about her training. She would have been capable of showing her passion for the dance, she was sure. An opportunity lost, but her heart was beating with excitement, the wife receding further into the background.

The Easter break was drawing nearer and when next she had seen him just outside his building, he had raised his hand to stop her, asked if she was going down to London for the duration, and if she were, whether she would like to join him and one of his doctoral students. He was driving down, his wife was staying on, and there would be plenty of room in the car. He didn't intend to drive beyond Clapham, but it was only half an hour on the bus across to Tooting. They were leaving in the morning and could be in London by the afternoon. The invitation seemed to come at a crest of a wave. She accepted and then spent the next few days wondering what she could get him as a thank-you present. It would be a long drive, and he would be saving her a train fare. She worried over the etiquette, not mentioning the lift to her friends for fear that they would tease her, uncover her crush. An hour spent looking online at titles classified as World Music was unproductive; from a shop on the high street she bought a box of chocolates.

In the car, some weeks later, he was in a T-shirt and jeans, unshaven, and looked younger, gave her a friendly greeting as he stowed away her rucksack in the boot. On being introduced, his doctoral student gave a peremptory grunt – she was an irritant, it was clear – and ostentatiously resumed the interrupted conversation, a discussion of his thesis, as she slid into the back seat. As they left the city, the student droned on, and Rita reached into her bag for her music player, her fingers brushing against the box of chocolates. The gift now appeared overly formal.

'So I'm saying that a Marxist reading reveals more of the reasons . . .'

'But you'll need to show that you've explored more than one angle . . .'

'Which is what I've done in chapter three . . .'

'Not nearly as rigorously as I think you need to . . .'

They carried on, and she stared out of the window. They were on the motorway, green around them. When she next tuned in, they were talking about music. He caught her eye in the rear-view mirror.

'Have you seen them, Rita?'

'Sorry?'

'Have you seen them live?'

She shook her head, embarrassed that she had not followed the conversation, worried he had expected that of her.

They made their first stop late morning, and as they queued up at a café, he said to her, 'Do you want to swap, sit up front for the next leg?'

She shook her head, 'No, I'm fine in the back, thanks.' He didn't press her, but smiled, then on reaching the counter waved her purse away and paid for her snack. When they returned to the car, she found she would again escape being called on for conversation: the other student slipped out a folder holding recordings of the demos of his band, which he played one after the other, pointing out in each the bass line he had contributed.

They stopped again at another services an hour from London, where they parted company with his student; for the rest of the journey, it would just be the two of them. After using the washroom, she found him outside, leaning against the wall, smoking. On seeing her, he waved the cigarette.

'Just the one. I'm supposed to have given up,' he said. He offered her the pack. 'Do you?'

She shook her head.

'Of course you don't. Being a dancer and all . . .'

He crossed one leg over the other, shook his head.

'I'm still not over how good you are . . .'

'I'm not that good . . .'

'You convinced me.'

She could have let it lie there, but she pushed herself.

'Perhaps,' she said, 'you don't have a good eye.'

He gave her a sideways glance, let his eyes run up and down her.

'I'll have you know,' and he blew out some smoke, 'that I have a very good eye indeed.'

He had accepted her offer. It was flirtatious, a compliment – she was sure of it. Her heart thudded against her chest. Then he turned slightly and made a gesture towards his car.

'I'm sorry it's not been much fun for you,' he said.

'I've not minded.'

'I could see.' He looked amused, as if he knew that she had been relieved by her relegation to the back seat, safe from any onus to make conversation.

She made a decision and presented the box of chocolates.

'These are for you. To thank you for the lift.'

'Well, that's sweet of you.' He straightened up and took the box from her. 'You really didn't have to.'

'Thanks for asking me along.'

'It's not a chore in any way. I wouldn't have offered . . .' spreading out his palms. 'Actually, I was looking forward to getting to know you a bit more.' He smiled, took another drag at his cigarette.

'I find you intriguing,' he said. 'You're so quiet, but you have these depths to you as well. And then,' he continued with an exaggerated flourish, 'and then when I saw how you dance . . .'

He was grinning, to temper his words, and she blushed. Yet it was what she had wanted: for him to see her, take note of her in a different light, not awkward as she always was around him.

He tucked the box under his arm. 'We'll open these in the car if you like.'

'No, keep them. They're for you.' She hesitated. 'And your wife.'

Now he blew some more smoke out, silently regarded her, his eyes slightly narrowed, as if acknowledging her parry. As she felt the colour rise again in her cheeks, wondering if she had gone too far, he reached forward around the back of her neck. She felt his fingers curl around her ponytail, and then he swished it gently into her face, as if it were the most natural thing to do: a gentle reprimand. Before she could react, he continued as if nothing had happened: 'As a mark of appreciation on my side,' he said, 'I'll let you choose the music we listen to for the rest of the drive.'

They walked back to the car. As he stamped out his cigarette, she searched the radio stations, unsure what her selection would reveal about herself. They pulled out of the services and continued on their way. He did not seem to want to talk, but hummed along to most of the tunes under his breath, never once denigrating her choice, tapping at the steering wheel. She found herself glancing at his hands: long fingers like a pianist, neatly cut nails.

They arrived at a large Victorian house in Clapham, and as he parked the car on the street in front he asked, 'Why don't you come in for a bit? Have a cup of coffee before you get on the bus?'

He was reaching across her, scrabbling around in the glove compartment to produce a large set of keys. When she had murmured her thanks, he continued, 'But once I get out of the car I'm on holiday. Don't think of me as a lecturer, all right? Just as Ben. Can you do that?'

She tried to smile. 'I'll try.'

'Good.' He smiled at her, and for a moment she thought he was reaching for her ponytail again, but he only reached behind to grab his bag from the back seat.

'Watch the step,' he muttered, the keys for the house between his teeth. He opened the door, stood aside for her to enter.

It was a wide spacious hallway, and she stepped onto the beautiful black and white tiles: a pattern that would stay with her and return to her, often, as if imprinted on her memory, a visual aide-memoire. There was a dark mahogany hall table holding a collection of photographs in thick heavy frames and on which he threw the car keys. 'Hang on.' He took her ruck-sack off her shoulder. 'I'll put this here.' He closed the door, led her down the hall and then down a short set of stairs to the kitchen. There were gleaming surfaces, large windows and a lingering smell of grilled fish. He produced a French press which he held out.

'Coffee? Or would you rather tea?'

'Coffee, please.'

There was a small washroom opposite, with shells in a glass jar balanced on the sink; the walls held framed photographs of a beach, a cliff. The mirror reflected her face, looking young and unformed. She quickly pulled her hair down from its band and brushed it, arranged it into a half-up, half-down style, tugged at her hoodie, touched some balm to her lips. He was arranging some cups on a tray when she re-entered the kitchen. His eyes briefly surveyed her hair, but he said nothing.

'It's a beautiful house,' she said.

'It is, isn't it.'

He motioned to her to follow him, and they climbed back up the stairs. The living room was a large area of wooden floors and leather sofas, rugs, two fireplaces. There were tall, wide windows, with ivory-coloured shutters, through which she could see a sloping lawn, a summer house at the end. Sunlight was streaming in, even though it had started drizzling outside. He laid the tray down on a side table and handed her a cup. She remained on her feet, taking in the room. There was one wall covered in African masks, another holding a large stretched canvas. There was a long, tall bookcase covering one wall, holding novels and large hardback collections of artists' prints.

It was a room that if she had drawn a house she wanted to live in would have fulfilled every aspect. So this was how he had grown up. He had made it sound like they might have had an upbringing in common, but she realised this was far from the truth. She stood for a few minutes looking at the titles on the bookshelves, absorbing the atmosphere, and when she turned she saw that he was watching her.

He came and stood beside her.

'These books,' she gestured to one shelf.

'My father's. Did I tell you he's a writer?'

He reached forward and slid one out.

'His most well known. He wrote it just before I left.'

'Before you left?'

He nodded. 'My parents were separated for many years. My dad stayed on in Harare while I came here with my mother. He only came to London ten years later.'

He opened the book – the spine had broken and some pages had been dislodged – then handed it to her. There was a cover featuring a dark hill of some kind, a streak of yellow, then the author's name: *John Martin*. She opened the book and glanced at the words inside.

'What's it about?'

She could feel her tongue relaxing, as if the drink he had handed her was laced with whisky. The warmth of the room, the pleasure of standing among beautiful, interesting objects, was working like a drug, as if this were not a living room but another universe, one in which she was a different person. He shifted onto his other foot.

'What's it about? Well, you have to read it and see. It's based on his childhood, growing up in Africa.'

She turned it over and looked at the blurb: *Surrounded by the open spaces of the Eastern Highlands of Rhodesia, a young white boy questions his parents' ownership of a farm* . . .

'I'll try and find you a better copy. I'm sure we'll have more.'

He let his fingers run along the shelves as he reached higher, his T-shirt riding up so that she saw a flash of stomach, a line of hair snaking down from his navel.

She averted her eyes and turned away, walked over to the painting on the opposite wall. There were five women bathing in the river, one baring her breast. A child was tied around her waist with a cloth, his fingers reaching for a nipple. The expressions of the women were haughty, and one woman, pausing as she was slipping off the cloth covering her upper body, looked directly at the viewer as if challenging this intrusion.

'Here you are.'

He came up beside her and held out a slim novel. 'Take it with you.'

'Will your parents mind?'

'They're away at the moment, but I'll tell them when they get back. They won't mind.'

'I love the painting,' she said.

'It's my brother's. One of his earliest actually,' he said. 'He's an artist.'

They stood side by side, looking at it.

'It's very good,' she ventured.

'It is,' he said, but did not continue.

'And is that you and your brother?' There was a photo on the mantelpiece above the fire: two boys, teenagers, with tousled dark hair, in a field of some kind.

He nodded. 'That was just before he went to art school.'

There was, next to that photo, another, which she did not mention: a wedding day. A slim, elegant blonde in a fetching cream-coloured dress; beside her, a tall, dark-haired, handsome groom. She blinked and turned away.

'And your father,' she asked. 'Does he still write?'

He nodded. 'He's working on something now. Not sure if it's a book or something else.'

She turned back to the painting. There was something hypnotic about the naked breast, the woman's beautiful face with its disdainful stare, the tones of her skin, the light reflecting in the river, more figures revealing themselves layer by layer. She was aware that he remained close, leaning against the wall, and when she glanced at him she realised what was making her heart beat faster: he was looking at her as if she were one of those women in the river.

'Come and sit.' He gestured to the sofa.

But she remained on her feet, placed her cup on a glass-topped table and pulled off the chunky hoodie she was wearing, leaving it on the arm of a chair. She moved further down the room, looking at the titles of the books, the painted ceramic pots; at one point she fingered a batik of some kind, pinned to a shelf. While she was inspecting the room, she could feel his eyes follow her movements, taking in her arms, her straight back and slender, supple body. She knew he was watching her, and she felt flutters in her chest, her stomach contract.

Eventually, he walked over to stand next to her. Pointing to the book in her hand, he smiled down at her and said, his tone light, 'I want a critique of that when you've finished.'

She nodded; the book slipped out of her grasp and fell onto the floor. They bent down in unison, nearly knocking heads, and he laughed, picked it up and handed it back to her. When she reached for it, he did not let go immediately, and she raised her eyes to meet his.

Time ticked by; she could not look away. His hands on the book: she could imagine them on her body. It was the moment when everything could have been different. She could have laughed and moved away, picked up some more books, and they could have engaged in a discussion over the merits of post-colonial literature, after which she would have excused herself, caught her bus. Later, she would understand: it was as if he were asking permission. That if she broke their gaze and turned away it would be the indication that he needed: that she was unwilling. As she didn't, he had received his signal.

'You're very lovely.' He spoke slowly and softly.

She opened her mouth, felt her face grow warm, and then seeing her reaction he seemed to change his mind. He smiled, but she saw his eyes were still dark with intensity. He touched her elbow lightly.

'Don't mind me,' he said. 'I don't have an English reserve.'

She was holding her breath, she realised; her mouth was dry.

'I don't mind,' she said. 'I mean, it's nice of you to say.'

He surveyed her gravely, then he reached forward and lifted some hair off her shoulder, as he had done before, but this time he kept hold of it, resting his hand briefly on her collarbone, before raising it so that the back of his fingers brushed her cheek.

'You're more than lovely,' he said with a quiet simplicity that seemed to take the words from his mouth and place them somewhere in her chest.

She did something she never would have imagined doing. She reached forward and with her fingertips touched his lips, then brought them back to touch her own: like a play-kiss, a child's game. He was quiet, looking down at her, and then his hand slipped behind her neck and he stepped in, pulling her forwards. Within seconds his mouth was against hers, the scratchiness of his chin scraping against her skin, the smell of his hair: tobacco mixed with a trace of shampoo. When he drew away, he didn't let her go but asked quietly, his eyes uncertain, do you want to leave, Rita? As she shook her head, she felt her heart pounding in her

28

chest. She opened her mouth, so that she could taste his tongue, and she let her head fall back, so that he had to move in closer.

Afterwards, all she could remember was how thrilling it was, the change in him. His strength, the way that there was an absolute certainty in what he wanted to do, where he wanted to touch her, as if he had imagined doing so before. He was breathing fast, his body pressing hard against hers, the feel of it so different from her own. His fingers were on her skin, pushing up her T-shirt, sliding her jeans down over her hips. She was being carried backwards; she was falling onto the rug. She was naked and then he was naked; his mouth was everywhere. When he entered her, she gasped and felt him stiffen against her in surprise, but she tightened her thighs against his, her fingers clutched at his hair, and then he was thrusting against her. The sunlight filtered through the shutters; the birds were singing outside.

4

S HE took the bus back to Tooting, down the Broadway, touching her lips with her fingers, reliving every minute, every breath, as the streets below her – the shops, the green spaces – all continued moving as if she was invisible, an onlooker on everyday life. She had wanted to stay on that rug with him for ever, as they were: there was no need to live any longer. When everything had stilled, he had lain with his face buried in her neck for some minutes, and she had listened to their breathing. Then he had lifted himself off her but kept his fingers on her throat, which he slid to her lips. When he leaned forward to kiss her mouth, he had said, you're so beautiful, and then in the same breath, I'm so sorry. The memory of that moment was one of the strongest she had: that along with the pleasure, there was remorse, the need for an apology. She was not sure to whom.

He gathered her clothes for her, and she pulled on her T-shirt. Looking down she could see the wetness and smears of blood on her thighs, the colours arranged as on an artist's palette. He pulled on his jeans and left the room, to return with tissues, a folded towel, which she took from him, wanting to gaze at him – this male person before her – the muscles in his arms, the breadth of his shoulders and his chest, his body tapering into his jeans. But she turned away and climbed the stairs to where he had pointed: the bathroom. She could not bring herself to step into the tub, gleaming white with brass taps, but washed herself from the sink. A messier proposition, with pools of water gathering on the floor. She mopped these up with several wads of toilet paper, flushed them away. Then she stood for a few seconds, trying to slow her breathing, her heart beating hard. When she came downstairs, she handed him the towel, which he took down to the kitchen, to a utility room, presumably to throw into the washing machine. There were so many practicalities. She felt a twinge of unease, a sense of something being done and needing to be erased.

'I should get back . . .'

'Yes, of course.'

He slung her rucksack on his shoulder, walked with her to the bus stop, his hands tucked into his pockets, then waited with her, not saying anything. When she glanced at him, he turned and smiled. Her bus arrived, and he kissed her quickly on the forehead, slipped her rucksack onto her shoulder. And then he waited on the pavement, his fingers drumming against his thigh while the other passengers boarded, until the bus pulled away from the kerb, and she looked for him. He waved goodbye.

Her mother was at home in the kitchen at the back and cried out on hearing Rita enter. 'I'll just take my bag up!' she replied in what she hoped was a jaunty, carefree voice, ran upstairs and then into her bedroom, the same bedroom she had slept in all her life, stood before her mirror. She had looked unremarkable in the guest washroom, even wan. Now her hair looked shiny, her eyes were sparkling, her lips indecently plump. She let her fingers run over her face, to make sure that she could still feel herself, then remembered his fingers, how she had let him touch her all over. She descended the stairs slowly. Her parents' ornaments and trinkets were displayed haphazardly, the wallpaper clashed with the curtains, the carpets were threadbare. The house remained unchanged, but she was.

When, later that evening, her mother called her to the phone, she heard his voice, indistinct, he was calling from somewhere noisy: sorry to renege, could you take the train back? Her heart plummeted into her stomach; her body was frozen cold. He would never speak to her again; she would be asked to leave the university. And because she was sure that if her parents' eyes met hers they would guess the truth, she tried her best to avoid looking at them, limiting her appearances over the following days. If they were hurt by her distance after weeks of absence, they did not show it, did not interrogate her, as if they were afraid of what they might uncover. Only when her teacher Jayshri called – she needed someone for a performance, there had been a drop-out due to illness – and Rita refused did her mother intervene, nonplussed. 'But she said it was a dance you were very familiar with, *mol*. Why don't you call her, find out . . . ?' She dug in her heels. There was no doubt that Jayshri would see on her face what had happened; the word *impure* would be emblazoned on her forehead. She had sinned: she had encouraged a married man, for why else would he have felt brave enough to do what he had done? A man whose wife was an invalid. This wife became now, in her thoughts, a consumptive, tragic heroine.

On Easter Sunday, she faked a stomach ache to avoid attending Mass with her parents: if she took the communion wafer it would burn a hole inside her. She spent the morning in her bed, only leaving it when the house was empty, to go and sit in her mother's sewing room, and then to walk in the park nearby. The fresh air was invigorating and outside of her parents' house she could view herself and her actions a little more dispassionately. She had chosen a university some distance away so that she would have space: space to do what? A boyfriend, a relationship: she had hoped for these. She had wanted, in effect, to confound all her friends who teased her for being too dutiful, too obedient. She had wanted to confound herself, be reassured that she was able to reveal herself, truly – be naked with a man – to dispel some of the intrigue that surrounded the act. Hadn't she spent the first term in awe of Julian, hoping she would catch his attention? When she had, she had been scared by him. You must be batting them away. And instead, the most inadvisable, inexcusable liaison, but one which had swallowed her whole.

But she could stand back from herself for long enough to see that she had never expected, except in those last few moments, for anything to happen between her and Ben Martin. Prior to feeling his body against hers, she had only ever imagined an intangible, unconsummated romance. But once she was in his arms, there had been no surprise, as if that moment had been preordained; as if her life until then had been a prelude to what was certain to happen. She could see now that he had not expected her to be so inexperienced: he would have seen her earlier in the year, with Julian, made his assumptions. The blood smeared on her thighs would have apprised him of the circumstance, added another distasteful dimension to the encounter. He had disengaged as a result; the moment had only been a moment. What did he know of her? And she of him? She could not have him: that was his message when he had phoned. He had discovered he loved his wife, his sickly wife. In sickness and in health. He did not want to betray her further. He was not cancelling a lift. He was cancelling her, erasing her as Julian had erased her.

Her brother and family arrived that afternoon, and everyone gathered around the table for the Easter meal. The smell of baked rice, spiced chicken, cardamom and cinnamon wafted from the kitchen: her mother's biriani. The meal began, her mother having slaved over several different curries, when the biriani alone would have sufficed, delighted to have the whole family together again. The room grew warmer as the dishes were opened, steam condensing on the windows. She regarded her family: her father, dignified, meticulously separating the meat from the bones; her mother perched at the end of her chair, ready to jump up at any request from her sister-in-law, who sat, solidly immovable in her chair, Mira on her knee, until the child squirmed off and then clambered onto Rita's lap. 'She missed you,' Joy said, ruffling his sister's hair and then his daughter's. After a cursory, are you feeling better? How are your studies? there were no more questions directed to Rita. As usual, she sat on the edges of the babble, allowing the talk to flow around her. On one side of the table, Joy held court – the sale of stocks and speculation on the market – their father grunting in response. She turned her head the other way: Rita's mother was nodding submissively as Latha pronounced that the chicken didn't taste quite right. She was suddenly repulsed by the stultifying, suffocating mundanity of it all. The table groaning with food, her mother nervously responding to questions, her father studiously chewing, her brother and his confidence veering into smugness. This was her life, and the life she had ahead of her. Was that why she had fallen for Ben Martin? Because he was a world away from hers?

She arrived back after the Easter break and avoided his corridor. There was no mention of her transgressions and no call to an office, no reprimand. She stopped cooking with her friends, started spending longer hours in the library, where she made copious notes while her mind remained blank. The physical action of putting pen to paper, seeing pages filled with closely lined script, in some way stifled her fears: that she was in the wrong place, that she did not fit in. The only place she did fit in were the lessons she continued to help with at the weekends, Maria commenting that she looked thinner: was she taking care of herself?

Weeks back from the break, she received an email from him, titled *Meeting*: *Hi Rita. We need to schedule a meeting. Please let me know if Wednesday at 2 p.m. suits you. Regards, Ben.* She did not reply, deleted the message, then later that day scoured her trash folder to find it again and see if there were any extra words she had not seen, any hidden message: she found none. She had two further meetings scheduled with him, but she went to neither. Then after exam week, the email, this from the student manager, saying that she was required to attend at least one meeting per term with her personal tutor, Ben Martin cc-ed in above, and records showed that she had not attended any. Could she please make her presence known to him?

When she knocked on his door, he was typing at his desk, and he rose to his feet, ushered her in and pulled out a chair, made a show of moving a pile of books, shuffling papers, and then, leaving the door ajar, sat opposite her. He was wearing his usual clothes: dark corduroys, a dark, collared shirt, the sleeves rolled up to his elbows. Her heart swooped as she remembered how his hands, now clasped between his knees, had touched her everywhere, how he had wanted to feel every inch of her body.

'You've missed a few appointments,' he said. 'And you've not replied to my emails. Did you get them?'

She nodded.

'I think you can do really well, Rita, and I don't want you to neglect your studies. Have you been keeping up with all your assignments?'

She nodded again.

'One of my colleagues mentioned that you didn't do as well in the exams as they had expected—'

'I'm trying,' she interrupted, and to her surprise her voice sounded firm. 'I'm trying my best.'

This time he did not look away.

'If,' he cleared his throat, 'if you would like to change personal tutors, I could find a way of getting someone else. I could find an excuse . . .'

She did not respond. He was silent, and she stared at her hands.

'I'm so sorry,' his voice was low. 'I don't know what came over me.'

She looked up. He had his elbows on his knees, his head bowed. He had one hand in his hair, his fingers pulling back, as if he wanted to yank his head off.

'I thought it would be best if you made your own way back here. That's why I rang. I found your parents' number on your records.'

She said nothing, and he continued: 'I want you to know that it was never my intention. When I offered you the lift? Invited you in? I never intended to . . .' His voice petered out.

Her skin felt cold, and she started to shiver.

'Are you OK?' His voice was full of concern. 'Do you want to say anything?'

She was quiet for some moments, but then took in a deep breath and spoke: 'You didn't make me do anything I didn't want to do.'

The silence between them extended, but she could not bring herself to look at him. She was still shivering. It was the hardest thing to be sitting across from him, when she could remember how warm he was, how his skin felt under her fingers, how his hands felt moving over her.

'That day when I was crying?' she started, and as if on cue the tears sprang from her eyes. He stood up quickly and closed the door, laid a hand on her shoulder briefly, then squatted in front of her. She raised her head and saw that he was watching her steadily, his eyes solemn.

'It was because of Julian. I suppose I wasn't what he wanted . . .' Her throat was tight and her voice was gargled. 'He dumped me pretty quickly—'

'Rita—'

'So don't worry. I've had practice . . .'

Her words sounded too trite for what she was trying to express. She was crying so much that she did not see him get to his feet again, turn the key. Then he was kneeling next to her, so that she was crying into his shirt, the smell of him, his chest, his arms around her. I'm so sorry, he was saying. Then, his lips against her ear, Rita, Rita, you have no idea the effect you have on me. I've not stopped thinking about you for one minute.

And then his mouth was on hers, and she could taste him again, feel his warmth.

He pulled her close, his hands moving under the jacket she was wearing, his tongue inside her mouth, so they were breathing the same air. She leaned into him, returned his kiss, it was so easy to do, and he pulled her to him, off the chair, so she was lying on top of him, so they were lying half under his desk.

She kissed him – a long, slow, searching kiss. It was just the two of them, in the dimness, behind the curtain of her hair falling around them, her body trembling with the release she felt, being back in his arms. She could feel his hands on the small of her back, pressing her to him, and then he started laughing, his body shaking against hers. You feel so good, he said, and she buried her face in his neck so he would not see her blush. He became serious, continued to stroke her. Did I hurt you, that time? he whispered, and when she shook her head, he said, I shouldn't have been so irresponsible.

It was only after a moment that she realised what he was referring to; it had not crossed her mind. She lifted her head from his neck and touched his mouth with hers, let her tongue trace his lips, and she felt his hands move, briefly clasp her breasts, before he exhaled heavily, settling them on her hips. I've not got anything with me, he whispered, and I don't want you to think I'm a brute.

She shifted slightly, and he drew his arms around her, holding her tight against him, as if they were now reunited, as if in celebration of what was meant to be.

But of course it wasn't. It wasn't meant to be, it wasn't right, it was wrong, so wrong. Her skin gathered goosebumps despite the warmth from his body, despite the clothes they were both wearing. The books in his office regarded them silently. When she gently pushed his arms away, rolled onto her knees and onto her feet, smoothing down her top, the photograph of his wife met her eyes.

'Can I see you again?' he said.

'I'm going home tomorrow,' she said. 'Summer holidays.'

'I see,' he said. But when they got to their feet and he turned to motion that he was about to unlock and open the door, he let his hand drop. 'Can I take your number then?' He looked so uncertain of her response, so unsure that she would hand over this piece of personal information, that she felt momentarily that the decision on which direction they would take rested within her control. When she nodded her head and complied, he folded the piece of notepaper and said thank you quietly, before pressing his lips briefly against hers. And then he opened the door so that she could step out. Back into the corridor, back into the real world.

5

THAT summer, she flew to India with her mother and father; the visit had been planned for many months. She had last been to Kerala three years earlier. Until then she had accompanied either both her parents or her mother alone on yearly visits: always in the summer, always upsetting any plans she had made for a holiday job or outings with friends. But when Mira was born, Latha had wanted her young sister-in-law to live with them to help with the baby, so that her career as a pharmacist would not be disrupted, and for the following three years Rita was relieved of the obligation to travel back with her parents.

The heat and the rains were familiar enough. But walking barefoot on the cool floors, hearing the rain outside, bringing with it the mix of odours – of crushed flowers and spices, of clean water and dirty water – she had stared at the land around her with amazement. For, suddenly, she felt one with it. The lushness seemed to mirror her lushness; the sensuous warmth complemented the sensuality she felt. Even the film songs which she understood just enough seemed to echo her feelings of total loss at the separation, at the ache of longing she had for Ben, for the six weeks she had been promised to her parents, here, rather than where she wanted to be: there, with him. How had she never felt this way before? And what could people see of her feelings on her face? There were the usual compliments that came rich and fast, an implicit insult to her mother: how could you produce so beautiful a daughter? Her mother, impassive, with only the set of her mouth betraying her vulnerability, was so absorbed by the complex emotions that returning to her childhood home and then her in-laws' seemed to entail, did not notice that her daughter beside her shone with a telltale lustre: lustrous hair, lustrous skin.

Her mother's parents were both dead, as were her father's, but her mother's last elderly relative, an aunt, was now old and frail; this visit was considered the last chance to pay respects. She knew her mother found the return painful; there was much rancour over her mother's barren years, only having Joy at a relatively advanced age and then, in an uncomfortable reminder of her parents' sex lives, Rita ten years later, her mother by then aged over forty. Her parents became parents again when most of their contemporaries in Kerala were looking forward to some years of rest before grandparenthood. After a visit to the small village, set on a lake with its water birds and buffalo, a few steps away from a coast dominated by soaring cliffs – where her mother appeared untouched by the beauty of the land but looked wounded, a visit during which neither of her parents translated much of what was directed at Rita in her great-aunt's thick dialect – they decamped further north: to the old rambling house that her uncle, Onachen, her father's younger brother, and only sibling of any worth, had inherited. It was the family home of his wife who had died many years ago, leaving Onachen and his daughter Seline as caretakers of the house and caregivers to Seline's ancient grandmother, Ammachi.

Seline was thirty, a graduate in chemistry, still single, having turned down the suitors her father had offered her some years back, when he was still of a mind to marry her off. That had all changed: they were now companions, business partners. As well as the house, Onachen had inherited an antique shop in Jew Town from his wife's family; Seline had sole charge of the business when her father travelled away to source the wares.

Seline had organised Rita's itinerary: 'Six weeks is too long just to follow your parents,' she said. Rita would help in the shop, and, more importantly, Onachen and Seline had a favour to ask of her. Their long-term plan was to renovate the old house and open it as a guesthouse. For this to be a success they needed to have good relationships with other similar operations, so that guests could be shared rather than competed over. One, established now for many years near the Dutch House in Fort Cochin, was owned by Onachen's friend, who was trying to entice guests to take dinner in the guesthouse by offering evening entertainment: a ruse learned from the expensive hotels on the mainland.

They wanted Rita to dance. She had to agree: it was impossible to deflect her uncle's and cousin's zeal. But some caveats: she would not wear the traditional heavy garments, as she would die in the heat. She would wear a costume not dissimilar to Maria's design. And if the first session proved too complicated – if the music system was temperamental, if it rained too much, if there was not enough room to dance, if she felt in any way that it did not work – she would not do it again. Of course, of course: her uncle, her cousin and her uncle's friend all reassured her with fervour. She remained unconvinced by their assurances, but when she and Seline made a reconnaissance mission, she was charmed by the environs. The garden was large, leafy, with fairy lights gaily decorating the edges. A thatched roof and a wide awning would protect the audience from any rain. There were tables dotted around with heavy white tablecloths and candles in old brass holders; these were lit when she arrived the first night. The small rectangular swimming pool, which acted as a buffer between the dance area and the guests, threw an ethereal light onto her that added to the atmosphere. There was an enthusiastic round of applause, whistles, after her performance, even though she had not done her best: easy to impress the uninitiated. More distracting were the comments some of the guests made – one older American man saying to his companion, sotto voce, She's a babe – and the hungry stares from the waiters. Seline sat to one side of the dance area: the chaperone.

Afterwards, the owner of the guesthouse insisted the girls drink coffee and eat a snack in his office, where they both sat primly, Seline having thrown a shawl over her young cousin's costume. It was agreed that Rita would dance three times a week for the duration of her stay: at that the owner smacked his lips, bowed and smiled obsequiously. They took their leave: thank you, Uncle. In the autorickshaw on the way back through the ancient narrow streets, they had held onto each other, in stitches at the owner's patent avoidance of what had become glaringly obvious: he would be reaping the rewards, gratis, from offering a talented, charismatic performer.

As always, she felt a closeness to her cousin: not old, not unattractive by any means, with her fine features and thick hair, but considered as such, in that unopposed, assumed way that Rita found unpalatable. It came from the same place that regarded her mother as faulty for bearing her children late. Why shouldn't Seline dance with her? she suggested. They could make up a folk dance. The guests would appreciate anything, really. But Seline had laughed heartily in response. 'Oh no,' she wiped her eyes. '*You* are what they want to see, Reetiekutty. Not someone like me,' brushing aside Rita's protests. 'No,' she continued, 'I'll be there to make sure you don't run off with one of the guests.' Then she guffawed at Rita's stricken expression. 'Come on, Reetiekutty! Don't be too serious.' It was what Ben had said. And perhaps then she could have shared with her cousin the news of her tryst, but immediately she dismissed the idea. Here, in this domain – another domain that made her who she was – what had happened, what might happen again, the pleasure she gained from something so wrong seemed wholly inexcusable, inexplicable.

Three weeks passed – halfway through. The morning had been spent with Seline in the shop, the afternoon with her mother, who was sewing a sari blouse for a neighbour: everyone it seemed was intent on occupying her every minute. It was a

42

hot night, a non-dancing night; the ceiling fan above her was ineffectual. She slept in Seline's room, but her cousin was working late on an inventory, and so she was alone. She sat up on the bed and pulled out her notebook. Before she knew it, she was writing his name and hers, in a heart, to join the others she had doodled, alongside the short phrases she had written, trying to express what she was feeling. Her mother entered, her hair in her bedtime plait hanging down one shoulder.

'Not sleeping, *mol*? *Urrannunnille*?'

She closed her notebook, shook her head. Her mother sat next to her, then leaned forward to bury her face in her daughter's hair. The gesture was familiar, loving, and her heart ached. There was such an essence of goodness in her mother, with her trusting nature that teetered on the naive; her own family had not appreciated her. How must it have felt, to be unvalued by your parents?

'Are you enjoying?' her mother asked.

She nodded.

'Thank you, *mol,* for coming with us like this. I know it's a long time, but you give me strength.'

'Are you all right, Ma?'

'Oh, you know,' her mother sighed.

She placed her hand on her mother's shoulder, bony under her touch. What did they talk about? Her mother always spoke in Malayalam; she replied in English. Most of the time their relationship consisted of being near each other, not conversing: in the kitchen, when she helped her mother with her sewing, at gatherings. It was as if they sought womb-like, silent interactions. Perhaps because a baby in the belly could not misbehave, collect misdemeanours, deceive. Her mother stroked her hair.

'Why was it such a big deal?' Rita asked. 'Why was it such a big deal that you didn't have Joychetta immediately? Why did they have to make you feel so bad?'

Her mother was silent for some time and then she spoke: 'You know, most couples have a baby within a year of marriage. Your father and I had to wait nine years before we could tell people we were expecting Joy.'

'It's none of their business . . .'

Her mother smiled. 'But it is, in a way. My parents were thinking, did we choose the right man? His parents were thinking, what's wrong with this girl? Why else get married if not to have a family?'

She said nothing, thought of the notebook under her pillow: his name, the silly love heart she had drawn.

'You didn't choose for Joychetta,' she said finally.

'Yes,' her mother nodded. 'He arranged everything himself, that's true. But that's not easy for a girl.'

She leaned her head on her mother's shoulder and felt an arm tighten around her.

'Maybe you can help me with some sewing tomorrow?' her mother said. 'I have three sari blouses to make. The lady gave it very late . . .'

She had smiled, squeezed her mother back, her heart pounding and hollow at the same time. Her mother's words hung heavy: why else get married if not to have a family? Why, she wondered, did Ben and his wife not have children? That night, she lay in bed, the notebook still under her pillow, and as much as she tried to indulge in bittersweet reminders of Ben Martin, of the illicitness but immutability of their affair, as she had done every night since he had held her and they had reconciled in his office, she found that it was her mother's face, that tortured expression, the burdened way she had comported herself in her childhood village, that filled her thoughts.

On returning another three long weeks later, she had only to wait a day before he called her. So he had kept in mind the dates she had given him, and any resolve to resist the temptation to see him again disappeared at the sound of his voice. He was glad she had enjoyed her holiday in India. Did she have many plans for the rest of the summer? He was wondering if she planned to return earlier than the start of term. He had some papers to organise, had he already mentioned them? Well, he had applied for some funds to pay for a research assistant. He knew of a room that was available at a decent rate – one of the administrators was looking for a lodger. If she agreed, perhaps he could make her lunch, over which they could discuss the details of her tasks.

Near midday, she rang the doorbell of his flat, in a converted old school near the river, to have him open the door with a happiness on his face that swept away any doubts she had harboured. He complimented her on her summer dress, kissed her on the cheek. There was no mention of the papers he needed organising, as if he had only given such a performance in case his phone was tapped. He had invited her so that he could see her again. His wife, it appeared, was away for the week visiting family in Brighton.

Standing at the island in their kitchen-living room, he stir-fried some noodles while she sat on a bar stool, feeling grown-up, feeling wooed: he wanted to feed and water her before anything else happened that afternoon. She ran her finger over the rim of her wine glass, her head becoming lighter. While they ate, he was full of questions: what was the monsoon like? This antique shop: what exactly do you sell? She described the heavy old wooden doors with their rich inlays, taken from decrepit houses and temples; the oars from the fishing boats that were in the boat races; the myriad brass vessels and door bells and prayer wheels that were collected from the remote, defunct temples in the mountains. As she spoke, he watched her lips, her eyes; he seemed ravished by her, and this made her articulate and breathless at the same time. After the meal, he filled her glass with more wine. What music did she like? The usual, she had replied, self-conscious. He said, I'll play you some tracks.

45

She moved over to the living area, where, above the mantel-piece, as in his parents' house, hung a painting: the viewer was on a rocky hill, looking down onto a valley of purples and browns and greens.

She asked, 'Is this your brother's?'

He glanced over and nodded, then added, 'It's the view from the garden of the farm my father grew up on.'

She inspected it. It did not have the wantonness of the other painting she had seen; there was a stillness to the landscape, evoking silence and warmth. She turned away and ran through the titles arranged on the shelves, just as she had perused those in his parents' house. She found his two books, lifted one off the shelf. *Daughters of Africa: Women's Stories from Post-colonial Zimbabwe*. It fell open at the acknowledgements page: *My gratitude to Patricia Zigomo-Walther for her invaluable assistance and guidance; and again to her and Michael Walther for their warm hospitality*. Some pages slipped through her fingers so she arrived at the dedication: *For Clare*. She snapped the book shut, returned it to the shelf. Next to it was another, authored by Patricia Zigomo-Walther, the strapline reading: *With an introduction by Ben Martin*. She was looking into his life, his achievements, none of which involved her. Her involvement: here, now, this living room, the bedroom down the short hall to the right.

He was ready, he said, bade her to sit on the sofa, which she did, curling her legs up beside her, while he knelt on the rug in front of his music player, his hair falling onto his forehead, his T-shirt stretched across his chest. He played several songs, drumming a beat on his leg: tunes she could not recognise. Erratic melodies and complex harmonies, mellow voices singing in languages she could not understand. He might have been trying to mask a nervousness: she saw how he fumbled once, putting in a CD. It was your birthday when you were in India, wasn't it? he said at one point, studying an album sleeve. I remember from your student records. Nineteen years old. Then, without lifting his eyes, I'm thirty-eight, a miserable old bastard. It was her moment for a clever riposte, but she said, without thinking, you're not miserable. He threw his head back and laughed with too much mirth for what her inadvertent wit deserved. But when he stopped, a smile on his lips, his eyes were grave. And then he stood up and walked to where she was sitting and knelt again, in front of her, his hands sliding up her calves, over her knees, under her dress and onto her thighs, leaned forward and kissed her on the mouth, as she felt her whole body tingle under his touch. When he stood up, he slipped an arm under her legs, picked her up and carried her to the bedroom.

This time was different. He undressed her slowly, unhooking clasps and opening buttons as if savouring every revelation. And when he pulled his own T-shirt off, and she placed her hands on his chest, slid them across to his armpits, then down to meet together at his navel, she felt him shudder beneath her fingers, as if he had waited in agony for her touch. Other than their own breathing, a silence around them, the room bathed in a muted light. Making her lie back and pulling a pillow under her hips, his head between her thighs; finding that she needed to bite down on her hand so she would not be too loud. Other differences: a condom, a whole bed to spread over, their limbs finding every corner. And then the feeling that he could not get close enough, his weight crushing her, hooking an arm under one of her knees, so that she could feel his every movement, feel him in every cell of her body. A sheet to cover themselves after, his arms pulling her close to his chest.

By late evening the August sunshine was still pouring in through the tall windows and they were still lying in the bed: in his bedroom, the marital bedroom. She had tried not to notice the many details of his wife: the pots of moisturiser on the dressing table, the flashes of colour from the wardrobe. In the bathroom which she had asked to use earlier, she had opened the medicine cabinet to see an array of vitamins and pills, hair accessories, dental floss. She lay on her side in their bed, trying to still the tenseness that was building in her if she let her eyes dart around the room. He seemed relaxed, guiltless, even when this was surely the ultimate in treachery.

'Should I return your dad's book?' she asked. Easier to speak of his father than it was to acknowledge that he had a present, a wife. He didn't answer at first; he was rummaging under the bed and produced a cigarette.

'Just the one,' he said. Then, 'No, keep it. They were glad to hear that I'd lent it to a conscientious young mind.' After which he turned to smile at her. 'Did you enjoy it?'

'I've not finished it,' she said.

'Finding it hard going?' He laughed. 'I won't pretend that my dear old dad writes the most accessible stuff. But his heart was in the right place when he wrote it.'

'And is that what it was like? When you were growing up?'

He shook his head.

'Not really. It's my dad's childhood, growing up on a farm. Mine was pretty tame. Very white, very middle-class, very bohemian. My parents are a couple of old hippies. That was probably the only point of note. We lived near the university where my dad was a lecturer. I went to the school where my mum taught geography, played cricket. Pretty normal stuff.'

He stubbed his cigarette out and turned abruptly to face her, pulling her closer. Then, 'Tell me more about yourself. You're very secretive.'

'I'm not.' She buried her face in the warmth of his cheek.

'You are. Like some kind of honey-trap.' He laughed, kissing her ear. 'Are you? Are you a spy, sent to seduce me?'

She shook her head, her heart soaring at the word seduce, so grown up, endowing her with powers she did not know she had. She felt his hands in her hair, gently tugging, then on her back, the base of her spine.

'What's your favourite book, Rita? Answer immediately, your first thought.'

'*Jane Eyre.*'

'Ah. Yes.' He leaned back on the pillow. 'The wife in the attic.'

There was a silence as they both contemplated his words. He turned to her. 'I don't have an attic, by the way.'

She smiled weakly. 'But you have a wife.'

He nodded, holding her eyes.

'How long have you been married?'

He tilted his head as if he needed to calculate. 'Nearly eight years.' Then, 'But we've been together for much longer.'

'How did you meet?'

'As undergrads at Oxford. At a party.'

She turned over; the tears had arrived unannounced and were hot, bitter, splashing onto the pillow.

'Rita.' He stroked her shoulder, touched his lips to her skin, then he moved in closer, slipping his arm around her.

'What do you want from me? Why are you doing this?'

He was silent for a long time.

'What is happening,' he said, his voice light, 'all of this. It's all me. You have nothing to feel bad about. Nothing to feel responsible for. It's all me.'

She did not respond, and he continued: 'I'm not without a conscience, but anything I say will sound patronising. That it's complicated. That it's not as simple as you imagine.'

'Is it because she's unwell?'

'No.'

'Do you sleep with her?'

'You mean?'

'Do you do all this stuff?'

He was silent for some heartbeats.

'Not for some time,' he said eventually.

'Do you still love her?'

He sighed; she felt his breath against her ear.

'The honest answer is probably yes, but in a very different way from when we got married or when we were going out.' He paused. 'We've known each other a long time.'

She let her shoulders slump, pressed her nose against the pillow.

'What are you feeling, Rita? Speak to me,' he whispered.

'Jealous,' she whispered back.

'Jealous?' He sounded genuinely surprised.

'I'll never be able to catch up,' she whispered again.

His body relaxed against hers; she felt the hair on his chest tickle her back.

'There's no need,' he whispered again. Then he kissed her shoulder and then her neck, his hands slipping onto her breasts. She was already turning back, her mouth yearning. 'Really no need to be jealous.'

'I love you.' She was helpless, could not stop the words or the gulp that accompanied them.

He was laughing, kissing her mouth, and she struggled, angry at his reaction, her hands in fists now against his chest, pushing him away. But he held her tighter, whispered, 'No, sorry, don't be offended. I'm just so very happy.'

After, she had used the bathroom again, this time refusing to succumb to her curiosity, open any more drawers. He had said before she left the bed, what you said, I feel it too. I just didn't want to do a vice versa. And it's something more: I want to dive into you, into your depths, protect you. And then he had caught himself, smiled ruefully: probably from men like me. She had mulled over his words, uncertain whether she had these depths he referred to, staring at her reflection in the mirror. Back in the bedroom, she had gone to stand by the window, look down at the street below and the river beyond, wrapped in a towel, knowing his eyes were on her. She turned to look at him as the shutter clicked.

'Couldn't resist,' he said. 'You just look so incredibly lovely with your hair all around you like that. That tan line on your shoulder.' But when he saw the flicker of uncertainty in her eyes, he tossed the camera aside. 'To capture the moment is all,' he said. 'To capture you.'

Later, she said she needed to leave, and he agreed, adding apologetically that the neighbours and the woman who owned the art gallery across the road were the sort to take note of comings and goings. A reminder that what happened between them needed to be hidden. He would walk her to the bus stop, he said, and when she slipped on her jacket at his front door, he straightened her collar, did up the buttons as if she were a child, as if he were wrapping a gift. Then he leaned forward, his thumb caressing the back of her neck and kissed her. Will you come back tomorrow? he whispered. That he felt he needed to ask her when she wanted to spend every waking and sleeping minute with him filled her heart. She nodded, and he kissed her lips again before they left the building. They arranged that they would meet the next morning in the departmental reading room: he would show her the documents that needed filing. The light was just beginning to fade. It was already nine o'clock: they had spent hours together. When they reached the bus stop, he whispered, See you tomorrow.

6

THE next morning she arrived at the reading room where the other assistant, a postgrad she recognised, had already started working on the papers. 'Matt, this is Rita. I thought you could do with the help.' Matt clearly thought otherwise but agreed to explain the filing system and colour-coded dots they needed to stick on each document.

'Right,' he said, his eyes fleetingly meeting hers. Her heart stopped, as, it seemed, did his. 'I'll leave you both to it then.'

That afternoon, at his flat by the river, after he answered the door, he pulled her inside to kiss her, carrying her backwards, tumbling onto the sofa, then off the sofa onto the rug.

'Forgive me,' he said, as he was lifting off her top. 'I just can't keep my hands off you.'

She kissed his mouth, her hands around his neck, revelling in the taste of him: 'Forgiven.'

There were four more glorious days, when they became reckless, and, despite earlier reservations, she stayed over each night. Evenings when he did not only undress her; he unwrapped her. He was, it seemed, interested in everything about her, and a seasoned inquisitor; she talked about herself more and more, in answer to his queries. Her family, her mother's sewing trade, growing up in London. Her cousin Seline, the stories of Kathak, her teacher Jayshri. The first night she stayed, he ran a bath: he wanted to share it with her. In the tub, she leaned back against his chest, between his legs, as he wet her hair and shoulders with a sponge, lathered her back and then her breasts and before long he was inside her again, his mouth searching round for hers, water splashing out onto the floor. She would wake to find his hand touching a part of her as he slept, as if to ensure she would stay near him, that she was real. Mornings were filled with the anguish of knowing that she would need to wait another eight hours before she could lie in his arms again. The first morning she took the earliest bus back, to let herself into the room she was renting, quietly, before her landlady woke. The next, more careless behaviour: he drove her back, dropping her on the street in front of her landlady's building. And with each encounter she became more adept at pretending that he was a widower of sorts, ignoring the photos, not many to be said, of him and his wife. She padded around their flat in bare feet, wearing one of his shirts.

Then his wife returned. He had warned her the previous night, driving her back to her lodgings just before midnight in a heavy silence, kissing her briefly on the lips with a sad smile: Good night, Rita. He still came into the reading room first thing in the morning, to greet Matt and her, but he avoided her eyes. It was the end, and she pined for him; each evening she was tempted to take herself back to his flat by the river. But she didn't, and there was silence for five days: no messages, no invitations. She could only imagine the scenario back in his flat: would his wife have returned, unsuspecting, and they had fallen back into the routine they must have shared for decades? Perhaps he had lied: perhaps he took his wife to bed, picking her up at the front door as he had done her, made love to her to assuage any feelings of guilt on his part or any fragments of suspicion she might have. How could she, a mere girl, displace a woman he had known since he was the age she was now, and a beautiful, accomplished woman at that?

The time passed inexorably slowly; every minute was spent wondering whether he would arrive suddenly at her side: come with me, Rita. In the evenings, she returned to her lodgings where the landlady, who had taken her in on Ben's request, expressed some surprise that she was staying in so much when the weather was so fine and, Rita knew, in contrast to her prolonged absences the previous week. On the Thursday afternoon, as she and Matt were packing away the boxes of files, he came into the reading room.

'Thanks, both, it's looking great,' he said. 'Let me invite you for a coffee – my treat.'

She had expected Matt to accept – he had fuelled himself on a steady supply of coffee and pastries everyday – but for some reason he shook his head. 'No, I'm good, thanks, Ben. I'll be off now, actually,' then glanced briefly at Rita. There was something in his eyes when he then returned them to Ben – a lack of surprise, or even a hint of disapproval – but she pushed the thought out of her head.

They went to the café on the square, as if both were thinking: better to be in plain sight. On entering, inevitably, they bumped into one of his colleagues, who was leaving, her young daughter in tow, and who offered them her table. She was a professor in the department but now, in a blouse and jeans, holding her daughter by the hand, appeared as human and harried as any mother.

Ben introduced her casually, 'Do you know Rita? She's working with Matt on my filing . . .'

'Lucky you,' was her response. 'How did you get any money out of the department?'

'It helps if you're on the committee for funding allocations . . .'

'I'll remember that,' she laughed, then, turning to Rita, 'Don't let Ben take advantage of you.'

Her words hovered above them uneasily as they ordered drinks and sat down. He said little as they sat opposite each other. She sipped her tea; he did not touch his espresso. He looked tired.

'Well, you and Matt will be done by tomorrow,' he said finally, 'And then will you hang on until the semester begins?'

'I've not decided,' she said. 'I was thinking of getting in touch with Maria to see if she needed any help.'

'Well, the room's available for another fortnight or so.'

'Yeah, I suppose . . .'

'I appreciate you coming back up to help out . . .'

She said nothing, only shrugged her shoulders, unwilling suddenly to keep up the pretence.

After some silence, he spoke again, in a low voice: 'I've missed you . . .'

She looked up into his eyes boring into hers and tried to steady her voice. 'Vice versa,' she said, and he smiled weakly in acknowledgement.

Then, 'You and Matt seem to have got on very well.'

She glanced at him. 'I suppose.'

They fell silent, and the silence began to unnerve her; the tears she was holding in were pressing at her eyelids. She was about to get up, leave − she had no wish for him to see her crying again − when he spoke again, quietly. 'If I seem a little off,' he said, 'it's because it's unbearable to be sitting here and not touching you. And I am stupidly, hellishly jealous of Matt.'

She looked at him in surprise; his eyes were full of suffering. He looked down at the table, his fingers casually toying with a packet of sugar, belying the emotion in his voice. She smiled at his words, at their ridiculousness, and somehow he seemed to know that, because he raised his eyes and met hers. For the first time she could feel what it would be like, when time had passed and she was more assured of herself, when she would and he would regard each other as equals. He gave her a slight smile in response, as if he was seeing into the same future, then he tore the sugar packet in half, spilling the sugar into the saucer of his cup. They watched as the granules rained down, as if he had made an ad hoc egg-timer for the next exchange.

She spoke quietly. 'Does your wife know?'

He shook his head. 'No. Pretending everything is all right has become a particular skill of mine.'

The bitterness in his voice took her unawares.

'I don't like seeing you like this,' she whispered. 'I don't like seeing you all sad . . .'

He smiled again, another smile which did not reach his eyes. 'Well, take it as proof then,' he said, 'of how much you mean to me, Rita.'

His words made her ache; her chest felt tight. 'Ben,' she said, then drew in a breath so she could continue, 'what do you want to do?'

'I want to be alone with you,' he said. Then, as if catching himself, he said, 'If you don't mind being alone with me, that is. Can we go somewhere else?'

They left the café, and as if they were both persons with a singular lack of imagination, they returned to his office. The corridors were by then conveniently still. But when they entered his room, he suddenly seemed unsure of how to begin. He sat down in his chair, pulling one over for her, in a parody of their previous meetings. When she did not take the chair but pushed it aside and sat in his lap, he looked grateful to her for making the first move.

She held his face between her hands and kissed him, as she felt his fingers unbuttoning her shirt, her skin melting at his touch. Then he ducked his head lower and put his mouth on her breast, his tongue slipping inside her brassiere, and as much as this gave her pleasure, she also realised that he was seeking a consolation, something she, her body, was able to give him. And the words that they shared afterwards, when she held him to her, as if she were the older and wiser, were as much part of why she loved him, why she could not consider not seeing him, not hearing his voice, whatever was at stake.

Back in the room she was renting, on the phone to her parents to whom she had invented a reason for her early return, she could barely concentrate, still absorbed by the memory of their love-making. His wife had returned, but they would continue: now she knew. Her whole body was still tingling, longing for the next moment.

But that next moment never arrived. The following day, there was an accident. A few lines in the paper reported that the car Ben Martin was driving, with his wife Clare Armstrong in the passenger seat, had swerved out of control, off the road. Both occupants were killed instantly.

In the last year of primary school, when she was not yet eleven years old, she had once, when walking home from school, been invited to a friend's house. She was allowed to walk home from school, but she was forbidden from making unvetted detours. She knew, however, that her mother was only due to arrive back later in the evening, so no one need know the actual time she had returned. But as soon as she entered her friend's house she knew she had made a terrible mistake: there was an air in the house that she could not define. The house, like all her friends' houses, was much better decorated than her own home. There was a vase of flowers in the hallway, the furniture matched, there were pictures on the wall arranged at pre-determined spaces: all unlike her eclectic home. It was not for lack of comfort that she felt uneasy; there was a sadness that pervaded the house.

The mother gave her a bright smile, and the father was home, another difference: her own father only ever appeared in time for a late dinner. Both parents had an air of forced gaiety on her arrival, exclaiming that her visit was fortuitous. They had a film the girls might want to watch. And her friend seemed changed too, her face become diffuse. There was no other way to describe it, like each of her features did not like the other. The sadness followed them into her friend's bedroom, which was, conversely, bright, full of books, a patchwork counterpane, cuddly toys arranged on the bed. She left later that evening, only to hear the following week that her friend had moved away, changed schools.

It was only years later, when she and the girl found themselves in the same class in high school, by then aged fifteen, that her friend revealed that her brother, three years her junior had died from leukaemia earlier in the year that Rita had paid an impromptu visit. Her parents, it appeared, never fully recovered themselves – her friend's words – and divorced a year later. Her mother had remarried, and she had a baby half-brother. She liked her stepfather, and her father had a new girlfriend. She was fine, her friend said, but Rita could only remember that sense she had of a deep disquiet, of not understanding her own intuition. The thought of the dead little brother upset her, the fact that her friend had spent all those interim years coping with that loss.

And when she had left her friend's house that evening, she had found that Joy was home for some reason – an unannounced appearance. He did not know that Rita was late coming home; he did not know of her subterfuge. But the fear that when later her mother arrived he would let slip of when he had seen her tainted the whole evening. On reuniting with her friend and learning of her little brother, she realised her own fears those years ago of being discovered for her detour were despicably trivial – nothing compared to the sorrow of a family who had lost a child.

Now, more than eight years later, she had the same sense of entering a sad house. But this time the sadness penetrated the buildings that she passed like damp, soaked the streets like rain. She walked as if she was always going to return home to find someone who would be able to divulge her misdeed. But it was more than a misdeed, more than a transgression. Willing everyone who saw her, who had seen her, whether by his side or not: Don't say anything. And again, her role – the disobedient child, the student-mistress – was diminished, belittled, when held up against the loss of two people. One a wife, a daughter, a sister. The other a husband, a son, a brother.

Part Two

7

THE back garden – where the tables were laid out and where the small band, friends of the groom's brother, were playing – was dusty. The guests had trampled over the patch of lawn, which was why the bride had insisted that they go back inside the house to take the photographs. But in each room they encountered groups of women taking shade from the heat, some in tight-fitting dresses which hugged ample bosoms, others with turbans and long brightly patterned kaftans, West African style. Only in the back, where it seemed the family stored the heaviest items of furniture, did they find an empty bedroom. The dark wood sucked out the light. He pulled the curtains as far back as he could, thinking that he would have to persuade the couple to take some more shots outside, which he did, in the bright glow before the sun began its descent.

Then, at the insistence of the mother of the bride, he joined the party, found himself handed a bottle of beer and a plate of rice cooked with tomatoes, grilled chicken and salad. He ate standing up, the beer in the crook of his elbow, while Gildo, whose half-sister was the bride, and who was by now quite drunk, pontificated. Taking his leave, he was kissed goodbye by several women, their lips impossibly soft against his cheeks, their hair and skin scented with rich emollients. The bride was the most tentative, worried about disarranging her elaborate hairdo, but in compensation she pressed herself against him in gratitude. Gildo accompanied him to the van, where he locked his gear in the back, declining any assistance from his now maudlin and emotional friend.

He drove back to the city, the windows rolled down, his head full of memories which returned with the soft kisses of the sweet-smelling women: of the city in southern Africa, on the shores of the Indian Ocean, where he and Gildo had formed their friendship. Of the power cuts and the heavy heat, followed by the deluge of rain. It was a lifetime ago, but this day was as hot as many he remembered. Before long the back of his shirt and the seat of his trousers were sticking to his body. It would rain later, but for now the air was oppressive. The sky was charcoal-coloured with delicate, lacy-white clouds, these becoming less distinct as he neared Lisbon, where the air was fresher, a breeze blowing in from the river. It was dark, a liquid oily black, when he parked his van on the street in front of his building, then half-jogged further up the road and flagged a taxi to Lucie's apartment. He let himself in and skipped up the stairs to the upper level, calling her name. She was in the bedroom, slipping bracelets over her wrists, and gave him an exasperated look when he appeared at the doorway.

'You're late,' she said.

'I'll take five minutes to get ready. You go ahead and I'll follow.'

She nodded, pressing her lips together. He pulled her into his arms and kissed her, but she tried to push him away, wrinkling her nose: 'You smell.'

He laughed, tightening his hold of her. 'After good honest toil.'

She leaned against him, but there was still a tightly coiled feel to her body.

'What's wrong?

She gave a shrug, seemed ready to brush him off, but then she said quietly, 'I had an argument with Josef.'

He massaged her shoulders, and as she drew closer he could feel both her breath on his neck and in his stomach the familiar knot of irritation at the boy.

'You're a wonderful mother . . .'

She left, soothed, trailing behind the scent of her perfume and of her guilty emotions. Her son now lived with his father in Cologne, sent back because he had been caught selling weed at the private international school where Lucie taught German, grudgingly, so that her son could enrol for subsidised fees. Now he was gone, four months had passed, and Lucie was still in Lisbon and still teaching; the small jewellery-making trade that was her passion was not as dependable a source of income.

He showered quickly and dressed – he always left a set of clothes in her flat – and arrived at the gallery, where she along with two others were exhibiting their jewellery. If no crowd had gathered, she would be a bundle of agony behind the serene facade. But as he ran up the steps he could hear a buzz and, thankfully, he had difficulty pushing open the door: there were at least forty people squeezed into the small interior. Lucie was in deep conversation with a woman whom he vaguely recognised. He relaxed: Lucie would feel vindicated; he could have a drink and enjoy himself. In the next fifteen minutes, he devoured two samosas and drank two glasses of the chilled vinho verde he normally avoided. He perched himself on a windowsill, behind a couple who were speaking animatedly in German: no doubt members of her set. When his phone vibrated against his chest, he lifted it out of his pocket and checked the caller. Because it was his father, he went into the corridor.

'Dad, how are you?'

'Are you alone, son?'

'No, I'm at one of Lucie's things.'

The signal was weak; he could hear his own words echoed back at him. He glanced at his watch. 'Let me call you back in an hour.'

'We may not be able to talk then . . .'

Something in his father's voice made him pause. He was due to visit his parents in London in September, but he realised, guiltily, he had also made tentative arrangements with Lucie to visit her son in Germany first. Perhaps his mother had got wind of this. He waited, but his father did not speak. The silence extended beyond what was normal.

'Dad? Is everything all right?'

'Francois . . .'

Now his father's voice broke, and to his shock he heard him crying: short gasps, high-pitched sobs. He walked down the corridor and out onto the fire escape. The night was black on this side of the building. There were no streets below, only an untidy patch of scrubland, a ditch and then, in the distance, some modern blocks of flats. Behind him he could still hear the babble from the exhibition.

'Is Mum all right? Dad?'

He heard his words repeated to him *Is Mum all right? Dad?*, his voice distorted, so that he sounded plaintive, like a small boy.

'It's Ben. Francois, Ben's dead.'

Then silence. He continued holding the handset to his ear. He stood on the platform that jutted out from the building, firmly anchored with concrete and steel posts; he would not plunge to the depths below. But his spirit had left his body and was watching him from above: in the midst of the dark, the light from his phone a pinprick in the blackness. Then the feeling passed, his spirit returned, he could feel his flesh and bones, a film of sweat making his palm slippery. His father was speaking again.

'Your mother is lying down. She can't speak. We've just been with the police. Ben is dead, Francois. And Clare too.'

'God, how . . . ?'

'She was with him in the car. It was an accident.'

For some reason, this was what made him jerk backwards. He had expected that his father would say: she has killed him. Why he felt that he would never understand, despite rehashing the exchange countless times over the following months.

He said, 'I'll catch a flight tomorrow. Don't worry. I'll be there.'

'We can talk more when you're here.'

When Lucie found him later, he was still gripping the railings. He told her, briefly, and then watched with a peculiar detached interest as she clapped her hand to her mouth. He was already feeling his spirit leave his body again, hardly hearing her voice, a hum in his head. He wanted to return to his flat, to be alone, but Lucie was already making excuses, leading him back to her car. They would drive to his flat and pack, but he would stay the night at hers, she insisted. She would drive him to the airport in the morning. The practicalities – booking a flight, leaving Lucie a short list of people she needed to contact in the morning to explain his absence for the near future – excused him from dwelling on the facts. When they finally turned in past midnight, there were only four hours to pass, as he lay on her bed – dreamless, sleepless – before they needed to get up again. She drove him to the airport and he caught a flight, during which the notes of a song played over and over in his head, drowning out the sounds of ordinary life around him. On the way to the airport he had said, you didn't tell me about Josef. What happened? But she had shaken her head, then reached across and laid a hand on his. He glanced at her. She looked older somehow from the previous night: the lines extending from her nose to the corner of her lips seemed more defined. He lifted her hand to his lips, which made her smile – a small sad smile – then she drew it away and laid it on the steering wheel.

His parents had shrunk; Clare's parents held pinched expressions. The police had no reason to involve themselves: an accident, and not uncommon on that particular curve in the road. The driver, Ben, might have been reaching for the radio, in a split-second might have strayed off the road. A sudden loss of control, an unusually steep verge: the car had been thrown into the air. Death would have been quick: this was the comfort the families could salvage from the tragedy. And the couple had died together. Neither would have to deal with bereavement, widow- or widower-hood. But no one voiced what they might have been thinking: it was also a complete erasure. With no grieving partner, the relationship, the romantic relationship, would be elided. Neither would visit the other's grave, excavate memories, tell anecdotes. The privacy that every couple guarded would ensure that several events of import to the lovers would be buried alongside their bodies.

He stood behind his mother, ran his fingers back and forth over the headrest of the armchair in which she was sitting, stroking the coarse material as if a pet. The room was small, with windows that looked over the hospital car park. The grief room. On a low table, there were a set of leaflets, fanning out, with a telephone number. No need to feel alone – speak to someone about your loss. The parents communicated in low murmurs. It felt awkward for them all to be closeted together. Neither family had, in reality, drawn very close; there were no grandchildren to knit them together. And each would have heard one side of the sorry tale: the long period of waiting for a pregnancy to take, then the IVF cycles – two failures – followed by Clare's elusive, lengthy illness. Only then had it been revealed to his parents that the extraordinary fatigue was a recurrence from her late teens. And over the years, each family tiptoed around discussions of Clare's debilitated state. He knew his mother was mystified by how the condition had entrenched itself. Its provenance was perhaps less baffling: Ben and Clare had agonised over the absence of a much-desired pregnancy. And then the IVF, usually so successful, had also failed. It was as if science was giving its own verdict on their compatibility.

Their families were now negative mirror images of each other. In one, there were two sons, the younger now dead; in the other, two daughters, the younger now dead. Unlike his family however, where the two sons were unmistakeably siblings,

Clare's older sister bore little resemblance to his sister-in-law. With dark lanky hair and the fatigue of a mother-of-three etched on her face, Jane was bulky, unlike her tall, thin, Norse-goddess sister Clare. His eyes were drawn to her: she had an easy, slovenly sexiness. Pushing her hair back, she revealed an armpit which sprouted some dark hairs. Then she turned and caught his eye.

'They're wondering whether to have a joint funeral.'

'It's hard to think about that now,' he said. Then, 'Are you OK?'

Her eyes filled with sudden tears.

'Not really,' she said, in a matter-of-fact tone. 'It's surreal. It just feels like it's the most unexpected thing that could ever have happened to us.'

She wiped her nose, unselfconsciously, on the back of her hand.

'I've always had imaginary nightmare scenarios, about being in a room like this, because of one of my parents or, God forbid, one of my children. But Clare? And not just her but Ben as well?'

He nodded but did not respond. What was he feeling? Grief? He would not call it that, not yet. Rather, a disbelief. He was standing here with these people, with years ahead, acres of time, when there would be a different calibration to his life.

After the hospital, the families congregated again in the flat in the old schoolhouse near the river. The area had been disused but was now sought after. Across the road was an art gallery; the river was lined with cafés. The police locksmith had been called out, replaced the old lock and left a set of keys with a neighbour. The neighbour appeared on cue, with a grave face: such a tragedy. They all waited as Clare's father turned the key in the lock, and then the men stood aside as if it were the women who would have the most courage for the first sight of the now abandoned home. They sat in the living room, speaking in whispers, each older couple sitting close, occupying a sofa each.

Above the mantelpiece hung his wedding present to the couple. Ben had instantly recognised the view, exclaimed with pleasure: a reminder of their holidays as children. Clare, he feared, had seen the present as more one-sided: a memory from which she was excluded. At one point, Jane moved to the kitchen, started boiling the kettle and opening cupboards, and he joined her. They produced six cups of tea, found a packet of biscuits which they laid on a plate. At another point, his mother rose to her feet and moved to the study that Ben and Clare had shared, a desk at either end. Through the door he saw her fingering the papers on Ben's desk, looking at the stack of books on the floor next to it. He went to join her, and she turned and gave him a tired smile, then leaned against him, so that he put his arm around her, kissed her forehead.

'There'll be things in the fridge, Francois,' she said, her voice low. 'Things that will go off.'

'I'll have a look in a minute,' he said.

'It's like time has stopped still, isn't it,' she said. 'Whenever we visited, things looked more orderly, like they'd tidied up for us. But it really feels like we're unexpected guests, doesn't it. Like we've intruded on something.'

He could think of nothing to say, but tightened his hold of her. Later, as the parents continued to talk in quiet voices, making arrangements to keep in touch regarding the funeral, he found the books his brother had written on the shelf in the living room and slipped them into his bag before they all left the flat, closing the door after them.

8

THE decision was made to have a joint funeral, if for no other reason than that both families were based in or near London. Perhaps among a crowded church the stilted relationship between the families would also go unobserved; any uneasiness his parents felt – neither of their sons bestowing grandchildren on them – would be less patent. He returned to London with his parents on the train. His mother fussed about finding a table, so they traipsed through three carriages before they could settle into their seats. There were, after a few stops, not many people around them, only two young women with headphones. His mother closed her eyes and his father folded his arms. They stared out of the window. The countryside was green and gentle.

'Do you remember when your Aunt Bea invited us to her fiftieth birthday celebration?' His father was speaking quietly, almost to himself. 'For some reason, we were held up just outside Bulawayo and we ended up waiting an hour nearly. As we sat there, this family went by, a family like ours. A man, his wife and their two boys. They were carrying bags of something on their heads, flour or maize-meal or something. And as we watched, the woman stumbled and fell. She fell flat, she must have tripped over something, but she was thrown headlong, her bundle went flying. Do you know,' now his father turned his eyes to his, 'I had never ever seen any of those women that I had seen all my days, all through my life, I'd never seen any of them fall or falter? I'd imagined them to be invincible.'

His heart was heavy when he regarded his father: the familiar strong jaw and brush of hair, but the shoulders looking less square, more bent.

He spoke: 'Was the woman all right?'

His father made a face.

'I would have thought the man would help his wife to her feet. I saw his lips moving, but he didn't offer a hand to lift her up. Perhaps his bundle was so heavy he didn't dare set it down. She picked herself up, the woman, dusted down her skirts, then retrieved her bundle, arranged it back on her head.' He smiled at his son. 'And they carried on walking, and I never saw them again.'

Beside him his mother whimpered, as if she were having a bad dream.

'Your mother,' his father said. 'I'm not sure how she will bear this . . .'

'I'll stay around, Dad. For as long as you need me.'

It was the first time he had stayed alone with his parents for many years. And just as he had found part of himself in Ben's flat, he found himself facing his painting in his parents' living room. The scene depicted the river that ran near to where he had spent his honeymoon: in Xai Xai, up the coast from Maputo, in a small beach hut, where he and Paula had made love and been bitten by mosquitoes with equal frequency and ferocity. The decision to stay in that beach hut had scandalised Paula's parents, who had imagined that their daughter would spend her honeymoon in Europe or at least at a resort in Mauritius: more befitting a Portuguese heiress. He stared at the image; the women in the river returned his gaze. Years ago, he thought. The man who had painted these strokes was now seventeen years older, and yet the women looked as fresh and luscious as when they had first appeared under his brush.

Over the days that followed, his parents kept him gentle company. For a large part of the day each retreated into their own space: his father to his writing shed, his mother to her

70

kitchen. He found a route that suited for his morning run, a field where he could do his sit-ups, with a football goalpost for his pull-ups. The rest of the day was spent doing odd jobs for his mother, who appeared to have an unwarranted concern about every fused lightbulb, squeaky door, every crack in the wall or loose floorboard in the house. The spare room needed a fresh coat of paint; the loft needed reorganising. The funeral loomed. Neither family was religious, but Clare's family had decided that the funeral should be held in the church in the village near Brighton where she had grown up.

A humid day, with a light drizzle; the church was full. Lucie flew in, held his hand during the service. But he found himself watching Jane, in the pew across from him, wearing a not unattractive but too-short dress, which exposed a series of light-blue veins on the backs of her thighs. She stood next to her husband, who had his arm around his wife's shoulder; in each hand she held a child. The third was nowhere to be seen, deemed, perhaps, too young for the solemnity of the affair. Clare's mother sniffed discreetly into a handkerchief, once turning to a grandchild and patting their head and then catching the living daughter's eye to exchange a glance. Beside him his own mother stood ramrod straight; his father beside her, his hands crossed in front. Was it easier? Having grandchildren? Knowing that your genetic material would extend to the next generation? He tried to focus, so that he could revisit the years he had shared with Ben, arrange them into some kind of chronology. But his thoughts were scattered, and he felt a mounting tiredness, almost boredom. What he craved most was to be alone, back in his flat in Lisbon.

After the service, he and his father stood together in the churchyard, while his mother and Lucie left with a cousin. A man close to his father's age approached them.

'Mr Martin? I'm Michael Walther,' then he looked around, 'my wife has just stepped out. I'll introduce you in a moment. My condolences.'

'Thanks for coming.'

'I'm not sure you remember, but we met several times in Harare. I was at the German Consulate, and you held some talks at the Goethe Institute . . .'

His father held out his hand again, and the man took it.

'I remember. The Thomas Mann season . . .'

'That's right.'

'And how is the Goethe doing?'

'I'm no longer in the foreign service,' was the reply. 'I'm a consultant for a bank now, in the City.'

'Well, I have fond memories.' His father made a gesture. 'My son Francois.'

'Yes.' The man shook his hand. 'Actually, we met some years ago, at one of your exhibitions in London. I am an admirer of your work. We bought a couple a few years back.'

'That's kind of you.'

Then they fell silent.

'You're probably wondering,' he said, 'how I know Ben. He was a friend of my wife, and he stayed with us when he was in Harare.' He broke off. 'Here she is. Can I introduce you to Patricia?'

She was much younger than her husband: elegant in a black trouser suit, her hair arranged in braids, then in a loose bun at the base of her neck.

'Mr Martin,' her voice was low. 'My sincere condolences.'

Then she turned to him. 'You must be Francois,' she said. 'Ben spoke of you often. We bought two of your paintings some years ago . . .'

'Your husband said.' He took her hand.

'It's such a shock,' she said. 'He had so much life left. And Clare too . . .'

'Will you come for some refreshments?' his father asked.

'No,' the husband said. 'Forgive us, but we need to be back in London by this evening.'

His wife spoke again. 'I was in touch with Ben just last month . . .' Her eyes filled with tears. 'He was such a good friend, and he helped me so much with my studies. You can be proud of him.'

Walther took his wife's arm and there was a pause after which he said, 'I'm afraid we need to go. Please pass our condolences to your wife and Clare's family.'

'Of course.'

There was a car waiting outside the church. A driver stepped out and opened the door.

'A nice couple,' his father said, and he mumbled his agreement. He watched the wife as she slipped into the car, her husband following. And then she turned around, to raise her hand in a goodbye. He recognised her name: he had seen it in Ben's books. A person who would have her own memories of his brother.

He was suddenly exhausted, an exhaustion which did not leave him during the small gathering at Clare's family's house. Lucie had already left by then, and he stood next to his mother while an uncle of Clare's made a brief speech, reminding the gathering that theirs had been a young love which grew with time, and that they had died together, Ben in the driving seat – a comment which might have been an indication that the Armstrong family would not let his parents forget that fact. At least they had each other in the after-life, if there was such a thing. The uncle stood down to an awkward murmur of thanks. His mother trembled beside him, her face blanched of any colour. He squeezed her arm, to reassure her; she smiled up at him, the weariness in her eyes making his throat tighten, before moving away to speak with Clare's mother.

While the conversations around him continued, he noticed a photograph on the mantelpiece. Ben and Clare at their wedding. Ben in a smart suit. Clare impeccable, with gleaming shoulders. He moved to the mantelpiece and picked it up. A warm summer's day, in the same village they were in now. Eight years ago: he was still living in Mozambique but beginning to feel restless. At the time, he was living with Gertrude, who was a medic for a Swedish NGO based in Maputo, and she had accompanied him to the wedding before paying a visit to her family in Stockholm. He remembered that she had laughed loudest at the short speech he had given at the reception, something that he was eternally grateful for and which added a few more months to their relationship. Then, later, he had danced with Clare, and she had accepted his compliment on her dress with her usual, perturbing, lack of expression.

But looking at the photo, his strongest memory was not of that day itself. On one of the days preceding the ceremony, he had taken his brother out for a drink. It was a hot summer's day, muggy and close. Ben had suggested a bar on the Common. They had, he remembered, talked about *Disgrace*. Ben had just started working at the university, a cause for some amusing comparisons. They had turned the conversation to their father, who had at one point been considered a great white African novelist, in the same league as Coetzee and Lessing. And then they moved on, with a fondness for nostalgia that seemed to arise because Ben's wedding spelled the start of a new era: real adulthood. For the first time as men, they turned to their childhoods, set, as Ben described, in a past that could not be recreated.

'It's something Clare and I always argue about,' Ben was saying. 'She keeps reminding me the country didn't disappear in a puff of smoke, that I've been back so many times. She thinks I've become obsessed with my childhood. But it's different for her, when she goes back to Brighton. I mean we were born in a country that had a different *name*. And going back like I do now, it's not the same. It's not just political changes, new inventions, me being older. There's a whole new quality to the light.' This with a sheepish smile.

74

'Well,' he had replied, 'we lived in quite a privileged bubble, didn't we? That must be different now.'

His brother shook his head. 'You'd be surprised. There's still a lot of separateness. Not just on colour lines. Political lines, rich–poor, Shona–Ndebele.' Then he paused. 'What do you miss most, Fran? Or do you miss it at all? You've hardly been back . . .'

That was true. He had left to study in Cape Town and moved on to Mozambique. Visits back to Zimbabwe became ever rarer; the family would congregate in London. He realised that little in his life now resembled his childhood in Harare, as if, rather than being an idyllic, loving period, it was a time he objected to.

'I don't know.' He racked his brain, then threw his hands up. 'Matilda.'

They both burst out laughing. She had been a round woman, permanently in knitted cap and grey dress that ended at her knees, shiny stocky legs on show, comfortable black shoes. She smelled reassuringly of carbolic soap, had a powerful hug that they sought when as young boys they ran to her after a fall or a slight. She seemed to be everywhere, all the time. In the mornings: laying out their shoes and bags for school. When they were older: their cricket kit. She would open the door to the little annex she lived in reprovingly when, in his teens, he returned home late, sniffing the air pointedly for traces of alcohol or worse. In the evenings she would be in the kitchen preparing dinner, except at weekends when their mother cooked. Any other time she was in the garden: weeding, raking, planting, watering.

Ben was grinning. 'It's hard to tell people over here about her. That we had a servant. It just sounds so awful, doesn't it?'

'Well,' he shrugged, glanced around him, at the drinkers gathering nearby, at the woman in a short red dress, who returned his look.

'You know I went to see Peter a few years ago?'
'Who?'

'Peter. Matilda's son. You remember him, don't you?'

'Vaguely.'

'What do you mean "vaguely"? I thought you guys were friends!'

The tone of his brother's voice had made his head snap back. His brother looked angry; his fingers around his beer were clenched.

'Jesus, Ben.' He held his bottle to his lips, then put it down.

There was a silence. Of course he remembered Peter; he had just been distracted by the woman. His brother's annoyance and the reminder of Matilda's son were unsettling. Peter. The whole 'friendship' had been another sop for the guilt felt by his liberal parents: they did not want their sons to grow up feeling superior. They had encouraged Francois to play with Peter; he had been too conscious of their reasons to tell them that Peter had a cruel, even unhinged streak, stamping on an injured bird once, then smearing the blood on his wrists with wonder. The afternoons when Peter came to visit were not his favourite: he was scared of him. Ben was still looking at him, and so he felt the need to elaborate.

'I'm not sure we could say we were friends. He was Matilda's son, for one thing. I was the son of the boss.'

His brother did not say anything but waited as if he wanted him to carry on.

He continued, beginning to feel uneasy with how he needed to justify his behaviour. 'He was some years older than me, right? By the time you left, I was what, eighteen? Peter would have been in his twenties, a grown man. He wouldn't have been visiting with Matilda. Even then I hadn't seen him for years . . .'

Ben was tapping a beat on his bottle now, his shoulders hunched.

'Well, I have. I saw him about two years ago.'

'Did you? Did you ever tell me? I don't remember . . .'

'I'm sure I did. Maybe I didn't. Anyway, I found out he was married and was living in Mutare. I met him and his wife. He has three kids now.'

'Well.' He took a swig from his bottle, unsure what to say. 'It's nice you looked him up.'

'Yeah.' Then relenting, 'Well, I was out there speaking to people for my research, you know? So it made sense that I should look him up.'

'What about Matilda?

'Peter said she died a year after Dad left.'

'Really?' Now he felt a shock, a sadness that made his body still. 'She can't have been old . . .'

He had stared down at his hands, surprised at how the news had made him cold all of a sudden. When he looked up, he saw Ben was watching him again, with an expression that grated, as if satisfied with the reaction that had been wrought from him. And because he felt then that he had been challenged and failed that challenge, because he felt that his brother had set him on the back foot, and possibly because when he met his brother's future wife she had left him cold, another memory surfaced, as it often did in times such as this. The memory of the girlfriend his brother had had aged sixteen: Denise.

She was the daughter of one of their neighbours – more than a year older than Ben, a few months younger than he. Her father was a property developer, at the time submitting plans for an upmarket cluster of shops near the racecourse further north in the suburbs. They had known each other since early childhood, and because they were more similar in age, it was she and Francois who were friends. Ben was the younger brother tagging along. Later she was sent to an exclusive girls' school and their interactions became less frequent. But they were neighbours, and the parents of each family threw them together. For some years, aged fourteen and on, he had to stay in the house with her after school until her mother returned from work: the parents did not want her to be left alone with the male servants. She was cut from a mould: a girl from a wealthy family. A girl whose affluence and access to luxuries would be untouched by the changing fortunes of the country around them. His wife Paula had come from the same mould. But his resentment, as he grew older, of an upbringing which robbed him of any of the romantic credentials that he felt an artist should have, had forced him to affect a disdain for Denise, pretend to regard her as a pampered princess. Those afternoons he spent as her chaperone were often an occasion for Denise to parade before him, with her long golden waves of hair, the soft swell of her breasts, while he sat outwardly indifferent but inwardly rigid with longing. For, in truth, he had loved her, loved her desperately for many years without having the nerve to approach her, fearful of jeopardising their friendship, but more fearful that if she were to rebuff him he would never recover from that humiliation.

Ben had not suffered from any such anxieties, and with a characteristic fearlessness had asked her out, cheekily, even when he was younger than Denise. He had spent the tenure of that relationship, many months, in a never-mentioned torture, intensely jealous of his younger brother, coveting the girlfriend who should have, he knew, been his. He was sure that she had been Ben's first, that his brother had lost his virginity to her, when it was he, Francois, who loved her. And when Ben had told him, carelessly, that they had split up, that he was going to London anyway, he had felt a rage at his brother and his casual conquest. Now, years later, the hurt returned. He took a long draught of his beer. The woman in the red dress was gone; Ben's eyes were wandering over the crowd around them.

He spoke in as offhand a way as he could manage: 'And have you looked up anyone else when you've been back?'

'Like?'

'Denise?'

'Denise . . .'

His brother had raised his eyebrows. Then he shook his head. 'No, no I haven't. She's still out there. I heard she was working for her father.'

'And you haven't looked her up?'

His brother shrugged. 'She's married, got a kid I heard. Why would I?'

There had been some kind of altercation at a table nearby which had distracted and amused them: at one point they had both caught the other's eye and grinned. But when things had calmed and they returned their attention to their own drinks, Ben had resumed their dissection of things past: 'And do you still keep in touch with Paula?' quickly adding, 'I'm not criticising you, Fran, I'm just wondering.'

He shook his head. 'Not really.' Then, as if to further absolve himself, 'She remarried not long after our divorce came through.'

Ben was tapping at his bottle again. 'What happened between you two?'

He was silent for some time, unwilling to reveal how little he understood of the whole affair. How love seeped out, as if their marriage was made of a fine mesh, unable to hold the concoction of their personalities, their differing ambitions.

He took a sip of his beer. 'We got married too young was the first thing.'

His brother remained looking at him, expectantly.

He laid his bottle down. 'And one day I just realised that we were only meant to be together for a finite period of time.' He stopped. 'I can't explain it very well . . .'

'You've done all right.'

'Well,' he said, after a pause. 'I'm probably over-romanticising things. There were lots of other reasons why we didn't work. I wasn't making any money at the time, for one. And her mother hated me . . .'

He could understand the interest his brother was showing. Even though Ben loved Clare and Clare loved Ben, it was perfectly natural before embarking on such a commitment to have some nerves. But then his brother spoke, his voice become almost disinterested: 'We just drop people, don't we, people like us? We just move through life picking them up and then leaving them behind.'

His brother's words bit into him. Did he think he had just dropped Paula?

He stirred. 'I think that's a bit harsh. We've moved around, that's what it is. It's natural that you can't keep in touch with everyone you knew.'

Ben fell silent, a pulse beating in his jaw. When he spoke again, his voice was low: 'That feeling that there is something bigger going on all around you, but that you're missing it, not quite getting it. Not quite being part of anything. I've never lost that feeling.'

'Hey.' He punched his brother playfully on the shoulder. 'You've forgotten how to drink, Ben. This is supposed to be a celebration . . .'

'No.' Ben's eyes had locked on his. Then his brother had grabbed his forearm, squeezed it. 'Fran, this is great, talking like this with you. It's been so long.'

Had that been an apology, an extending of the olive branch, as if Ben had intuited that he had opened old wounds?

From two tousled-haired boys they had become men. When had they as brothers decided to diverge? As young children and young teenagers they had done everything together: it made logistics more convenient for their mother. She had also treated them as one entity: 'Boys, time for school,' 'Boys, cricket kit to Matilda, please,' 'Boys, your father wants you in the garden.' Francois had possibly been a shade more aligned with their father than Ben, but only a shade. Both parents treated their sons with commendable equality. Then his mother made the decision to leave for 'home': England. Francois refused to join her as she had wished; he had been already accepted at Michaelis in

Cape Town. Ben had accompanied their mother and ended up at Oxford.

And for the six months previous to all that, there had been the girlfriend, Denise. Someone who seemed to have been sent by the gods in order for the brothers to form their own separate selves. To see each other as men, stake their own territories, their own areas for success. What would have happened if he had one day taken Denise aside, declared his love and lust for her, reminded her that his brother – two years younger – could not make up for the experience in matters carnal that he had garnered in that significant head start? What would have happened if, having bared his soul to her, she had chosen Ben after all? He had never told his brother about his feelings for Denise; he should have, and put the saga to bed. She was an ordinary girl from a wealthy family, a category into which nearly all the women he had slept with fell into. He was relieved to feel only a light interest in Clare, so worried had he been that some genetic defect would ensure that he lusted after his brother's loves There had only been that one time, and then soon after his brother had left with his mother, to London. When he and his father had visited them, that first Christmas, there was already a shift: childhood had ended.

He closed his eyes, leaned against the mantelpiece, the murmur of people behind him a backdrop for the ache in his chest as he thought of his brother. They had been formed in one country and had each embarked on life in another. But they would forever have the memories of those shared first years, before they were scattered like leaves thrown up into the wind, to hover for years before fluttering back down. To settle together again, slightly misaligned, never the same as before.

9

IF he had stayed married to Paula he might have offered his parents grandchildren, a thought that nagged at him over the days that followed the funeral, after he left London and returned to his flat. Lisbon was now home. From his spell in Cape Town, he had been absorbed into Mozambique, then slunk away to Portugal: a journey in reverse of the explorers from centuries previous. When all of his immediate family had removed themselves to Europe, he had felt an urge to move closer to them. But he had no wish to live in London: he needed a geographical buffer. Gildo had helped with his decision, having moved to Portugal himself the year before. Those first few months after he arrived, he walked all over the city, climbing its steep hills, listening to the snatches of conversation and scouring the faces of its residents for reminders of its colonial past. It was his first time to live in Europe, aged thirty-four, and if he had not fallen in love with the city, facing out to the Atlantic, turning its back on the petty obsessions of other neighbours, he might not have stayed.

It was decided Lucie would visit her son, as arranged, but alone. After dropping her off at the airport, he returned to his flat feeling lighter and annoyed with himself for feeling that way. With Lucie now gone, he could wallow, but wallow with a purpose. He had brought back his brother's books; it was his intention to read them. He was ashamed that he had never read beyond the first pages, and he felt that finally immersing himself in what Ben had spent years working on would be a fitting homage to his younger brother. He phoned the college and arranged another week to himself before he resumed his commitments, which at that time of the year were few. He called Gildo, who immediately entreated him to stay with them, but he refused. More than anything he needed to be alone, devote his thoughts to Ben. He threw open all the French doors in his flat. The sun was still high and strong, and so he lay naked on his bed, picked up the first of Ben's books, his doctoral thesis, published eleven years previous. *My Land, My People: Land Reform Through a Human Rights Perspective in Zimbabwe.* The dedication read: *To my parents, John and Louise Martin*, and on the acknowledgements page, the final sentence: *And to Clare Armstrong: for keeping my feet on the ground, wherever I am.* His eyes moved up to the other people mentioned: himself, Patricia Zigomo, then four lines' worth of names. Samuel Mutadzwi, Annie De Houwer, Johnson Gomo: the list continued. Who were these people? His own life seemed monkish in comparison. He read and re-read the names, then skated through the contents page, to the introduction, which he must have read at some stage, although he had no recollection.

The possession of land – who it belongs to, who has a right to cultivate, build, inherit – is a defining trope of human history. That the land belongs to the peoples who occupy it on discovery is itself a concept that eludes careful dissection. For without discovery, without contention, possession becomes an abstract rather than a hard-fought accomplishment. When Ian Smith unilaterally declared Rhodesia's independence from Britain, he unleashed a long and protracted war for sovereignty between the two main tribes – the Shona and the Matabele – culminating in the Lancaster House Agreement. Solomon Moyo, Zimbabwean poet, writes on this treatise in his anthology, *Seeds of Struggle*: 'Before the ink had dried/ the seeds of a new nation had been germinated/ nurtured/ thrived/ only to await a cutting down/ and burning/ a scorched earth policy/ *in utero*.' What Moyo alludes to is the essential flaw in the agreement. That is, the assumption that a transfer of power to the indigenous peoples would automatically ensure the protection of the most vulnerable members of society, women and children. On Robert Mugabe's ascendance to power . . .

He turned the pages, browsed through the long bibliography at the end, then picked up the other book, *Daughters of Africa*. This, dedicated to Clare.

Ten narratives of women from varied socio-economic backgrounds in the southern African country of Zimbabwe illustrate the realities of life in the post-colonial state. I use the women's life stories to illustrate the complexity of discussions related to land tenure and land titling; discussions that have divided gender specialists. While some believe that customary law is entrenched beyond removal and that reform, thus, has to focus on making those same laws stronger and fairer, others reject these decisions, arguing that change will only manifest itself if women's land and property rights are enshrined in statutory law.

The latter position, considered by many as an act of rebellion, conversely, persists with the convention that statutory law is paramount. Others, however, point to the complexities involved with land rights, and beg further considerations of pre-colonial aspirations and individuals' rights. All these perspectives, when viewed together present the most persuasive argument: that women's rights are interwoven with land appropriation; that before and after colonisation, continuing after independence and beyond, actors in land reform have located the struggle in the women's struggle. Gender non-specialists all ascribe to the need for statutory commitment, but the stories these women tell reveal less emancipation and equality than is afforded by rule of law.

Lydia, introduced in Chapter 3, is a solicitor specialising in women's issues, and based in Harare, the capital city of Zimbabwe. She completed a law degree at the University of Zimbabwe, and followed this with a Master's from Witwatersrand University in South Africa. She has achieved academic and professional success even though her parents, because of their involvement in the freedom struggle in the sixties and seventies, did not have as much education. She speaks of their very traditional, conservative values, and the fact that her female cousins living in rural areas of Zimbabwe have been disinherited from the land . . .

His brother had given the women pseudonyms, and their ages ranged from late twenties to seventies. But for each woman, the picture he had in his head was Matilda. He thumbed through, skimming through chapter after chapter, and then turned the book over and stared at the back cover. *Martin writes with clarity and honesty on contentious issues of rights and rites, bringing a much-needed perspective on the human rights issue underlying land reform and appropriation.* The inside of the back cover read: *Born in Zimbabwe, then Rhodesia, Ben Martin completed his doctorate at Corpus Christi College Oxford and is on the editorial board of The African Studies Journal.* His brother, the Africanist. Ben would not have seen every painting he had completed, but he might well have seen a greater proportion of his oeuvre than he, Francois, had seen of his younger brother's.

The sun had begun its descent, and the breeze had begun cooling his flat. He placed the two books one on top of the other onto his chest. They weighed little – as much as a bag of sugar, as much as a newborn baby – and he remained as he was until the sun disappeared and darkness gathered around him.

A month later his father called to let him know that their wills had been read and that Ben and Clare had, in the event of no children being issued, left their flat and its contents to their siblings. His father had already spoken with the Armstrongs. Neither set of parents particularly wished to be involved in any dealings and both would be grateful if their children shouldered that responsibility. He received this news and made arrangements to fly over with some discomfiture. His property portfolio was increasing exponentially, as if a malicious reward for his brother and sister-in-law's childlessness. He was already named on the deeds of his parents' large house in Clapham; as an appetiser, he now had half a share in another flat in a desirable location. Both investments outstripped the value of his flat in Lisbon and made his savings and income from a fairly successful career even less precarious. At least Clare's sister did not have the embarrassment of being a sole beneficiary: there were her children, who would presumably benefit from their aunt's generosity. Before he left Lisbon, Patricia Zigomo-Walther called; his mother had given her his number. Her voice was comforting, with its low tone, the familiar accent. She was sorry she had not spoken properly to him at the funeral. There was a gathering in her London pied-à-terre, she said, on the day that he was flying in: a gathering of what she described as her Zim Circle. Most of them had known Ben and would like to meet him.

He had always avoided such expat enclaves. In Cape Town there had been the usual disgruntled old Rhodesians, clinging on to an older time, bemoaning the imminent changes arriving in South Africa. He had shunned any clique made of people with similar backgrounds to him, causing some consternation, but he was determined to stretch himself out of the cocoon he had grown up in. The result: he fell in love with Paula, another art student with a privileged background, but one who had the added piquancy of being faulty in her English and whose home was Maputo, war-torn and dilapidated, an injured beauty of a city.

There were fifteen or so people crowded into the living room at Patricia's flat, most of whom were academics specialising in sub-Saharan Africa; only a few were transplanted Zimbabweans or South Africans. Standing out, sitting in a chair wearing a maroon jumper, a woollen cap on her head, feet pushed into ill-fitting shoes, sat a woman: Patricia's older sister,

Tsitsi, just off the plane from Harare. Much older sister, he thought, shaking her hand. Her eyes avoided his, and she held the crook of her elbow: both actions sending a shockwave of memory through him. She said something to Patricia, her eyes focused on her knees, and Patricia replied in kind in Shona, then turned to him: 'She met Ben a few times and wants to convey her condolences.' He turned back to her – Thank you – and the sister nodded. She looked uncomfortable, out of place in the smart modern flat.

Patricia was moving around the room with a plate of snacks, throwing her head back to laugh when the only young man in the room, his dreadlocks tucked into an oversized green and yellow cap, said something to her in Shona. Then she turned, saw him watching her and approached to refill his glass. She whispered, 'Will you stay, please? When the others go?'

As he nodded and she moved away, he heard a voice by his elbow: 'Francois? Annie De Houwer. Ben and I worked on a project together.'

'I recognise your name.'

'And I recognise yours. You were at Michaelis, weren't you? My sister Ella studied there as well. Not sure if you crossed paths?'

She had a fine pair of green eyes, and he smiled into them. 'I hope we didn't. I was a bit of a prick in my youth.'

She laughed out loud, exposing a row of white teeth.

'I'm sure you weren't. Or if you were, wasn't everyone?' Then she closed her mouth, her lips turned down in disappointment. 'I'm on my way out, I'm afraid. I've been here for ages.' She placed a hand on his arm. 'But tell me, how are you? I'm just devastated. And how are your parents?'

'They're well, considering. It's been very strange.'

She made a sympathetic noise, scanning the room, 'Well, I'd say most of us in here knew Ben in some capacity.'

'That's nice.'

'Keep in touch, will you? Patricia is a brilliant social organiser. She'll make sure we meet again.'

He was approached by several people whose names he recognised, as if characters from Ben's books were coming to life. All spoke warmly of his brother. When the guests took their leave, Patricia's sister rose to her feet, heavy-bottomed, and the two sisters went together to another room. Patricia reappeared alone a few moments later. 'My sister is just having a rest before we get the train to Maidenhead.' She straightened her skirt and then raised her face to his. 'So, how are you?'

'It's strange,' he said, 'and hard for my parents.'

She nodded, made a clucking sound. 'I should have invited them as well. I will. But I wanted to see you alone.' She smiled. 'Would you like a coffee?'

As she went to the kitchenette, he moved to the other end of the living area, where a sofa was positioned to look out of the window. A stretched canvas hung on the adjacent wall.

When she reappeared, he pointed to it. 'João Pinto,' he said.

'That's right,' she said. 'Of course. You were in Maputo, weren't you?'

'He was one of the artists we sponsored. It's great to come across his work like this.'

'I wouldn't say we are patrons,' she said. 'I for one don't know enough about art. But we like to buy from artists we know something about. João stayed with us a few times in Harare.'

She poured the coffee. 'Milk?'

'Just black, thanks.'

She held out a cup. 'Yours are hanging up in our house in Maidenhead.' Then, 'I'll just make sure my sister's all right . . .'

She seemed nervous; he had presumed her husband would also be present. Now, he looked around the flat again and spotted a photograph of two little girls with honey-coloured skin and darker, candy-floss hair. When she returned, he gestured to them: 'Your daughters?'

She smiled, nodded.

'They're gorgeous.'

'Thank you.' She stood smiling, looking at the image a little longer before saying, 'I have a regret. I've not taught them Shona. I should make more of an effort, because when we go back, they're not able to really feel part of it all, you know?'

She gestured to the sofa, and he sat down while she settled opposite him, curling her hands around her cup.

'Do you go back often?' he asked.

'Once a year as a family, to see my mother. She refuses to move from Chinoyi. I go by myself a few more times as I still have my project, and the house in Chisipite . . .' She sipped her coffee. 'Do you?'

He shook his head. 'I haven't been back since my dad left.'

She made that same clucking sound. 'You know, you must come back with me sometime. You could stay with us and you could take a walk down memory lane.'

His memories would be patently different from hers, he thought, but it was a kind offer, and he smiled his gratitude.

'And so Lisbon is now your home?'

'I like it,' he said. 'It reminds me of Maputo.'

'I know what you mean. We went once a few years back.'

Then she laid her cup down, leaned back and folded her arms, a wide smile on her face.

'You really do look alike,' she said.

He let her eyes slide over his features.

'Get a haircut, shave a little more closely . . .'

'Lose a bit of weight . . .'

'I didn't say that! Of course not!' She laughed, her shoulders shaking – it was pleasant to watch her amusement. And then she stopped. 'I'm glad you came, Francois. It's nice to talk with you. I hope we'll keep in touch.'

Her voice quietened, and there was a long pause before she spoke again.

'You see, I was so fond of Ben.' Now she was pulling a tissue from a box on the coffee table. 'Excuse me,' she said, and blew her nose, then stayed still, her eyes no longer on him but on some far corner of the room.

'He just gave me so much confidence,' she said suddenly. 'I told you I grew up in Chinoyi – you can imagine. He always said that *I* helped *him* out on his projects. But I feel it was the other way. He really encouraged me. He helped me more than he needed to . . .'

'It's nice to hear,' he said. 'I suppose I didn't see that side of him.'

'I want to do something,' she said. 'This is what I wanted to tell you. I want to set something up, a bursary or a fund, in Ben's name. I've already spoken to Michael, and when we have a clear idea we'll approach the university.'

'That's very kind of you.'

She looked up at him, and then she lowered her eyes.

'I was probably a little in love with Ben,' she said, pulling at her sleeve. He put his cup down and was surprised when she chuckled, wiping the tears away from her eyes.

'Your face!' Then she smiled. 'Nothing ever happened.'

They were silent and then she laughed again, a throaty laugh.

'The first time we met, I wasn't married yet, and he invited me for dinner. I remember thinking it was a date, but he told me soon enough he had a girlfriend, back in England. It was Clare.' She smiled. 'He took me to Da Guido's, do you remember it?'

He nodded. An Italian trattoria in one of the shopping areas in the Avenues, a criss-cross of tree-lined streets near the centre of the city.

'And I was thinking, cheapskate, why not the Sheraton or Meikles – that was where all my friends got taken to. But then I realised – Guido's, that was where everyone went. By everyone, I mean all of you guys.' She raised her eyebrows. 'You must remember what it's like back home.'

He nodded and she smiled.

'And Ben wanted to show me off in a way. Not as a date. But just the normality of it: two people having dinner. I think the waiters minded more, when I spoke to them in Shona . . .'

He could picture the scene well, and he appreciated her retelling of it. He let his eyes move over her: a beautiful woman, but her choice of husband would lend status and provoke censure in equal measure from all sections of the society. An irritation with his conservative childhood environs returned. It never took him long to remember why he had wanted to leave.

'I never really got to know Clare,' she was saying.

'I'm afraid I never really tried to get to know her,' he said, an admission he found was easy to make with Patricia in front of him. 'They got married and then soon after I moved to Lisbon, so it wasn't like I was far away. But we just never seemed to coincide with each other.'

She was quiet. Then, 'Were you not close to Ben?'

He crossed his arms. 'The funny thing is I think we were,' he said. 'We just didn't need to see each other much.'

She reached forward, stirred her coffee, her eyes still on him.

'Why did you leave Maputo?' she asked.

'I was running the cultural centre,' he said. 'It was the most enriching experience. It was an incredibly productive time of my life. But in the end, I just began to feel differently somehow.' He paused, choosing his words carefully. 'I began to feel like an interloper.'

She smiled, and seemed to turn his words over in her head.

'We all belong,' she said finally. 'If I didn't believe that, I'd never be able to hold my own here or there or with my husband's family.'

She was thoughtful, genuine. He knew that he would get to know her better and that would help him remember Ben. He spent the rest of the afternoon talking with her. She showed him some photos she had taken when Ben had last visited Harare. His brother looked tanned, at ease. In one, he had his arm around Patricia; they were both smiling, not at the camera but at each other. They talked until she and her sister had to get their train, and they all left the flat together. He accompanied them to the station and onto their platform. He offered his hand again to her sister, and then to Patricia, which she took. And then she pulled him closer, reached her face to his, so they stood cheek to cheek for some time. *Fambai zvakanaka*, she said in his ear, which he understood with a jolt. She laughed her throaty laugh. So you remember what that means, she said, and he nodded, the response *sarai zvakanaka* on the tip of his tongue. But he did not say it, only held her again to him before letting her go. Go well, stay well.

10

H E stayed a night with his parents before taking the train up
north, where he had arranged to meet Clare's sister, Jane.
He ordered some packing boxes and bin bags, picked up the
keys from the solicitor and then arrived on the street, a cool light
glinting off the river to his left. The cobblestones reminded him
of Lisbon, but the buildings were freshly painted, groomed,
unlike those on his own street. The art gallery across the way
was just opening up, the owner giving him a curious stare.

While he waited, he sent a message to Lucie. There was a
sense that the relationship was holding its breath, waiting to see
who would exhale first and take the other's hand. When they
met, Lucie had just separated from her husband, who remained
for a year in Lisbon out of sight. She had been adamant that her
son, then a sullen twelve-year-old, take priority. He had
complied with her wishes, careful not to over-step. But the
separateness of their lives meant that the woman he had been
with for four years had been hardly acquainted with his brother.

'Sorry, am I late?'

She had arrived at his side, a faint sheen of perspiration on her
face, pulling a small travelling case which, to his surprise, she
handed to him absent-mindedly. He took it and set it down next
to his feet.

'No, I've just got here myself.'

He bent down instinctively to kiss her cheek, but she mirrored
his movement with such eagerness that he retreated slightly,
then moved forwards again to avoid causing offence. They
embraced in an awkward hug.

'You didn't go to the hotel first?'

She shook her head.

'I came straight here. I'd rather crack on.'

He eyed her sideways: she was wiping her forehead with the back of her hand, and he caught another glimpse of her under-arm hair. He picked up her suitcase and followed her to the entrance. As he opened the door, he asked after her children, to which she gave a vague wave of her hand. Then they entered the flat.

It was very quiet inside with the door closed behind them and all the windows shut. They stood together for some moments on the doormat, as if each was unwilling to be the first to move further inside. Then he put her suitcase down, took off his jacket and hung it up on a hook, offering to do the same for her.

'I brought us something to drink,' she said. Diving into her handbag she produced a bottle of gin. 'They'll have tonic in the fridge, I'm sure they will. Could you make me a gin and tonic? Have one yourself. I'll be back in a minute.'

She went through to the bedroom, and he could see her entering the bathroom and closing the door. He glanced at his watch: it was only midday. He moved into the kitchen and opened the fridge. Sure enough, at the back, on the bottom shelf, were a row of tonic cans. Perhaps this had been a family tradition that Jane was sure her sister would uphold. He found two tall glasses in another cupboard and measured out the gin.

'Great. Thanks.'

She had brushed her hair and patted some powder on her face. She smiled, clinking her glass against his.

'I don't make this a habit,' she said. 'But these are exceptional circumstances.'

They sipped their drinks and then discussed. They agreed that large items of furniture would remain in situ, until they decided whether to rent or sell. Clothes and books would be donated. Any objects of sentimental value would be boxed separately to go to the respective family. It was as if the siblings had been enlisted to proceed with a divorce settlement. Belongings of the couple were now being deconstructed, each item reverting to the original single owner. The exception was his wedding present, the painting above the mantelpiece; his parents had already relinquished any claim, offering it to the Armstrongs. On this, Jane would consult her parents. On a more practical note, the fridge needed to be completely emptied, which he offered to start with.

The decisions made, he moved to the kitchen area, just as Jane's phone rang. The next hour was spent throwing away everything that remained in the fridge and freezer, quickly filling a black bin liner and then another, while Jane was involved in a protracted conversation. The old Victorian-style pulley that was raised near the ceiling in the utility nook carried his sister-in-law's underwear, his brother's running gear: their last laundry load. He lowered the pulley and shoved everything that was on it into the bags, then passed through the living room and walked out, down the stairs to the street, where he located the large skip that served the block of flats and hurled the bags in. When he re-entered the flat, he saw Jane sitting on the sofa with her feet on the coffee table, the phone in one hand, her gin and tonic in the other. As far as he could tell, she ran a business and was on the phone to one of her employees.

'You should find an order sheet in his file . . .'

He worked quickly, around her, and then moved to the small study. There were two laptops. His father had requested Ben's, and any of his brother's notebooks or drafts of writing. What about Clare's laptop? A decision for Jane. The shelves of books: he skimmed the titles, all academic. They could be donated to the university. He would box them and ring the library for some advice. Eventually, Jane ended her call, and he could hear her moving around. When he came back into the living room, several hours had passed and it was nearly dark outside.

'Would you mind?' she said. 'I know I haven't done much. But maybe we could get something to eat? Blitz the rest tomorrow?'

They left the flat and took a bus uptown to their hotel, where she checked in before they searched for a place to eat. They found an American-style grill, with exposed brickwork and heavy wooden tables. As they waited for their food to arrive, he looked at his phone: no message from Lucie. Jane was tapping furiously: bedtime routines had been transgressed was what he could discern. Eventually, she sighed, pushed her phone away and picked up her glass of wine. The next day, they both knew, they would have to clear out the bedroom. A strange turn of events, when he would step into his brother's most private space. Perhaps she was thinking the same thing, because she said, 'All her clothes. It's going to be odd.'

Then, 'And how are your parents?'

'Coping. And yours?'

'The same. Very upset still. We all are.' She plucked at a thread on her sleeve. 'We're just grateful that it seemed to have been very quick. You know, that they didn't suffer.'

'Yes.'

They both looked out the window, across the broad street.

'You know he strayed from the flock, don't you?'

She moved a strand of hair away from her mouth.

'The fold I mean. You know he had an affair, don't you?'

Her tone was perfunctory. She picked up her napkin, folded it in half and then again.

He set his glass down.

'No. No, I didn't.'

She nodded, a large oversized nod, looking down at the napkin, which she opened up and started folding again.

'About a year and a half ago? With a colleague. Who has since moved away.'

He looked at her and she smiled, a different smile to her usual: crooked, more weighted to her right side. There was a sudden strong resemblance to Clare, he realised, despite their different colouring.

'How did you find out?'

'She told me. But not then, not when she was in the middle of things. Last Christmas. We went out, just the two of us. You see, he never admitted it. But she knew.'

He tightened his hold of his glass.

'How could she be so sure?'

'There were signs. He was always in meetings. Classic stuff. She just knew.'

'But,' he tried to control his voice, 'if he was upset about their,' he stumbled over the grammar, 'their IVF, he might have just been finding somewhere quiet, somewhere to gather his thoughts . . .'

'She knew, Francois. Ben had an affair.'

The complacency in her voice was unpleasant, and a sudden anger erupted inside him. He released his glass, afraid of snapping the stem, and picked up his cutlery, tightened his grip, looked down at the table. The waiter arrived with their plates and then left.

She leaned back against the banquette. 'I mean, you seem astounded. Is it so surprising, given what they went through? All that messiness?'

He was silent; she was watching him with frank interest.

'So you really didn't know?'

He shook his head.

'He never kind of confided in you?

He refused to answer, picked up his fork. It was his signal to her and she, at least, recognised it. She fell mostly silent, occasionally checking her phone through the meal and rewarding the small screen with a wry smile. He only spoke at the end, to ask her if she had finished, and when she nodded, he paid the bill and they left. Back at the hotel, they arranged to meet in the lobby after breakfast. For a moment he was tempted to invite himself to her room simply to see her reaction: she would be able to form a delightful opinion of two marauding brothers. But it was only a flash, less driven by malice than from a restlessness that plagued him for the remainder of the evening, as he stood under the shower, then flipped through the channels on the television in his room until he felt he could sleep.

The evening had cast a pall over him. Whatever had happened with Ben, whether he had indeed been unfaithful, this seemed to shrink in size compared to the other discovery: his brother had not sought his advice, his counsel. He remembered there had been one rather morose visit to Lisbon, some years ago, which his brother had initiated because the warm weather would 'do Clare some good'. The couple had spent a long weekend with him. They had strolled along the narrow, cobbled streets; they had spent hours sitting in the sunshine at cafés in the squares. He remembered that Clare had been particularly enamoured of the flaky custard pastries, *pasteis de nata*. But after the initial enjoyment, she had become withdrawn, unreachable. Ben had tried rather obviously to compensate for Clare's silence, and he had rather uncharitably resented his sister-in-law's aloofness. It might have been the time when he could have encouraged Ben to talk about their struggles, shown himself to be a support. He hadn't. It was not for a lack of empathy or sympathy; he had simply assumed that Ben would know that he had these feelings, that he loved Ben, without the need to be explicit. But he might have been wrong. Ben had always been more of a talker.

The next morning when he went downstairs, Jane was waiting in the lobby. This time he picked up her suitcase before she handed it to him. She looked tired and did not attempt to make conversation. They rode the bus in silence, which continued as they opened the flat, but both exchanged a glance before they went into the bedroom. It was a large room with tall sash windows looking onto the cobbled street and the river beyond; sanded wooden floorboards with two oriental rugs, one at the base of the large wrought-iron bed, the other under the window. There was a bedside table and lamp on either side of the bed, each holding a pile of books. Seven weeks had passed since the couple had got up, got dressed, made the bed and left their flat.

Outside, a light rain was falling. Jane moved to the window and stood looking out, and he followed her before stopping a few feet away. He was still angry with her.

'I'm sorry about last night,' she said suddenly, then half-turned, so that one side of her face had the grey light falling on it. 'They worked through it, whatever happened, didn't they? I should have let sleeping dogs lie.'

He could not think of how to respond, and so he said nothing. She gave him a slight smile.

'I think I was cross with her for telling me. And then not talking about it again. She had that way: of letting me in so I could play the big sister. And then closing a door with me left outside, feeling stupid.'

He went to stand near her.

'She could be like that.' Now the tears were running down her cheeks. 'She made me feel a frump. *You* try and keep it together when you have three kids under seven.' She wiped her eyes. 'But of course it was her way of coping. She so desperately wanted children of her own . . .'

He stepped forward and put his arm around her shoulders.

'This has been an incredibly difficult time,' he said. An anodyne commentary, but all that he could think to say. She gave him a small smile, then briefly laid her head on his chest. They stood by the window, each offering the other light pats, little squeezes: tactile consolations, a primate ritual. Then she straightened her shoulders.

'I'm not going to stop long,' she said. 'I'm worn out.'
'That's fine.'
'I've changed my flight to leave early afternoon.'
'We should be done by then anyway.'

They moved apart, like a splitting shadow, like an egg that separates to form twins but instead produces two sibling-less adults. He walked to a bedside cabinet, opened it and closed it. 'Clare's side,' he said to her. It was obvious anyway, with a bottle of hand cream, and a pair of glasses crushed between her piles of books. She nodded and opened one of the sliding wardrobe doors, then the other.

'They were very neat, weren't they?' she muttered. 'You should see my husband's clothes.'

He was glad she had mentioned her husband: it served as a reminder of their earthly lives. He moved to the en suite, the only bathroom in the flat. The laundry bin was half full, and he picked it up, tipped the contents into a bin bag, followed this with the bottles and jars from the medicine cabinet. He knotted the bag, left the flat and chucked it into the skip. Wasteful, death was. He had thrown away foodstuffs yesterday, medicines and clothes today. He watched a swan float on the river, before turning away and mounting the stairs back to the flat. Jane was sitting on the floor on the other side of the bed, her legs tucked under her, engrossed in a notebook. He squatted on his brother's side of the bed, quickly glanced under it – empty – then opened the drawers on the bedside table. There was a collection of documents, old passports, several battery cases, two small notebooks. He skimmed through them. The small pages were covered with notes, tightly squeezed writing, related, he could just make out, to Ben's research. These would be passed on to his father. Under all the junk, a small green oblong: a camera. He picked it up: it was a good make, light in his hand. He leaned back on his haunches and turned it on.

It was the first photograph on the roll – the last his brother had taken – and his breath was suddenly gone. He looked up – Jane was still reading, turning a page – and then looked down again at the small screen. The window he recognised instantly: he had stood in front of it a few minutes ago. He saw a bare back, a long line of neck, a towel held together loosely at her chest. As on Jane's face earlier, there was the effect of half-in, half-out of shadow, but the sun was brighter, higher, a summer sun, and the face was younger, soft-skinned: a girl, really. He saw a movement in the corner of his vision: Jane had raised her head to him, and he slipped the camera into his pocket, gave her a wide, foolish smile, his heart pounding. He opened his mouth to say something, anything, but at the same moment her phone rang: her husband calling to arrange where and when he should pick her up.

He stood up with a sudden energy, swept the books off the top of the cabinet and into a box, threw away the assorted collection of batteries, a torch, junk from the drawers, then straightened up and moved back through the living room to the study, where he stood in the middle of the room, breathing deeply, Jane's voice rising and falling in the background. There was nothing: nothing in the shelves that stared back at him, the walls, the blinds; nothing to explain why his brother had a photograph of a half-naked girl on his camera.

The next hour passed by as if speeded up. He accompanied Jane, who looked pale and pensive, to the stop for the airport shuttle bus, and then walked around the city for the next two hours before his train was due to leave for London, resisting the urge to put his hand into his pocket for fear of finding the camera was still there. On the train, he took it out and held it in his palm: it now seemed to weigh much more. He was unwilling to look through the photos with his fellow passenger, an elderly woman, by his side, not sure what other poses he might find. When she got off the train, he moved into her seat by the window, and then, trying to dampen down the furtiveness he was feeling, he clicked through the camera roll.

There were few pictures, ranging from months before: the camera was not often used. Several were of a cover of a journal: perhaps his brother needed to upload an image to a website.

There was only one of Clare, from the previous year, holding up what appeared to be a long string of garlic: an inside joke. Then, after a few more, he arrived at the girl. Now, in the privacy of the train, he allowed himself to peruse it carefully: a tumble of hair, large eyes, high cheekbones, a slender body. She was beautiful. But young: there was no doubt. The date read from a couple of months previous, a week or so before his brother had died. He switched the camera off, leaned back and stared outside, remembered the conversation with his father the last time he had made the same journey: I'd imagined them to be invincible.

When his parents asked after the flat, in tired voices, each wondering whether they should have accompanied him, he reassured them that there had been no need. The most essential tasks had been done, and he would come back again in good time after he had had a chance to discuss with Jane what she saw as the way forward. Of the photograph he had found, of the butterflies in his stomach when he thought about his brother, he made no mention. He flew back to Lisbon the following evening and saw Lucie waving to him. There was, however, a slight stiffness about her when he took her into his arms. He was being given a reprieve: he had not, the last few weeks, been very good company. But as they drove back to the city he asked if he could come to her flat, and she held his eyes for a moment before nodding. They made love quickly, without speaking, and then lay together, the windows flung open, the curtains pushed aside, looking at the night sky from her bed. She had her head on his chest, and he stroked her back as she described her doings of the last few days.

But his mind was elsewhere, in another space, another time. He was back in Maputo: the sun was setting, and it was that time of the day when the light seemed to cling on, unwilling to plunge the city into darkness. The air was redolent with the smell of drains and exhaust fumes, mingling to form a heady mixture. He was in a taxi, halted outside a restaurant in the Feira

Popular, with its esplanade of white plastic tables and chairs. And through the window he could see the girls, emerging like birds of prey, their legs shiny and long, drifting between the tables, leaving a lingering presence of cheap perfume. One girl caught his eye: a slim girl, her hair in beaded cornrows. As she walked towards a table, he could see a scar on the back of her right leg, like a zip that beckoned to be unfastened to reveal her flesh and bones. She sat down at a table where a middle-aged man with a red beard was nursing a glass of whisky. When she smiled encouragingly, she revealed a missing front tooth which, rather than making her unattractive, lent a sordid realism to her attempts. Years later, lying now with Lucie, her skin under his fingers, all he could think about was the young girl with the zip on her leg, and all he could feel was sorrow, a stab of concern about how her evening had ended.

He was back in that taxi, he was leaning out of the window, his arm hanging down the side of the car, the wind blowing in his hair. He was closing his eyes, feeling the taste of salt air on his tongue on a hot humid night. The taxi was swinging away, so the girl was now out of sight, never to be seen again.

11

AT the weekend, he drove out past the familiar stretches of land and arrived at Gildo's house in time for lunch. His wife Jacinta came out as he was parking his van and kissed him, ran her fingers through his hair, pushing it back off his forehead. He held her for a little longer than necessary, enjoying the feeling that he had known these two people for many years, from a different life; that despite the passing of time, relationships could survive. Gildo hugged him, pulled him into the house. It was after the meal, when Jacinta insisted that they leave the clearing up, their daughter was due back from a friend's and would help, that they took a few bottles of beer each up the road that led to a hill, a rocky outcrop overlooking the other houses and their gardens, where they had often sat and drank. He slid the green camera out of his pocket, turned it on, and with now practised touches found the photograph on the roll. He handed it to Gildo.

'I found this on Ben's camera.'

Gildo set his bottle down, took the camera and peered at the small screen, then let out a low whistle.

'That's his flat. She's in his bedroom,' he continued. 'I haven't told anyone else, not showed anyone else, not even Lucie.'

Gildo was holding the camera closer, his eyes darting over the picture.

'Indian?'

'Looks like.'

His friend scrutinised the screen for some moments longer, then gave another whistle and handed the camera back, picked up his bottle of beer, held it to his mouth.

He felt a wave of irritation. 'So what do you think?'

Gildo gave a small wave with his bottle: '*Estava foudando ela.*'

The pronouncement, crude as it was, yet summing up the situation perfectly, was wholly unsatisfactory.

'But who is she?'

The words, unspoken so far, exploded from his lips, and his friend raised his eyebrows, shook his head.

'I mean she's young, right? A student of his?'

Gildo sighed, then spoke: 'We can assume.'

'He was having an affair with a student?'

When his friend did not respond, he continued: 'Gildo . . .' he gulped. 'I mean. Do you think Clare found out? Do you think they had a fight? In the car—'

'Francois, whatever or whoever, don't make a nightmare—'

'I can't stop thinking . . . was that why—'

'It was a car accident. Like Lady Diana—'

'What was he doing . . . fucking around like that?'

'Maybe Clare was fucking around too. Did you check *her* camera?'

He wanted to hit his friend, but instead he threw his bottle against the rock on which he was sitting, and for some reason it didn't shatter as he had expected, but bounced back up and smacked him on the cheekbone, the remnants of beer it contained dribbling down his chest.

Gildo was laughing, wiping him down, '*Hepa.* Are you OK?'

He nodded, pressed his hand to his face.

'Let me see.'

His friend pushed his hand away, held him by the sides of his head, then clapped his cheeks. 'Just a bruise. You're still beautiful.'

'Gildo,' he said, still holding his face, 'I don't think this was the first time.'

His friend looked at him. 'And so?'

He shook his head, frustrated. What was he hoping to get from Gildo? His reaction was so . . . *African*. Gildo, married to Jacinta for fifteen years, had not, he was sure, remained faithful all that time. He was always making jokes about his polygamous heritage: jokes which had a ring of truth. And yet, was he, Francois, any better? He had stayed faithful to any woman he was sleeping with, yes, but that was sometimes only a matter of months, weeks, days even. A serial monogamist. His short marriage had been his longest relationship. And what of his brother? Ben and Clare had been under enormous strain, compounding the ordinary wear and tear of a long relationship. Yes, he was shaken by whom his brother had chosen to have an affair with: a very young woman. A girl. But he could not be sure that he would act any differently if placed in the same situation. He was angry with himself and the moral high ground he seemed intent on occupying.

The bottles of beer were finished too quickly. They returned to the house, where Jacinta exclaimed in shock on seeing Francois's face, berated Gildo's sanguinity. He sat in the kitchen, his friend's wife tending to his cheek, a clear view of her cleavage, her breasts at one point brushing against his chin. He wanted to bury his face in them. She smelled of the cream she used to straighten her hair, the rich aloe vera which she used on her skin. She smelled of sunsets and a warm wind blowing: a Maputo night. Gildo lingered in his eyesight, his face indulgent, before announcing that he would take Francois out that evening to a bar in the small town, run by an Angolan, who, after a discreet word from Gildo, brought them drink after drink. Francois sat in a warm bath of hospitality, the dark faces and cadences of the language taking him back. If he had stayed on the continent he had been born in, kept a foothold on behalf of his parents and brother, his family would still be intact. The feeling grew and grew the more beers he downed. When Gildo helped him into the taxi later that night, he leaned against his friend.

'Don't you miss it?' he asked. 'Don't you miss Africa?'

If his friend responded, he didn't hear.

He woke the next morning to Jacinta's voice scolding their daughter in the kitchen: the sounds of domestic life. Later that day, Gildo drove him back in his van to Lisbon, stayed a few hours, before taking the train back to his wife and daughter.

The weeks passed. It was winter in Lisbon, a rainy, windy season. He spent most of his energies at that time of the year preparing canvases, soaking them with gesso, grounding them with different colours. It was routine, therapeutic work which set him up for his more productive months, when he had no commitments to the art college or the Gulbenkian. One evening he looked at the students gathered around in a semicircle. The class was working on a still life. They appeared impossibly young to him, out of reach. Good lines, Isabel, he said, smiling at one, and she looked up in surprise: he rarely commented so early on in the process. She had almond-shaped eyes, rimmed with eyeliner; the whites shone pearly and untouched. When a nervousness crept into her expression, he patted her shoulder, carry on, then went to the front of the class, stared out the window. The only sounds were of brushes against canvas, the scrape of a stick against a palette: the soundtrack to his life.

He received an invitation to submit for an exhibition in London – *Hearts of Darkness* – the coming spring; the curator was a contemporary from Michaelis. The remit: to explore love and lovers, sex and sexuality, through a global dimension. Would he have an artwork he was working on or even a completed canvas? He knew why he had been approached. He had produced a series of paintings which had received much acclaim, of sex workers in Maputo, a project set up by a Mozambican friend who was running an HIV awareness centre in the Alto Mae area of the city.

But because his mind was still full of the events and discoveries of recent months, he found that whatever he sketched or outlined in preparation for the exhibition was banal; his thoughts kept returning to the photograph on Ben's camera. He had at one point considered cropping the photo, then sending it to his brother's former colleagues: recognise this girl? But even from neck up the viewer would be sure of her nakedness below. He would be compromising his brother, and this stranger. Instead, he found himself sketching her. Before long he had six drawings scattered around him. Her proportions were like a gazelle; in one picture he drew her with hooves at the end of her legs. In others, he drew her naked. He needed little imagination to sketch her buttocks and hips, her breasts, decorated with – somehow he knew – dark nipples. It was unlikely that she shared the same history, the same kind of life and livelihood as the girls he had painted in Maputo. But he could not shake off the sense that there was a thread connecting them, even as he balked at assigning his brother to the same category as the girls' clients.

Youth and beauty were always a currency, sometimes a bane. It was the expression in the girl's eyes that was most arresting. She was looking back at Ben, but she was also looking at him, the viewer of the photograph. What had happened after this moment? He was sure that this image followed love-making. Had they made love again after the shutter had clicked? He chose a small canvas, cutting it carefully, then prepared his paints: an activity that always soothed him. A portrait, up to her chest, her neck and shoulders gleaming, as Clare's had done in the wedding picture.

He had been warming up some soup on the stove when Lucie appeared one evening at his flat. They greeted each other with a kiss, but neither could ignore the rarity of the occasion: she hardly ever arrived unannounced. Their whole relationship, he could see, had been conducted as two busy, independent adults. Nothing like the way his brother seemed to have been enmeshed with people. She accepted a bowl of soup; he poured her some wine. She wanted to know if they should go to the beach the next day: they could brunch at one of the cafés. He agreed and noticed with some guilt the release of a tension in her eyes. As he started clearing the table – he never left dishes for the next day just as he kept his flat, aside from his atelier, in meticulous order, old-womanish traits she liked to tease him over – she took her glass to the other side of the room, where under the skylight the light fell onto the small painting.

'Who is she?' she said.

She was looking at the canvas, at the messy pile of sketches on the floor, had not noticed the photograph he had clipped up, on the other side of the room. She stood between the two, as if the timeline had become skewed. The canvas was his present. She was his past. The girl, his future. He gestured to the photograph, and she turned.

'I found it on Ben's camera,' he said.

She stood stock still, and he took a moment to survey her. He knew every inch of her body, he knew what she liked to hear, he knew what she liked him to do in bed. But at that moment he felt as distant from her as if an ocean divided them.

'When did you find it?'

'When we were cleaning out his flat.'

'You never told me.'

'I'm telling you now.'

'Who is she?' she repeated.

'I don't know.'

'So Ben was having an affair with this girl?'

'I think so.'

She was quiet. The flat had become so silent he could hear her breathing.

'Why are you painting her?'

'I don't know.'

She paused. 'Do your parents know?'

'No.'

'Anyone else?'

'Only Gildo.'

'Gildo . . .'

She turned and stared at his canvas for what seemed many minutes. He was unsure what to say, where to stand.

She asked again: 'Why are you painting her?'

He came closer to her, then changed tack and sat on the edge of his worktable.

'I'm not painting her,' he said. 'At least, I don't feel like I am. I don't know her. I'm painting what Ben saw. I feel like I am looking through his eyes. I can't explain . . .'

She came to stand in front of him. He slid his hands over her hair, down her neck, then moved his hands to grip her shoulders, his thumbs caressing her collarbone. She was watching him, her expression cool, the amused smile on her lips not reaching her eyes.

'Try,' she said. 'You want to bring her to life? Are you going to exhibit this picture so she sees herself one day in a gallery?'

'Of course not . . .'

She moved away so he had to drop his hands.

'Does it help you, Francois,' she said, 'to imagine this girl?'

He saw that now she looked aggrieved, the expression on her face at odds with the nonchalance of her tone.

'Lucie . . .'

But she shook her head, as if pre-empting any attempt he would make to lie to her.

'Why didn't you tell me?'

'I don't know.' He clasped his hands together. 'I feel . . .' he hesitated, 'that we haven't talked properly for some time. I didn't know how to bring it up.'

'And Gildo? What did he have to say?'

He shrugged and was relieved when she did not press him. She returned to stand in front of his canvas, and he went into the kitchen. At one point, he glanced through the hatch. She was smoking a cigarette, sifting through his sketches, tapping her ash into her glass. Then she appeared behind him in the kitchen, not to help but to sit on the stool watching him, until he turned around and tossed a tea towel at her. He felt another pang of guilt when she smiled, came to stand next to him, started drying the plates and glasses.

'I'm forty-seven next year, Francois,' she said.

'I'm planning for your retirement, don't worry . . .'

She elbowed him playfully, but he could see her eyes were sad.

'I just meant . . .' she began, but didn't finish.

She meant many things. She was a woman who had a son who lived in a different country, a woman who guarded her independence just as she admitted her physical needs. She was older than him. The age gap had never been an issue for them; if anything it had been part of the attraction. But perhaps he was being disingenuous: he might have appeared too unrooted, inconstant for her visions of the future.

After they had washed up, he asked her to stay the night, and she agreed. That itself was another indication that things had changed. He would have preferred a reluctance, for she did not like waking up in a bed other than her own, she had told him. Usually, she would entice him back to her flat, which was bigger and more modern, so that they could plan the next day while having a last drink together on her balcony. Tonight she pulled on one of his T-shirts as bedtime wear. They lay together on his bed, facing each other. He stroked her thigh, and she watched him, her expression meditative. It pleased him to see her in his clothes, and when he kissed her and slid his hand between her legs she pulled off the T-shirt. They made love tentatively at first, as if testing the waters, and then resumed their familiar positions, each with the knowledge of what the other enjoyed. But her words earlier had touched a nerve, and he suddenly had a sensation that it was not Lucie moving above him but the girl, with her silky hair falling onto his face, into his mouth, with her small breasts and wine-coloured nipples. The vision unnerved him and, to exorcise his thoughts, he flipped Lucie onto her back, was much rougher than usual. Afterwards, as she slept, on her side, turned away from him, he found that the sensation had not faded. He felt the girl was still in the room, with him, some-where he could not see her, waiting.

12

THAT Christmas he arranged to spend the holiday fortnight with his parents, while Lucie returned to Germany; she would bring Josef back with her for the second half of his college vacation. When he arrived at his parents' house in Clapham, he rang the bell to be greeted by his mother, her face alight with love for him, her only son now, and he felt an ache in his heart. How must it be to be healthy, cognisant, vigorous, when your child is cruelly not allowed to age? His mother took him up the stairs to the room he always stayed in, sat on the bed as he unpacked. He noticed how small, how delicate she appeared, dressed in her usual flowing layers: a Persian scarf around her neck, a long multicoloured skirt. Her right hand was in a bandage: a gardening accident brought on by impatience. His father, it seemed, had suggested that they go out for Christmas lunch at a nearby hotel.

'Excellent idea.'

'Saves me cooking and worrying about what will set me off,' she said. 'Plus I'm a bit useless with this on,' she motioned to her hand.

He sat down next to her, took her other hand, massaged it between his. She smiled, slipped an arm through his.

'I hope we didn't spoil any plans you had with Lucie.'

He shook his head, then smiled at her ruefully. 'I'm not sure she's going to put up with me for much longer . . .'

'Oh, darling.'

She was silent, then she squeezed his arm. 'These things either make you closer or pull you apart.'

'I'm not sure it's even about Ben,' he said. 'I'm just a difficult bastard.'

She tutted. 'No, you're not'. Then she spoke as if he were fifteen years old, suffering from his first, unrequited, love. 'You're kind, handsome, talented.' He started laughing. 'You just haven't met the right person.'

'Maybe you're right, Mum,' he said grinning. 'Maybe it's them.'

She smiled back. So they could still smile, laugh; life would go on. He could see ahead to their very old age, and then they would die, and he would be the last of the line. But he would leave something behind: his paintings.

His mother rose to her feet. 'Wait here.'

He could hear her in the next room, and he lay back so he was resting on his elbow.

She re-entered, holding a small booklet.

'Look what came in the post.'

On the cover, a black and white print of a photograph: Ben sitting in a circle of children with wide white smiles, skinny dark limbs, clapping hands. One boy had his face turned to the camera, his hand halfway towards meeting the other. His brother was leaning back slightly, his long legs awkwardly crossed, but laughing. There was a cross, and the letters RIP printed in heavy black letters. He lifted his eyes and met his mother's. She was watching him, her lips set in a sad smile. Inside, there was a letter to his parents signed from Agatha Chiweshe – Mother, SOS Children's Village, Waterfalls, Harare – along with others written by five children, aged ten to fourteen, their handwriting fastidious, their sentences short but heartfelt. Each expressing the wish that his parents be well, and assuring them that Ben would be remembered for his goodness.

'I had no idea,' his mother said. 'When he used to go back, he didn't say that he always stopped by. Your father and I give a regular donation, but Ben actually went there, spent time with those children.'

They fell silent, both looking at the small booklet in his hands.

Finally, he said, 'I'm not surprised. He seems to have touched everyone he met.'

'It's so sad,' his mother continued. 'I know what people think. They give Clare the monopoly on the disappointment that they couldn't have kids. But Ben felt it too . . .'

Her voice broke, and he slung his arm over her, so that he was crushing her into his chest. They remained like this for some time until she whispered, smiling, 'Not very comfortable', and he released her. She smoothed her hair and glanced at him.

'Actually,' she said, 'your dad and I want to do something, in Ben's memory.' She paused, took his hand again. 'Patricia Walther got in touch a few weeks ago, and she wants to set up an award of some kind, for students from Zimbabwe, in Ben's name.'

'I remember she mentioned something like that . . .'

'Well, both your dad and I thought that was a very generous thing for her to think of. And well,' she smiled half-apologetically, 'we want in on the action. So we thought we would also contribute, not as much as the Walthers, but, well, she agreed immediately and even said we should help her in the selection process . . .'

'Mum, that's a wonderful idea.' He hugged her again, and she started laughing. When he let go of her, he saw there were tears in her eyes.

'I'm cross for not thinking of it myself,' she said.

'Don't be silly . . .'

'But anyway,' she wiped her eyes, 'what do you think? *Really*, I mean?'

'I *really* think it's a wonderful idea.'

'For postgraduate study, you know? A distance doctorate or master's most likely, and for something women-related, because that was Ben's field.'

He squeezed his mother's hand.

'Anyway,' she straightened up. 'Patricia said she wanted to see you again. She said she'd call. She might be tied up with the kids over Christmas, though.' Then she patted his arm. 'Come. We'll find your father in his shed.'

As they walked downstairs, she paused again: 'Have you been in touch with Jane about the flat?'

He shook his head. 'I'll try and ring her . . .'

That evening, he sent Lucie a message: *How are you doing?* Within a quarter of an hour his phone beeped. *All good here.* Then, a minute later: *Miss you.* It was impossible to tell what would happen between them. Perhaps they would stay good friends. He seemed to have accumulated a bevy of such friends: exes. The exception: his only wife, ex-wife, Paula, the person whom he had discarded.

He went for an early-morning run the next day, then took his mother to the Tate Modern on the Embankment, where they had mulled wine and mince pies in the members' section, looking down at the river. On Christmas Eve, they drove out of London for a country walk. The hotel Christmas lunch the following day was serviceable. Later, they spent the evening in front of their log fire, his father dealing inexpertly with a jigsaw puzzle, a pursuit he had never seen him engage with before, while his mother showed him her genealogy project. By then he had drunk nearly a bottle of red wine, to avoid smoking more than his quota of cigarettes: exchanging one evil for another.

He was amused to see his mother clicking expertly through websites. So far, there were no surprises, nor any inconvenient ancestor. Her family had been in Lahore, then-India, for two generations before returning to England, after which her father joined the police in the 1950s, in then-Rhodesia. His father's family arrived in England at the turn of the twentieth century from France, before moving to South Africa. As she talked him through the family tree, his mother seemed unconcerned that she was speaking with the end of the line. Or maybe she was taking comfort from the intricacies of their extended family – the first, second and third cousins, their spouses and children – beyond the limits of their nuclear family. His eyes were heavy, and he drifted off for a few moments, came back when she was tidying her papers away and shutting off her laptop. She was saying, 'I mean, people find it so hard to talk to you that they just don't talk to you at all.'

He roused himself. 'You mean about Ben?'

She nodded.

'Who do you mean?'

'I suppose no one we're *really* close to. I'm probably being over-sensitive. But friends I've made here. The ladies from my book group . . .'

He made a sympathetic sound.

She stopped still. 'I should phone the Armstrongs . . .'

For some reason he could picture Jane, reading out a card from a board game, sitting by a fire just like theirs, in a very short dress and woolly tights, her legs tucked under her like that day at the flat.

'Wait until tomorrow. It can be a Boxing Day thing to do . . .'

His mother sighed. 'You're right, it's a bit late now.' Then, 'We were so touched when Ben's student came to see us, weren't we, John?'

His father grunted.

'That goes there,' she said suddenly, picking up a piece and handing it to him. His father gave her a long look before placing the tile in its slot.

'His student?'

'Lovely girl,' his mother said. 'Indian. Of course, I bored her with my stories of Grandpa in Lahore.'

He tried to keep his voice steady.

'How,' he said, 'how did she know where you lived?'

'Ben gave her a lift down once,' his mother said. 'I remember him saying actually. Because her parents live not far away. And he lent her one of Dad's novels. Which one was it again, John?'

His father mumbled, and his mother continued. 'That's right. She wanted to return it. Of course we said to keep it.' She was quiet for some time and then repeated, 'I was so touched that she'd made the effort. She stayed for an hour or so.'

'And,' he spoke slowly, 'you said her parents live nearby?'

'Yes, but we ordered her a taxi to get home. It was dark by the time she left, and you know what buses are like . . .'

So: whatever he had thought, whatever he had expected when he painted that painting, it had worked. Someone who was not real became real. An image from a photograph became flesh and blood. There was no chance that this was not the girl. Why had she made herself known? He was unwilling to quiz his parents, both of whom were still innocent of the affair, but later he went to the hall table and found in his mother's extravagant swirls an address written down on a notepad, and beside it, a name: Rita.

It was an unpretentious road off the high street, a small gate leading to a park just visible at the end. He located the house easily. The front garden had been covered with concrete, and the curtains in the windows looked old fashioned and tired. He spent a few moments standing on the street, allowing himself to acclimatise. If this was indeed her parents' house, then it was clear that the girl had done well to gain entrance to a prestigious university. And there, she had met his brother. He rang the bell, and the door swung open almost immediately. There stood a woman whose eyes widened in surprise before one hand went to her neckline.

'Good afternoon,' he said, his best smile on show. 'Is Rita in?'

'No.' She hesitated. 'You are . . . ?'

She was flustered, smoothing down the shapeless gown she was wearing. Older than he had imagined, with hair streaked grey, heavy eyebrows but smooth skin. He had not prepared an excuse, half-hoping that he would find the girl conveniently waiting for him outside the door. He made a spontaneous decision.

'I work at the university . . .'

It was enough. Her face cleared; she beamed. 'Oh! Come in! Doctor . . . ?'

'Martin,' he said.

She showed no reaction to his name, only opened the door wider. He stepped into the entrance hall.

'Come in, please. I am Ushmi Kalungal, Rita's mother.'

He held out his hand and she took it.

'It's a pleasure to meet you.'

She had been expecting someone else, otherwise she might have substituted the grey slippers she wore, a hole at the toe, for something smarter. And then, as if she knew what he was thinking, she spoke: 'So sorry. The house is messy.'

'Please don't worry.'

'She went to the park with my granddaughter. Please come. Sit, sit.'

The living room held two shabby sofas, a coffee table placed on a violently coloured rug. The walls were mostly bare aside from a picture of an Indian-looking Jesus, surrounded with a wreath. On one side stood a synthetic Christmas tree; the lights were not turned on.

'I'll call her.'

She went into the hall, and he heard her speaking on the phone, in another language, in an excited voice, two sentences that he didn't understand; and then she came back in, still holding the phone.

'She is coming.'

She sat in a hard-backed chair in front of him, her fingers twisting in her skirts. The aromas – heavy spices, oil and meat – made his mouth water and, again, as if she could read his mind, she asked, 'Some tea? Coffee?' Then, 'I made some samosas?' A pause. 'Beer?'

Tempting, very tempting, but would that be the done thing? he thought. To have a beer and samosa with the mother of the girl his brother was having an affair with?

He cleared his throat.

'No, thank you. I wouldn't want to trouble you.'

'No trouble!' she was on her feet already, so he said hurriedly, 'Really, please, I'm not hungry', his stomach growling in protest.

She sat down slowly, and he snatched at a way to distract her.

'Did you have a good Christmas, Mrs . . .' he struggled to remember her name.

'Kalungal,' she spoke quickly, smiling. 'Yes, but quiet. Just Rita, my husband. My son and family were not with us.'

'I see.' He smiled back, laid his arm on the armrest.

'So,' she said. 'You teach Rita?'

He made a movement with his head, then gestured to the photos on the mantelpiece. 'Your granddaughter?'

'Yes,' she laughed nervously. 'She likes photos! Always a big smile.' Then something outside caught her eye. 'Ah, she is coming,' and she went into the hall.

He saw her through the window, walking at a pace down the street in front of the house, turning into their path. In short black jacket, her face hidden by the hood, skinny jeans tucked into boots: her clothes hugging her delicate frame. She was a slip of a girl: a child carrying a child on her hip. He got to his feet, flutters in his stomach, and he had a sudden desire to turn and leave through the back door. He heard her mother's voice as she opened the door, the same excited tone, and then silence.

She stepped into the room, the child still on her hip, small hands gripping the collar of her jacket, her own hand pushing back her hood so he saw the drops of rain on her cheekbones, the makings of a spot on her chin.

'Rita,' he said. 'It's good to see you.' His realised his hands were shaking, and he put them behind his back.

She said nothing, her face a mask, her lips pressed together. The child wriggled, dropped to the floor like a cat and went out of the room. The mother returned to her daughter's side, spoke rapidly, and the girl shook her head, then spoke, reluctantly: 'My mother asked if you are staying for tea.'

The sound of her voice flooded into him; he could see her

lips move as she formed the words. After months, a picture had come to life.

'Oh no,' he said, then turned to the mother with a smile. 'Actually, I wondered if I could invite Rita out for a coffee. There's something I'd like to discuss . . .'

His voice trailed off, and so he turned and smiled at the girl, then clasped his hands in front of him. 'Perhaps you could suggest somewhere?'

She did not reply, her eyes had not moved, and then he saw a small nod. She turned and walked back to the door. He held his hand out to her mother.

'It was so nice to meet you . . .'

'Thank you for coming. Please, next time stay for dinner.'

He almost raised her hand to his lips, as an apology for his lies, and then he followed the girl out of the door. It had started raining, softly.

She was walking rapidly, with long strides, and he kept pace, glancing at her, and once he glanced back. Her mother was still standing in the doorway, a bewildered expression on her face. Then they reached the end of the street, turned the corner, and she swung around to face him, her eyes flashing. He stopped in front of her, his eyes involuntarily taking her in, her form, her face: his brother's inamorata.

'Rita,' he started, then stopped. 'I'm Ben's brother. Francois.'

She nodded, opened her mouth, closed it and then opened it again.

'How did you find me?'

'My parents had your address. For the taxi.' And then, as if she needed reminding: 'You went to see them.'

She nodded again. He realised he had his hands stretched out in front of him, as if he wanted to catch her. He let them fall down to his sides.

'I found the photo that Ben took of you.'

She digested his words.

'Your parents didn't recognise me.'

'Well, they've not seen the photo.' He smiled but she did not return the favour, and his smile faded. She did not say anything, only stared at him.

He gestured at the rain, 'Look, shall we find somewhere to sit down?'

But she ignored him: 'You came to see my mother?'

'No. I came to see you.'

'But you spoke to my mother . . .' her voice was rising.

'Well,' he said, 'you spoke to mine.'

She was breathless; her cheeks were flushed. 'You told her you were . . . him.'

'No, she came to her own conclusions.' It was not quite a lie, he told himself. Near to one, but not quite.

'She told me, "Dr Martin has come to see you".'

He was quiet.

'That must have been a shock for you, but like I said, your mother—'

She turned away suddenly, striding up the road so that he had to jog a little to catch up.

'Can we talk? Can we go somewhere and sit down?'

She was crying, he could see, and he felt a brute, a bully. But at the same time he could not stop himself. 'I just want to know what happened. I want to know about Ben . . .'

'Why?' her voice was strangled.

'When did you last see him?'

She shook her head.

'Did he—'

'I don't want to talk about it. I don't want to talk to you.'

He reached over and put a hand on her elbow, which she shook off with a sudden violence. But she did stop walking and stood still, looking down, her breath coming fast.

He swallowed.

'OK. I can see that. But I'm staying with my parents for a few more days. Can you call me and we can go for a coffee or something?' He fiddled in his pockets, found a pen, an old tube ticket. 'My number. Please call me.'

He wasn't sure if she would, but she took the piece of card. She stared down at his number.

'Will you call me? Please?'

She raised her head, and he saw the heart-shaped face, the smudges under her eyes but the soft freshness of her lips, her bruised expression, and he thought, *Ben. Christ.*

'I saw him the day before . . .' Her eyes were huge.

'I see.'

She looked shell-shocked. Perhaps he was cruel to have looked her up, remind her of what had happened.

'I haven't told my parents,' she said.

He said nothing. Beyond her physique he had made few assumptions about her, and now the question arrived: what had he expected? Certainly he had not expected the surge of sympathy that rushed through him. He was confronting a broken spirit, that was clear. And along with this came a recognition of a purpose, as if his brother had left the photograph knowing that he, Francois, would feel exactly such a sympathy for this young and lovely and vulnerable individual before him.

'I've not gone back,' she continued, her words tumbling out. 'I've not gone back to uni. I'm not sure I'll go back.'

A tear rolled down her cheek. He reached out tentatively with one hand, touched her shoulder, and when she did not flinch he did the same with the other.

'Please,' he said. 'Please tell me what I can do,' he gave her shoulders a small squeeze. 'I want to help. I know Ben would want me to make sure you were all right.'

She raised her eyes; her eyelashes were clustered together.

'How can you know that?'

'He was my brother,' he said with as much confidence as he could muster. 'I just do.'

Part Three

13

WHEN she arrived at his office that morning, he was not there as they had arranged. Waiting outside, someone had told her the news. She stood aside as the hushed, shocked conversations ensued. Ben Martin had been a valuable member of the faculty. He was so approachable; he never made you feel dull. For his wife to die as well? Such a tragedy. Each comment was a reminder of the marriage, of the connections that each of them had to so many people. When Matt arrived, he had surprised her by enveloping her in a hug, crushing her face against the tattoo on his upper right arm, then said, let's go somewhere else. I'll buy you a drink. Could he see? Did he know? She refused, untangling herself from his embrace. She returned to the room she was renting and lay on the bed, staring at the ceiling until late into the night.

Some days later, she took the bus down to the river. The windows of the flat stood dark and empty, the occupants gone. If only she could go inside one last time, look on at his (her) books, look out from his (her) window, choose something as a memento. There was a movement in the large window on her right. The owner of the art gallery had been arranging something on a stand but was now eyeing her curiously. It was possible that she was recognised: she had passed in front of this window every time en route to her assignation in that glorious week. The woman stared; Rita could not look away. Eventually, she cast her eyes downwards, turned and walked away. That evening, she decided that she could not remain. She sent an email to the two friends she was due to share a flat with in the new term. She would be letting them down: they would think badly of her. There would be rapid, quick-fire, appalled condemnations of her last-minute decision. The judgements they would make upset her even as there was a derisive voice: and what if they knew everything?

How could she tell her parents that in her first foray as an adult she had amassed so much darkness? She had not the bravery to go somewhere alone, and so she alighted on Rosemary, a friend whose parents had no contact with hers. These parents had bought a flat in Cambridge as an investment when her friend had been accepted to read law. Rosemary, after the initial surprise, went silent on the phone when Rita explained: she would tell her parents at Christmas but needed a place to stay until then. She would pay her way of course, she would find a job in Cambridge. When her friend finally spoke, it was with a kindness that made tears pool in Rita's eyes. The other bedroom was already taken, by a paying tenant who could not be asked to leave. But there was a small room off the living room, a study of sorts but which already held a single futon. Would that do? And then her friend's voice lowered to a whisper: you're not pregnant, are you, Rita? When she had responded, no, no, it's nothing like that, I'm just stressed out, she had for a fleeting instant a vision of herself: her swollen belly holding a precious, living, breathing memento of Ben.

A few days after the decision was made, there was a brief and startling encounter with Julian, in a shop in town. She pretended she had not seen him, but to her embarrassment he had come over and asked after her. They spoke inconsequentially for a few minutes; he was friendly and relaxed. He was not a monster; he had clearly wanted to make amends. She could have behaved with more equanimity after their entanglement, but she had taken another road to more ruinous consequences.

The study in Rosemary's house in Cambridge would serve very well. Over the next months, if she feigned an inordinate interest in her studies, her parents need never know that she was not where they imagined her to be. She found a temp job as a data-entry clerk at a genito-urinary unit at the nearby hospital. She was taken into the manager's office on arriving for her first day and reminded that the patients' privacy was paramount: the conditions they might suffer were intimate and not to be disclosed to anyone. If she were to encounter the name of someone she thought she knew, she was beholden to come and inform the manager immediately. The clandestine nature of the post was an extension of what she had become accustomed to, only now the secrecy was sanctioned. She assured the manager that she was capable of great discretion. And over the next weeks she was left alone with her thoughts; the other clerks were not inclined to chat over coffee breaks, most sitting in silence with their phones. She paid a share of the bills, but Rosemary refused any rent, pointing out that Rita was sleeping in a glorified cupboard rather than a room. When the year was drawing to an end, Rita took her friend out to dinner to thank her. What will you do? Rosemary asked. Come clean, she had replied, but even as she said the words, she was not sure that she would.

In late December she took the train into London. Only months earlier, in India, she had travelled back on the train from her mother's family home, with her wounded mother, her stoic father, wondering when she would see Ben Martin again. This time, no matter how fiercely she longed for it, she knew she would never see him again. As she approached the house, she slowed down. She could hear voices inside: her brother and family had arrived for a pre-Christmas meal. They were all gathered in the living room; five pairs of eyes turned to look at her. Her mother had been talking, holding Mira on her lap. Her brother Joy rose to his feet.

'Reetie. How are you doing, little sis?'

He stepped across the carpet to give her a firm hug.

'Chetta . . .'

She turned to her sister-in-law, leaned forward to kiss her cheek.

'Chechi.'

'Still too thin,' Latha's mouth was turned downwards. Then she prompted Mira: 'Say hello, *mol*.'

The little girl unfolded herself from her grandmother's lap and approached Rita, who knelt down.

'Hello, Reetieaunty.'

She clasped the tiny body to her. 'Hello, Squirrel,' she whispered, 'I missed you.'

The child giggled.

'How's your tail?'

Mira turned around briefly, smiling widely.

'Ah,' said Rita. 'Still nice and bushy I see.' Then she stood up, the child still in her arms.

'Shall I take her to the park? Before it gets too dark?'

'No sit, wait,' her mother protested. 'You've just got back.'

'I'm fine,' she said. She could use the time to compose herself. 'Would you like to go on the swings?' she asked her niece.

The child looked tired: sitting on her grandmother's lap must have made her sleepy, but she nodded obediently. Within a quarter of an hour they were leaving the house, Rita piggy-backing her niece to the small playground in the corner of the park at the end of the street. The wind was cold, and Mira's nose was red. She wanted to go on the see-saw, and Rita helped her onto the seat, then sat on the other end, deliberately suspending her niece far up high, watching her cackle with delighted laughter. It had been months since she had last seen the child, but she had come passively. Would he have felt the same way about her: that she was a docile, malleable accomplice? She looked across the park; his parents' house was no more than a bus ride away.

'Reetieaunty.'

A shoe had fallen off, which she picked up and pushed back on the small foot, pressing the Velcro down. It was too raw to be outside, the light was fading anyway, but she was loath to go back to the house.

'Come on, Squirrel.'

They walked back briskly, hand in hand. Now that the return to the warm house was guaranteed, the child began to chatter. They re-entered. The men remained in the living room, where she deposited her niece; the women had moved to the kitchen. Her mother had prepared a feast. Another meal during which she let the Malayalam flow over her; at least Mira stayed close, on her lap. After Joy and Latha had left, Mira now asleep on her father's shoulder, she went upstairs into her bedroom. She plugged in her laptop, waited for it to boot up.

There was a knock on the door.

'*Mol?*'

Her mother came inside and sat on the bed. 'Don't work too hard. You look tired. *Ivvide irrike,*' she patted the bed.

It was her mother who looked tired, but she obeyed. Her mother put her arm around her, stroked her hair.

'Did you eat enough at dinner?'

She nodded.

'You know Seline has been unwell?'

'Unwell?'

'Have you been in touch with her?'

She shook her head, remembered with some guilt how Seline had emailed her some months back, asking after her.

'Onachen phoned,' her mother said. 'She hasn't been taking interest. Not even in the shop.'

The shop, Seline. They were speaking of a different world, but it was her world. The thought scared her. Impossible to reconcile, impossible to reconcile what she had done with whom she was supposed to be. Now she wanted her mother to leave for fear that she had powers hitherto unknown: that she could see into her daughter's heart. But her mother, unaware of her disquiet, stayed on as Rita unpacked her suitcase. While she placed her pile of T-shirts in her wardrobe, her mother talked about the arrangements for Christmas. Finally, she discovered a pair of jeans which needed washing, which her mother took away.

When her mother had gone, she reached into the zipped compartment of the suitcase and pulled out the book, stared at the cover. He had held it on one side and she on the other. And looking down at the novel as she had done that afternoon, she saw beyond it to the floor below: to her feet in the lace-ups she had been wearing, and beneath her feet the rough coir rug that covered that part of the room. Not the soft, fluffy wool rug he had laid her down on, so that as she had felt his weight on top of her, she had also felt as if she had a long-haired warm animal against her back. The sensuality of the memory made her catch her breath, and she let the book slip out of her hands onto the bed. She undressed, her heart beating, and crept to the bathroom. The hot water gushed against her body as she stood under the shower, her palms over her face, trying to still the images which spooled out in front of her like a collage from a film. She turned off the water and tiptoed back to her bedroom. There was no noise from her parents' room.

She had spent many nights thinking of his wife, punishing herself by remembering the woman who had been his chosen companion. We've known each other a long time. But all these weeks, months, it had never occurred to her to look beyond. Perhaps it was an unconscious fear of uncovering a network, a web of people who knew him better, who had more claim to his loss than she. She reached under the bed and pulled out a shoe-box covered with a colourful fabric: a memory store. Into it had gone her favourite notes from friends, some photos, programmes from her dance performances. Would this be where she kept this book? To join her other innocent, childish keepsakes? But she turned away, opened her laptop and typed his father's name.

A short biography revealed that he was born in the Cape area of South Africa in 1945 to English parents but moved to

Rhodesia aged ten. He grew up on a farm in Inyanga, and studied later at the University of Cape Town. He married an Englishwoman, Louise, whose grandfather had served with the Secretary of State for British India. The couple settled in Salisbury, later renamed Harare, where he taught at the university and wrote five of his eight novels. The entry finished: *In 1998, John Martin moved to London, where he now lives.* She skimmed through the list of search results, mostly reviews of his books, mentions of his name related to talks he delivered. And then, published in a newspaper supplement, an essay written, the introduction read, after the death of his son, Ben, in a car accident.

The darkness outside her window – she had not drawn the curtains – was that navy blue of winter nights. She saw her reflection in the window, the pool of light cast by her desk lamp, her eyes staring back as if a stranger's. Minutes passed as she kept her head turned away from the screen, and then, as if in slow motion, she turned back and read.

I arrived on this island twelve years ago. A few weeks earlier, if asked, I would have said that I have never felt at home. My eyes crave the austere beauty of plains covered in a brown, dry grass, the silhouettes of trees against open land. My ears long for the sound of people speaking across the street to each other in a language I never learned but which I can recognise in a second from a babble of a hundred. My bones miss the heat of a long, silent afternoon. In Africa, if I looked up I saw the sky was blue and everlasting. I exchanged that sky for London's, and a few weeks ago I realised what I have never allowed myself to think. I am, in effect, an émigré. I have left my home and it is unlikely I will return. It is possible my home will now welcome me back only as do the new owners of the house you sold, who rarely want you to revisit. But burying a son in the soil; well, that makes a place a home.

This island now holds the remains of my younger son and his wife. If I do not mention her again, it is not because I do not grieve her loss to this world. Only that the vacuum she has left belongs to her parents. I do not intrude on their sorrow, just as they do not intrude on mine. Rather, ours. For my son has left his mother bereft. Because we were foolish, I spent ten years away from my wife. My wife clung to her youngest, Ben; his brother, Francois, remained closer to me. When I finally arrived on this island, I was determined to re-acquaint myself with my younger son. But he was grown, a man. He had achieved, excelled. Slowly we began to find each other again, like an old jigsaw that you find tucked away in a cupboard. Once you start it you remember how often you used to make it, how the pieces have their familiar nicks and scrapes, telltale signs of where they should fit. My son and I renewed our friendship.

My last conversation with him: he was editing a collection of essays and his wife was in good health all things considered. He wondered if his mother and I might be free to visit in a fortnight, as he had bought tickets for a concert. If I had known that was to be our last conversation, I would have interrupted him and said, My boy, do you remember the afternoon in the Bvumba, we were camping, and only you and I, your mother and your brother arguing over the tent, saw the gazelle, come to inspect us and then leave, as if revealing herself only for our delectation?

Now my wife moves next door in her room. I hear the sounds of drawers being opened and closed, chairs creaking. I can imagine her movements. We have decided to return to the old days, when from across the length of the great continent, over a sea, we would imagine each other's daily lives. By re-enacting the decisions we made when our son was alive we have solace. When we decide to speak, I will tell her: my heart is broken.

The tears had arrived on seeing his name, in print, embedded in the sentences; she did not continue reading. In those few lines she felt she had learned more about Ben than she had ever known. She did not recognise the writer from his novel: grief had made his words cleaner. She returned to the blurb at the beginning: *One of Africa's most celebrated writers, John Martin, writes on the death of his son.* She stayed for some moments reading and re-reading that sentence, trying to breathe regularly, then she typed his brother's name in the browser. The first return detailed a forthcoming exhibition: *Hearts of Darkness. Contributors include Francois Martin, who is based in Lisbon.* Lower down there was a Q and A interview in a magazine. The photo showed a full head of dark hair, a strong resemblance to Ben. *What's in a name? Francois Martin explains how his parents' whim has caused a lifetime of explanations.* Her eyes dropped further down and she read on:

My parents are ardent Truffaut fans. The story is that my father invited my mother to watch *Jules et Jim*, which was showing in the only cinema in Salisbury, and their love blossomed. So, when I was born, they named me after the director. But 'Francois', spelt without the cedilla, is a fairly common name among Afrikaners of Huguenot descent. People have made all sorts of assumptions about me, especially when I lived in Cape Town. It means that I've spent my life talking about my parents and their love of Truffaut's work. Which, on reflection, might not be such a bad thing.

She closed her laptop. It was as if she were intruding on this family. He had compared them: it makes us different people, that dislocation, he had said. And yet, her own family's journey, her parents' journey from Kerala to South London, and frequent visits back and forth, seemed one-dimensional, neat and delineated, compared to his family's diffuse, sprawling connections over three continents, over an empire. She had only thought of him as himself, but she realised that he was composed of those around him. Perhaps there lay the reason for his interest in her, all those questions he had asked. He was searching for her story, knowing before she knew herself that she had one to tell.

She rode the bus in reverse, her fingers on her lips just as before. These lips, his lips. Seline had replied that morning: *I am fine, do not worry about me.* She sounded stilted, writing in English for Rita's benefit. *I am taking supplements for more energy. This year it was so hot, even after the rains. I got a stomach infection. Please write and tell me about your friends and studies.* As she read her cousin's words, she thought: she does not know me. I deceive everyone near me. It was three days to Christmas, four until she told her parents. She saw the bus was nearing a junction: this was her stop. There was a bustle, the shops were decorated gaily, excited children scampered, the restaurants were full. There seemed to be an excess of consumption, taunting her over the emptiness inside her. She was glad when she turned off the high street and into the quieter residential roads. She had worried that she would not recognise the house, but it stood at the end, its walls painted an elegant cream.

She expected the house to look smaller, but it was as she remembered. Not even a year had passed. The door was closed. She had no idea if anyone was inside, if they still lived there. She stared at the door and immediately could see herself inside, her lace-ups on the black and white tiles. She had followed him into the kitchen, watched as he rifled familiarly through cupboards. Had she known then what would happen? No. What had happened had taken them both by surprise. An alchemy, a natural event, like a rainstorm which arrives without warning.

She crossed the road and came to a halt near the path leading to the door. The front porch was clean, with lavender bushes and pots. So, one continued to tend the garden even after one's son has died. She found her feet starting to move, heard her boots crunching on the gravel – watch the step – and then she was standing right in front of the door. The knocker was heavy and brass; she had not used it before. After a minute, she heard footsteps in the hall. The door swung open.

'Mrs Martin?'

'Yes?'

Her soft silver hair was cut into a fringe, then fell long to between her shoulder blades. She was dressed in a long-sleeved blue dress, beaded necklaces at her throat, beads dangling from her ears. Her right hand was bandaged and was hindering her efforts to place the spectacles, hanging around her neck, onto her nose.

'Yes?' she repeated, when the glasses were in place.

'Mrs Martin,' she began again, 'I was a student . . .' She stopped.

His mother was silent, her hand still on the doorknob.

'I just wanted to say I was sorry to hear about . . .' she pulled out the book from her bag, 'about Dr Martin. And to give you this.'

His mother made no move to take it, but stared down at the book.

Then, 'Please come in.' She stepped back, held the door open, the dizzying pattern of black and white tiles now revealed.

'I don't want to bother—'

'Come in, please. Out of the cold.'

She stepped in, and his mother closed the door.

'I didn't catch your name?'

'Rita.'

'Rita,' his mother repeated. 'That's a pretty name. Not one you hear very often.' She smiled as she looked at her. 'I'm Louise,' then briskly, 'I was just going to take some tea out to my husband. Will you join us? I'm sure he'd like to meet you.'

'I really didn't mean to—'

'You can help me carry the tray.' She motioned to her bandage. 'My hand, you see. It's terribly painful. I'm so cross with myself. I should have worn gardening gloves, but I find them so unbearably awkward to take off.'

Unbeerably awkward to take orf. His mother's accent was a surprise, the unexpected vowels, the denser tone. She was already moving down the hallway, expecting to be followed. Down the stairs into the kitchen. The room had the same four walls, but the surfaces were in more disarray. His mother was placing cups on a tray, filling a teapot, finding a sugar bowl, teaspoons, placing biscuits on a plate.

'Will you manage this? If it's not too heavy?'

And then she was following his mother to the glass door at the side, leaving the house as she had never done before, stepping onto a small patio and down the path leading to, she could see now and couldn't remember if she ever noticed it before, a summer house made of wood. His mother rapped on the window, 'John, we have a visitor.' It was dim inside, but his father was rising to his feet and turning around at the same time. Tall, kind eyes, with a head of brushed-back hair, he squinted at Rita. She deposited the tray on the table in the centre of the small space and straightened up. There was a silence as she stood between these two old people, but not that old, neither much older than her own parents.

'John, this young lady is one of Ben's students, come to see us. Rita, this is my husband John.'

'He never taught me,' she said, as if this detail were more important than all the others she would not tell them. 'I was one of his personal tutees.'

They both looked on at her.

'I came to return this.' She plunged her hand into her bag and brought out the slim novel again, then held it out to them with both hands.

Neither made a move to retrieve it.

'He lent it to me . . .'

'I remember.' His father spoke. 'He mentioned giving

someone a lift, lending them the book.' Then he shook his head. 'There's no need to return it,' he said. 'Keep it.'

They were still for some moments, then his mother spoke, 'Sit down please, Rita. Have some tea.'

His father sat back in his chair at the desk, and she sat on a small armchair, his mother opposite. A writer's shed: books in piles, a surprisingly modern laptop, a beautiful old schoolteacher's desk. His mother poured tea, added milk, passed a cup to Rita. Then paused, her hands folded, the bandaged one below, and said, 'I do appreciate you making an effort to come all this way . . .'

'I don't live far. My parents live in Tooting.'

'Even so . . .'

They were quiet, each sipping their tea: so quiet she almost started giggling with nervousness at an image that arrived of the three bears.

'And what are you studying, Rita?' This from his father.

She set her teacup down.

'Anthropology.'

'Interesting.'

She could have nodded, said nothing in return: that was her habit. But she had placed herself in this little shed, and she owed his parents something, didn't she?

'My parents have a different opinion,' she smiled.

They fell on her words with eagerness; she understood that they needed her to talk, spend time, so that they could soak up this reminder of their son.

'I should have been a doctor or a lawyer or an accountant,' she continued, 'like my brother.'

'Good careers,' his father said. 'But we can't have everyone being a doctor . . .'

'I read somewhere,' his mother interrupted, 'that a degree in anthropology sets one up for a host of career paths . . .'

'Well, what we learn from studying others,' his father continued, 'is that there is by no means only one way of building

137

society or indeed sustaining society. But also that we have so much in common with each other . . .'

The conversation flowed. From her studies, they moved on to living up north, and then on again. Louise's father had been born in Lahore. Was Rita . . . ? Yes, she complied. She was four when she came to England. Yes, she visited quite frequently as a child, and she had last gone back in the summer. No, she didn't really speak the language, but she could understand it well enough.

'Do you remember, John,' his mother was saying, 'how my father would talk about India, even though he was only eight years old when he left? It never left him, his memories of the climate and the food. He talked so fondly of the house and his ayah,' she looked at Rita apologetically. 'They all had one in those days. I'm afraid it was all very colonial . . .'

'Did he ever go back?' she asked.

His mother shook her head. 'No, he didn't. And I've never been myself. But I can honestly say that my father never felt at home here in England. When he was older, he went to Rhodesia; he was in the police, and I grew up there. There's no one left in India. I mean,' she coloured slightly, 'none of my family.'

They fell silent, and then she turned to his father. 'I enjoyed your book very much.'

He raised his eyebrows, gave a little shrug, but she could see he was pleased.

'You must be one of the few people to have read it in the last thirty years,' he smiled.

'Are you working on something now?'

He shook his head. 'Just essays and articles mostly. I get too distracted by the cricket these days.'

His father folded his arms, and his mother laid her bandaged hand on the armrest of her chair. An attractive older couple. How had he described them? A couple of old hippies. They were attentive but not curious or prying. They were both warm, cultured and interesting people: fitting parents to have produced their son. They did not know how she had loved him, and she was unsure whether that knowledge would have consoled or appalled them. She got up to leave, started collecting the tea things on the tray.

'Well, thank you for having me . . .'

'It's been a pleasure,' his mother said. Then, 'John we must order a taxi for Rita. It's so dark now.'

'There's no need . . .'

'Nonsense. We have an account with a local chap. Just give me your address . . .'

They ignored her protests, accompanied her back into the house, then to the door. When the taxi pulled up, she turned to say her goodbyes, and to her surprise his mother clasped her in an embrace. 'It's so kind of you to pay us a visit,' she said. 'We didn't talk about Ben, but I feel that he's been with us.'

She could not reply, but turned to his father, who leaned down and kissed her cheek. 'Thank you, Rita.'

From inside the cab, she waved goodbye. His parents stood together, silhouetted against the light from the hall.

She slept fitfully, the voice of Seline mixing with the voice of Ben Martin: don't be too serious, Rita. Instead collect adultery, deception; preserve them and nurture them, put them in that box under the bed you are sleeping on, a box of mementos. She had simply wanted to return the novel, hadn't she? Or was she aware then that she was making her presence known? That a few days later, more confirmation of what had happened would arrive: a brother would appear and remind her that yes, she was that girl.

14

THE old tube ticket, his name and phone number scrawled across it, stayed with her for some days. He had left her on the corner of her street, as she had asked him to do, but with a heavy reluctance: she could see he did not believe that she would call. Why did he want to see her? He did not appear the type to jeer at salacious details, and she knew she did not appear the sort to offer any. He was, simply, grieving his brother. She remembered his paintings: he was the creator. He had said, later in that interview she had read: *How often do you see African subjects in a painting in the Louvre? I want to turn things on their head a bit. Show African themes through a Western prism. The story of my life, really.* She could not be as eloquent as he. After going to see his parents and enjoying their erudite but unassuming company, she had been doubly unable to speak to hers. They remained unaware of her circumstances, oblivious of her whereabouts the last few months.

When she called him, the gratitude in his voice was palpable. She had a few commitments with her parents, she explained, but would he like to meet just after the New Year? Yes, he agreed, perfect. He named a café, and before ringing off he thanked her. She had used her phone: he would have her number now. Slowly, slowly, she was revealing herself, as if she were a photograph being developed in a dark room. Her mother, after commenting on him when she had returned home that afternoon – such a nice man, I'm pleased to have met one of your professors – had not mentioned him again. Hopefully his visit would be forgotten in the bustle of the upcoming events: a gathering of the community, New Year's Eve at Latha's sister's pile in Croydon.

And then, on a bright, cold day, she arrived at the café he had suggested. He was not there; she ordered a drink and sat down. It was nearly a quarter of an hour later when she saw him, striding towards the building, his eyes searching for and then alighting on her in the window. She thought: it could be him. The same dark hair, the same build.

'Rita, I'm so sorry, please forgive me.' It was his accent which distinguished him from his brother: the skewed vowels that he shared with his parents, the heavier intonation. 'I got off at the wrong bus stop. What can I get you?' His eyes settled on her half-finished cup with disappointment.

'I'm all right, thanks.'

'Are you sure? A croissant or something?'

She hesitated for a fraction of a second, and so he pounced. 'I'll get a couple. And is that tea? I'll get you another. Won't be long.'

As he queued up at the counter, he did not turn around once. It was as if he were afraid that if he did he would invoke an unlucky charm and she would disappear. The barista took a disproportionate amount of time to organise the simple order on a tray, long enough for her to become nervous of how their conversation would develop. By the time he arrived at their table, she had contemplated several times slipping out quietly.

'Sorry for the wait,' he said, unpacking the cups, saucers, knives, little pots of jam and butter as if the agreement to meet with him merited nourishment. He didn't speak, waited for her to pour milk into her tea, split open the croissant, but the silence was not uncomfortable. At one point, he reached over when she was struggling with the small pot of jam, opened it and handed it back to her.

Then he smiled.

'I'm so glad you called,' he said.

She decided to share what had swilled around her mind over the last few days.

'I thought about what you said. How you found that photo of me. It must have been . . .' she hesitated, 'weird for you.'

He half-shrugged, then, after a few moments, he said quietly, 'I didn't find anything else related to you.'

No notes, no diary entries, no poems which needed finessing. She had left no trace, and the only evidence that she had been there, that the whole affair had actually happened, was a photograph.

'Where did you find it?'

He shifted in his seat. 'On his camera.' Then, 'When we were clearing out the flat.'

He did not elaborate, and so she asked, 'We?'

'Clare's sister,' he said. 'Clare's sister and I were clearing out the flat.'

'And,' she spoke slowly, 'did you show her the photo?'

He shook his head. 'No. I took the camera away with me.'

'And you didn't tell your parents?'

He shook his head again, cleared his throat.

'They were very touched that you went to see them.'

'I'm not sure why I did . . .'

'But I'm glad you did,' he interrupted. 'Otherwise I may never have found you.'

'But why did you want to find me?'

He was quiet for a long time. She took a sip from her cup, noticed that her hand was trembling.

Finally, he spoke: 'You meant something to Ben. He wasn't the sort to do things lightly.'

She felt her eyes fill with tears, and his face fell.

'This must be very hard for you,' he said.

She blew her nose. 'It must be hard for you as well,' she said eventually.

She looked out the window, could feel his eyes on her. What was he thinking as he looked at her? So this is the girl! He would have found that photograph months ago. That was a long time to be aware of the existence of a person but have no knowledge of where they were or who they were.

'You said,' he spoke, 'that you haven't been back to university. Would you tell me about that?'

She hesitated, found her throat constricting. 'I can't go back.'

A gentle probe: 'Why not?'

'Well,' she felt as if her tongue was loosening, 'I'm worried people will find out about me and Ben,' she took a breath, 'and what they'll think of me. And whether I'll get in trouble. And there are just too many places where I know I'll be thinking, that's where he was standing or that's where we . . .' Her voice petered out.

'But your degree,' he said. 'What I mean is, if you don't want to go back, which is understandable,' he added quickly, 'maybe you should try to transfer to another university.'

It was not something she had considered. She sipped her tea without saying anything.

'What was . . .' He stopped and started again. 'Did Ben teach you? Is that how you met?'

She shook her head. 'I never took his classes. He only taught second years and above. He was my personal tutor. I had these meetings with him about general stuff.'

She could feel the colour rising to her cheeks. From that description it was hard, even for her, to imagine how a liaison could have emerged. He nodded, did not press her, and she looked out of the window again and then back at him.

'Ben's wife,' she said. 'Clare. How are her family?'

He laid his spoon down. 'Well, it was a shock.' Then, 'You have a brother, don't you? And a niece? She's adorable.'

She smiled. 'Yes, she is.'

'How old is she?'

'Three.'

He folded his hands together. He had the same nice long fingers, neat nails. Had she not read somewhere that twins

143

separated at birth often pursued the same hobbies, wore the same hairstyle? Perhaps it was the same for two brothers, separated in late adolescence: they adopted the same grooming habits. A wave of lethargy washed over her. There was no reason for this conversation, was there? Perhaps it was his artist's mind: the need to shade in the backdrop, add light and dark, shorten or lengthen shadows and shapes.

'I never found out,' she needed to ask, 'about the funeral.'

He waited for some time before he said, 'There was a joint funeral. Near Brighton.'

In death they had rediscovered each other. An image flashed before her, coruscating, of the two of them, lying under metres of soil, their skin brilliantly white, bloodless, mud in their mouths. Turned to each other, their fingers entwined – and she felt the nausea rise in her throat. We've known each other a long time. Friends, lovers, spouses, now death-mates.

She pushed her plate away and slipped her arms into her jacket. 'Well, thank you.'

'Please don't go yet . . .'

He looked crestfallen, as if he had imagined that they would spend hours, the whole afternoon together, in facile, unfettered conversation. Could he not see?

'What can I tell you?' she asked. 'I have nothing to offer you except for details of our affair. Is that what you want?'

The words sounded grandiose, incongruous in the setting.

'Of course not—'

'Well, then what else can we talk about? It lasted a few weeks, no more. I can count on my hands the times we spent together.'

Her voice had risen, and the couple at the table next to them with their toddler were noticeably quiet. She left the café, and only when she reached the lights to cross over the road did she notice that he was standing next to her and, further, that she was unsurprised that he was.

'You don't have to tell me what happened,' he said. 'It's not about that.'

The light turned green, but she didn't cross the road.

'I just hope to . . . I don't know . . .' He had pushed his hands into the pockets of his jeans and was standing humbly before her, his hair falling onto his forehead, looking much younger than he would be, as if he was stumbling over asking her for a date. 'Spend a bit of time with you, before I go back.'

She remained silent.

'I live in Portugal, you see.'

'I know,' she said. 'I looked you up.'

He was quiet for some time, as if processing what this said about her.

Then he said, 'I mean, is there anything I can do? Do you want me to go back with you? We could find out about re-registering . . .'

She shook her head. 'I can't go back.'

She should have turned to leave then, but she stared at her feet. He seemed content to stand with her, for many minutes, not speaking.

'I still haven't told my parents that I didn't go back,' she said finally.

When she did not continue, he asked, 'So where did you go, I mean, after the accident?'

He seemed concerned about her welfare, but then, hadn't Ben? Before he left her with the immense, unseeable, unwieldy, indescribable black stone that had lodged itself in her chest.

'I stayed with a friend, but I can't do that again.' She turned to face him fully. 'I'll have to tell my parents. And I'll be all right.'

She held out her hand. 'It was nice meeting you.'

He took her hand, but he didn't let it go. He was half-smiling, shaking his head. 'I can't end it like this,' he said, his voice apologetic. 'I'm afraid I just can't say goodbye when I don't know what you're going to do.'

'I'll be all right,' she repeated. 'Thanks for your concern.'

His eyes were fixed on hers for a long time, as if willing her to say something, but she remained silent. Then he let her hand drop, without taking his eyes away from hers. 'If you think of anything, and I mean anything,' he said, 'that I can help you with, will you,' now his voice was almost pleading, 'will you please call me?'

She nodded, smiled briefly and then skipped across the road. She did not turn back; she had no idea how long he stood on the pavement. It was later that night, in her bed, her mind a tumult, that she realised that there was something that she wanted. It was late, but she called him and he was not miffed, rather unambiguously relieved. He was so pleased she had asked. Of course he would; he completely understood. And it might be a good idea. It would let her have some kind of resolution to a very difficult few months. They could take the train down to Brighton later the next morning and visit the cemetery. She would be able to say her goodbyes.

She had only visited the graves of her grandparents, in verdant, mossy graveyards in Kerala. Each grandparent had a large head-stone, a fat slab of concrete, an epitaph in flowery language. This cemetery felt bleak. Two small stones, each with the same brief message: *In loving memory.* The same year of birth, the same death day. They were so low, so close to the ground, that she bent down so she would not be towering above them, mocking them with her erect, alive body. She felt a sadness engulf her, not just for Ben but for this couple interred in front of her, for she could see there was a forgiveness, both now lying side by side. She tried to pray but could only snatch at generic, well-memorised venerations. She tried to speak to him but only got as far as, Ben, I just want to say . . . For what did she want to tell him? That she understood now that he had never been hers alone? She found herself projecting his image – looking down at her smiling – onto the small stone bearing his name; Clare's stone remained blank. And then she closed her eyes, shook the memories away. It was inappropriate to remember their intimacies when his wife lay beside him. She emptied her mind so that all she did, for an endless, silent tranche of time, was stay still before them, welcoming the chill on her skin, the freshness of the air. When she rose to her feet and turned away, some words finally arrived: I'm sorry.

It was afterwards, when they were on the train back, that she became aware of him again. He had stayed in the background, as if he understood she needed her own moment, and only after this did he make his play. If you like, he said, you can come and stay with me, until you make up your mind. He understood why she was disinclined to return to the same university, but there were other places. Maybe she should investigate transferring to another institution, then present her parents with a fait accompli.

She had asked him then, 'Aren't you married?'

'I was married,' he said, 'but not any more. I have a girlfriend.' And then, as if pre-empting any questions, 'I'll tell her,' before continuing: they did not live together, she would have her son visiting anyway. She would not mind.

'Did you tell her about me?' she asked.

He had taken a few seconds before saying, 'Yes.' Then, 'Does that bother you?'

She nodded and allowed her hair to fall forward so he would not see her face.

'I know I did something wrong,' she said. 'I'm not proud of myself.'

He had remained quiet. His eyes were dark with concern when she looked up at him.

'Rita,' he spoke quietly, 'if we need to apportion blame or responsibility or whatever, then Ben comes out of this worse off.'

She contemplated his words.

'Because I'm younger? I'm not a child.' She tried to sound detached, mature, as if inspecting her handiwork. 'He said that himself once,' and then glanced at him. He was watching her, hungry for just that kind of comment: for her to narrate the words she and his brother had shared. 'He said I needn't worry. But of course that's not true. I'm just as at fault.'

He said nothing and she asked, 'Does anyone else know?'

He shook his head, a brief movement.

'Thank you,' she whispered, ashamed at how grateful she was that he had not exposed her deceit.

He was quiet, his hands tapping a gentle beat on his thigh; hadn't Ben had the same habit? But the man sitting beside her was different with her. There was a deference, a restraint. Any such caution on Ben's part had been short-lived. She looked out of the train window. They were leaving the graves behind, the two bodies which weren't even bodies: they were ashes. It was only because of her upbringing that she imagined them as whole, under the earth. Just as even now in her mind she relocated their gravestones to a graveyard in Kerala, the coconut trees whispering above them.

15

HE lived on the top floor, no lifts he apologised. He carried her suitcase as she went up ahead, climbing and climbing up the dingy stairwell, while he intermittently banged on the stair-lights, which glowed dully in the gloom. At the top, there was a tiny landing with two doors on either side. 'The one on the right,' she could hear him say behind her, and then he was stand-ing next to her, her suitcase still in one hand while he used the other to turn the key in the lock, over and over. He opened the door, stood aside for her to pass in front of him, then stepped in himself and closed the door. 'Over here,' he moved to the left down a small corridor, 'is the kitchen. Small but perfectly formed.' Then he opened the door at the end through which she spied light spilling into a small bathtub from a skylight above, a plant sitting on the end, 'Bathroom,' and then walking back towards her and leading her forwards, 'Living room cum everything else.'

It was a large open area, spanning the width of the building. The dark wooden floorboards gleamed in the light falling around them, dazzling her after the gloom of the stairwell and entrance hall. As well as tall windows punctuating the walls, there were two floor-to-ceiling French doors to the front, two more to the side, each with its own small balcony, hemmed in by a wrought-iron railing. As she walked into the space, she saw to her right a bed and wardrobe; in the middle section a sofa and coffee table. There was a small table with four chairs in front of the hatch through which she could see the kitchen. And then, at the other end, under another skylight, a sudden chaos. A stack of canvases, pots, cloths, a wooden bench, an easel: his studio.

'When I bought it, there were three small rooms,' he was saying. 'I knocked all the walls down and ended up with this. It works better. At least,' he smiled down at her, 'it does for me.' Then, 'Do you want to give me your coat?'

She slid it off her shoulders, then bent and unzipped her boots, slipped them off.

'Shall I leave them here?'

'That's fine. Thanks.'

He led her to one of the French doors, pulled at the handle, swinging both glass panes open. They stepped onto the small balcony. 'In the summer, I leave them open all day. We get a great breeze up here. Just take care.' The city tumbled down the hill before them.

He walked back and picked up her suitcase. 'You take the bed,' he said. 'There's a camp bed over there,' he pointed to his studio, 'that I use sometimes anyway. That will be my wing.' He set the suitcase down next to the bed.

'It's all very open-plan,' he continued, 'but I'll be there on the camp bed and you'll have your own space. Actually,' he paused, thinking, 'I have a screen that I can put up.'

He went into the hall and returned with a dark wooden frame, a spray of orchids and lilies on the material stretched across it.

'It's nice,' she said, for something to say.

'It comes in useful.'

'For what?'

He seemed to avoid her eyes. 'If I have a model over . . .'

She said nothing more. He arranged the screen at the foot of the bed, then started pulling the bed sheets off, and she walked to the other end, tucking in the fresh sheets, while he produced another quilt from his wardrobe and threw it over the bed. Then he left her, so she opened her suitcase and took out a few things, laid them on the window ledge. When she looked up, she saw that he had moved to the kitchen, and after some hesitation she followed.

'Can I help with anything?'

He had his head in the fridge, raised it at her voice. 'There's nothing to help with. There is literally no food in the house.' He smiled, shut the door. 'Why don't we go out for a bite?' he said. 'I'll show you the square and where the supermarket is, and we can set ourselves up a bit?'

She used the bathroom, which was pristine but spartan: no sign of his girlfriend's toiletries. They left the flat, and he gave her a key, showed her how to turn the locks. They walked down the hill towards the main shopping area, the Baixa, and then up the opposite hill.

'This place,' he said, holding the door open, 'my favourite place. I first came when I moved here; I was renting on this side of the city. I'd just left Mozambique, and I remember coming here and thinking as I sat down, this is my new life.' He led her upstairs where there were more tables, a view of the street below. 'They do a nice seafood rice here. Does that suit you?'

'Yes, thanks.'

'Would you like some wine?'

She shook her head.

'I'll just give our order.'

She heard him speaking in Portuguese downstairs, and laughter: he was obviously a regular customer. He came bounding up the stairs carrying a stick of bread, a bottle of mineral water and two glasses. He sat down, and as he poured their water he resumed speaking as if he had not stopped.

'I sat here, actually, this same table. And then, over there,' he pointed, 'a couple sat down. And then the man gets up and walks over. Turns out they lived in Maputo and were on holiday. They recognised me from the cultural centre I helped run. I remember thinking, I'm not leaving anything behind me, I'm just adding on.'

He smiled, acknowledging the end of his anecdote.

'Ben said once,' she said, and she noticed how his ears pricked up, 'that we were the same, him and me, because we were both kind of immigrants, or at least children of immigrants. But when I think of my parents, they left India to go to London, and that's that now. It seems so much more uncomplicated than your family.'

He laughed. 'I've not seen it that way before.'

'We only ever go back to India. But where would going back mean to you?'

He took some time. Their plates of food arrived, delivered by a woman who kissed Francois on both cheeks, then laid a hand on his shoulder affectionately as they chatted.

'It's interesting you mention Ben,' he said when the woman had left. 'because he had such an affinity with where we grew up. I'm not sure I do . . .'

He had not answered her question, only alluded to another. She ate quietly. He was similarly quiet, but attentive: tearing her off some more bread, topping up her water. They had nearly finished their plates before he spoke again.

'I have a good friend from my Maputo days, who lives further along the coast from here. He's invited us to a party at the weekend.'

'What about your girlfriend?'

'She's busy at the weekend with her son. I'll phone her tomorrow and ask them to come round for dinner or something this week.'

He was not looking at her but wiping some crumbs from the table onto his palm.

'Is she cross with you . . . ?'

He looked up, abashed, his face breaking into a smile. 'She might be.' Then, 'But it's not just about you.'

'Do you not want to get married again?'

'I'm not the marrying type,' he grinned. 'Too set in my ways.'

'But you don't mind having me around.'

His smile disappeared, and he spoke hurriedly. 'Not at all. You can stay as long as you want.'

She looked out of the window as he went downstairs to pay. There were few people on the street outside; even though it was a capital city, there was an unhurried, contemplative air. They stopped at a supermarket back up the hill where he bought some supplies, then walked back towards the flat, as he pointed out landmarks: if you use the castle to orient yourself, it's impossible to get lost. That's where you can buy a tram ticket; if you're stuck, go and see Jorge in there, he speaks very good English. Then they reached the square, which she recognised, and they sat on a bench, outside the church, listening to a busker, until night fell and the wind became too cold to be sitting still.

Back in the flat, he insisted that she use the bathroom first; when she returned to the living room, she saw he was in his studio area, papers scattered around him. He did not turn around, evidently trying to give her some modicum of privacy. Good night, she called out, and only then did he turn halfway around, good night, Rita. She lay in the bed, her eyes not fully closed, so she could see when he dropped out of his clothes, walked across the room in his trunks to return later, a towel tied around his waist, drying his hair with another. His body was hard and male, and disconcerting. He had the same broad shoulders and chest tapering to his waist, the same long muscles, the same line of dark hair bisecting his lower abdomen.

She was unsure whether she would ever sleep, she was so aware of his presence across from her. Earlier that day, they had met at the airport for only the fourth time, as very new acquaintances. Now they were sharing a bathroom, sleeping metres from each other. She could hear him turning the pages of a book, and then the sound of it falling to the ground with a thud. She got up from the bed to use the toilet a last time, and when she was tiptoeing back she could not stop herself looking across. He was fast asleep, half on his stomach, one arm under the pillow, the quilt pushed down to his waist. His whole demeanour was of satisfaction, a job well done: that he had found her and brought her back with him. She climbed back into the bed, pulled the quilt over her, counted the diamonds in the patterns that the windows threw onto the wall before falling asleep.

16

WHEN she blinked awake, her first impression was that she was in heaven: the room was filled with a golden light. She peeked around the screen and saw Francois. He was sitting at the small table near the hatch, his legs stretched out before him, a pot of coffee at his side, scooping what looked like porridge from a bowl, already dressed in a pair of cargo trousers and T-shirt. She wriggled under the quilt, pulling on the pyjama bottoms she had taken off for the night, then sat up. She peeked again and saw that he was keeping his eyes considerably averted. There was nothing she could do about her hair, which would be a mess; there was nowhere she could wash her face before she presented herself. She swung her legs off the bed, pulled on a zip-up over the T-shirt she slept in and walked out from behind the screen.

'Good morning,' he said, without raising his head. 'Coffee? Milk?'

'Yes, please.'

He poured her a cup and waited until she was seated before looking up, his eyes crinkling apologetically.

'You don't have much privacy, do you?' he said. 'I should have kept those walls up.'

She shook her head. 'It would spoil the whole effect,' she said, 'It's like waking up in the mountains or something. At the top of the world.'

'That's a nice way of putting it. Thanks.' He looked pleased with her announcement. He passed her the coffee, and she tucked her feet up in front of her, blew on the hot liquid.

'Did you sleep well?' he asked.

She nodded. 'Did you? You must miss your bed . . .'

'I don't. Like I said, I often sleep on the camp bed. Do you want porridge? Or toast?'

She watched as he buttered a slice of toast and pushed it over towards her.

'You'll see that I don't,' he said, paused and used air quotes, 'go out to work as such. But I've got to meet some people today and be various places. I'll be back about five or six, I think. Will you be all right on your own?'

He reminded her about the keys, then stood up, stacking the plates and placing them on the hatch. Then, pointing to her end, 'I'll just get a few more shirts and things.'

'Yes, of course.'

She sipped her coffee as he opened his wardrobe, pulled out a set of neatly folded clothes. He caught her eye as he walked back across, and she said, 'Sorry to chuck you out of your wing.'

'Don't be silly,' he said. 'That's the last time you need to say that or even think that. I'm an old itinerant at heart.'

When he left, she walked across the room and opened one of the French doors, leaned on the railings. To her right, she could see the castle, on top of the hill of green trees. The white houses with terracotta-tiled roofs spilled down the incline until they disappeared into the flatness near the port, the Baixa. To her left she could glimpse the river, so wide that it appeared as if it were the ocean that it fed into some miles further ahead. Directly below, the narrow cobbled street. The grey stones were neatly inserted into their positions, mesmerising – as mesmerising as a pattern of black and white tiles.

She closed the doors and turned back to the room. He had made the camp bed neatly; on the floor next to his bed was the small pile of clothes. She pulled off her zip-up so she was in her thin night T-shirt, and lifted the first item – a long-sleeved shirt – slipped it on. The shirt fell to the same part of her thighs; it swamped her shoulders in a similar way. He had a pair of trainers shoved to one side, and she stepped into them, took a few steps around the flat to the window, and then into his atelier.

Unlike the rest of the flat, which was minimally furnished, here there was clutter. There were wooden frames of various sizes and several uncompleted canvases. She had not imagined this to be the way an artist worked, but maybe ideas came and went and had to be recorded for later, like jotting down notes in a notebook. There was a stack of canvases on one side, leaning up. One, sandwiched between two larger frames caught her eye, and she slid it out. A figure, naked from the shoulders up, looking over her shoulder. A rush arrived, like boiling water poured into her veins. It was her.

To capture the moment, to capture you. When she had stood at the window, she had known Ben's eyes would be following her, just as she had known they were on her as she admired the women in the river. The man who had painted those women was the man who had painted this image, which rendered the tones of her skin and the planes of her form with much more subtlety, grace and harmony than she felt she possessed. It was an unsettling thought: that he had painted her before she had met him. Her heart was beating fast, and she had to take a moment to breathe. She stared at the canvas; the brushstrokes were evidence of what he had taken in. She knew that to evoke such a rich facsimile of a person, he would have spent much time considering the flat two-dimensional image he had found. She could imagine him lying on his bed, or leaning out of his balcony, toying with the controls of the camera, zooming in and zooming out, sliding across one way and then the other, as if she had emerged from behind his screen and was posed in front of his easel, while he held a large magnifying glass in his hand.

But then hadn't she done the same: examined the photograph which accompanied the interview she had read without his knowing, scrutinised his features? His wide, open gaze framed by the thick dark eyelashes that he shared with Ben; the dimple that nestled in the stubble on his cheek – this, unlike his brother. She had not then transferred these aspects of him to another medium – she had not his talent – which is all that he had done. She waited until she could feel her muscles relax. It was his idiolect, to paint. The kindness and consideration he was showing her: she should not forget that. She pulled his shirt closer around her. If she was wearing his clothes, sleeping in his bed, how could she object to him painting her eyes and mouth and hair? She slid the painting back into place in the stack, went back to his camp bed and sat down.

On the floor next to her feet were a large glass of water and a book that she recognised immediately. There was a piece of paper, folded over with notes scrawled across it, which he was using as a bookmark. *Daughters of Africa*. She forced herself to open the book, found the page, *For Clare*. His words survived even if they hadn't. Ben and Clare. Clare and Ben. There was no reason why it should be, but somehow she was sure that the book in her hands was the same book she had held in his flat that first time she had visited, he had made her lunch. She closed her eyes and lay down on the camp bed, the trainers slipping off her feet, the shirt enveloping her like a blanket. His pillow smelled of washing powder, shampoo and another musky male smell. She opened her eyes and turned to the page where Francois had placed his bookmark.

The commonly held assumption that women's rights to land are weaker than men's has recently been contested, with scholars such as Goodwin and Sithole arguing that across a diverse continent, with varied socio-historical contexts, the realities must be more complex than imagined. Letitia is a case in point. Finding herself pregnant at the age of nineteen, she married and had three more children with her husband, Munyaradzi. He died suddenly from a heart attack, and she approached his family in the Eastern Highlands, who offered her some land in Mutare. She joined the Manyame project – a project which engages women farmers to grow the herbs and plants used to produce the essential oils and natural remedies for the Western market – and she is now a small-scale farmer on the land she was given by her late husband's family.

Letitia's story reveals a paradigm that has been neglected in academic literature, that of land acquisition through kinship not only inheritance, and of women's rights to land decided on a familial basis. What Letitia's story also shows, however, is how colonial discourses on land and the uneasy relationship between colonisers and the indigenous people in positions of power have led to the very chequered nature of land appropriation, and the patchwork of policies available in a country such as Zimbabwe, and indeed over the continent.

The phone rang, startling her. She had not noticed that he had a landline in the corner of the room. She did not move – Francois would call her on her mobile, surely – and the voicemail kicked in. His instructions were brief, in English. There was a pause and then a woman's voice: *Francois, hi, it's Jane. I was wondering when you were next planning to come over to London. There's something I'd like to discuss. Um. Better in person.* A pause. *OK, let me know.*

The phone message stirred her. She sat up, closed the book, slid his shirt off, refolded it. She stood up and patted his camp bed so that he would not see the impression her body had made. Then she pulled out her laptop from her suitcase, set it up on the table. She spent an hour looking at university websites and sent off two requests for further information, an email to her parents telling them she was working hard. The lies came easily after months of practice. Then she changed her clothes, pulled on her jacket and went downstairs onto the street and up the incline to the square, where she sat on the wall overlooking the city for some time, listening to the busker, the same from the previous evening, who smiled and bowed at her in recognition. When she left, he gave her a wave, which she returned.

She found her way back to the supermarket, bought two pieces of fish and a few more vegetables and spices. The least she could do was cook dinner, which she did. And when he returned, his surprise and appreciation was gratifying. He ate heartily, complimenting the meal and querying after the spices she had used, where she had bought them. He stopped her when she began clearing the table – the chef doesn't wash up – only allowing her to dry the dishes with a tea towel after she insisted.

When they had finished and were leaving the kitchen, he said, 'I'm meeting Lucie and Josef for a drink. There's a singer I know who's playing in a bar just down the hill. Would you like to come along?'

The suggestion of a dinner en famille had not been well received, as she had expected. He must have called his girlfriend during the day, been rebuffed.

'Should I?' she asked quietly.

He stopped in front of her, gave her a sheepish smile. 'I think she should meet you,' he said. 'So I'd be grateful if you came.'

She murmured her agreement, and then as she moved away to her end of the room to change into a warmer top – the temperature was dropping – she remembered: 'You've got a voice message,' she said. 'Someone called this morning.'

As she brushed her hair, she heard him play the message. *Francois, hi, it's Jane.* She glanced around the screen: he was standing with his hands on his hips, listening, then he bent forward, deleted the message. She watched as he stood still for some minutes, then turned around, 'Ready?'

She walked towards the entrance hall but then stopped and gestured to his studio area.

'I hope you don't mind, but I looked at some of your work.'

'That's not a problem.'

'I saw the painting,' she decided to say. 'Of me.'

He had been slipping his jacket on, but he slowed down; he was not brushing off her discovery. He moved closer, his eyes searching hers.

'I found that photo on Ben's camera,' he said, 'and somehow it felt like the right thing to do.' He paused, 'You can have it if you want.'

'I'm not sure I'd hang it up.'

'I'm not as good as I think I am then.'

She did not return his smile. 'That's not it . . .'

He was quiet, and then he reached forward, gently squeezed her elbow. 'I should apologise for painting you without asking you first.'

She shook her head, tried to smile, but her lips felt dry.

'If we hadn't met,' she ventured, finally, 'what would you have done with it?'

His eyes had not left her face, and he spoke quietly.

'I might have shown it somewhere.'

Then, as she watched him, she saw his eyes soften, waiting for her reaction.

'For me to see it?'

'Or,' he hesitated, 'or someone who knew you . . .'

A phone call, an email from a friend. Hey, Rita, there's a painting of you in an exhibition! The likelihood of such a coincidence manifesting itself was slight. No, he had painted her to try to get under her skin, and under his brother's: give warmth and flesh to an ephemeral glance over a shoulder, to the two people on either side of the exchange.

'Well,' she said, trying to smile, 'I came in from the cold, didn't I?'

'I'm glad you did.' His grin was full of relief, gratitude, and he touched her arm lightly.

Out of the corner of her eye she could see, behind him, the canvas, propped up on the ground, but she had no wish to look at it again, and it appeared unlikely that he would pull it out and explain his work. She had been quiet; she felt his hand on her arm again – shall we? – and she allowed herself to be led outside the flat.

As they went down the stairs, she asked, 'Can I give you some money? For the flight and expenses and everything?'

He shook his head. 'Don't worry about that. I owe you for a delicious dinner anyway.'

'It wasn't that special.'

'It was to me.' Then he stopped. 'Really, Rita. I didn't ask you to stay because I wanted you to pay for lodgings or anything. Did you have a look at some universities?'

She nodded.

'Well, that's great. That's what you should be worrying about.'

She couldn't tell him that none had excited her, that the prospect of studying again now seemed old-fashioned, as if it belonged to a different era. But that was why he had invited her. Because he knew she would not stay with him for ever. They walked in silence down the hill, down a steep cobbled street cut into the side of a rock face, and when she glanced at him she saw his expression was filled with trepidation, like a small boy caught red-handed. It would be awkward, this meeting with his girlfriend.

Lucie was striking: toned and tanned. Dark hair cut close to her scalp, black eyeliner, nude lips, with a sculpted figure, wearing a tight black sleeveless top, black jeans. They kissed on the lips in greeting, Francois and Lucie, while she and the son skulked in the background: the children.

'Nice to meet you.' She had a sultry voice and offered a firm handshake. 'This is my son, Josef.'

A beanpole, nearly Francois's height, gangly, with brown hair lying around his ears.

'This is Rita,' Francois said, and then played the host: what drinks did everyone want? Would a carafe of wine be a good idea?

'Just orange juice for me, please,' she heard herself saying. He went to the bar, and she followed him involuntarily with her eyes, and then returned to see the woman, Lucie, watching her, her expression not cool, not unfriendly: non-committal.

'So how do you find Lisbon?'

'It's lovely,' her voice sounded gushing. 'And it's so sunny.'

'Well, we get the rain, wait for it.'

'I love the architecture.'

'You haven't been before?'

She shook her head.

'Well, you must ask Francois to show you the coast,' the woman said generously.

He returned with a tray, handed out the cola and orange juice, lifted the carafe and poured Lucie a glass of wine before pouring one for himself, then sat back smiling. His efforts were almost comical, and she felt some pity for him.

'Good to be back, Josef?'

His mother pouted. 'He's hardly been home. He's been meeting friends nearly every evening.'

'Have you settled in Cologne?'

The youth grunted. What did he know about this assembly? It was unlikely that Lucie had shared all the details with him, but then how could she be sure?

There were a few chords, and the musician began to play: a welcome distraction. She saw Francois and Lucie speaking, in low tones, their eyes on each other's lips. There was a tension between them, the way he touched her arm with contrition while she sat unmoving, holding her head turned away from his. A memory: sitting above Ben and Clare in the library, he was looking up at her. She turned away and focused on the singer, a young man in a beanie, with a guitar. He sang in English, mostly covers, strumming expertly, and she found herself tapping her foot.

'*Obrigado*,' he said when he finished his set, this directed at Rita, who blushed and glanced back to see Lucie watching her, an amused smile on her lips. But she was not supercilious, not hostile. How must she feel that Francois had brought back the embodiment of his brother's infidelity? That the person was now sleeping in his flat, in his bed?

She stood up.

'I'll make my way back,' she said to Francois. 'Thanks for the drink.'

He started to get up.

'No, stay,' she said. 'It's so close and there are so many people around. I'll be fine.'

Then Lucie spoke: 'Josef will go with you, to the door,' and she said a few words to her son, who began to unwind himself. When he stood next to her, the sensation that they were siblings, asking permission from their parents, persisted.

'He knows the way,' Lucie continued. 'I'll see you again, Rita,' and she stood up to kiss her cheek.

She left with Josef, who trudged next to her up the incline, not saying a word, until they reached the entrance door. 'Thanks,' she said, and he was gone. She was already in bed when she heard Francois return, heard him run the shower and then pad across the room. She peered around the screen: he was lying on his side on the camp bed, a small lamp poised so that he could read. He had picked up the book, *Daughters of Africa*, was finding his place; she could see his head bent over his brother's words. She turned over so she faced the window, and watched the night sky. She had not heard his voice in those words; he had not introduced her to that world. He had kept her separate; she was nowhere to be found. Her name was not written down in any of his books. Just as Lucie did not leave any belongings in Francois's flat, she had left no trace in Ben's life.

17

THE next day she woke earlier, to the sound of Francois walking across to the entrance. He was wearing running clothes. The door closed with a soft click, and she was alone. She did not want to impinge on his lifestyle, but if she was here sleeping in his bed, then Lucie was not able to. She would not have breakfast: she felt suddenly unwilling to be sipping his coffee and eating his toast when he returned. She washed and dressed quickly, slipping her laptop into her bag. At the door, she stopped, wondering whether to leave a note on the table, but if she did he might feel he had to do the same whenever he went out. She had her phone, he had his – that would suffice. She ran down the stairs, munching on an apple, and stepped out onto the street. It was fresh, not very cold.

She meandered down the hill towards the Baixa. It was invigorating to be plunged into strange, unfamiliar surroundings. Aside from the frequent returns to India, school trips, one week when she had accompanied her friend Priya and family to a resort in Spain, she had not left London. Tooting and the Bhavan in Kensington had formed the margins of much of her life before she went away to university. Lisbon was an unforeseen destination. A tram hooted beside her, nudging her elbow; it was a beguiling city. By now more people were appearing, walking purposefully, on their way to work. She would benefit from a routine, but for now she would imbibe the mellow environs. Just before the short stretch to the Baixa, she turned into a café, managed to order a milky coffee and a toasted baguette. As her order was being prepared, she sent Francois a text: *Gone out for a walk*. Her phone beeped soon after. *That's great. See you later. F.* Then she seated herself near the window. The coffee was hot and strong, and she ate the baguette hungrily. The waiter approached with another toasted slice and said something, smiling. When it was clear she did not understand, he said in English: of the house. It was only after he had left her that she understood: *on* the house.

When she opened her bag, she extracted not her laptop but her notebook. She wrote 'Anthropology One' at the top of the page and then listed all the modules she had taken in her first year, the marks she had received. She had done best in 'Ritual and Symbols in Religion', even though her final assignment had been completed in a rush. She chewed on her pen as she looked at the names of the courses she had followed: not she, another person. Her pen began to doodle and then began to write: *crying in his office, in the café queue, in the park (with Clare), in the library (with Clare), in the café (his invitation), outside on the street after the performance, in his car, in his parents' house*, and then she stopped. There was no point. She had been to the graves, hadn't she? She had met his parents; she was staying with his brother. Life was moving on; new scenes were being written. But as she stared at the page, the events she had listed revolved, each in their own sheath of light, which reflected onto the pages of her notebook. If she wanted, she could pierce one with her pen. Which to choose? She twirled the pen between her fingers and then descended: standing in front of Francois's painting at their parents' house. Ben was leaning against the wall, watching her.

The chair opposite her scraped, and she looked up. He was wearing the same beanie, today with a dark hooded jacket: the singer from last night.

He smiled and said something, and she cleared her throat, 'Sorry, I don't speak Portuguese.'

'I can join you?' he asked in English, and she nodded, quickly looked down at her words and laid her hand over them. It was an obvious attempt and he noticed it, smiled again and gestured to the pages: 'You are writing something?'

'Just . . .' she could feel her face becoming warm, 'just some notes.'

He sat down, offered to order her another coffee, and then when she declined ordered one himself. His name was Moises; he lived on the next street. Was she visiting with Francois? No, she wasn't related; he was a friend. No, she wasn't an artist or an art student. Well, she wasn't sure just yet when she would be leaving. Yes, that would be nice, if he showed her around one day. After he finished his coffee, he got up to leave. But before, he swooped down and kissed her on one cheek, then the next: a warm, welcoming local custom. He was always in this café, he said before he left. She could find him easily.

She watched him walk up the hill, towards Alfama. He was nice; she would enjoy his company. She already knew the busker to wave at and this singer, Moises, to talk to; she could imagine living here and making a life. She left the café. Today the Baixa was bustling, and she wandered through its shops. In one, a type of newsagent's, she perused the notices pinned to a corkboard. A few offered English lessons, and she considered this possibility before dismissing it: she was not qualified in any way, would not know where to start. And then down one narrow street she found a small dance studio: Ana Dourado, Escola de Dança. She went in and with a mixture of sign language and pidgin Portuguese learned that there might be a need for her: most of their students attended the international school on the other side of the city and spoke only English. Come back on Monday, *segunda-feira*; Ana would be there.

By now it was four o'clock. She had been out for hours, but she did not want to return too early. A shopping mall provided a distraction for another hour, and then she walked back, up a different steep incline, past a different row of decrepit apartment buildings, without too much worry that she would find her way.

He was right: the castle and the river were two excellent landmarks. It was dusk when she let herself into the flat. He was in his old cargo trousers, in his studio area. His flat was his workplace as well as his home; she was a double intrusion on his life. She was of a mind to turn and leave again quietly, but he looked up and smiled: 'You've been out a while.'

She nodded. 'I looked around.'

She took her boots off and walked into the living area, and he came towards her as if to give her a kiss in greeting as he had done with Lucie. But he stopped some feet away.

'I sent off some more requests,' she lied.

'That's great,' he said. Then, 'Are you hungry? I was just going to start cooking actually.'

'I can make dinner,' she said, 'if you want to carry on working.'

He shook his head. 'No, no. I can't have you cooking every day. I might get used to it.' He was grinning now.

'I don't mind . . .'

'You can help me. I was going to make some pasta. Does that sound good to you?'

As she unloaded her laptop, unpacked her bag, she saw that he was fiddling with his music player. A symphony flooded in. He stood for some moments, savouring the music, then he turned to her.

'Mahler,' he said. 'Do you know him?'

She shook her head.

'I read a biography a while back and something stuck with me. He said, "What is best in music is not to be found in the notes".'

He listened for a few moments, then he smiled: 'Maybe it's not the time for Mahler.' He ejected the CD. 'Let's listen to a bit of Cesária. She's from Cape Verde.'

The soulful voice seeped into the room as if patterning the walls with the melody: wistful, poignant, mournful. She had heard it before, with Ben. An image arrived which stopped her heart: Ben, in his flat, kneeling on the rug in front of her, moving closer to kiss her. And just behind him, within her vision, Francois's painting, the landscape. So, he had been there with them. Just as his five women in the river had been witness to the two of them on the rug in his parents' living room.

She noticed he was watching her. Perhaps he was waiting for her to offer her judgement.

'It's beautiful,' she said, and he smiled as they moved to the kitchen.

'Did you see anything interesting on your travels?' he asked, pulling out two saucepans from the top of the fridge. He handed her a bulb of garlic, 'Could you . . . ?'

'I saw the singer from last night,' she replied.

'Ah, Moises. You'll find that in Alfama. You'll keep bumping into the same people.'

'He said he'd show me around some time.'

'Mm,' he was smiling but said nothing more.

She sliced the garlic as he opened two tins of tomatoes.

'I also went into this dance school,' she said. 'They might need a teacher for Saturday or evening classes.'

'Well, that's very resourceful of you,' he said, pausing before lighting the hob with a match. 'Have you done that sort of thing before?'

'At the weekends when I was at uni.'

He nodded, smiled, but again did not say anything else. He did not make any pretence that he wished to chat. And, on her side, she did not want to pave the way to a similar conversation, a reminder of an invitation. The night of the performance, the frankness in Ben's voice: you took my breath away. The memory arrived and stood behind her like a shadow, as if the dead brother was watching the living brother: playing the same music, talking of the same things. Francois seemed oblivious of the spectre sharing the kitchen; he was frying the garlic and opening a packet of spaghetti at the same time.

The music soared, and he started to hum along with it. The kitchen was small; their elbows brushed against each other. But everything was neatly arranged, with military precision, dispelling any stereotypes of the chaotic artist.

'That should reduce a bit,' he said. 'Will you join me for a glass of wine?'

He cut some slices of cheese which he arranged on a plate, tucked a bottle under his arm and produced two wine glasses from a shelf above her head.

'After you.'

In the living area, he said, 'Tell me if you get too cold,' before throwing open one set of doors, pulling two chairs and a small table forward so that they sat facing the vista of the castle on the hill. He held out his glass and touched it against hers. 'Cheers.' Then after taking one sip, he moved towards his studio area and reached under the camp bed to produce a packet of cigarettes.

'You don't smoke, do you?' he said, and when she shook her head, he continued, 'Just the one. I'm cutting down.'

They listened to the same music, said the same things, had the same vices. Maybe they even shared the same ambitions, taste in women. But Lucie was dark where Clare had been fair. Older. And yet, both women had the same composure, the same controlled mien. She sipped the wine. It was an unhelpful habit, to keep comparing the two brothers.

'You're reading Ben's book,' she said, gesturing towards the bed.

'Yes. Have you read his stuff?'

She shook her head. 'Not really. Only bits.'

'I've got his first one here as well,' he said. 'If you want to read it. I found it a bit technical.'

He balanced his cigarette on the balcony railing and walked over to the bookshelf.

'Here you are.'

Again, the sensation that she had seen this book in his flat. *To my parents, John and Louise Martin.* She had met them now and could picture them reading this same dedication, exclaiming with pleasure. *And to Clare Armstrong: for keeping my feet on the ground.* And now they were both below the ground, together.

She said, 'Do you know all the people in Ben's books?'

'The people he interviewed?'

'And the people he mentions in his acknowledgements?'

He shook his head. 'I've met one or two, but only just recently. Patricia Zigomo-Walther for example.'

She recognised the name and could not stop herself from asking 'Who is she?', hoping he would not hear the curiosity in her voice. 'I mean, she's in his acknowledgements as much as Clare is, really.'

He might have glanced at her, but she was looking away, affecting indifference.

'She's a friend of his,' he said. 'Her husband is German. He was a diplomat or something in Harare.'

She held her wineglass between her knees, watched the lights come on in the building below.

'Actually,' he stubbed out his cigarette, seemed to hesitate, 'she's been in touch with my parents about something she wants to set up. A named scholarship of some kind for Zimbabwean students,' and then he paused before saying, 'in Ben's memory.'

She knew the sort: there were other bursaries offered by success-ful alumni, a reading room that was named after an old professor. Ben would be remembered, his work would be appreciated, while someone would also be given a chance to better themselves.

And me? She could not stop the thought from entering her head, nor the bitterness that accompanied it. She would have neither ignominy nor fame: no one knew about her. She was shocked to feel her stomach lurch at the prospect: to be forgot-ten, swept under a carpet, hidden. But she had set that sentence for herself, by removing herself from the university, when – why not? – she could have knocked on someone's door: you need to know something about Ben Martin.

'How,' Francois was speaking slowly, 'how do you feel about that?'

She turned to him. He was tuned into her; she could hear the gentleness in his voice. He could discern what she was thinking, even if she would prefer that he was ignorant of her petulance. It was a monumental effort – her features felt turgid, fossilised – but she managed a small smile: 'That's a lovely way to remember him.' Saying the words almost made her believe them, feel the sentiment.

He accepted what she said without responding. She picked a slice of cheese and nibbled on it, but when she tried to swallow, her throat was tight. When he got up and moved back to the kitchen, she did not join him. And after, they spoke little, only commenting on the meal. As they washed up, he said, 'I'll just finish off what I was doing,' and squeezed her arm gently. There was a melancholy to him tonight. She did not sense any regret or rancour over her presence in his flat, and yet he seemed to be mulling over something; perhaps he was thinking of his brother. Perhaps the evening before with Lucie had not ended well. Whatever, he was carrying something inside him.

She had a shower and returned to her wing. As she was pulling on her night T-shirt, she peered round the screen: another habit she was developing. He was standing before the easel, engrossed, a small brush in his hand. She slipped into the bed, studied the cover of Ben's book. There was a grainy photograph of a group of men in military-type fatigues; to one side, a woman in a similar outfit was holding what looked like a shovel. She stared at the woman: she had an open, brave expression, even though the men standing near her were carrying machine guns of some kind. There is a world out there, the photograph seemed to be telling her. She opened the book:

The Land Policy Division (LPD) of the World Bank claims the new directions of its policies offer better outcomes for women's aspirations to land tenure and titles. Yet there is a divergence in approach and ideology beyond the LPD as demonstrated in the African Division. Here, one set of gender specialists argue for top-down reform, so that statutory law safe-guards the rights of women to land, especially after widowhood. However, others such as the Gender and Law Reform in Africa group (GLRA) insist that customary systems must be enshrined, arguing that state reform has had little benefit for women. The discourses surrounding these issues themselves perpetuate another discourse: that women in Africa are silent witnesses to struggles for their rights, a discourse not uncommon in past times of the coloniser–colonised. By regarding women as passive witnesses to change, global organisations ignore the many women's groups and rights activists that make changes themselves before decrees are issued. An example that will be discussed in Chapter 2 is the Manyame project (an initiative founded by Patricia Zigomo-Walther, a contributor to the chapter) in which small farmers, all women, cultivate the herbs and plants that produce the essential oils that are sold in Western health outlets.

She read many pages, turning over and over, the sentences bleeding into each other, until her eyes felt heavy and she returned to the first. Patricia Zigomo-Walther. Another person from his world. She looked up and realised that it was dark around her; Francois had also turned in. She pulled the quilt closer around her and shut her eyes, the words swimming in front of her, along with an image of the young man in the beanie, her notebook, before she fell asleep.

18

SHE got up as soon as she heard him stir, pulled on her pyjama bottoms and a hoodie, and crept across to the kitchen. His preoccupation the previous night worried her. Her presence might well be weighing on him, even if subconsciously. She was intruding in his space; she was preventing him from spending time with his girlfriend. Perhaps she was an unwelcome reminder of secrets the brothers kept from each other. He had been so pleased with the dinner she had cooked, and she found that she wanted to please him again: he was so gallant, so thoughtful, endearingly undemanding. As she was lighting the hob, he appeared at the hatch. His expression was quizzical, amused.

'Pancakes,' she said. Then she faltered, 'I hope you like pancakes . . .'

'I do,' he grinned. Then, 'This is very nice of you . . .'

'Leave it to me.' She tried to sound forceful. 'You go and enjoy the view or go back to bed or read or whatever. I'll call you when breakfast is served.'

He said nothing, but smiled and then bowed in agreement. When she started laying the table, she saw that he was sorting out his sketches from the previous night, back in his cargo trousers and T-shirt.

'Ready,' she said, and he straightened up and sat down at the table.

'Coffee?' She left it black and passed it over, and he accepted it with a smile. When she served him his plate, he ate in silence but with his customary gusto. When his plate was clean, he reached across to the bowl of fruit perched on the ledge of the hatch, his fingers curling around two tangerines, one of which he peeled before handing it over to her. He lived alone, had no children, but it came naturally to him – like a gardener tending his plants. A clip here, a prune there.

'That was delicious, thank you,' he said, opening his own tangerine. Then, 'You'll be glad to know that we don't have to worry about lunch today. We're going to that party, remember?'

She laid her cutlery down, picked up her cup.

'Is it a special occasion?'

'I was the photographer at my friend Gildo's sister's wedding last summer. I think the couple had a late honeymoon and have just come back.'

'Is it a formal party?' she asked. 'I'm not sure what to wear.'

'It's not formal, no,' he said. 'But the women will all be dressed up. The men less so.' He smiled. 'A Mozambican *festa*. Everyone should go to at least one in their life. Lots of food, wine, beer, music. I think you'll enjoy it.'

She did not respond, and, as if he could read her mind, he added, 'Don't worry about what to wear . . .'

'But will they be expecting Lucie?'

'She's doing something with Josef. I called Gildo and his wife and told them I had a friend staying. They won't mind. They'll be happy to meet you.'

He stood up, gathering their used cutlery. 'We'll be driving there and back, so I won't have much to drink,' then added with a smile, 'but you can let your hair down.'

'I'm not much of a drinker,' she said, and for some reason she felt her face growing warm at this admission. He didn't seem to notice.

'Neither am I, really,' he said. He started stacking the plates. 'So,' he continued, 'we'll leave about twelve o'clock. I've got a few things I need to do before then . . .'

'Leave the washing up,' she said. 'I'll do it.'

He smiled, nodded, 'OK, thanks.'

She heard him leave the flat while she cleared the rest of the table. She washed up, drying and returning the plates and cutlery to their places, taking care to maintain his orderliness. And then she went to look through her suitcase. She was not one for gatherings, even less so if she knew no one and did not speak the language. But it was clear Francois wanted to go, and if he could be considerate to her, she should pay him back in kind. She inspected her clothes. It would have to be her fail-safe mini-dress in purples and blues, dark tights and her perennial boots. She showered, dressed and was slipping in a pair of dangly earrings when he returned, a roll of material under his arm. He was humming as he entered but stopped short when he saw her.

'Nice dress,' he said.

She felt a glow. She looked well: she had seen so in his expression.

'Is this the right sort of thing?' she asked, even as she saw his eyes move over her before he turned away.

'Yes,' he said. 'Perfect.' Then he strode over to his studio, laid the material down. 'Quick shower and I'll be good to go.'

She lay on the bed with the book, read and re-read the dedication and acknowledgements pages – *To my parents, And to Clare Armstrong* – heard the shower running, and then he was padding across to his pile of clothes.

'Rita?'

He was wearing the smartest clothes she had seen him in: dark trousers and a dark-grey, collared shirt, the sleeves rolled up to his elbows. The resemblance was now even stronger. He could easily step into a lecture theatre, give a seminar, deliver a paper at a conference.

'Shall we?'

When they reached the street, he pointed to a dusty van: 'That's me, I'm afraid. It's clean inside, don't worry.' Then he opened the door for her with a little bow, '*Senhora.*'

She climbed in and he closed the door, then jogged across the road to a small shop, emerging a few minutes later with a crate of beer and two bags of groceries.

As he slipped in behind the steering wheel, she gestured behind her, to the back of the van, at his supplies.

'Do you go camping?'

'Every year. And fishing.' He smiled. 'I'll take you,' he said. 'But we'll wait a couple of months for the weather to warm up a bit.' A couple of months. He did not seem to be counting down the days to her departure.

They drove off and in minutes were on a ring road, driving past the airport, heading west. He was relaxed beside her; the melancholy from last night, if that was what it had been, had disappeared. His hands were on the lowest curve of the steering wheel, his eyes on the road. He had his head leaning against the back-rest, his hair falling onto his forehead. He had the same dark hairs on his forearms, the same long legs. She looked out of window: the sky was a brilliant blue above, the colours as distinct as if they had been drawn by a child.

They arrived at a white-painted house to the sound of music playing, the smell of meat grilling, shouts of laughter. As if he could sense her apprehension, he took her arm and guided her through the side gate into the back garden.

'This is Gildo.' A large man, as tall as Francois but wider, took her hand, then leaned forward to kiss one cheek and then the other.

'Welcome,' he said in English, spoke to Francois, then back to her, 'I introduce my wife, Jacinta.'

A small, curvaceous woman, who also kissed her, pressed her shoulders in a quick embrace. And then she had a glass of sparkling wine in her hand, which in her nervousness she gulped down – it was delicious, the bubbles sparkling off her tongue – as if it were fruit juice, before her glass was filled again as if by magic with some heavier red wine. Beside her, Francois was talking to another man; then he was joined by Gildo, who said something that made the others laugh.

She was glad she had worn her dress: the women were beautifully attired. A young woman – busty in a slinky, sparkly green dress – approached to kiss Francois on both cheeks, pressing her chest against his in slow sensual motion, while he stroked the small of her back with obvious enjoyment. This was how grown-ups acted: the thought entered her head just as she saw her wine glass had been refilled yet again, somehow. She was pondering this, did not notice the young man standing in front of her until he spoke, in English, to Francois.

'Your friend is very beautiful,' pointing to Rita.

Francois turned, let his eyes sweep over her in mock appraisal, before replying to the young man, 'She is.' Then he turned back to her, smiling: 'This is Gildo's nephew.'

'I can dance with her?'

Francois was laughing: 'You have to ask her.'

Gildo appeared, spoke rapidly in Portuguese to the young man, then in English: Be gentle with her.

Her cheeks were burning after the exchange over her, but when the nephew held out his hand, she took it. It was flattering: to be complimented, invited, appreciated. The young man wore a tight white T-shirt, biceps bulging, his hair in shoulder-length braids. He put his hand on her back as he led her to the dance area. I am Ricki, he said conspiratorially, his breath tickling her ear, his eyes locking hers. Rita and Ricki. She wanted to giggle, but he was so serious she was sure she would offend him. There was not much for her to do except allow Ricki to move her around, and when he gave her space to move by herself she was rewarded with a murmur of approval – *boa, boa* – his eyes resting frankly and admiringly on her legs.

Francois, she saw, showed no inclination to dance, but was talking to another woman, who had slipped her hand into his shirt and was caressing his chest, while he looked down at her, smiling. Her attention was then taken by another young man who asked her to dance, and then another, and then she was reclaimed by Ricki, who was more confident now. He pressed his lips against her ear and placed his hands on her hips, moving her against him. She was surprised she did not mind. It was, in fact, nice to be touched. At one point, he clasped her bottom, and then his hand was removed quickly with a muttered apology, as if it had acted of its own accord.

When Jacinta pulled her away, laughing, pressing a plate of food into her hands and another glass of wine, she found she was ravenous. She saw Francois leaning against the wall at the other end of the garden, stabbing at his plate, talking to another man, and went over to join him. Immediately he turned to give her a smile, before pulling a chair over so she could sit next to him. When everyone had eaten, the music started again and Ricki appeared, holding out his hand, to lead her back into the dance area. And then finally she saw Francois, amongst the other couples, holding Jacinta tightly to him. They were swaying to the music, her cheek was pressed to his, and she was whispering something in his ear. The sun sank, and the night air grew chillier; the wine kept flowing, and in the end Jacinta had to prise her again from Ricki's arms. Francois had said they were leaving.

'That was nice,' she said as they drove away.

To her surprise he burst out laughing, and it was only after he had laughed for some time that he said, 'You certainly made a splash.'

She blushed, and he patted her arm briefly, smiling. 'That's a good thing, I mean. I'm glad you enjoyed yourself.'

'I did.'

'Good,' he repeated, then turned to her. 'You're allowed to, you know.'

She smiled back at him, a warm feeling spreading through her: the wine.

'They're so welcoming.'

He nodded.

They were silent; she looked out of the window. She was a little drunk, but it was an agreeable feeling. She reached forward and touched the glass.

'Do you want to open it?' he asked. Perhaps he was worried that she would be sick, but she felt only pleasure from the light-headedness. She shook her head, her thoughts scattered, floating with the wine, the music replaying in her head, the shouts and claps when the young man had put his arm around her waist and turned her to him. Be gentle with her. Her eyes were closing, she was falling asleep, and then she woke, her mind clear.

'What was wrong with Ben's wife?' she said. 'What was wrong with Clare?'

He turned to glance at her briefly. 'I thought you were asleep.'

She shook her head again, sat up straighter. 'Why was she ill?'

'Some kind of stress-related fatigue,' he said.

She waited for him to continue, and when he didn't she asked, 'So she was stressed about something?'

He shrugged his shoulders, and she could immediately feel his reluctance, which with the clarity she had acquired caused her to pursue her line of questioning.

'Was it their marriage?'

'Most probably.'

His response came suspiciously quickly; she swatted it away.

'What do you think it was, Francois?'

He stared at the road so intently that she turned to follow his eyes. There was nothing to see, so she turned back to look at him, his profile. He was silent for so long she thought she would have to prompt him again.

'They'd been trying to have kids,' he said finally. 'And it wasn't working. That could have triggered it, along with other factors.'

The words entered her like a stone: rather, as if a bag of stones were poured into her, through her ears to fill up her limbs.

She found her voice: 'You mean, they wanted to have children and they couldn't?'

He gave a sideways nod: a tiny movement, as if to undermine the enormity of her discovery.

'Were they trying for long?'

'I think so.'

'And she was upset?'

He nodded.

She stared out of the window. It's not so simple. She remembered how her mother had comported herself in her family home, how she had appeared shrivelled by the derision she had sustained. She was back in the bedroom in the old house, lying under the fan, her mother sitting beside her. She had asked her mother: Why did they have to make you feel so bad? But in the end her mother had produced two healthy children, unlike Clare. Clare's chances for motherhood had been stolen; a car accident had robbed her of the opportunity to recover.

They turned off onto another road, long and straight, the gentle brown hills now indistinct in the darkness that had gathered around them. She was still light-headed, but her stomach felt twisted. He didn't speak, as if he wanted her to fall asleep, move on from their conversation.

'But,' she persisted, 'if they really wanted kids, why didn't they adopt or something?'

He tapped on the steering wheel. 'I think by then she was ill and things were complicated.'

She didn't say anything else; she didn't have the words. She caught sight of herself in the side mirror. She could not rid herself of her exterior decorative self; she would forever look vital, vibrant, even if the person inside was warped, had died. She was a girl in a pick-up. A girl to pick up.

'He told me he felt happy with me,' she said, but she was not sure he could hear her; part of her simply wanted to see her lips moving in the mirror. 'Did he want children as well?' she asked in a louder voice.

'Yes, I think he did.'

'But then they stopped trying.'

He turned to face her more fully, his eyes glancing back to the road as he spoke. 'You can have a nap if you want—'

'Do you want me to shut up?' she grinned, surprising herself; it was the last thing she felt like doing.

'No, of course not . . .'

But then she did not speak; her tongue felt swollen, as if she would choke, and for the last few miles she resorted to her favourite pastime: revisiting their encounters, the pathetic little list she had written in her notebook, as if those events were hermetically sealed from the world around them. But the sheath of light that held each was now less bright, dulled.

It was not because he had fallen head over heels for her, not because she had arrived and opened his eyes to the constraints of his marriage. He had embarked on their affair because he was hurting, aching inside. They were aching together, Ben and Clare: bereft, baffled. Clare wore her torment on her sleeve, sat in the wheelchair like a throne. And Ben? Had he really believed he would find solace by betraying the woman who would be the mother of his children? An image played before her: Joy carrying Mira on his shoulders. She could not envisage her brother in a clinch with someone else; was that because Mira was a small, warm living being? If the child was not born, was just a figment – desired but not formed – did that make it easier to be unfaithful? And if Ben had been a father, with a small child holding his hand, would she have let him make love to her? That must have been the added, indefinable ingredient to their coupling. He had not simply desired her; he was pouring his agony into her, into her body. Those depths he had said he felt in her: he had found a vessel for his sadness.

She didn't talk. When they had driven a few more miles, he asked if she wanted the radio on. She shook her head; he left it turned off.

'Do Gildo and Jacinta know about me?' she asked finally, when they were re-entering the city.

He glanced over at her. 'Know what?'

'Do they know about me and Ben?'

He didn't respond immediately – they were negotiating a tight bend, a white, domed building to their left. They turned into a narrow, steep cobbled street. He seemed to spend a long time adjusting the gears, looking into the wing mirror. She felt an anger rise into her throat.

'They know, don't they?'

Again, he didn't reply, but parked in a space a few metres from the door of his building. He switched the engine off and turned to her.

'Yes,' he said. 'I told Gildo. He will have told Jacinta.'

He was looking at her, his hands in his lap. His expression as always seemed to be searching hers for some kind of sign.

'Why did you tell him?'

She felt her voice shake just as she asked herself: what does it matter?

He let his eyes fall briefly to her hands, then raised them.

'I guess I needed to share it with someone.'

'When you found the photo.'

He nodded.

'But you shared it with Lucie.'

'Only after.'

'After what?'

He hesitated. 'After I started painting you.'

She opened the door and got out of the car. It was dark now; the air was chilly. It had not even been a week, but she felt as if she had lived here all her life. She had never had an argument with Ben. She had felt an angry humiliation when he had laughed at her declaration of love, but he had erased it instantly, absorbed it by his touch. Here, with his brother, it seemed was the next instalment of the serial: now the couple fights. She walked around to the back of the van where he had put the bags of groceries and reached for one.

'Don't worry I can carry—' he began, but she ignored him, lifted the bag out, heard the bottles clink together, then walked up the street, feeling her calves ache with the incline. He fumbled with his keys, dropped them, picked them up, opened the door.

On entering the flat, she kicked off her boots and went into the bathroom. The mirror reflected her face, just as it had done in the washroom at the services, his parents' bathroom, before and after sex, among his wife's toiletries. She could hear Francois opening and closing cupboards, putting things away in the kitchen, and left the bathroom to lean against the door jamb of the kitchen. He was tidying away the bags of fruit and juices; a box of eggs lay open and a frying pan was heating on the stove.

'I'll make an omelette,' he said, not looking at her. She could see his shoulders were braced, as if in anticipation of how she would respond.

She slid a bottle of wine from one of the bags, twisted the cap.

'Want some?' She didn't recognise her own voice.

He glanced at her and nodded, started cutting some tomatoes. She took two glasses out, poured two generous measures, slid one over towards him – Cheers – and swallowed the wine, all the while ignoring the tears that had arrived unannounced in her eyes.

When she picked up the bottle again, he set his knife down and watched her pour herself another glass.

'Drink some water with that as well.'

His voice was gentle, concerned, even fatherly. She wanted to throw the wine in his face, but she turned away. 'Can I put some music on?'

It was bubbling out, at last, what was inside her. Who were these men, like characters from a fairy tale, these brothers: Ben and Francois? Who were they and why did she feel like she was at the centre of a no man's land between them, their eyes drilling into her? The thought excited her as much as it infuriated her. She found his CD player, struggled to focus on the controls, her finger sliding over the buttons, missing, then choosing the first album that came up, an up-tempo dance beat.

He entered the room with the two plates in his hands, which he laid on the table, then turned to retrieve the glasses and cutlery from the hatch. The bottle of wine remained behind in the kitchen, and as she walked back down the short hall she heard him, 'Rita . . .'

She poured the wine as she walked back, splashing some on the floor, on her dress and onto her collarbone, from where she felt it trickle down her chest, just as she had felt the blood trickle down her thighs, that first time. Then she leaned over and poured some more into his glass as well, giving him her widest, brightest smile. She noted his unease with satisfaction and was tempted for a moment to sit in his lap. What would he do? Lift her off, or swivel her around and kiss her on the mouth? Would he taste the same: did brothers taste the same? Did they have sex in the same way?

'Come and eat something.'

'I'm not hungry.'

He cut his omelette into pieces and ate. An obvious ploy: parents used it all the time to entice their children. Delicious, he should say. Are you sure you don't want to eat anything? When she sat down in her chair and picked up her fork, the relief on his face made her giggle, and then she found she couldn't stop, started coughing over the morsel of omelette stuck in her gullet. He poured her a glass of water and slid it over, but she shook her head and drank her wine. She could not face any more food, and, pushing her plate away, she stood up and carried her glass to one of the French doors, moving her hips to the music.

At one point, she turned around to see that he had left the room, was back in the kitchen. He had taken the plates; she could hear the water running. The castle was lit up now, dignified above them. The washing hanging from the terrace opposite fluttered in the breeze. He walked back into the room and went to the other set of French doors, opened them out. When she craned her neck around, she saw that he was smoking a cigarette, his elbows on the railing, tapping the ash out onto the street. She felt her heartbeat slow down; her head ached, but then she shook herself: not yet.

She swung back into the room, walked over to him and leaned her back against the railing so she was facing him. His eyes were on the street below, and he did not look at her when he said, 'I'm sorry. I can see you're upset.'

'I'm not upset.' She could hardly hear her voice for some reason, but she must have spoken, because his eyes flickered over to her and then down again. His expression, soft and gentle, smote her, but she steeled herself, rallied.

'What did you think,' she said, 'when you saw the photo Ben took of me?'

He flicked his ash, spoke quietly. 'What do you mean?'

'I mean,' she leaned sideways, then tilted her head so she was looking up at him, blocking his view, her hair falling onto his arm, 'what did you think of me?'

He straightened up slightly, but he did not move his arm.

'Did you think I was pretty?' She laughed, but then the tears returned, and she had to turn her face away before he could see them. One splashed out onto his arm, but he seemed not to have felt it.

'Did you?' then leaning sideways again. 'Do you?'

She felt his hand on the back of her head, like a caress, a gentle touch. Where was his cigarette now? Was he setting her hair on fire? She sprang away, giggling.

'Rita, please . . .'

'Now that I'm here, in the flesh, do you want to paint me again? Paint me now.'

The idea took hold of her: why had she never thought it before? This was why he had invited her, begged her to let him help her. He could paint her if she came back with him: a parting gift from his brother. From me to you. Didn't artists always paint women in the nude? He had seen her barely clad in a towel; now he could see her without. She didn't need the screen, right here. She was tugging her dress over her head, but it was caught in her earring, so when she felt him pulling it back down, his fingers brushing against her ribs, she could not see him. Her hair was in her eyes, clinging to her cheeks, which were wet with tears. She felt his hands at her waist as if arranging the dress more becomingly over her hips.

And then they slid around her, his arms entwining with hers, so that his whole body was against her back. His face was in her hair, and she could feel his warmth flooding into her. Her own body was shuddering, so that it felt that he was protecting her from an earthquake, not holding in her sobs. And only after many minutes, when she slid around within the circle of his arms, when she lifted her chin to his face, did she see the sadness in his eyes, so that she had to close her own because it was too much for her to bear.

Closing her eyes was a relief; he was saying something to her which she could not hear. She was back in Ben's arms, their future ahead of them, because if she believed nothing else she needed to believe that they had had one.

Part Four

19

HE had returned to his parents' house late in the evening after walking for hours, having tried to make the journey back from Tooting to Clapham on foot. When he was well and truly lost, he gave in and hailed a cab. London was familiar but still confused him. He let himself into the house, but then he exited the front door again quietly and walked round the side of the house. The light was on in his father's shed. He walked across the lawn and tapped on the door, then opened it and went inside.

'Hello, son.' His father looked as if he had sat where he was, pen in hand, for a while, without writing anything on the notepad in front of him.

'May I?'

'Of course.'

He settled on the armchair, and his father turned his chair around. 'There's still some tea in the pot . . .'

'I'm fine.'

He wanted to say, I've found her. The encounter with the girl had proceeded as differently as he could have imagined, but in truth had he even imagined it? From gazing at an image he had found a voice, a face, a hand in his, a body. He had even met her mother, as if he were a suitor asking for her hand.

'I've not asked what you're working on at the moment,' his father said, leaning back in his chair. He was wearing his usual heavy fisherman's sweater, corduroy trousers. He had aged well, exuding the sensitivity expected from a writer of his calibre, overlaid with an unconfused maleness; both he and Ben had inherited these same attributes. From their mother, they had received different things. Although people always commented on the brothers' likeness, he knew Ben had his mother's eyes and mouth. Whereas he had acquired his mother's instinctive wariness of good fortune.

He shook his head. 'I've been invited to submit something for next spring. Still thinking about it . . .'

His father nodded. The writing shed was cold, but his father seemed unwilling to leave. They stayed quiet for some moments, then his father picked up a manuscript from the desk, bound in a soft cover, showed it to him: 'I'm reading this again.'

It was Clare's Master's dissertation, written nearly fifteen years ago: a study of three writers. His father smiled. 'I'd forgotten how good it is,' he said, then passed it over.

He stared at the cover page, turned it over and over in his hands, then opened it. He would not read it, he knew. He could not even remember if he ever had. He had neglected his sister-in-law, and by proxy his brother, who had invested nearly eighteen years of his life with the writer of the manuscript he was holding.

'You know,' his father was saying, 'she came to talk to me about her plans to do a doctorate once. It must have been ninety-eight or ninety-nine or something. I wasn't long in London. It would have only been the second or third time I'd met her.' He paused. 'I can honestly say it was the most intimate conversation Clare and I ever had.'

They were both quiet.

'She didn't really need my advice,' his father continued. 'But I was touched that she asked.'

'I wonder what she made of us all,' he said.

His father laughed. 'Yes, I know what you mean.'

What would have been *his* most intimate conversation with Clare? He sifted through his mind; they had rarely been together on their own. There was one exchange: when Ben and Clare had come to Lisbon, to recuperate after the last failed IVF treatment, just before she succumbed to her illness. They had stayed in his flat; he had given them his bed and had slept on the camp bed. It was the first morning. Ben was having a shower, and he and Clare were taking in the view from one of his balconies. She was not yet aloof: that would come later in the visit. She was still relaxed, smiling up at him as he pointed out some of the sights: the Tagus, the castle, then, just visible, the Sé. This place suits you down to the ground, Francois, she had said. He had not been sure what she had meant; he was not even sure she could profess to know him well enough to make that judgement. She had continued: I envy you, you know. You're such a free spirit. How had he responded? He had made some joke; they had laughed. Not long after, Ben had joined them and she had repeated her diagnosis. He remembered a brief instance of incomprehension had flitted across his brother's face.

Could that count as an intimate conversation? He had suspected that she had been implicitly accusing him: that rather than being a free spirit, he was selfish and self-centred, disinterested in commitment, marriage, family life. He felt that none of these descriptions suited him. Yes, he had divorced Paula, but not because he didn't want to be committed. Only because he knew that he couldn't be committed to *her*. And what followed in his life seemed governed as much by chance than by any effort on his part to engineer where he lived, who he was with.

He handed Clare's dissertation back to his father.

'How are you doing, Francois?' His father's voice was low.

He waited. His father never asked extraneous questions; he deserved worthy responses.

'At a crossroads,' he said finally. At a loss, he added to himself.

He knew that he could have said to his father then, I've met her, and so have you. The girl Ben chose, possibly to usurp Clare. But he didn't, and then his mother was calling them in to have dinner.

It was some days later that the girl phoned him, and they met in a café. And it was later that night when he had returned again to his parents' house – this time with an unshakeable sense that by letting her go he was letting his brother down – that she had phoned again and asked to see the graves. By then it was clear he would not be able to dismiss the girl, return to Lisbon without seeing her again. He had in fact already planned to return to her parents' house and lie in wait: stalk her, stake her. But twice by then she had herself initiated a meeting; she was as well – even if she would not admit it – unwilling to let go of him, the reminder of his brother.

Watching her stand quietly in front of the small stones, then lower herself so she was sitting on her haunches, her hair falling forward so it eclipsed her face, reading and re-reading the epitaphs, he had been free to observe her, as if she were his muse. She was young, heartbroken. The affair: it had consumed her. The death of his brother, and of the woman they had both betrayed: these lay heavily inside her. His heart had gone out to her, and it was then that his role presented itself to him. He would bring her back with him, shelter her, until she was ready to face the world again.

It was still dark when he woke; the sky was only just turning a rose red. He rolled off the camp bed. His leg felt numb – he must have slept in an awkward position. He glanced at the other end of the room. She was still asleep, her body curled up on its side like a foetus. He changed quickly and quietly, slipped out of the flat, then down the stairs onto the street. The air was clear and chilly; his lungs drank in the sweetness. Thinking of his lungs always pushed him to run faster and go further; he would never give up, he knew, but he had managed to cut down to the occasional, restorative cigarette. He followed his usual route. Then, returning to Alfama, he ran repeatedly up and down the steps, punctuating each couplet with pull-ups on the handy children's swing frame at the top and press-ups at the bottom, his hands slipping on the chilled cobbles. An old woman pulling a wheeled basket passed, chuckling, '*Bom dia, meu filho.*' When he had finished, he jogged down and found a bench near the Panteão. The Feira da Ladra was setting up for the morning. He waved to some of the regulars, and when one offered him a cigarette, with a cheeky smile, he shook his head. He sat back on the bench and watched the stall holders arrange their tables, then looked across past the white dome to where the land fell away, the cliff beyond which lay the river.

He had held Rita for what seemed an age; the music had continued playing, as if they were supposed to be dancing, not simply standing entwined but motionless, his lips in her hair. Her breath fanned his neck; her body was pressed against his, whether purposely or not, but in a manner which was trustful, yielding, disarming. He had been holding up her weight for some minutes when he realised that she was asleep, the deep sleep of the young. So he had scooped her up and moved to the bed. The feel of her in his arms – her head against his shoulders, her silky hair spilling over his one arm, the feel of her thighs on the other – only emphasised the intimacy of the moment. They were alone in his flat, it was dark outside, there was no one to intrude. He had laid her on the bed and crouched down beside her. There were tracks from her tears on her cheeks. Her lips were puckered, plump. A sleeping beauty, waiting for a kiss from a prince. He observed the drops of red wine on the front of her dress and a streak on her chest, a sticky reminder, considered undressing her, so she would not sleep in her stained clothes. But the thought of peeling off her dress, pulling her tights over her hips to bare her delicate hip bones, her neat briefs and slender legs, just as once his brother would have done, was suddenly, shockingly appealing, and it was this realisation which made him rise abruptly to his feet and take a step back. He had thrown the quilt over her and returned to his wing, turned the music and the lights off, and lay down on his camp bed, his heart pounding. At some point, in the stillness of the night, he had fallen asleep.

He shut his eyes, and when he opened them all he saw was the soaring white dome, the trestle tables, the benches: his adopted home, but now he felt the familiar restlessness that had usually presaged a change in his circumstances. He folded his arms, scuffed the ground with his toe. That evening at the bar, Lucie had said, she cannot compensate you. It was one of the very few times when Lucie's English failed her, when she used a word incorrectly. Usually these moments endeared her to him; that night he had remained unmoved. She meant: she cannot replace your brother. But it was just as possible that she meant, she cannot compensate for . . . for what? Whatever, he could not push aside the feeling that Lucie was now in his past: he had moved on. We just pick people up and drop them, Ben had said, those years ago.

He watched his foot make circles in the ground, as if attempting to hypnotise himself, place himself in a trance, so he could behave and speak as he should, not as he truly wanted. For the truth was that he was not only enjoying Rita's presence in his life, he was beginning to feel that she *belonged* to him. The evening before, at the party, Gildo's nephew had been shamelessly transparent in his designs. But what was also patent: the young man meant nothing to Rita. It was as if the pleasure of her company was only on loan from him, Francois. Her eyes kept travelling back to his, even as Ricki's hands were on her body, as if seeking permission or approbation. She had sought him in moments of respite, sitting in his shadow, her knees brushing against his leg; if he reached out, he could have stroked her hair, her face. And then, after, her anger, the music she had played, the coquetry she had mocked him with, her body in his arms, and the sadness that emanated from her like radioactive waves – all had imbued the evening with a sensuality that had derailed him. When he had laid her on the bed, he had wanted to make love to the girl.

He watched the smoke curl from a chimney pot ahead, much as it would curl from a cigarette, which he was now wishing he had accepted. The stall holders were numerous, and groups of bargain-hunters were gathering in wait. He stood up, flexed his arms and legs, waved a goodbye to the regulars and jogged back to the set of steps which led to his street. She was still asleep when he let himself back in the flat, and it was only after he had showered and was pulling on his jeans that she awoke. She raised herself on one elbow. Her eyes were unfocused, but otherwise her face was unravaged from the events of the previous night – a gift of youth. He slipped on a T-shirt, turned to her.

'Good morning,' he said.

'Good morning.' Her voice was a whisper.

'How's your head?'

She tilted it one way and then the other.

'Terrible.'

'I'll get you some aspirin.'

In the kitchen, he found a packet of soluble tablets and returned with a large glass of water. She moved her feet to make some room in invitation, and he sat down on the edge of the bed, in awe of the vast reserves of trust she placed in him. He should not offer Rita refuge and then re-enact the situation she had fled. His thoughts of earlier seemed now even more misplaced.

She gulped the water and then put the glass down on the floor next to her.

'Sorry for behaving badly last night,' she said in a small voice.

He smiled. 'Was that the worst you could do?'

When she smiled back, bashfully, he felt a tug of some kind inside him. He stood up.

'Give me your dress when you're ready, and I'll put it in the washing machine. I'm not sure it will work . . .'

'It's my fault.' She fell back on the bed, her arm over her eyes. He moved into the kitchen and heard her footsteps behind him as she entered the bathroom. The shower started running. He would suggest they visit the Gulbenkian; they could play tourists. He could be guide to the enchanting city; last night could be forgotten.

He was making the coffee when he heard his phone ringing in the living room, then click to voice message.

Francois, hi, it's Jane again. Could you phone back, please? There's something I'd like to talk about. It's to do with Clare and Ben. I went back . . .

He rushed through to the other room.

'Jane? It's Francois.'

'Oh, hello there.' Her voice sounded even more clipped and English on the phone.

'Sorry I didn't call back. I've been up to my eyes . . .'

'Yes. Actually, I should have got in touch when you were in London, but what with Christmas and the kids . . .'

'Yes, of course, don't worry.'

He waited.

'Well,' she said. 'I went back up. You know, to the flat. With my husband this time. So we could think about what to do.'

Part of him could pretend to himself that he expected her to ask: which was more pragmatic? To sell or rent? Realistically, how often were either of them going to go up north? But the other part of him, already braced for the next thread to be teased from the fabric of his brother's life, was not surprised when she said, 'There's something bothering me, about Clare and Ben. I'm quite sure Ben was having an affair. A different one, I mean. Recently, I mean.'

He paused; his heart was racing again. The girl was still in the bathroom, out of earshot.

'Really?' he said, trying to keep his voice indifferent. 'And what makes you think that?'

'Well, firstly, her writing,' she said. 'I've been reading what she was writing. It's a journal, of a kind.'

He remained silent. Let her do the work, he thought.

'In an entry from a month before the accident, she made a note that Ben was acting strangely, *like the last time*. She must have been referring to his last affair.'

'Did she always keep a journal?'

'Not when we were young, but she might have started later. Maybe it was part of a therapy—'

'So she doesn't have one dating from when you think Ben supposedly had his first affair with a colleague?'

She seemed taken aback by his tone. But he was allowed to be irate: any brother would defend his younger sibling, wouldn't he? He swallowed down the bile that had risen to his throat.

'He *did* have an affair—'

'What I mean is, that sentence is rather vague, isn't it? She could be referring to anything.'

There was a silence.

'There's more.' She spoke again. 'When we were up there, we popped into that art gallery, you remember? The owner got chatting with us, and she mentioned that Ben had a visitor when Clare had been away.'

He said nothing.

'An Asian girl. The gallery owner said she saw her several times.'

After a long pause, he spoke, trying to keep his voice unconvinced.

'Well, it could be that he was helping a student out with something. There's no need to read anything more into it.'

'I didn't expect you to be so . . . defensive.' Her voice was cold.

Well, what did you expect, he wanted to shout. Rita walked back into the room, her hair wet around her shoulders, wearing a short mauve-coloured towelling robe, bare-legged, barefoot:

for all intents like his young lover after a post-coital morning shower.

'Jane,' he said. 'Sorry. This isn't a good time—'

'I just wanted to ask if you found anything among Ben's effects—'

He did not hesitate. 'No—'

'that might have made you wonder—'

'No, nothing comes to mind. Look,' he glanced at his watch as if he were really going to keep a promise. 'Shall I call you later? I'm sorry, but I've got something on and—'

'Just a minute.' Her voice was icily calm now, commanding. 'You know what the university is planning, don't you? I just think if Ben was unfaithful that it's a bit ironic—'

'The university?'

'A scholarship or something in his name. For *female* students to do research into *women's rights* issues.' Then she paused. 'Didn't you know?'

He scrambled around under the camp bed and looked at his mobile: two missed calls from his mother yesterday.

'Yes, well, someone Ben worked with, Patricia something or the other. She and her husband are setting up a fund. When my parents told me, I just thought: if they only knew.'

'You haven't spoken to your parents?'

'My parents? No, I've not spoken to them.'

'It's probably better not to,' he said. 'When you're not sure of the facts.'

She was silent.

'OK,' she said finally; her tone was brittle. 'OK.'

'Yes, take care.' His own voice sounded hideous. 'Give my regards to your family, hope you're all—'

She had hung up.

He turned back and saw that Rita was behind the screen. She had only heard his side of the conversation and would not be able to understand much. He picked up his mobile: his mother had left two messages. He went through to the kitchen and played them. In the first she relayed what he already now knew. The fund that had been mentioned was coming into being. His mother read out the proposed description: *The Ben Martin Award for studies in women's rights issues in sub-Saharan Africa is a £10,000 yearly award offered to a female Zimbabwean or Zimbabwean-origin student who is engaged in research in the stated field. Applicants are requested to submit a letter to John and Louise Martin, and Patricia Zigomo-Walther, sponsors of the award. This award has been set up in memory of Dr Ben Martin, of the Centre of African Studies. Applicants for the award can be studying distance and part-time.* What do you think, Francois? his mother asked. Let me know if you have any suggestions. In the next message, she repeated the news, adding that there was no hurry for him to call back; she knew he was very busy.

He held his phone to his ear for a few more seconds, his heart aching at the pride in his mother's voice. His parents deserved to commemorate their son. He would not allow Clare's sister and her entitled tone rile him. And what did she know of Ben? He was one-dimensional to Jane: a sentence in a journal. Whereas for him, Ben was a myriad memories, arguments, resentments, laughter and sadness.

But, despite his anger, he could empathise with her dogged-ness: she was trying to make sense of something from her dead sibling's life, just as he had tried, those months after finding the photograph. He could picture her with a tiny axe, chipping away at Clare's gravestone, brushing away the fragments of stone until she found the message her sister had left for her. And then?

He closed his eyes, covered them with one hand. He needed to admit that as much as apprehension at the recriminations that could be directed at Ben, his reaction to Jane was about his unwillingness to burst the bubble of the last few days, to have the girl, Rita, taken from him. He put the phone down on the surface next to him, stared at the familiar objects in his kitchen, trying to see beyond them, trying to dampen down the feeling that was tightening his chest. He could hear her moving next door, unaware of the chaos of his thoughts. This girl: his brother's inamorata.

20

THEY left the flat and walked to the square, then down to the metro station. She looked fresh and bright now, with her hair brushed back and tied in a ponytail, as graceful in jeans and T-shirt as she had been in the dress the night before. When he had suggested that they spend the day together, explore the Gulbenkian's art collection, her face had lit up: she was the type who appreciated small gestures. Now, she met his eyes and smiled, and he felt that tug again. She was so trusting; he could be leading her anywhere. Why should she believe he was taking her to a museum; not a cave, a cellar, a prison? An image from the previous evening arrived: Gildo had offered her a cone, and she had licked the ball of chocolate ice cream with rapid flashes of her tongue, without any inhibition. A reminder that she had not long left childhood behind her and it could still be lapping around her ankles.

Leaving the metro, they walked through the garden and towards the museum, nestled among the greenery. There were few visitors: some families, a handful of tourists. He went into one of the back offices where he picked them both passes for the day, and led her to the main rooms. He had no real wish to be a guide, and he was pleased she did not seem to expect it of him. She wound her way through the paintings and installations, reading the information cards. Once, she stood in front of the painting of the boy by Manet, turning to catch his eye, smile, before turning back to it. He left her, to talk to the curator, with whom he would be examining the final-year installations at the degree show later in the week. When he caught up with her, she was in one of the rooms at the back, gazing at a large canvas nearly five metres in length. He watched as she read the information card, then laughed as she looked up, astonished.

He moved closer so he was standing next to her. He had called this painting *O poder delas*. Two *mestiças*, reclining against a tree. The clothes covering their upper bodies undone and in folds around their waists, tools in their hands clasped on their laps, a mound of sweet potatoes beside them. The colours he had used for the women's skin – ochre with tints of light yellow – were not dissimilar to the palette he had chosen for his painting of Rita. But these women's bodies were stockier, and their breasts were rounder, heavier. He turned away.

'It's one of the reasons I came to Lisbon,' he said. 'So I could have the chance to do something like this. You know, have both creative freedom and the luxury of being paid a commission.'

He waited and then asked, 'What do you think?', surprised to feel his heart beat faster in anticipation of her response.

'It's beautiful.' She exhaled the words. 'They're so beautiful and calm and wise.'

Her pronouncement pleased him – more than he had expected. And then he felt an annoyance at himself, for behaving no differently from Gildo's nephew: a kid trying to impress a girl.

He waited a few more moments and then said, 'For me it's a love poem to the women of the island. To their beauty and resilience.'

'It's an island?' she asked. 'In Mozambique?'

He shook his head. 'Cape Verde. Some years ago, I stayed there a few months.'

'How long did this take you?' Her eyes were still travelling over the canvas.

'How long do you think?' he smiled.

'I don't know.' She shook her head. 'A year?'

He laughed. 'Ten days.'

204

She laughed back, her eyes wide with disbelief.

He nodded. 'Ten days. Not including all the preparation. I made the frame here in this room, and prepared the canvas. When that was all done, I got permission to stay overnight in the building and worked like a madman . . .'

'That's amazing . . .'

'Well, it's preparing a raw canvas that takes time. And the oils. But what I was going to do, I had it all planned out already. In my head and on paper.'

She was still shaking her head in wonder. He could forget who she was, he saw. She could become his. The thought settled into his mind, as light as a feather, and he shook it off, took her elbow. 'There's more. Let's leave me well alone now . . .'

She allowed him to lead her away, and they continued through the other rooms together. But as they stepped out into the courtyard, she stopped, put her hand on his arm. 'Thanks for showing me your painting. I feel, I don't know, privileged for seeing it.'

He was touched by her words, and the response came easily: 'The privilege is mine.'

It was warmer outside now. The gardens enveloped them; the foliage was lush even though it had not rained for the last fortnight. She walked along the path through the garden that led towards the fountain in the centre, and perched on the edge. He followed and sat down next to her. They both watched the people walking through the trees ahead on the paths that traversed the bushes, the tall grasses and flower beds.

'It's such a nice city,' she said.

'I couldn't leave Maputo for just any old place.'

'What's it like?'

'Oh, well,' he smiled. 'Dirty and crumbling. Throbbing.'

She leaned back slightly, dipped her fingers in the water, swirled them around.

'How do you know Gildo?'

'I met him soon after I moved to Maputo, and we became friends,' he said. 'The country was still in a civil war, and for a few years I just did my own stuff. Then after the war ended I started running art-therapy groups, you know, to help with post-traumatic stress disorder. I think I kind of capitalised on the zeitgeist. We got a lot of funding from foreign governments, a lot of attention from Western media,' he shrugged and smiled. 'It became a bit of a success, and I became a bit of a name. Well, Gildo was also the architect for the cultural centre we built.'

She was quiet, then said. 'That sounds wonderful—'

'I'm no saint,' he interjected. 'It raised my profile no end, and I could do all sorts of things for myself because of it.'

'It still sounds like a great project.'

'It was. It's still going strong. One of the men who came to us early on is now running it. It's broader now, not just PTSD but other mental issues.'

'Do you go back?'

He shook his head. 'No. This is home now.' He paused. 'I wouldn't want to go back and have people think I'm checking up on them.'

She was quiet. 'I've not done anything nearly as interesting or as important as that.'

She was looking away. He chose to say, 'When I was your age, neither had I.'

She was moving her fingers forwards and backwards, as if stirring the water would encourage a genie to arise, to do her bidding. What would she wish for? That his brother would come back to life?

'Did you always want to be an artist?'

He shook his head. 'Actually, for ages I wanted to be a photographer. All through my teens and even when I first went to art college.'

'Do you have any photos back at the flat?' she asked him. 'That you could show me?'

She was hoping he would have some of Ben, he realised. Perhaps she had no memento of him.

'I'll dig some out when we get back,' he said.

She smiled her thanks, then returned to the water.

'You and Ben. With your books and your paintings . . .' she was still smiling, but now looking at him askance. 'Ben writes about women and you paint mostly women. What does that say about you both?'

He laughed. 'I'd not seen it that way actually, but you're right.' He spread his arms out. 'Well, I like women. I like looking at them. There are so many I admire, not anyone famous, just ordinary women. They are for me the more interesting sex by far.'

She was making circles in the water, and then she lifted her fingers and splashed some water onto his chest.

He laughed again: 'Was that the wrong answer?'

She shook her head. Then she ducked her head away and said softly, 'Your parents must be very proud of you.'

He shrugged. 'They're the kind who never pushed us. They're just very supportive.' There was a silence, and then he asked quietly, 'What are your parents like, Rita?'

She took her time. And then she answered a question he had only thought, not asked.

'They're not like you think,' she said, turning away from the water so she was looking ahead. 'If I tell them what happened, they wouldn't hurt me or disown me or anything. They wouldn't lock me up and throw away the key. They've always been gentle, both of them. They're older than most of my friends' parents, maybe that's why.' Then she whispered, 'But they would feel very let down that I've left university. And they'd be shocked at what I've done and who I am.'

He was silent, watching her. Now she was playing with a bangle on one wrist. He had to resist the urge to reach forward, lift up her ponytail, place his fingers on the nape of her neck. He looked at his hands, pushed them into his pockets.

'They're quite religious, you know?' She was speaking quietly. 'I mean, everyone in India is; they're not unusual in that way. Sleeping with a man before marriage would be enough of a . . .' she stopped, then said, 'would be enough to disappoint them. But that he was married? And now he's dead?'

She looked up at him suddenly. Her eyes were large, dark pools: 'Did they die, did they have the accident because of me?'

He had made the same conjecture, hadn't he? He remembered Gildo's words: don't make a nightmare. He touched her cheek for an instant, her eyes did not leave his, and then he said, 'We won't know, Rita. But what we do know is that people die in car accidents all the time.'

She shook her head, as if in disagreement, then turned again away from him so he could not see her face. He could not tell whether she had felt his touch, or decide whether he should have made the gesture. His mind was cluttered, and he tried to breathe deeply, regularly. The sound of the water falling behind them was soothing; he listened to it until she spoke again: 'Do you miss him?'

'It's not sunk in, I don't think,' he said. 'But I guess it will sink in later, when I want to phone him about something and then I'll remember I can't. And when my parents get older and frailer, and I won't have Ben around to talk to about them.'

She nodded, but he knew she was showing her understanding of something else: that grief was not momentary but everlasting. From this day on, he would forever feel Ben's loss; he would not be presented with a replacement brother. He glanced at her: she was staring at her hands. Would it be easy for her? To replace Ben?

He suggested that they walk around the garden, and then they took a different route back to the metro stop so she could see more of the area. By the time they returned to his flat, it was getting dark. He had picked up some ingredients for a soup, and a stick of bread, all she said she could manage to eat; she was still suffering from the effects of the previous night. When the soup was simmering, he rummaged through the cupboard in the hall and pulled out his files of photographs, which he deposited on the dining table. She sat down opposite him and watched as he flicked through them.

'I'll have some of our old house, I'm sure,' he mumbled, just as he found the first, taken outside their home, by his mother most probably. He and Ben stood with their dog, aged eight and ten, he guessed. Two toothy boys, dark hair in pageboy cuts, very short shorts and T-shirts. Then several taken by himself, with the camera he had saved up for, bought in London on one of their visits to see his mother's family. Angled shots of the house, a rugby game, and several from the Eastern Highlands where his father had grown up on the farm. There were arty shots of his parents, mostly taken when they were obscured in some way. One of Ben, taken from behind: his brother was sitting on a rock, facing the hills before him. Several photos of Matilda, hanging up clothes, digging in the garden. One when she was polishing a row of shoes, another when she was staring into the camera's lens with impatience. Then amongst another selection taken at the racecourse in Borrowdale – he remembered going with a friend whose parents owned one of the horses – a picture which he had not taken: an old photo of his wedding day.

He stood next to Paula, whose long dark hair was arranged in a chignon, wispy strands framing her face. Their parents and siblings were aligned on each side. He slid it over to Rita and was surprised to feel a sharp stab of jealousy when she halted, breathed, God, that's Ben, her fingers briefly touching his brother's image. Much younger, but unlike the previous photos of boyhood, recognisably the Ben whom she would have known. She did not speak for some minutes, and then she asked, 'How old was he here?'

'Well, I was twenty-three, so twenty-one or thereabouts.'

He watched as she gazed at the photograph; his brother would be close to the age she was now. It was as if time had spun her back, so she could meet him as a peer. She said nothing for some minutes, and then seemed to make an effort. 'Your wife is very pretty. I mean your ex-wife was very pretty. I mean I'm sure she still is . . .'

He smiled, and she gave up.

'How long were you married?'

'Five years.'

'Clare isn't in the photo.'

'No, she didn't come. The wedding was in Joburg. Johannesburg. I think they might have just started going out or something.'

He skipped through some more photos. Out of the corner of his eye, he could see her put the photo down, reluctantly. Then, as if to lance a boil, he slid another over towards her: Ben in Lisbon, not more than four years ago. He couldn't remember if he had come alone or with Clare, but Ben looked well. He was leaning against the wall in front of the castle. The wind was in his hair, the sun in his eyes; he was squinting into the lens, and he seemed to be in mid-sentence. He radiated a vitality that set his face aflame.

He felt tears spring into his eyes, at this reminder of his brother, at how when he took this photo neither knew what the future held in store for them, but the girl was too engrossed to notice, and he could blink them away. She touched her fingers to the image, her lips parted, and his heart suddenly ached, then burned. Whatever he and Rita had shared a short while earlier, those moments by the fountain, they were not what she had shared with his brother. Ben had made love to her: he would have held her naked body against his, coiled her hair around his hands, he would have heard the sound she made when she arrived at her climax. He stood up, went into the kitchen, repelled by the prurience he seemed to have acquired, knowing at the same time that *that* was not what hurt most. His brother had not only made love to the girl. He had touched her: under her clothes, under her skin, touched her heart, because it was clear that she had loved him.

He turned the soup off, collected two bowls from the shelf above and sliced the bread, washed up the things that remained in the sink. Then he spent a few moments gripping the edges of the kitchen surface and breathing deeply. When his pulse had slowed down, he glanced through the hatch: she was tidying the photos away, dry-eyed, slipping them back into the file.

He walked back into the living area.

'You can keep it, Rita,' he said. 'That photo of Ben, keep it.'

She didn't stop returning the photos to the file. Then she slowed down, shook her head and looked up. Her face had that same bruised expression he had seen that day he found her, when they had stood opposite each other on the street near her parents' house.

'No, I shouldn't,' she said. 'It wouldn't be right.'

He didn't press her, and she smiled wearily. He picked up the folder and placed it on the bookshelf. If she wanted to find it again, she knew where it would be.

Up and down, up and down: his feelings, her feelings. From the lightness he felt from being with her in the gallery, laughing in front of his painting, sitting by the fountain in the sunshine, to a heaviness when he looked at her, at her youth, her loveliness, reminders of his brother and what he had delivered into his midst. They ate their soup quietly. He put on some music, Debussy this time, to accompany them.

After they had eaten, she insisted on washing up, and then sat on the sofa with her laptop while he tidied things away in his atelier. Later, she told him she was nearly dropping off: she would turn in. He opened his own laptop and dealt with his emails, mostly concerning the degree show later in the week, another reminder about the exhibition in the spring, then climbed into his camp bed, turned on the small lamp and opened his brother's book.

The country won its independence in 1980, after twenty years of unilateral independence under Ian Smith. During that period, whites and blacks lived segregated lives, if not as well documented or draconian as the infamous apartheid rule in neighbouring South Africa, persistent enough so that by the time Grace was born, in 1975 in Salisbury, the city was a patchwork of colours: the white population occupying the desirable Northern suburbs, such as Mount Pleasant and Borrowdale, the Indians congregating in the Belvedere area, the Coloureds (the mixed race peoples) in areas such as Hillside and Braeside, with blacks mostly found in commuter satellites such as Chitungwiza.

Grace left school at sixteen, in 1993, when Zimbabwe was in the midst of an economic boom. By 1998 she was working as a hairdresser's apprentice, at a chic city-centre hotel, Meikles, a Harare institution. She lived in a women's hostel in the Avenues area of the city and met a Mozambican man, with whom she had a child. He left her as a single mother when he returned to Beira, his hometown, a year later.

The political changes that ensued had been forecast, but the speed at which events took place had not. Mugabe's decision to honour the terms of the Lancaster House Agreement to the letter cemented his statesmanship in the continent, where leaders were too often ridiculed as peddlers for the West. Mugabe reinstated the system of two-tier citizenship lauded by Ian Smith, with a reversal of fortunes. The economy began its decline. By 2003, the women who still attended the beauty salon on the rooftop of Meikles hotel were only told how much the cost of their treatment would be at the end of the session, because of constant changes in the value of the currency. A few months before the end of 2003, after five years of service, Grace lost her job:

G: I lost my job and I have a son. He was now ten years old and I couldn't look after him. So I sent him back to my village, to my grandmother.

I: Did you not have family in Harare?

G: My mother, she had died of AIDS two years ago. I found a job, in Sam Levy's [Sam Levy's village, an upmarket shopping centre] but Borrowdale is too far. I pay too much for the CO [commuter omnibus] so I need to move now.

I: Where will you go?

He closed the book, laid it on the floor beside him and turned off his lamp. He did not need to look behind him to know that Rita had fallen asleep; he knew by now the rhythms of her breathing. He lay for some minutes in the dark, and then he sat up, felt for the book, walked across to his bookshelves and placed it in a gap on the highest shelf.

He had been reading his brother's book because he had hoped it was a way of communicating with his dead sibling. But it wasn't; it wasn't the Ben he knew in those words. These were hard-working and courageous women whose personal struggles pointed to grander narratives. But they were not speaking to him: only to the researcher in front of them, Ben. He had never had that relationship with his brother, who was only that, his brother. If he expected to read something directed at him specifically – Fran, take care of Rita – he would not find it in the works his brother had published years before the girl had arrived in their lives. From now he would have to listen to himself, and those still in the living world. The man who had written the words he had immersed himself in the last few months was gone; he, Francois, remained.

21

THE women's voices reverberated in his head as he slept; the feel and look of the photographs he had nearly forgotten about drifted in and out of his dream-vision. He heard the rustle of the quilt as the girl got out of bed while he was still lying down. He pulled on some clothes and walked through to the kitchen to brew some coffee, heard her leave the bathroom, and then she appeared at the door.

'Coffee?' he asked. 'Porridge? Toast?'

'I'll grab a piece of toast in a bit,' and then she hesitated. 'Should I go and see the lady at the dance school? Find out whether she needs anyone?'

'Sounds like a good idea.'

'Just in case I can pick up a few hours.'

'Go for it.'

'It might keep me out of your hair a bit.'

'Well, you don't have to worry about that, but you might enjoy it as well.'

As he was having his coffee at the table, she emerged from behind the screen in a short maroon skirt, a dark fitted top.

'You look nice.' More than nice: she had touched some colour to her lips and to her eyes.

She smiled. 'Would you give me a job?'

'Absolutely.' He raised his cup in a salute. 'Good luck.'

He heard her pull on her boots at the front door, and then she was gone.

Without leaving his chair, he reached behind him and lifted the folder of his photographs off the shelf. The photograph of

Ben was still at the top. He laid it to one side and leafed through the others until he found a photo he had taken of his parents in the garden. He examined it closely and saw what he was looking for, what had been troubling him through the night. There was a vague form in the background, moving between the bushes like a ghost. A shimmer of long fair hair, long limbs: Denise. She would have been visiting, and he might have tried to include her surreptitiously in the shot. He had no memory of such an entrapment, but judging from the age of his parents, it would have been the right period of time. It was probably one of those days when she joined the family for lunch, while he burned up with jealousy across the table, before Ben would walk her back to her house. Down the road they would go, hand in hand.

His phone beeped and he stood up, retrieved it from under his bed: Lucie. *Can you meet me after my classes at 2 today? And come back for late lunch?* He stared at the message. This was how they had made arrangements over the last four years, but she had not done so for some weeks now. *Love to,* he replied. *See you then.* He walked back slowly to the table. So, Denise had returned to jostle with Rita in his thoughts, and as if she could sense this, Lucie had reasserted her presence.

He had cleared the breakfast things when the doorbell buzzed. He dried his hands and went to the door with a sense of foreboding that yet another woman he had either lusted over or wronged would speak to him through the intercom. But within minutes he was opening the front door with some surprise to Gildo, who appeared at the top of the stairs, panting.

'Did we organise something?'

'You mean, "Good morning, Gildo, my old friend. It's nice to see you" . . .'

His friend pushed past him and walked into the living area, his head turning one way and the other. '*A menina?*'

The girl. Even he himself, in his head, still referred to Rita as 'the girl'.

'Out,' he said.

'Out?' Gildo looked at his watch, then glanced over at Francois, at his papers and materials.

'I know it's hard for you to believe,' he said, 'but I don't sit around all day.'

His friend ignored him. 'Where did she go so early?'

'There's a dance school in the Baixa. She wants to find out if she can teach some classes.'

Gildo was smiling. 'Well, she can move, as we saw . . .' Then without waiting for any response, he walked over to the screen at the foot of the bed, drawing a finger along the wooden frame before moving forwards and bending down to inspect the toiletries Rita had set out on the windowsill.

'Looking for something?'

'No, no.' His friend grinned, straightened up, turned around. 'I've got a meeting later in Graça. I thought I'd take you out for breakfast.'

'I've already eaten.'

'Come and join me for a coffee. And you can watch me eat a *prego*.'

Gildo wanted to revisit an old favourite. A shack behind the Panteão, on the side of the hill facing the river, which served an old-fashioned steak sandwich: a heavy breakfast, but one which would transport them to the *barracas* in Maputo. He knew he would be tempted into having a half portion. While he gathered his keys and jacket, his friend continued to circumnavigate his flat, until he said, finally, unable to keep the irritation out his voice, 'Gildo, what are you doing?'

'Imagining, Francois,' still grinning, 'Just imagining. Very nice. Very intimate.' *Muito intimo.*

'You know my flat is what it is.'

'I do. Certainly, I do.'

He ignored his friend's antics. He knew already what was being implied, and he refused to join in on the tease. On the way down the hill, Gildo spoke of the family's plans for the spring school holiday. They would be going to the Algarve, where Jacinta's family owned a restaurant. They would be spending a week there, no more, because their daughter wanted to revise for exams. She was incredibly driven, like a changeling; they could only sit back and watch her in amazement. Jacinta secretly wished she would study medicine, but neither wanted to place further pressure on her shoulders. Young people nowadays seemed to crumple under the difficulties of the world.

They arrived at the shack and ordered their sandwiches, two coffees and a bottle of mineral water to share. Because he knew why his friend was paying him a surprise visit, and to avoid any accusations of avoiding the topic, he decided to say, 'Rita enjoyed your party.'

Gildo was drinking, motioned with his palm, swallowed and said, 'She's a nice girl.'

'Yes.'

'Sweet.'

'I agree.'

'And she looks like her photograph. You understand what I mean.'

'Mm.'

A short pause, then, 'When did you decide to bring her back with you?'

'Well, I never thought I'd meet her or find her or whatever. I didn't plan anything.' And he found himself continuing, peevishly, 'I told you she went to see my parents.'

Their sandwiches were called out, and Gildo went to fetch them. For some minutes, they ate in silence. Again the thought arrived in his head: let him do the work.

Finally, Gildo spoke, wiping his mouth on a napkin, enunciating his words with relish: 'And *her* parents, her *Indian* parents, are happy she is staying with—'

'They don't know.'

His friend nodded, placated. 'I thought so.'

When he made no response, Gildo put his sandwich down, making no effort now to hide his exasperation. 'Do you think this is a good idea? That they think she is one place, but she is in a different country?'

'She'll tell them when she's ready, I'm sure.'

'*Está fraca*, Francois,' chastising, shaking his head, '*muito fraca*.'

'Gildo, I know she's fragile.' He wiped his mouth with a napkin, placed the remnant of his sandwich on the plate. 'That's it exactly. She didn't know what to do or where to go. I just want to give her some breathing space.'

'And nothing more?'

He glared at Gildo, who met his eyes coolly. It was unpleasant to be found out: he had no intention of admitting to his thoughts over Rita.

Instead, he said, 'You're making this into something that it's not.'

'I'm opening your eyes.'

He pushed his plate away, threw the napkin into its centre.

'This is between Ben and me.'

His friend raised his eyebrows. 'Ben is dead.' His voice was low. 'But this girl . . .'

'She's of age. An adult. She came of her own free will.'

'*Free will?*'

Even as he had said the words he had cringed, but now he stared defiantly at Gildo, whose voice was rich with scorn: 'You don't have a daughter, Francois. And neither did Ben.'

The words cut through him. Gildo did not look away, but a shadow moved across his eyes. The silence between them lengthened and yawned, stretched its limbs, then looked at one man and then the other, expectant.

Finally, he spoke, slowly, holding Gildo's eyes. 'All the women,' he said, 'all the women you've had. You've been thinking, she is someone's daughter?'

Gildo grinned, his teeth a flash of white, bowed his head as if to accept the challenge, but his eyes were angry. Then his smile fell away, and he growled, '*Filho de puta*. Why can't you see when someone wants to help you?'

'You're helping me?'

'Do what you like, *filho de puta*.' His friend picked up the menu card, tossed it over. 'Do you want anything else?'

He shook his head, his heart thumping with anger. Gildo left their bench and walked over to the cash desk, paid for the meal. When he returned to stand next to Francois, he picked up his glass of water and drained it. 'I have to go,' he said.

They stayed like this for some minutes, the heat between them faded. Both men watched the street where opposite them a narrow alley led further down the cliff. Gildo relaxed, leaned against the bar, and he in turn allowed his body to uncoil.

'You never met my father.' Gildo spoke suddenly, his voice moderate, light. 'He was from the bush, you know, a real man of the land,' grinning now. 'It was my mother who made sure we all went to school, spoke Portuguese, had the good manners for society . . .'

He tried to smile back, to show his friend that he wanted, too, to end their rendezvous well.

'In my father's tribe, in the villages, this still happens in some places. If a man dies, then the younger brother becomes responsible for the widow and children left behind, so she stays in the family and she will be looked after. But you know, Francois,' he leaned down so that his lips were an inch away, 'sometimes the brother can choose if he wants to marry her. He can have sex first with his brother's widow, to cleanse her of spirits. After that, he can decide if he wants her or not . . .'

'Why are you telling me this?'

His friend straightened up, his fingers mussing Francois's hair. 'To remind you how uncivilised we Africans are. Those Africans you love so much . . .'

He shook him off, slapped Gildo's hand away. 'Fuck's sake.'

His friend was laughing now, but the jollity was a veneer – that was clear to see.

'I'll mind my business, Francois . . .'

'*Espera,*' he said impatiently, and they were silent for some time. More people were entering the shack, and there was now a queue for orders. Most had the look of having arrived in Lisbon from further afield: from islands in the Atlantic, or from the countries that dwarfed their old colonial master with their sprawling land masses: Brazil, Angola, Mozambique. All gathered now in the shack in search of a reminder of what they had left behind.

'You're worried that something will happen between me and Rita,' he said eventually.

Gildo raised his head, looked him in the eye: 'It's inevitable, don't you think?'

'I'm not like you.'

'Yes, you are, Francois. Yes, you are. Tell me you haven't thought of it?'

'I haven't thought of it.'

'You're lying. Lying. And you're making her lie to her parents, to everyone. Like your brother made her lie.'

'When did you become a professor in moral philosophy?'

'When I finished my degree in architecture. You didn't know?'

'Thanks for breakfast.'

'OK. OK.' His friend laughed, collected his keys from where he had left them on the bar, slipped his jacket back on. 'Just let me say my last word, Francois. Don't think I don't see what you are feeling. It's difficult to lose a brother.' Then he clapped him on the back. 'Are you going back to your flat?'

'In a minute.' He paused. 'Thanks again.'

'*Até a proxima.*'

He knew there would be a next time: before him stood his closest friend, who had, as always, upended him. He took no pleasure in hurting Gildo, who loved Jacinta, who was a better husband than he had been or could be. He had an image of himself, Ben sitting by his side, while before them was a court-room, a judge in wig and gown, regarding them over his glasses. Yes, the court accepts your noble intentions – here he exchanged a look with his brother, who raised his eyebrows slightly – but, and the voice changed, so the judge became Rita's mother, pulling at her shapeless house-dress in distress, but she is bright, she is sweet.

He left the shack and walked up the hill. He took his time: there was a heaviness in his step. The stairwell of his building appeared even gloomier than usual. The steps seemed to have doubled in number, felt endless, as if he were climbing higher to acquire something more portentous than a better view of the city: an answer to something. He opened his door; his feet led him to his bookshelves. He ignored his file of photographs and reached higher, lifted the book, *Daughters of Africa*, from where he had placed it only the previous night. He found a cigarette, which he lit, opened one set of French doors and leaned against the balcony railing. Gildo's lecture had reminded him of a passage he had read some weeks before in the introductory chapter. It only took him a few minutes to find the section.

The Matrimonial Causes Act passed by the Zimbabwean government in 1985 ensured that a woman would not be stripped of property when widowed or divorced, and enshrined in law the man and woman as equal owners of land and prop-erty. However, I argue that continued social practices, and the sexual obligations they entail, diminish a woman's ownership of her own body or sexual behaviour. Rather than being a lament on the social mores of a nation, the practices I describe below give context to the complex struggles women face when aspirational and ambitious. The negotiations the women undertake in managing the varied niches of their lives illustrate the underlying thesis of this book: that the daughters of Africa are the driving force of change.

He skimmed through the paragraph, turned the page:

> In a polygamous culture, control of the sexual encounter is still a male preserve, and husbands are excused infidelity or have multiple wives. Social practices such as lobola (where a dowry is paid by the future son-in-law; one which increases with the 'mombe yechimanda', a reward to the bride's family for preserving her virginity), the tradition of kupindira (where a man's impotence can be hidden by a younger brother engaged to impregnate the wife) and the tradition of muramu (where the younger sister of a wife is considered the husband's 'junior' wife) . . .

Not here. His eyes zigzagged over the text until he found it:

> The persistent tradition of levirate marriage imposes the brother of the late husband on the widow. Shona culture is not alone in affording brothers with such entitlement. Indeed, in disparate cultures, over millennia, brothers have been endowed with a powerful oneness, regarded as unitary. In fact, levirate marriage is a feature in Central Asian, Jewish and Kurdish communities. There is even mention in the Old Testament, where Onan marries Tamar, the widow of his brother. What all these practices shine a light on is how sibling relationships are intensely gendered, so that brothers share and inherit property: be that property land, a house or a wife.

He dropped the book onto the floor, stared down at the cobbles below him. The previous night he had not found Ben in the words he had written. But now he had resurrected his brother's voice to confirm a nagging suspicion: that despite his awareness of the shaky morality of his feelings, he was beginning to believe the young girl, Rita, who had been introduced into his life by his brother, was an inheritance.

So: he had been wrong. Despite the skin they had been given, which would forever make them stand apart from other men, they were not in fact interlopers; he and his brother were indeed sons of Africa. The spirits had entered their bodies, whispered in their ears, infused their thoughts. His now came thick and fast, unfurling like the smoke from a witchdoctor's fire, rising and falling to the backbeat of a drum, ululations and stamping feet. The dancers swirled and leapt, landing on dusty ground, spinning and weaving around the flames, their faces aglow; the beat of the music matching the beat of his heart in his chest.

22

H E spent the rest of the morning unable to settle down to anything. After trying unsuccessfully to clear away some of his paperwork, he walked over to Rita's wing. He stood above the bed: his bed, but it looked like it belonged to her now. She arranged her pillow under the quilt; he always left it on top. She had tucked the ends of the quilt under the mattress, something he never did. She had, in a few days, transformed the small space into her own. On a clothes hanger, hooked to the side of his wardrobe, was the short mauve towelling robe which she wore after her showers. He could immediately picture her wearing it as she walked across the room from the bathroom. He turned his back on her things and returned to safety, which lay beyond the wooden screen. He sent a message, *I'm going to Lucie's, back later*, and then left the flat. He wished not to be reminded of her, but, as fate would have it, he saw her walking back up the hill, returning to Alfama.

The sun was on her face; several men turned to watch her pass. She possessed many gifts; no wonder it was easy to think of her as a reward, a prize. Towards the top of the hill, one man spoke to her. She would not have understood what was said, but she could guess, and he saw her give a shy smile and increase her pace. And then a young man detached himself from a group, calling out something that made her stop. She allowed him to draw up to her, allowed him to hold her waist as he kissed her on one cheek and then the other, after which she smiled up into his face. He gestured up the hill, and she nodded. They carried on walking, the young man pressing his hand to the small of her back in a semblance of guiding her: Moises, with his guitar and his charm.

He turned away and tried to still his thoughts, racing, ricocheting off one wall of images – Rita, turning to meet his eyes in the gallery – to another – Rita bending over the photograph of his brother, which became Rita bending over Ben, her hair falling onto his face – to another – Rita, naked, in front of him, an inherited wife. Approaching the stop, he had to make a conscious effort to lift himself out of the mire of his brother's words, his brother's mistress, to appear normal and happy when Lucie came out of the school.

But she had appeared light-hearted herself, greeting him with a breezy kiss, pushing her sunglasses up on her head so he could see her eyes were bright. They climbed into her car, and as she drove back towards her flat, she told him she had felt, in her last visit, that she had reconnected with Germany, not just because her son now lived there but because, she explained, as you grow older you cling on to things that are familiar from your past. She wanted to go back home. The weekend had been busy with packing Josef off back to his father's and making several phone calls which would allow her to make the same journey before too long. She had handed in her notice that morning; she hoped to tie up and leave Lisbon in a month. Her parents had offered her their annex to live in and from which she could start up her own jewellery-making business. And being closer meant she could help her parents more as they became older. They lived not one hour away from where Josef lived with his father; she would not be near enough her son to annoy him. And she had felt, when he had visited her, that he had grown from a boy into a young man, someone who was now able to love her more.

All this she told him as she negotiated the narrow streets and as they neared her flat. Her tone was one of light regret; her timbre was optimistic. Never once did she mention that she felt her announcement would surprise him in any way, nor, after an initial casual enquiry, did she mention Rita. Things were different, she insisted, ever since Josef had moved. This is not just about you, Francois, she said, smiling, pre-empting any attempt on his part to admit any guilt. He knew that this was a reprimand of sorts: she did not want him to claim their relationship as his alone to orchestrate and to dismantle.

He was sure there was an anger somewhere in her; perhaps there was also somewhere a wish that she could have steered their relationship into deeper waters. For their first years together, her son had dictated their relations, as well as providing an excuse. When Josef left, they had accepted that neither of them wanted the intimacy of living together. That might have changed as they grew more used to being unencumbered, or it might not have. Whichever, theirs was never going to be a farewell that was acrimonious, but rather a celebration of what they did very well. So, as he had half-expected they would, they made love: in the living room, on the rug, as if to remind themselves of the freedom they had to ignore the domesticity of the bedroom. She had gathered the ingredients for a risotto, but first they sat on the sofa with a glass of wine to toast her new adventure, and he found that she needed only to stop a moment, take his glass out of his hand and put it down, touch his lips with hers, before he responded to her signal and was pulling her to him. They had last spent a night together just before they had each gone on their separate Christmas holidays, three weeks earlier. Each had returned in the new year with a companion: Lucie brought Josef, and he had brought Rita. And now, despite Lucie's declaration of intent, he found that she needed him to fill the role that he had occupied for her, and she for him, one last time.

Yet he could not let go of Rita, of the understanding he had arrived at: that he wanted her to be his. And in a grotesque reversal of loyalties, as if to mitigate the feeling he was betraying her by making love to Lucie, she filled his thoughts. Imagining that it was Rita in his arms was disturbingly easy, erotic; when he came, the pleasure was so intense that he blacked out momentarily, then, returning, he threw himself off, his hair matted with sweat, his heart pounding, to fall into a very short, very troubled sleep against Lucie's shoulder. He could only hope that Lucie would mistake his ardour for regret that this would be their last time. And when he awoke and met her eyes, saw with relief a glimmer of self-satisfaction, he was glad he had deceived her, glad of her erroneous conclusions, because she deserved better than to be used as a conduit for the desire he felt for his brother's young lover. She deserved to feel she had punished him in some way, rather than learn of the murky moral swamp he was letting himself be sucked into.

They ate a lunch which was more like a dinner, as darkness fell, and stayed on her balcony for hours after, talking about the many common interests which had sustained them through an enjoyable four years. But before that, after they had dressed and as she was making the risotto, he had sneaked a message to the girl – *Might be late* – feeling guilty, like an unfaithful husband, worrying that she would guess his exploits, the reason for his delay.

He left Lucie's unscarred, reflective, but impatient suddenly to get home. He decided to walk; by the time he had got to a tram stop or even found a taxi, he could be halfway there. But more than time, he needed to relinquish Lucie, needed to gather his thoughts before he saw the girl, Rita, whom he seemed now unable to not think about. It was past eleven when he finally arrived at his building. He climbed the stairs, banging on the lights as he ascended, and opened the door to his flat quietly. It was in darkness, which was good; by the morning he would be more objective. But after he had slipped into his camp bed, he heard her get out of the bed and move to the bathroom, heard the toilet flush, and then her feet were padding down the short hall.

'Rita?'

Her footsteps paused, and he leaned out of his bed. She was standing with one foot slightly raised, like a cat.

'Did I wake you?' he asked.

She shook her head. 'No I couldn't get to sleep for some reason.' And then she came closer. She was wearing only a thin T-shirt, her hands weighing down the hem, demurely, so that it reached the tops of her thighs. He shifted across a little as she had done the previous morning, and she accepted his invitation, stepped forward and sat on the edge of his camp bed.

'Are you cold?' He reached for the pile of clothes he had set on the floor beside him. 'Here. Put this on.'

He saw a flash of her cotton briefs, a triangle where her legs met, as she raised her arms above her head to slip them through the sleeves, and then she was enveloped in his jumper, the deep red bringing out the red in her lips, her hair cascading around her shoulders.

'It looks good on you,' he couldn't stop himself saying. She smiled, hugging her knees, then said, 'I've never seen you wear it.'

'No.' He pushed his pillow aside so he could prop himself up on his elbow more securely. 'There's usually only one really cold day in the winter when you might have that pleasure.'

The moonlight fell onto them, so they were in a grey circle in the darkness of the rest of the flat. There was something so guileless about her that it was easy to imagine her completely oblivious, unaware of the intimacy they shared: the moonlight, the bed he could pull her onto. She had her eyes on her feet, and he found his own travelling over her legs, long and lovely. What would she think of him if she knew that just hours earlier he had imagined lying between them? And how would she feel if he were to tell her: I thought of you. He was sure that if she knew it had been a separation between him and Lucie, the girl would not imagine the sex, not envisage a last parting act of intimacy.

She had had an affair with his brother, but this seemed to have left her an innocent.

'Well,' she said, looking up with a smile, 'I've got a job. Sort of. The lady, she's called Ana, said she needed an assistant for the kids' classes, and she'd even pay me five euros an hour.'

'Congratulations.'

'I'm still looking for a transfer,' she said, 'don't worry. It just means I can pay my way a bit while I'm here.'

'Well, I don't mind about that you know.'

'And I borrowed a book from your shelf,' she was saying, as if the day they had spent apart needed to be filled in with details of what each had done. She paused before saying, 'I couldn't make headway with Ben's book.'

'I told you it was technical.'

'Maybe I was reading it for the wrong reasons.'

He had thought the same; they had arrived at the same point at the same time, but he said nothing, then, 'What have you chosen?'

'A Henning Mankell,' she laughed. 'Did you know him in Mozambique?'

'Only to say hello to.'

She hugged her knees tighter. He sat up straighter, and he saw her eyes move for an instant over his torso, his bare chest and arms, and then away, and he saw the beginnings of a flush rise to her cheeks. So, she noticed him. She was not blind to his naked-ness, his proximity, and he could feel himself grasping at that thought even as he tried to discard it.

She made to stand up, and he spoke.

'Do you want to go out for a walk? If you can't sleep?'

She hesitated. 'Don't you have that busy day tomorrow?'

He glanced at his watch. 'It's not too late. Only half past eleven. We could go to the Miradouro for a bit of air.' He nearly added, and then tuck you into bed.

She moved back to her end of the room, and he dressed. Did he want to help her sleep, or was it imperative that he change the dynamic, get them both out of the circle of moonlight, off the bed, out of the flat, to help him push away his thoughts? His brother's book regarded him balefully from the shelf. He pulled his jacket off the peg, resisted the urge to take his packet of cigarettes, and slipped a bottle and two glasses into his pockets. She reappeared in a pair of jeans, still wearing his jumper, and he held her jacket for her while she slipped it on; then clicked the door quietly shut behind them.

The night was misty, cold, their breath coming out in puffs as they climbed the steep cobbled street to the square and then walked to the wall that overlooked the city. They sat with their backs to the church, their legs dangling over the edge of the wall, so that the vista of the city lay before them. The café-bar to their left had closed, and there was no one around. He pulled out the bottle and showed it to her, 'Would you like a small shot to warm you up?'

Her eyes glittered in the dark, and she nodded. He measured a finger carefully, and passed the glass to her, poured a double for him. They clinked their glasses, and she took a tentative sip, then started coughing, her hand to her chest.

'Take it slowly,' he smiled.

The whisky warmed his gullet, settled somewhere in his chest. He thought of Lucie: he was not heartbroken, but there was some regret there, that he had treated her shabbily, had not nurtured their relationship but allowed it to float as if on a wave. He saw his glass was already empty, and he poured himself a little more, then glanced at the girl and held the bottle up: 'More?'

She smiled, nodded. 'If you think I can handle it.'

'Of course you can.'

They were quiet; the city was aglow below them, a sea of small shimmering lights in the mist, in patterns that belied the rough and tumble nature, the haphazard shambolic feel. He had fallen in love with the city because it had not felt European, but more like it was pivoted in readiness to leave the mainland and float out into the world, leaving the hills and mountains behind. There was always, when he looked out of his window, or stood at this point, the sense that if he wished he could set out. This restlessness, this holding on to the land by his fingertips, this might have wearied Lucie.

She said, 'We should play that game.'

He looked at her. She was smiling widely, and so he raised his eyebrows.

'Which game?'

'You know those questions, by, was it Marcel Proust? If we answer with honesty, we reveal our true nature.' She laughed. 'Apparently.'

'I think I know what you mean.' It charmed him to see her in a playful mood. 'But I don't know them by heart.'

'We can make our own.'

She had a glint in her eye, and so he smiled, nodded.

'When and where were you happiest?' she asked, tilting her head and touching the glass to her cheek.

He thought for a moment. 'Twenty-seven years old, living in Maputo, preparing for my first solo exhibition in Joburg.'

She raised her glass to him, saying nothing, and so he asked: 'When and where were you happiest?' and then immediately regretted, hoping she would not resort to moments with his brother. But she thought for some minutes; the answer did not come immediately.

'The summer after I finished my A levels and I knew I was going away to uni.'

So: the anticipation of freedom rather than the reality. Freedom to make mistakes, freedom to lose your heart.

She swung her legs for some moments and sipped her drink. Then, 'What's your favourite book?'

'*War and Peace*,' he said without hesitation.

'Oh wow,' she said. 'Heavy.'

'Well, you asked. And what's yours?'

'You can't just copy my questions . . .'

He laughed. 'OK, next one will be original. Your favourite book?'

She was quiet for a few moments, then she said, '*Jane Eyre.*'

'Good book.'

The whisky was like golden nectar, and he felt his mood lifting.

'I'm just warming up,' he said. 'You ask another, and I'll think of one in the meantime.'

'OK.' She still had the glass to her cheek, and then she moved it away and looked at him sideways, lowering her lashes, 'What most attracts you in women?'

He gave her a stern look.

'Rita,' he said, 'are you behaving badly again?'

Her shoulders shook with silent laughter; she pressed the glass against her lips.

'Well,' he sipped his drink deliberately, enjoying himself, 'I'd say intelligence.'

She rolled her eyes.

'I'm not saying anything more,' he grinned. 'My turn. What is your proudest achievement?'

She thought for a few moments. 'This performance I did at the Indian High Commission a couple of years ago, of Kathak.'

'And what is Kathak?'

'A classical Indian dance.' She paused. 'It takes years to learn.'

'That sounds impressive.'

She was still swinging her legs, but now lowered the glass away from her face and placed it between her knees.

'Have you ever said I love you without meaning it?'

'Hey, come on,' he said. 'Play fair.'

Her eyes gleamed, but she did not look away.

'Possibly,' he said eventually. 'When I was younger and more foolish.'

She inclined her head, but there was a slight dimming of her expression as if he had disappointed her; perhaps he should have lied. He was enjoying himself, but he should not forget that she was still young enough for her visions of romance to be grounded in true love, illicit or not.

'My turn,' he said. 'Where is the most beautiful place you've ever been?'

She sipped her drink and then spoke. 'Where my mother is from in India. There's this lake surrounded by trees, and a kind of bridge made of earth running across it so you have to walk in single file to get to the other side. The trees are green palms, and the water is green, and then there is this thin red-earth bridge.' She stopped. 'It's beautiful.' Then she turned to him. 'You'd like it.'

He smiled. 'Sounds like I would.'

There were some shouts behind them, and two motorbikes roared up in the still of the night and stopped some feet away from them. He laid his hand on Rita's knee to reassure her – provoking further catcalls – before remembering that she would not understand what the young men were saying. When they turned their bikes and roared away, he took his hand away and saw that her body had stilled. Her hands were cupped around the glass, now empty, against her chest, and her eyes darkened as she said, 'My turn.' Then, her voice low, 'What would you say to Ben if he were standing in front of us right now?'

Her question hung in the air. But it was not unwelcome; he found that he wanted to answer it. He breathed out.

'There are a lot of things I should tell him,' he began. 'Like that I've finally read his books, or at least long sections of them.' He smiled weakly at her. 'But I'd probably tell him about something that happened when we were still living at home.' The night seemed to thicken with his words. 'It's years ago, years and years. There was a girl I was terribly in love with. I never told her, which is my fault. But Ben went out with her. It's all come back for some reason, and I can't stand not knowing if he ever knew how I felt about her or not.'

She was quiet for some time, and then she said, 'I think he mentioned her once.'

'Really?' He stared at her, stunned. 'Denise?'

'He didn't say her name.' She paused. 'He made a joke I think, that he might have married her, if he'd stayed.'

His heart was hollow: was it the farewell with Lucie, the reminder of Denise, the whisky, the circumstances of sitting in the dark with his brother's young mistress? That his brother had revealed the depth of his feelings for an old girlfriend to the young girl beside him, that at least Ben had had those feelings and the relationship was not merely a taunt, was disorientating. He should not have chosen to tell the truth. Something generic would have worked. But he had a wish to open a wound, stir his hand into its flesh, and so he said, 'Can I copy your question? What would you say to him?'

She put her glass down beside her, then shoved her hands into the pockets of her jacket, kicked at the wall with the back of her heel.

'I'm so angry with him, Francois,' she whispered. 'He should have told me about the children thing.'

He didn't respond, and then she continued, her voice still a whisper. 'I'd like to think that if I'd known about what they'd been through, him and Clare, I would have acted differently. He told me they weren't really sleeping together any more; I didn't think to ask him why. He just used me, he used me to—'

'It was more than that, Rita,' he interrupted. She turned to hold his eyes. 'I'm sure it was more than that.'

She didn't ask him again, what she had already asked, that day he had found her: how can you know that? She looked away and slipped her hands between her knees. Impossible to know you, he wanted to say, without feeling something for you. Her hair fell forward, hiding her face from him. He watched her. They had arrived at his brother again, which was why she was sitting with him, in the dark, in this city, on its castle walls. All those years ago, they had both wanted the same girl, Denise. And now, this girl, Rita.

She shook her head, turned back to the view, the mist engulfing them. He cleared his throat and picked up his glass and hers, slid them back into his pockets. The atmosphere had turned, and he searched for the strength to pull himself away from his thoughts.

'What did you do today?' he asked eventually.

'Oh well,' she tucked her hair behind an ear. 'I bumped into Moises on the way back here, and he introduced me to some of his friends. We all went for a coffee together, and then I went back to the flat.'

He nodded, saying nothing, and then watched her as she reddened.

'I think he likes me,' she whispered.

'I'm sure he does,' he smiled.

'But I'm not sure,' she faltered. Then, after a long pause, she said, 'I'm not sure about anything. I feel like I have no right to be thinking about anything that makes me happy or makes me feel good in any way.'

He watched her; her head was bent again.

'But it's nice for you to meet people,' he said eventually, and added, 'and people of your own age.'

'I'm no good with people my own age,' she replied.

There was silence again, and then she shook herself, as if trying to throw off the moroseness that had settled between them. She turned to him: 'And how is Lucie?'

He hesitated and then said, 'She's going back to Germany in a few weeks. She wanted to end things between us in an amicable fashion.'

'Oh, I'm so sorry.' Her fingers went to her lips, and then she touched his arm briefly. 'Are you OK?'

He thought for a few moments. 'I am,' he said eventually, then with more honesty than he expected he would show the girl, 'But I'll miss her.'

'I'm sorry,' she repeated, her eyes holding his, 'if I've played any part in that.'

'You haven't.' He touched the ends of her hair briefly, and her eyes dropped quickly to his fingers. 'Really. It was a long time coming. We'll still be friends, keep in touch. I'm sure of it.'

They ended there. He suggested they go back, and she agreed. They walked back across the square and down the street in silence. When they were back in the flat, she took off his jumper and folded it, handed it to him, and then as he took it from her she reached up and kissed his cheek, so that for a brief moment he could smell her hair, feel the softness of her lips. He wanted to press his hand to the small of her back, as Moises had done earlier, then pull her closer into him and kiss her mouth. But he didn't, and she moved away. So that they settled back into their positions, the windows letting in the moonlight, on opposite sides of the room.

23

HE left the flat just before sunrise. He needed to clear his head after a fitful night's sleep: the whisky had only served to make him feel thirsty and restless. He did his press-ups in isolation, ran back to the flat where Rita was still asleep, showered and left just as she was waking. He had started avoiding her: an unsatisfactory state of affairs, but his thoughts were too confused, and he did not trust himself. Neither did he want her to feel he begrudged her presence, and so he wrote a note, telling her that the degree show was open to the public from midday onwards, and she would enjoy it. It was in the college just down the hill on the way to the Baixa.

The café held the usual regulars, and he ordered breakfast while catching up with several others with whom he had comfortable, unassuming friendships: his life for the last six years. On first arriving in Lisbon, he had taken some time to adjust to living in Europe, but not long. He had dipped in and out of the lives of several amorous but undemanding women before his convenient and pleasurable attachment to Lucie. But nothing had yet given him cause to feel as much turmoil as the arrival of Rita. He drank his espresso, ate two large croissants and conversed with Fabio, who had also been invited to be an 'esteemed observer' of the students' work. He tried to shake off thoughts of the girl as they walked back up the hill and entered the exhibition space, where he saw several faces he recognised from the classes he had given over the years. It was a few hours later that he realised his phone, which he had turned to silent, was vibrating against his chest, and he remembered suddenly how it had done the same that night, nearly six months ago, when his father had called to tell him Ben had died.

This time it was his mother, whom he had forgotten to ring back. He cursed himself, answered guiltily, but she brushed his apologies away impatiently, 'Darling, is this a good time?' Her voice was tight with tension; it was not a request. He moved outside the chamber and went to stand in the landing, the staircase before him leading to the exit, his mother's voice continuing, louder now in the silence of the stairwell.

'I'll start at the beginning,' she was saying. 'It's all been very strange. You remember I told you about that student who came to see us? Ben had lent her your dad's book?'

His skin contracted, and he felt goosebumps appear on his forearms. He opened a door and moved into an empty room.

'Yes,' he said.

'Well, I phoned Marc Duplessis a few days ago, you remember, the South African? Ben's colleague?'

'Yes.'

'I was so touched, you see. I wanted to send her one of Ben's books, but I wasn't sure whether she would have a pigeonhole in the department, you know? Well, Marc said, Francois, that that young lady hasn't been back to university since last summer. She didn't re-register.'

He didn't speak, but let his mother continue.

'The thing is,' she was saying, 'Marc was very strange, very odd. And when I explained how thoughtful she had been, he became *cagey*.'

She paused, as if expecting a reaction, and in the silence he could hear a hissing sound in his ears, as the truth leaked out. He could picture his mother with her soft hair, her swirling skirts and delicate wrists. She would be holding the phone to her ear, unsuspecting, unprepared for what she would learn of her son, her youngest. He gripped the phone and pressed it to his ear as if by doing so he could delay the moment, arrest her words.

'But that's not it,' she was continuing, 'I wouldn't have given that another thought. Except that he got back in touch today, Marc that is, to say the Armstrong family have been in contact with the university. They're unhappy that they weren't consulted about the award. Well, I have no idea why they think they should have been consulted, Clare didn't work for them, but then Marc said they're also requesting that the university investigate Ben's relationships with his students.'

By now her voice was showing her distress. 'Francois, I mean, what on earth are they *implying*? That Ben was having an inappropriate relationship with a *student*?'

'Mum,' he interrupted without preamble. 'Ben was having an affair with the girl. Rita. He was having an affair with Rita.'

Saying her name provoked an image of her: in the Gulbenkian, in front of his painting, her face lit up. As if she had just realised that she had her life ahead of her, to appreciate the beauty of art and of other things; that she needed to forgive herself. Perhaps he had in some small way helped her reach that point: that could be his defence. His mother was quiet for many minutes, and then the questions came quickly.

'Are you sure?'

'Yes.'

'Rita? The girl who came to see us?'

'Yes.'

'And when was this? Do you mean recently?'

'Just before the accident.'

His mother fell silent again; all he could hear were noises in the background, very faint noises coming from afar.

When he had phoned her, twelve years ago, to tell her that he and Paula were divorcing, she had been similarly quiet on the other end. His father had just joined his mother in London; his parents were cohabiting after ten years' separation. If there was any couple who could appreciate the vagaries of a marriage, it was his parents. But he had found himself listing all the expected reasons why the decision had been made. Only when he had finally dried up, unconvinced himself by the litany he had recited, had she said, simply, her voice full of love – Francois – and this had plucked the truth from his heart, so he had continued, without thinking: I'm no good as a husband. Shouldn't she have the freedom to find someone who is? His mother had been quiet for a long time before giving her verdict: I have faith in you, son.

Because he had in mind her voice from all those years ago, when she said 'How do you know all of this?' he was shocked to hear how she had aged. He had never thought someone's voice could change, but his mother's had.

'She told me. You see, she's with me now,' he said. 'She's been staying with me, here in Lisbon.'

She accepted the news mutely, so he continued.

'She felt she couldn't stay on at uni after the accident. And her parents don't know that she hasn't been back.'

'But how did you meet her?'

That was a story for later, he thought. A photo, a painting, a note on a hall table: details for later. His mother's breathing was audible now, and she did not press him. Perhaps she was unready to hear more. Then she asked, 'Do you have to get back?'

'Don't worry about that.'

She fell silent again, and he waited. Then she spoke: 'I remember when Ben told me about them, him and Clare I mean. By then they'd been trying for children for a year, and they'd decided to visit the doctor. It was his first real trial, you know? Ben was so gifted. I know both of you are gifted, but with Ben everything seemed to come even easier.'

He crossed an arm across his chest and tucked his hand into his armpit, as if by holding himself he would be better protected from his mother's words.

'He was telling me about how things were tricky between him and Clare. I think he expected words of wisdom from me.'

She snorted. 'Me! I left your father because I didn't know how to talk to him. I felt,' she hesitated, 'incompetent and ill-chosen to be giving him advice.'

She stopped speaking, but resumed a few moments later.

'But that was years ago. It could have been five, six years ago or something. So all this time, it didn't go away. I wonder what their life together was like, the day-to-day. If they ever found comfort in each other or if it was just all too painful.' Then she sighed. 'I thought she was a lovely girl. Rita, I mean.'

He cleared his throat. 'She is.'

'But she knew he was married?'

'She knew.' And then he added, his heart aching as he spoke, 'She loved him, and he loved her. It doesn't make things better, but I'm sure of that.'

Again, it came back to his brother, and now he felt an anger at Ben, which made it difficult for him to hear his mother, who was saying something, her voice indistinct at first, then becoming clearer: 'This is an awfully heavy burden for her to be carrying.'

Someone knocked on the door, and he turned around, held his finger up, one minute, and turned back again, not seeing anything, his eyes blinded by a white screen of anger.

'You can't know how devastated I feel, Francois.' His mother sounded drained. 'I was all for fighting off the Armstrongs. But how can I defend my son when what they suspect is true?'

His heart went out to her. Whatever failings they had as parents, he was sure his did not have many. He had only felt love from them, an acceptance of whatever he decided: his refusal to accompany his mother to England, his impulsive marriage. They had been immensely proud of the cultural centre he had established in Maputo. They had both visited, braving his chaotic schedule, Paula's family's incomparable superiority. Then his divorce; his erratic, chopped-together lifestyle. His childlessness.

When he did not respond, she spoke again: 'Francois? Surely you can see that Rita shouldn't be staying with you?'

He shut his eyes, almost plugged his ears with his fingers.

'She can't stay with you, but I'm happy for her to stay with us. We have the space for one thing. And when she's ready, I'll go with her to her parents. That's better than . . .' she hesitated, 'the situation as it is.'

'She may not want to leave . . .' He stopped himself just in time to drop the 'me'. She may not want to leave me.

'I know. I know, darling,' and the way she said it he had for a horrifying moment a certainty that she knew everything: how he felt about Rita, how he had had her in his mind and body for the last days, months, since seeing her photo. How he could not shake the feeling that she had been given to him, that she belonged to him now.

'But let her make that decision. Promise me you'll tell her that she can stay with us.'

He covered his eyes with his hands. 'Yes. I'll tell her.'

The line went dead, his mother's energy expended, and he threw his phone down, so it clattered to the floor, the facing and battery pinging out. An immature reaction, befitting his puerile behaviour of late. Now, silence. He could hear nothing around him, only the sound of his blood pumping through his veins. He could not even see what was in front of him; he was in the muffled vacuum of his thoughts.

He had been asked once: why become an artist? The answer presented itself as a vision: of the raw, empty canvas, alone and untouched, to be tended to, nurtured, before he layered his colours on its bare form. It was never the finished product that mattered to him, even when that was what remained, but how he changed in himself when an idea took hold: he could feel it inside him, scratching at his abdomen, seeking release. Rather than the creator of a piece of art, he often thought of himself as an excavator. He was only finding what was already there on the canvas, peeling off opaque strips that hid an object of beauty from view, exposing it for the rest of the world to see. And what he found was never inanimate to him; it was a tale that spoke out from the brushstrokes. His brother wrote about women; he painted them. She had asked him: what does that say about you both? He had wanted to say: I want to give them a stage from which they can tell their story. Ben had the same intention. It seemed that he was destined to uncover how similar he and his brother were; was it then so surprising that they would love the same women?

His focus returned to the room he was standing in, to the window at one end which offered a view of the river, and the sounds of people gathering across the hallway. They were similar, he and Ben, but they were not boys any longer. They were men, each exposed to different experiences as adults, with little commonality to their everyday lives. He remembered his mother's words: their day-to-day. Ben's would have included many things his did not: lectures, seminars, research trips, a wife at home every night. And then, the girl: Rita.

The door opened: the departmental head.

'Francois? *Pronto?*'

He picked up the parts of his phone and clipped them back into place, slipped it back into his pocket and re-entered the hubbub. He tried to divert his thoughts as he wandered through the chamber, joining in the discussions with his colleagues and contributing to the evaluation of the artworks on display. The students responded conscientiously to the questions that were posed, and he nodded sagely along with the others. But his mind was elsewhere, there were flutters in his stomach, and while no one could suspect, the voice coming from his lips was not his.

24

A T midday, the doors were opened. Members of the public and the families of the candidates poured in. Before long, the chamber was full of noisy chatter and exclamations. He left his colleagues and moved to stand on a small dais from where he could have a view of those who entered. He could not be sure that Rita would visit, but he was not surprised either when, through the crowd, he saw her. He watched her from his vantage point for some minutes. She had dutifully picked up a pamphlet at the entrance and was reading the names of the contributors, identifying their artworks then standing in front of each with respect. In the sea of people, he could still pick her out with ease. He could have watched her for hours, but not many minutes had passed when she raised her head and scanned the room, met his eyes, the trust that then arrived in her expression giving him a pang. She weaved her way towards him through the gathering, her eyes shining.

'It's such a great atmosphere,' she said when she drew up to him. Then, looking around, 'And have they all passed?'

'It's not a pass-fail thing. More like putting them forward for awards and exhibitions and suchlike.'

'Oh, I see.'

In front of them a young man was being squeezed on either side by two smaller, rounder elderly people: grandparents most likely.

'Actually,' he said, and he could hear his voice sounding brusque, 'I wouldn't mind some air. Shall we go out for a bit?'

She looked surprised at his request: she had not long arrived.

'OK . . .'

'I've seen too many of these to be too excited by it all . . .'

He regretted the cynicism in his voice; she bit her lip, perhaps embarrassed of her earlier enthusiasm. But he hardened himself against her and led her out of the chamber, down the stairs and into the street. Across the road stood the Plaza do Sol; on one side, a kiosk where he could buy some cigarettes, but he would not. He had no wish to give her the impression that he needed any crutch, any fortification. He held her arm as they crossed the road to the viewing point, the river ahead of them in all its splendour, and pointed to the café a few steps further.

'Would you like a drink?'

She shook her head. Her eyes were on his face even as he looked out to the Tagus.

'There's something, isn't there?' she said. 'There's something wrong.'

He shook his head; he could feel a nerve pulsing in his temple.

'There is,' she said.

'My mother phoned,' he said. 'She's upset about something, that's all.'

She was quiet, then she said, 'About Ben?'

He found that his hands were bunched by his sides. He pushed them into his pockets and said, 'There was a suggestion. Someone she spoke to at the university suggested to her that there was something between you and Ben.'

The colour left her face and her features tightened. 'Who was it?'

'One of Ben's colleagues. Marc?'

She nodded. Her face had become so pale that he pulled one of his hands out of his pocket and took hers. It was small and cold in his. He said quietly, 'I told her everything, Rita. About Ben and you. And she knows you're here with me now.'

She slowly drew her hand away from his grip. He wanted to press his palms against her skin, block her pores to stop the light that had been inside her from seeping out. He remembered that night when he had held her: the feel of her skin, the smell of her hair, the way her body bent into his arms when he had lifted her up. He did not just want to hold her in his arms; he wanted to relieve her of the weight she held inside her. His mother had said: this is an awfully heavy burden for her to be carrying.

'Your mother . . .' Her voice was low.

He said nothing. She folded her arms around herself.

'What does she think of me?' she whispered.

He shook her head. 'It's not like that.'

They stood like this for many silent minutes. She was half-turned away now, looking at the river. He gestured to it: better to talk of something else.

'Down that river,' he said, 'and into the Atlantic Ocean, the armada would have sailed. To Africa, South America. To India.' He smiled, but she was looking away and did not see him. He abandoned his hackneyed recital and leaned against the railing, letting his eyes take her in, wanting her to know that he was doing as much. But her gaze was fixed on the water.

Finally, she spoke: 'My parents came in the other direction. Not by sea of course.'

He had not heard many mentions of her family; he had no idea how often she had phoned or emailed them while she had been here, but, he realised, only a week had elapsed.

'I know my father has never really adjusted,' he said. 'Not with being in London itself, but with not being in Africa.'

She was quiet for some minutes and then asked, 'Did you read what he wrote? About Ben dying?'

He straightened up.

'No, I don't think I did . . .'

'I found it on the Internet,' she said. 'When I looked you all up. Before I went to see your parents . . .'

She stopped speaking, pressed her lips together. His eyes ran over her features, the curve of her cheek, the cusp of her lips, her slender throat. Her hands were at her sides now, her elbows bent. It felt like a lifetime ago that Rita was not in his life; it felt unseemly that his parents had met her before he had.

'Rita,' he said, 'my mother wants to help. She wanted me to tell you that it might be better if you stayed with my parents in Clapham.'

She accepted his news without any surprise. After some moments, she said, 'Why does she think I should stay with them?'

'She said my flat's not big enough. And also,' he hesitated, 'she said she'd be happy to go with you, whenever you want to talk to your parents.'

She stood still, and he watched her. She did not appear so young to him now; she was pale but composed, her eyes were dry. She held herself erect, and despite the uniform of youth that she wore – the jeans, the boots – she looked elegant and poised. Then she turned, and as the moments passed, her eyes held his, steadily. They seemed to have unfathomable depths, which opened into her heart. He could hear it beating, a rhythm that matched his, thudding against his ribs, his insides melting into his stomach, down into his legs.

'And,' she said, 'what do you think, Francois?'

What was she asking him? He waited until he knew he could speak in a normal voice.

'If you want to, I'm happy for you to stay here. I've enjoyed having you around.'

She tilted her head without looking away.

'That's nice,' she said quietly.

There was a shout from across the road: someone was waving at him.

'They're starting the awards,' he said. 'Look, I'll tell them I can't stay—'

'No, don't,' she interrupted. Her voice was strong now. 'You shouldn't let them down.'

She took his hand, squeezed it, then dropped it.

'Go,' she said. 'I'll be fine.'

'There's a dinner after, but I won't be very late . . .'

'Don't worry about me.'

His heart was heavy, suddenly, in preparation for what was to come, but he gave her his most winning smile.

'We can talk more later. We'll figure this out,' he said.

He continued smiling, then reached forward and chucked her under the chin, and she rewarded him with a twitch of her lips.

'I'd better go.'

'Yes, OK.'

He turned away. There was a large group of people suddenly walking towards him, some kind of group, arrived to see the cathedral, the Sé, chattering excitedly to each other. He waited for them to make space for him to tunnel through them, and reached the end of the esplanade to where there was a crossing over the main road. The people milled behind him, but he did not hear what they were saying. There was a hum in his head, Mahler's Adagietto, as loud as he had ever listened to it; louder than when he had played it on returning to Lisbon after Ben's funeral; louder than that night all those years ago in Maputo, when he had learned that one of the girls he had painted had been strangled by her client and was only found days later in a miserable squat in Alto Mae; louder than a morning many aeons earlier, when he had woken up from a dream where Paula had walked into the sea and drowned herself because she had learned that he no longer loved her. The hum stayed in his head as he walked through the last dregs of the crowd, back into the building. When he reached the top of the stairs, he looked out of the window and saw her walking back up the hill, taking long but slow steps, the fingers of one hand on her lips.

It was later than he had envisaged, when he could finally extricate himself from the panel, the examiner from the Università de Belle Arti in Rome, the group of excited students, and then from his colleagues and friends who refused to let him leave after the meal had ended but dragged him to a bar for a celebratory cognac. The building was quiet, and from the street he could make out that the lights in his flat were turned off. He had a feeling of déjà-vu, returning from Lucie's the night before, calling out to the girl as she crept back to bed. He was hoping she would be properly asleep tonight. He wished to delay any discussions of plans or his parents' invitation until the morning, and was relieved when he opened the door and saw the flat was indeed in darkness and very quiet. Then, closing the door and stepping through to the living area, he saw that the screen was folded, lay leaning against the wall, the bed was neatly made, and her suitcase was gone.

He walked around the room, from one end to the other, along the edges, as Gildo had done just the morning before, not expecting to find her curled under a table or behind a chair, lying in wait to spring a mischievous surprise, but simply so that he could see what she had seen before she took her leave. When he reached the bookshelf, he saw that the file of his photographs was on a different shelf: the shelf he had placed it on that night after the Gulbenkian, not where he had left it the morning that followed. He opened it: the photo of Ben, standing in the wind, leaning against the castle wall, was still there. She had had a last look, but she had not taken it with her. He walked back to his studio area and looked through the stack of canvases: the painting remained, too. He looked at it with disdain: it captured nothing of her. He stood up, glanced around. She had taken nothing it seemed. Even the note she left on the dining table was pinned in place under the books he had lent her: Ben's book and next to it the Mankell.

He went into the bathroom and turned on the shower, let the hot water wash the day away, then walked back drying himself, tossing the towel onto the floor, to pick up the note from the table. He slid into the bed – his bed, her bed – the note in his hand. He turned his face into the pillow. He could smell the scent of her hair; the sheets were perfumed with the body lotion she used. The note read:

Dear Francois,

If I keep hiding away and lying to everyone, I'll never grow into the person I was supposed to become, before I met Ben. But at the same time I know that I can't ever become that person, because meeting him changed me. But I do need to grow and accept that I have hurt many people. I hurt Clare. I've hurt your parents, her parents, my family. And I've hurt you, because you'll remember Ben differently now. I'm going back to tell my parents everything, because I owe them my honesty. I won't keep in touch, because any responsibility you feel you have for me must end now. You've done more than you ever needed to and I'll always be grateful.

Rita.

Such eloquence, he thought; she sounds older than her years. He lifted the paper away from him, as if invisible ink would reveal a hidden message: a love poem, a secret address where he would always find her, where he could wait for her. But there was nothing. Even if there had been someone to hear him, he could not speak; his voice was choked in his throat. The only thing that broke the silence was the mantra repeating in his head: go well, stay well.

Part Five

25

SHE arrived in Ernakulam in the early hours, after an intermi-
nably long flight. When she came through customs, she saw
her uncle, Onachen, standing in the arrivals hall. Her ribcage
ached with the weight of her holdall, and she felt dishevelled
and in need of a shower, but the languorous warmth of the air
and the familiar sounds of greetings and instructions being
shouted in Malayalam lifted her spirits immeasurably. Her uncle
clasped her to him briefly, his chin grizzly, his eyes tired: hello,
mol. They drove through the quiet streets. She opened the
window, felt the breeze in her hair.

For the first time, on this return, she did not have her
parents with her to orchestrate, delegate, translate. Onachen
had been told that she had had a love affair. No more details
were needed for him to understand the gravity of the situation,
and grave it certainly was, he commiserated with her parents.
But Onachen's disconnection from the rest of the extended
family located far away in the hills, and his adeptness at deflect-
ing disapproval and curiosity – which Seline's debilitation and
spinsterhood had already attracted – determined that he would
be the most suitable guardian for Rita. Seline was still unwell,
and he would appreciate Rita's help in the antique shop; she
had been such an asset the last time. Anyway, her visit was just
that: temporary, only to let time pass. Rita could resume her
studies later.

Latha had enrolled her on some online courses and would be
posting some materials. Keep up to date, it will make it easier
when you get back. It was her way, Rita knew, of showing her

gratitude: that Rita did not insist on remaining in London, in her home. Indeed, why should she be treated like a pariah when all she had done was fall in love? But as the scandal at the university grew, so did the danger of the spotlight falling on the family. There had been one conversation she had overheard, that week when she first returned, when her parents had summoned Joy for his support and his advice and he had appeared at the house every evening. This affects all of us, Joy was saying. All of us: me, Latha and Mira too. She knew her brother loved her; he was only expressing what they all knew. It was the mention of her niece that had strengthened her resolve. Her involvement with a lecturer, the subsequent death of both the lecturer and his wife, and the speculation that it was the discovery of the affair that had led to the accident: these were not her burdens alone. There would be whispers among the other Malayalees who worked in the hospital with her father, the ladies who provided her mother with her trade. Latha's family – Mira's other grandparents, her other aunts and uncles – would regard her parents and Joy with disdain: what kind of family? What kind of daughter?

As she had expected, rather than venting fury on her, her parents had crumpled on her news, looked broken themselves. The first night back in her bed, her childhood bed, late at night, her mother had knocked on the door and sat next to her, stroked her hair: a simple gesture which made Rita's tears flow onto her pillow, her mother then whispering, *karayanda, mol. Karayanda.* For hadn't her mother cried tears for years, been denigrated for years, on account of not producing a child? These memories had left her parents aged, deflated. Rather than pass judgement, her mother made a request: that she attend church the next day and make confession. A request which made Rita hurt as much as if she had been struck: her mother was as worried about her soul as about her person.

Whether the priest would recognise her voice and form – he had known her since she was a teenager and had heard her

254

childhood trespasses: I have disobeyed my parents, I was angry with my friend – was not a likelihood she wanted to dwell on. When she kneeled in the darkened cubicle, she whispered, bless me, Father, I have sinned. Then, I slept with a married man. There was a pause, and she saw the priest shuffle his feet.

'Just the one time?'

'No,' she whispered. 'Many times.'

He cleared his throat.

'And then you repented?'

'Yes, Father.'

'And so you ended it?'

She chose to say, 'Yes, it ended.'

He was quiet, then, 'You understand the seriousness of your actions?'

'Yes, Father.' Her palms were now sticking together.

'I see,' he said. And then after a long silence, he said, 'You are young and attractive now, Rita, but when you are older and married and not so attractive you will want to be able to trust your husband.'

She felt her face grow hot with shame. 'Yes, Father.'

There followed a monologue on the weakness of the flesh, delivered, she felt, in a rather lukewarm manner, as if the priest were so disappointed in her, he did not himself believe in her redemption. She was given her penance: three prayers, which she recited quickly after, her mother kneeling beside her on the pew. As they left the church, her mother patted her arm but, heartbreakingly, did not appear convinced that the ritual had saved her daughter.

And when, not even a week after she had returned, a letter arrived from the university – addressed to her but read by everyone around the dining table – written in a very neutral register, asking whether she would like to discuss the reasons for her non-registration, she knew then that somewhere a ball had started rolling. But rather than gathering in its descent leaves and earth to fatten it up, it would be eroded, thinned, grazed, so that at the bottom it would sit raw and exposed: Ben's legacy.

She wanted no part in that. It was impossible to explain to her parents that she had been utterly willing: she had wanted to be desired, touched, even owned by Ben. Her family had asked her whether she wished to make a complaint; after all, it was clear this older man had taken advantage of a young girl. But their queries were half-hearted. Better for everyone if they moved on, avoided any attention. A towel smeared with blood thrown into a washing machine, a photo ripped up. Of Francois she had said nothing. She had discarded her phone without replying to his messages so that no one would know of him. She had only, after all, stayed with him for seven days. The lucidity and fullness of those seven days: these would remain her secret. They did not belong to any account of her wrongdoings, why she was where she was now. For a tale was never a truth; but only what the narrator wanted to tell.

The sun was rising and the sky was turning a fragile grey-blue, more traffic was gathering, and the familiar colours were emerging: the endless green, the red dust, the blue sky. Before long, they were on the bridge crossing over from the mainland onto the peninsula. The car swerved suddenly: a man on a bicycle had swung in front, a pile of sacks balanced on the back, teetering dangerously, and her uncle hooted angrily.

'*Karutha*', then he turned to her. 'Sorry, *mol.*'

They drove up the dusty, bustling road in Mattancherry. To one side, under the shade of a banyan tree, there was a cluster of vendors selling fruits and biscuits. Along the rest of the road, before the turning to the quiet street leading to the synagogue, the stalls displayed garments and trinkets. Onachen's next exploit, he was telling her, was to make good on their dream: to renovate the house and open some rooms to guests. The old house was crumbling, but they were in a prime location – the halfway point between Jewtown and Fort Cochin – and tourists loved old houses. This house had been in Seline's mother's family for at least a century. 'When you are feeling better,' he said, as if she were suffering from an ailment, 'you can give me some ideas.'

On her arrival at the house, she had had a shower, washing away the journey but also, she felt, preparing herself for a new life. Her environs had changed; time was slow. She could learn to forget. Seline had moved downstairs, and Rita could have her own room. That first morning, she knocked on her cousin's door, heard a mumbled response. It was stuffy inside; Seline lay in a crumpled kurta, sweat stains at her armpits. She gave a small smile when she saw Rita: 'Reetiekutty.'

She sat down next to her cousin, trying to hide the shock she was feeling. Seline's face was blurred, her lips were cracked, her hair needed washing.

'Will you come for some breakfast?'

Her cousin shook her head but offered no excuse. Then closed her eyes as Rita sat for many minutes until she stood up and left the room. Onachen had laid out some coffee and bread on the table on the veranda.

'There could be a small fountain; the sound of water is relaxing,' he was saying. 'We could make the two downstairs rooms en suite, more privacy. Then the big living area . . .' He seemed intent on looking to the future, when he and Seline would resume their partnership.

'How long has Selinechechi been like this?' she interrupted, and her uncle stopped mid-flow.

'About one month,' he said after a pause. 'Maybe a bit longer.'

'Have you seen a doctor, Onachen?'

He nodded, his features sagging momentarily. 'It's not serious,' he said. 'Her mother was like this sometimes. After some rest, she will feel better.'

Then he moved on: the antique shop needed to be manned, it was still the high season. If Rita could help, then, when Seline was recovered, things could go to plan.

She was unconvinced by her uncle's optimism and disturbed by the change in her cousin. It was a macabre thought, but it was as if the illness that had plagued Ben's wife had left her body like a malevolent spirit and settled into someone else, someone who would suffer for Rita's misdeeds. She had never known Clare Armstrong or seen how she had suffered, physically or mentally. Now she could witness the effects in Seline, a fraction of the person she had been just a few months ago; her uncle, deprived of his beloved child, his companion. Rita was now in the midst of such pain. Not an observer or an intruder but an actor in a family's drama.

Her parents called her every day for the first weeks; she made the same responses: yes, I'm all right. Yes, eating well. In fact, she had little appetite: the heat, the boredom, the repetitive, limited curries that Marykutty, who tended to the house and Ammachi, produced. It had been less than a year since she had last been, but there were many changes: no visits to the other guesthouse, no giggling with Seline. Her daily trajectory was a few metres across the road and down the lane to the antique shop, and then back to the house. There was a steady stream of visitors to the shop – it was on the lane leading to the synagogue – a steady stream of interest in her. But Onachen and his scowling assistant, Noble, loomed large; perhaps Onachen was more alarmed by her fall from grace than she imagined. She missed her cousin; the days were long and the nights were hot, uncomfortable.

One afternoon, she opened the door to the front bedroom, which was now unoccupied. Previously, it had been the main bedroom, for Ammachi and her husband; now it was used mainly for storage. It was the coolest room in the house, never having the sun fall in it, and sheltered from the heat of the roof by two storeys. She pushed the bags of rice and boxes of dried produce to one side; she had space to move and, with the fan on its highest speed, a type of breeze. In here, she could practise Kathak when the rest of the household and the street were having their siesta.

It had been several months since she had danced – the last time had been at Onachen's friend's guesthouse the previous summer – the longest hiatus in her life until then. When she slipped on the heavy ankle bells and made her first steps, her elbows bent and level with her shoulders, singing the taal's rhythm herself – *thaa thaa thay ha thaa thaa thay* – her love of the movements and what they brought to her flooded back and filled her heart. The rhythms took over her body. She spun, found her centre, leapt and then crouched, one knee bent, the other leg straightened to her side – *thay ha thay ha* – then she slid back into standing position, her arms raised, and spun and spun. By the end of the afternoon, she was drenched with sweat, exhilarated; her muscles were aching. If she could do this a few times a week, she need not fear her body atrophying like she felt her soul was. But, as well, the tears were rolling down her cheeks; her heart was in her throat. For along with the joy of retrieving something she loved came an understanding of the dance that had eluded her until then: as if she had had to live, err and survive to acquire a oneness with the elements it celebrated. The fire between her and Ben, how she had felt that to be with him was to breathe air, be watered; his death and this exile had turned her to wood. Now she would need metal, resilience, to continue living when he was gone and she was alone.

If her family ever wondered at her dedication, practising diligently, writing out new sequences which she performed for herself alone, in the front room, and in the drier months, outside in the yard, they never spoke of it. For, she could see, they feared that her gracefulness and litheness shone too brightly. It was never mentioned that she should share her talents, perform to an audience; she never asked. She had asked too much of her family already. She did not tell them that each dance she wrote told the tale of what had happened, that each stanza had its own tempo, and that as she did not have a tangible memento of the events that were etched in her memory, she was making her own.

26

THE street in front of the antique shop – with its craft stalls and Internet cafés, the tea shops and spice galleries – was her window to the outside world. Aside from the hours she spent there, her time was spent in the house in Mattancherry, where she found herself waiting for the others to retreat to their rooms for the afternoon siesta so she could return to the front bedroom, now her dance studio. Other than the burst of vitality which her dancing awoke in her, she felt listless. She found she was reluctant to begin the courses that Latha had recommended. Her cousin's ailment infected the household, which seemed to wait for Seline's recovery in a stupor, one in which she, Rita, could not contemplate laying down stepping stones that could lead her to a future.

More than a month had passed when one morning she opened her cousin's door: 'Selinechechi, let me wash your hair.'

'I washed it the day before,' came the muttered reply.

'Not properly. Come with me.'

Rather than closing her eyes and turning over as she had done previously, her cousin gave a small smile: Rita had, without thinking, spoken in Malayalam.

She helped her cousin up. Seline gave off a stale, sad smell. She led Seline outside, to the courtyard in front of the veranda, the kitchen building to one side, and settled her cousin on a chair in the shade. Then she went back, stripped the bed of its sheet, threw open the windows, tied back the light curtains. Marykutty was outside the kitchen door, Ammachi beside her on her cot, pounding rice for appam, but had stopped to stare.

Then, as if she understood what needed to be done, Rita saw her put down the mortar and enter the house: she was going to sweep out Seline's room.

Her cousin's hair was plentiful but greasy. Her stomach turned as she soaked it using mugs of hot water from a bucket beside her, then lathered it with shampoo.

'Smells nice,' Seline mumbled.

'Because you're worth it,' she replied smiling, but the joke was lost on her cousin, who nodded absent-mindedly. She left Seline with her hair in suds while she drew some more hot water into the bucket, carried it back to the chair in the courtyard, avoiding looking at the dirty water that flowed in muddy streams into the vegetable patch behind. Seline sat passively, her hands folded in her lap, her eyes half-closed. Then she spoke: 'I hear you in the afternoons. You are dancing?'

Rita nodded. 'Otherwise, I'll be out of practice, and I wouldn't get any exercise.' She paused. 'Do you want to join me?'

'No, no.' Then, 'But I like hearing you.'

Her cousin's hair looked so full, glittering in the sun, that Seline herself now looked even more unkempt.

'Will you take a bath now Selinechechi?' she asked tentatively.

'*Venda*,' Seline replied, then stood up, tossed her hair over one shoulder and walked back into the house.

It was a step. Marykutty related the incident to Onachen when he returned. He looked joyous: 'Her mother was the same, *orkkunnunille*?' Rita was pleased to give her uncle happiness, but she was also frustrated: did Seline not need medication or therapy? It was derisory, this fatalism – like mother, like daughter – which came from the same place that had branded her cousin not marriage-worthy, had branded her mother as faulty. And she knew she herself would enter the family's mythology: your great-grandmother, Rita. She fell to temptation, she brought shame to the family, she was a step away from being a *veshya*.

And then she was startled by her own convictions: that she would in the future marry, have children, who would have children and on and on. Had she learned nothing? Had she not learned that nothing could be predicted, presumed, that life was governed by the throw of a dice, a turn of phrase? Two hands steadying her as she walked blindly down a corridor. How could she know that she would be privileged enough to have such a life: of love and children of her own to cherish? But she could not shake, along with her fears, a sense of belief in herself. She had made a mistake, a grievous mistake; she needed to confront herself and what she did. The sense of belief arose from this understanding: that she had the strength to do so.

Seline began to appear at breakfast. Eventually, she started coming to the shop for increasingly longer periods. The accounts were in dire need of her perusal; Rita was starved of company. Now that her cousin was there, Rita appreciated the activities around the shop. In the mornings the grill was lifted, and they sat, open-fronted to the shady street. Her desk was positioned near the front, she had a stool, but she found she could not sit still all day and often spent hours dusting the shelves: a repetitive task, but at least it allowed her to finger the wares, which were exquisite. There were the usual cluster of brass ohm signs, bells and Buddhist bowls. But there were also real temple doors, carved gods in teak, tiny jewelled instruments and tools, and, her uncle's pride, the *chundan vallum* which hung along one side. This was what caught most visitors' attention, even though it was not for sale. And this was what spurred most visitors to engage Rita in conversation: what exactly is this? From a description of the boat races they would move on: you speak excellent English. Eyes would surreptitiously move over her face, her frame, an invitation would ensue. At this point she could feel her inner doors closing, like the doors of the temples in the hills. Now, rather than Onachen and Noble appearing in the shop, having heard a male voice intersecting with Rita's, she only had to glance to one side, into the office. Seline did not even bother to look up, but there would be a smile playing on her lips.

Some months later, when Seline's previous energy and vim were nearly restored, Onachen insisted that the girls have a day out together. He would arrange a driver to take them where they wanted: the shopping mall on the mainland, the beach further up the coast? In the end, they decided to do everything: start the day watching the temple elephants being bathed in Kodanad, before returning to the city, its shops and its beach.

They stood on the banks of the river as the mahouts led the elephants to be washed in its water. There was a smattering of others – tourists, two families with young children – the banks so high that they had a near-aerial view of the splashing below. The river was wide at this part, the hills framed in the distance by the blue sky and a line of coconut trees. The mahouts were sinewy, with dark bodies, red mundus tied around their waists. They called to each other, barking orders that were lost on the tourists: *Eda cherrakan, nee naannayi cheyyukkannum!* They slapped the elephants' legs, scrubbed their backs, while the elephants, large and grey, like oversized boulders, luxuriated in the attention and the warm waters of the river.

Afterwards, she sat side by side with her cousin on a rock, and perhaps because after all these months – she counted, more than four since she had arrived – she had forced herself to empty her mind of thoughts, it was especially unexpected when, as she faced the river, the words rushed into her head, like a ghostly bell – Ben and Clare, Ben and Clare – as if a child were calling out for assistance from down a well. She felt that familiar ache that she had suppressed for the last months, and her cousin beside her seemed to sense a change.

'What happened, Reetiekutty?'

She had not spoken of it for months, even though memories of what had happened had become part of the tissues and cells of her body, implanted themselves in her tendons and muscles.

'He was married,' she said quietly. 'And then he died, in a car accident. With his wife,' adding in a whisper, 'I loved him.'

But without any embellishments, without allusions to the sensuality, the struggles of childlessness, without describing these dark betrayals, the announcement fell flat: an anticlimax. A few sentences had sufficed to relay the events.

Seline said nothing, only remained looking out at the river, until Rita asked, 'Is it worse than you thought?'

She was surprised to see her cousin chuckle in response.

'No one could have wanted them both to die. That is a tragedy, yes,' Seline said finally. Then she looked at Rita: 'But it's no worse than many stories I've heard.'

Below them the mahouts were leading the elephants away, down a path back to the temple. The tourists were gathering near their coach; a child was smacking her mother's legs in excitement as the older sibling cavorted on the rocks.

'Which is harder?' Seline asked, in English now, turning to look at her. 'That he was married or that he died?'

She waited: they had time, and she needed to give herself a chance to find the response. It arrived, eventually, but it was an understanding that she would not share. That he died with his wife, because now she's with him and I'm left behind. This realisation shamed her, and she shook her head.

'I don't know,' she said.

She glanced at Seline, who was watching her.

'This is what makes us strong, Reetiekutty,' her cousin said. Her tone was soft but decisive. 'That we make mistakes, but we learn from them and carry on living.'

'But,' now she had found her voice, 'that's what is so hard. That I love living. Isn't that unfair? That I should be alive and they aren't?'

'If everyone stopped living because someone they loved died . . .' Her cousin sighed, turned back to gaze at the water.

She realised she was speaking to her maiden-cousin, who, it

was very likely, had never had a relationship. Seline was looking out onto the river, which she would have known all her life. Before moving into the old house in Mattancherry, her cousin had grown up in a village not far from where they were sitting now, where she would have swum in this same river. As children, she and Joy had kept each other company: both, at that time, sibling-less. And if her own parents had not decided to leave Kerala, she, Rita, would have grown up like her cousin, surrounded by the coconut trees and rivers, with the mountains to one side and then to the other the sea. All a reminder that they were clinging to the end of the great peninsula, and that beyond lay the vast waves of the ocean. It makes us different people, that dislocation: his words.

Her cousin was sitting still, outwardly serene. Seline was better, but she was not the same as she had been the previous year, when she had exuded vigour and confidence. Rita had never thought in those days that her cousin might want her life to be different. But sitting next to her now, she saw tiny lines near Seline's eyes: from too much laughter, or from a disappointment somewhere, at some time?

She spoke softly: 'Are you thinking of your mother?'

Seline shook her head, smiled. 'No. Not really. Of course I do, sometimes. Not now.' She took Rita's hand, placed it in her lap. 'Now I'm thinking that I enjoy living too, sitting here with you, by this river.'

She hesitated, then whispered, 'You don't want to get married, *chechi*?'

'I'm not the marrying type,' Seline smiled.

It was a common enough phrase, but she had heard it before, and the image of the speaker flashed before her: the room they were sitting in, the sight of him breaking pieces off the stick of bread for her. For a moment she felt her head spin; for a moment she could not discern if she were remembering Ben or his brother, and she had to place her hands face down on the rock

266

beside her so that she could feel something solid – hard, cool – beneath her fingers and remind herself where she was.

Her cousin was continuing: 'And I don't think my mother was either. That was part of her problem.' She turned now and held Rita's eyes. 'She lived a life that was not of her choosing. My father will never admit that.'

She returned Seline's gaze, taking the moment to regard her cousin: the sweep of hair from her forehead into the single plait, the angles of her face.

'And is this life the one you have chosen?' she asked quietly, unable to prevent the tears that filled her eyes as she said the words: she was so full of love for her cousin.

'Actually, yes, Reetiekutty.' Seline smiled, squeezed her hand. 'I get ill sometimes; it might happen again. But, yes, this is the life I have chosen.'

Later, as they climbed down the rocks and walked on the track back to where their driver was waiting for them, another name chimed like a bell in her head – not ghostly this time but sonorous, like a symphony – a name which stroked her with his gentleness, his tenderness. She had avoided thinking of him, even as she had submerged herself in revisiting her entanglement with Ben. She had not returned her thoughts to those interim weeks, to all that had happened before her return to the crumbling house, her uncle and her cousin.

The rains arrived: the afternoons were spent with the thundering sound of the monsoon on the rooftops. After, her parents arrived for Christmas. Her mother's chest heaved with emotion on seeing her, as she held her in a long embrace; her father kissed her forehead, patting her shoulder awkwardly. Good to see you, *mol*. If she felt she was in exile, she realised her parents felt the same, in exile in London. Mira had sent a stack of pictures for her Reetieaunty, brightly coloured crayoned rainbows which sang out from the paper: Joy and family would be visiting next spring.

By the time her brother and family arrived, Onachen and Seline had started overseeing the renovations to the old house, and Rita had been given more responsibility over the caretaking of the antique shop, with Latha commenting on how efficiently she had adapted to her new circumstances. It was after her brother and family had been and gone, after another season of rains, that her mother broached the subject on the phone one evening: do you want us to try and arrange something?

She understood their line of thinking: she needed to be protected, and Onachen could not be her guardian for ever. Perhaps, too, they felt she could not be entrusted with her own safety: she had proved herself an unreliable self-adjudicator. Yes, she had now a history which would complicate matters, but she had youth, good looks and a British passport to redress the balance. There was, her mother continued, a pharmacist, from Kottayam, who was interested. His parents had both passed away: this fact given with the implicit coda that it would immediately smooth the way for a marriage to a fallen woman such as Rita. Perhaps next year? She did not reply immediately. She had completed the courses Latha had enrolled her on; and she had also registered to complete a distance degree with a college in Surrey. Whether she engaged with her studies from Tooting or from the house in Mattancherry now did not matter. She felt, just as she had always done, that the space around her was irrelevant; she was a person who dwelled in her thoughts.

But did she want to return? And as a wife? If she had learned anything else of herself it was this: she was only in India because she herself felt that was where she needed to be. Her family had not forced her into anything, just as Ben had never forced her into anything. She could now offer them a neat ending to the whole episode. The obstacle: her insides were steeped with memories of what had happened, which clung to her muscles, her tendons, her nerves. How could she grow if she could not remove them from her body, to a place outside her? And if she did, would she then be able to return herself to the living world?

That evening, she told her mother in answer to her question: she did not want to go back to London, not yet; she would finish her degree. And as for the other matter: she would think about it. And then, alone in her room later, she extracted her notebook and stared at it, an idea forming inside her, inside her body, it seemed, as if a small heartbeat had begun.

27

B Y late March he had a canvas ready for the *Hearts of Darkness* exhibition, which needed to be shipped to London in time for the opening. The weather was warm and dry; he kept the French doors in his flat open. Lucie had left a month earlier, and this was the time of year when he planned his travels: once he had flown out to Cape Verde and then São Tomé; one year he had set off with Lucie for the south of the country, driving across the border to the Andalusian coast. Most years he had gone to London on his own and from there elsewhere. This year, he would be doing the same: staying with his parents for two weeks while the exhibition ran, after which he would accompany Patricia, her sister Tsitsi and her two daughters to Zimbabwe. Neither parent had wanted to join him on this return to his birthplace; both had quietened, exhausted by the events of the last months.

The morning after Rita left, that morning back in January, the rain had arrived. The streets were slick with water, the cobbles slippery, the alleys dank and damp. He remembered thinking: she never saw it like this. She would carry a halcyon view of life in Lisbon: a city of sunshine, cafés and parties. His mother had been quiet when he had phoned her that same morning, asking only one question, what's that noise? To which he had replied that it was the rain on the skylights in his flat. He had told her that the girl must have taken a taxi to the airport, boarded one of the many flights that left for London. He told his mother that he had sent messages and that when he had not heard back, he had called; her phone was turned off, and he had not received a reply to that or any of his subsequent calls.

Within a day, his parents had more to worry about. The Armstrong family were insisting that the university investigate whether Ben Martin had had a recent affair with an undergraduate student in his department. They also asked the question: had there been others? Surely this possibility – that Ben had preyed on young female students in what would be a clear abuse of office – must be investigated before an award in his name was to be set up? The following weeks were spent on tenterhooks. His parents were on the phone to him nearly every day with updates. The university was taking the allegations seriously. Colleagues had identified a student who had not returned and whom many suspected had engaged in a relationship with Ben; contact had been made. Days passed during which the student was given an opportunity to lodge a formal complaint, be offered extenuating circumstances, and be granted any assistance for a deferral. While the Armstrong family pressed for details, the university insisted that they had a duty of care to protect the identity of the student and had instructed all members of staff to respect such a duty. A few days later, his parents learned, the student had sent a formal response to the Dean of Student Services: no complaint would be lodged. Further investigations had not revealed any other cases that needed to be reviewed concerning Ben Martin. The university's sigh of relief was audible even from hundreds of miles away. But the misconduct committee had requested in the same breath, his mother told him, that while they wished that the award be upheld, under the circumstances and out of respect for the Armstrongs, that the family consider renaming it. The wrangling had blown a frost between the families, and a tacit understanding was reached: ties would not be maintained.

It was at the start of the most fraught few weeks his parents had ever endured, when the memory of their son was to be sullied, that his father had phoned Francois: if anyone needs to know what we know, about Ben and Rita, it's Patricia. He offered to fly into London, but his parents dissuaded him; he suspected that they wanted him to maintain as great a distance for as long as possible from Rita. His mother was firm: she would talk to Patricia in the first instance. Patricia phoned a few hours after his mother had left her.

'You know what, Francois?' she said, and he clutched at the familiar tones of her accent, just as he clutched at the phone. 'You know I'm jealous of that girl, that she could make him so crazy to risk everything.'

He had remained quiet, and she had grunted. 'Jealous, you know?'

He spoke: 'Patricia, he really valued you. That's clear from all his work . . .'

'Sometimes, though, Francois. I just wonder . . .'

Why was he reassuring a married woman over his brother's infatuation with a young student? It seemed that everyone had their own reaction to the news. It was only to Gildo that he said, when he had gone over the following weekend, when they were alone, Jacinta out of earshot: *deixou-me*. She left me. And as he had always known he would, Gildo had not made a barbed comment or even chided him, but simply held his arm tightly. *Coragem*.

Patricia rang back a few days later; her voice was more measured. She had talked to Michael, she said, and she had already told his parents their decision. The award was not dependent on Ben Martin's canonisation; his good work and his friendship had not changed with the revelation of the affair. The award could be named after her project, Manyame, but his parents could still be involved in the selection process, and to all intents it would remain a memorial to Ben. That was when she had extended her invitation: come with me, Francois. We can walk down memory lane. After he had agreed, she had said, before ending the call, but remember, you don't have to be your brother.

With Rita gone, he could regard himself with more censure: the circumstances of how they had met could not be changed and neither could the fact that he had fallen in love with her. But even as he wanted her, he knew that his position was tenuous. His brother had propelled the girl into a world which had overwhelmed her; he could not assume that he, Francois, was the right person to see her through to the next stages of her life. She had removed herself for a reason. Perhaps she had sensed his desire for her and this had concerned or even frightened her. This, he would have to accept. More difficult was to stem his concerns for her welfare, of how her family would react to her return. Arriving in London before he flew out with Patricia, after his commitments at the exhibition ended he excused himself from his parents, retraced his steps to the semi-detached house on the quiet road. As if he were reliving his first visit, her mother opened the door, again in a shapeless gown, but this time her eyes widened with recognition, and there was no invitation to enter. She stood in the doorway, uncertain, choosing her responses carefully. She made no mention of his last visit, nor any mention of the week that Rita had spent in Lisbon. She only said, in response to his question, she is not here. Might he know when she will be back? A long pause. She is not here; she is in India. He nodded, smiled. That's nice, his skin tightening. What had she said? They've always been gentle. He could only hope that she knew her parents. He knew at least that Rita had indeed returned to her parents, not absconded somewhere else, disappeared, to struggle somewhere, alone and scared. Please, he said, when you speak to her next, please give her my best wishes. The next day he flew out with Patricia's entourage.

At the airport, Patricia was asked, in Shona, but he just about understood: this is your husband? A friend of my husband, she had replied, her eyes cast down, her voice subdued, respectful. She was playing a role, to offset her obvious wealth, her two honey-coloured children, who were hanging off his arms, grinning, as if to deny what she had said. Patricia had commented: they like you, Francois; you have a way with children, don't you? Did he? Gildo's daughter was the only child he had really known, and even then, when she became a teenager she had drifted from his company. But he could see that Patricia's daughters were taken with him, assuming a familiarity almost instantly. In transit, they had taken turns to ask him to draw something for them: their mother had revealed he was an artist. When they had exhausted subjects for his sketches, they took turns clambering onto his shoulders, patting his head and tugging at his hair as if he were their pet, while their mother and aunt remonstrated with them. He had waved away their worries. If the girls tired themselves, they might sleep on the plane, which they did, head to toe, using their mother and aunt as pillows; for this, they shunned Francois. The officer at the airport had stared wordlessly at Francois's passport, turning page after page, his expression bored. Finally: and what do you do? I'm an artist, and then immediately the officer nodded, stamped their documents, waved them through, as if this were the exact profession that would be welcomed in the country, to solve its ills. For something had died, a spark had been lost, a joy. It was no longer, in this way, the country in which he had grown up.

His family had lived in a large bungalow in the suburb of Mount Pleasant; his father would cycle to the university. A sprawling house but not ostentatious. It was cold in the short bitter winters; they used the open fire in the living room. There were rugs on the parquet floors, faded furniture, books everywhere. They no longer owned the house, and he returned to stay in Patricia's modern, elegant villa, which bore little resemblance to the old comfortable family home he had grown up in, in a different part of the city. When he went for a run in the area, he became breathless; he had forgotten that the city sat at a high altitude. There were groups of women sitting by the sides of the roads, with sacks of fruit, cigarettes and other items; street vending had been rarely seen in this part of the city when he was growing up. It was different, going back. What had Ben said? There's a whole new quality to the light.

He could not be his brother, as he had agreed with Patricia, but he wanted to do something while he was in Harare. And it was Patricia's idea that he bring his camera and take photographs of the children in the children's village that Ben used to visit, so that they could each have a portrait of themselves and of their foster families. These children did not cherish their childhoods, Patricia had said. It was all about moving them on, onwards, into adulthoods where their lives would be no less precarious. An easy request for him to comply with; the reward was far greater for him. It was touching how long the girls especially, budding into adolescence, took over their toilette before appearing before him, completely unadorned, their hair cut in short burrs. He could have finished in a day, but he took more than a week, simply to extend the pleasure his project was clearly giving. And then he took more photographs of the centre and the staff, for a book that Patricia was editing.

On their last day, they were surprised with an afternoon tea and a large cake. The staff who worked in the centre seated themselves around a table in the hall; the children took the bottles of cola that Patricia had brought as a treat outside. A thick slice of cake was put on his plate, alongside a strong mug of tea. Aside from the older man who worked in the kitchen, he was the only adult male at the table, and as if in synchronisation with his thoughts, Patricia turned to him.

'This lady, Agnes,' she said, gesturing to the woman sitting on his other side, whom he recognised as one of the house-mothers, 'she wants you to know that she is one of the women Ben wrote about in his second book.'

She was small and plump, mid-forties, he guessed, with shining eyes and teeth.

'He called me Annabel,' the woman said quietly, and then laughed, her bosom shaking. 'I didn't like the name.'

Annabel, Chapter 7, he thought as he held out his hand. He had not reached that far in Ben's book, had returned it to the shelf without retrieving it again. Perhaps he was worried which other messages, or even edicts, he would receive from his dead sibling. Agnes took his hand, and he found he did not want to let it go. Her lips were stretched wide, but her eyes were full of sympathy. She had watched him work, this last week, without revealing her presence in his brother's publications, one of the daughters of Africa. Perhaps, just as Patricia had advised, she had wanted him, first, to carve his own role in the children's village before reminding him of Ben's. 'We pray for you and your family,' she said. Perhaps it was the generosity of the sentiment, when they were surrounded by children who had suffered more loss in their short lives than he ever had, or simply that he would have to get used to the sudden waves of grief that would swell and ebb unannounced all through the rest of his life, but his throat tightened as he held the woman's hand, whose story Ben had listened to. The two women moved closer; Patricia squeezed his arm, and Agnes did not let go of his hand, while with her other she pushed his mug of tea closer. As the cake dwindled and the children ran in and out, he talked with the woman, a simple activity which gave him immense comfort. He could imagine Ben with his recorder, perhaps under that tree in the yard against which some of the smaller boys were kicking a makeshift football, sitting with Agnes. Now he, Francois, was listening to the same voice.

There were a few family friends – his parents' friends – who still remained in the country and who wished to see him after such a long time; a few parties to which he took Patricia as his guest, where she demonstrated the panache with which she could comport herself. In each he introduced her: she was a good friend of Ben's. The weeks passed quickly. He now had a visa and he would be travelling by bus to Mutare, then over the border to Mozambique; for his plan was to travel by land down to Maputo, where he knew, conversely, he would feel more at home than in the land of his birth. The week before he left, he took Patricia and the girls out for lunch at Da Guido's: he remembered how she had enjoyed that first quasi-date with Ben. And while the setting was as pleasant as ever, the bushes surrounding the outdoor tables smelling of jasmine, when they parked, young boys appeared like wolves, offering to look after the car in exchange for a few dollars, something he could not remember happening in his childhood. And as they tried to order from the menu, the waiter kept apologising: sorry, sir, that is not available. Ingredients had become scarce. The two girls began to giggle at the charade, mimicking the hapless waiter behind their menu cards, while Patricia scolded them, vexed and embarrassed. Afterwards, he offered to drop Patricia back at the villa while he took the girls off her hands: the animal reserve on the other side of the city would still be open, wouldn't it? The girls enjoyed the outing, bounding ahead up the viewing platform, shouting excitedly at the rather dry-looking elephants and giraffes that had come sauntering forwards to the watering hole. The trio attracted much attention; most would assume he was their father, and he did not disoblige. The reserve was slightly worse for wear, but it was still uplifting to be reminded where they were: under the roads and the houses was the savannah. The land that Ben had written about – fought over, cheated of, ravaged – was the land on which he and his brother had grown up. The sun was hot and the sky clear; when the girls clamoured for an ice-cream he agreed – he would square it with their mother. Did you say thank you to Francois? Patricia asked on their return, and then she laid her hand on his chest. She called back, Francois. Denise.

When he had mentioned casually to Patricia that he might try to catch up with a family friend, she had responded immediately: that old girlfriend of Ben's? His brother had met her, apparently, several times. When he called Denise, he was struck at how normal it felt to be speaking to her. How little trauma he felt. This woman who had come to embody any disgruntlement he felt towards his younger brother. Time was a healer in matters of love, and with that reflection, he fleetingly thought of Rita: perhaps she too would heal, over Ben.

Denise had two sons, just as Patricia had two daughters; it seemed only he and Ben had not created offspring in their image. The children were on holiday, they might be under-foot, but would he like to come over for lunch? It was a mansion, surrounded by a fence and burglar alarms, perched at the end of the city, a sloping view from the sunken living room. She kissed him on the cheek in greeting, then tried to wipe away the smear of lipstick that remained. She was nervous; who wouldn't be? More than twenty years had passed; they had both grown older. She looked exactly how he had imagined she would age: her skin slightly weathered from constant exposure to the sun's rays, her hair styled carefully with highlights, she had kept her figure. But all he felt on seeing her was affection, like finding a much-loved childhood toy; not regret. The boys scampered around them – come and meet an old friend of Mummy's – then swooped off to the swimming pool at the bottom of the manicured lawn. A maid brought drinks on a tray.

'Lilian, this is Ben Martin's brother, Francois.'

The sympathetic cluck, 'Nice to meet you, sir,' and then she stood, uncertain, her eyes sliding up to his face. She had noticed the resemblance.

Denise's dismissal: 'Thank you, Lilian. You can serve lunch in half an hour.'

She leaned back and surveyed him.

'You look well, Frannie.'

'So do you.'

She waved his words away. 'You must pass my condolences on to your parents.'

He asked after her father, whose business she was now over-seeing. Her husband would be joining them later in the afternoon; he wanted to meet Francois. She asked after his work, he mentioned the photos he had taken for Patricia, she murmured her approval. They ate the lunch Lilian had prepared – too much meat, too much butter in the vegetables – a meal that suited a wintry climate rather than the clean heat of the day. But that was their way, he remembered, to carry on as if the land had been swapped overnight while they were asleep; they would carry on wearing the same clothes, speaking the same language, eating the same food, even while all around them swirled a different people, different customs. Denise's sons played to their audience, misbehaved until their mother called for Lilian, who came to corral them, her face full of disapproval, this expression giving him a pang: a reminder of Matilda's rebukes. Custard and fruit for dessert, which the boys were allowed to have if they took their bowls to the step outside Lilian's kitchen. And then, as they were having coffee on the patio overlooking the lawn, he said, 'I never knew that Ben kept in touch with you.'

'Well,' she smiled. There was a small smear of lipstick on her front tooth: a lone discrepancy in her otherwise immaculate appearance, which made him feel even more affection for her. 'He was like that.' She looked at him. 'He was always reluctant to talk about you when I asked after you—'

He laid down his glass. 'I'm surprised.'

'I'm not!' She laughed. 'He was jealous of you, Frannie. He knew it was you I always carried a torch for—'

He stared at her.

'Oh, I know I never showed it. I had old-fashioned ideas that the boy should do the asking—'

Her sons came running over from the swimming pool, with their lithe bodies, spattering water from their hair. There was an

279

argument between them, and she got up from her chair, her voice now higher pitched with irritation: 'I told you Mummy had a friend to visit, and if you can't play nicely . . .' It took some time to sort out, and then he watched her as she walked back across the lawn, her hips swaying, looking more self-conscious than before.

'I missed a trick,' he said when she sat down, smoothing her skirt over her knees. She laughed, pushed her hair away from her face, colouring slightly. 'Oh well, it's all water under the bridge.' Then she paused. 'I wanted to look you up a bit later, in the Cape, but you were getting married.'

He let his eyes focus on the view: that particular palette of greens and browns, the flat-topped trees. He was not unused to the sun in Lisbon, but here the sun was more confident, fiercer, the brightness less forgiving. He glanced at Denise; she was toying with the bracelet on her wrist – perhaps she was thinking of his brother, or even of him. He remembered how he used to stay with her, those afternoons, alone in her parents' house: had he not had ample opportunity to hold her, declare himself? Perhaps, he thought, he had never really wanted to make her real; she was more enticing, more arousing if she were unattainable. Ben was brave, craved reality. Whereas he, Francois, even then, idolised the story wrought from the visual. It was this aspect of himself that gave his art the quality that was most admired. But Denise's words did not dismay him; it was, rather, like hearing an account of a different person, one he had left behind. When he went to Cape Town, the desperate love he had for her, and its twin, the jealousy he had for his brother, eventually both faded into a sullen resentment. He had transferred his love to Paula, which in turn had faded, and on and on. Now he was sitting with the girl that his brother had taken from him, while his mind, his heart – even as he tried to push away the thoughts – were full of images and sounds and scents of the young girl his brother had left for him – Rita – as if the interim years of his life were only to be bookended by his brother's loves, both of whom he, too, loved.

She was speaking again: 'But there was something else, Frannie.'

He looked at her. Her eyes were full of tenderness, and she seemed to hesitate, as if she was worried that she would hurt him.

'When Ben and I were going out, I fell pregnant.' She was speaking slowly and softly. 'My parents sent me to a clinic down south. They didn't want your parents to find out and interfere.'

There was silence now: even her sons seemed to have quietened in order for him to hear what she said, unimpeded. The scene in front of him, the palette he had just admired, had become more parched, lost some of its colour.

She gave a small smile. 'Ben felt terrible about it. That's why he kept in touch, and that's why he didn't talk about me.'

He immediately wanted to leave: stand up and walk out, get into the car and drive away. It took all of his will to stay where he was; he could not desert Denise. But the shroud that her news cast over the afternoon, over all he saw, was less about what he had learned than a realisation that arrived with tremendous sadness: this was death. Secrets that you stored up became open for public discussion, without any chance for explanations or mitigations. A past that cannot be recreated: Ben's words all those years ago. A young boy and girl, bound together by something they had created which would never again be recreated – Ben's child, his parents' grandchild – a bond that remained even after what had been created was destroyed. Did Ben ever tell Denise about him and Clare, their struggles and disappointment? Had he even told his wife about his putative, curtailed fatherhood? Now his brother was laid open as if on a slab; his wounds were on display. Dying left you with no privacy. And he ached for Ben, who had tried his utmost to be good, fighting against whatever circumstances he found himself in – some of his own making, true, but who tried his hardest to be good, do good. In dying, all his weaknesses and flaws and fears had come to the surface, as if he had not been cremated but instead thrown into a river, only to rise and float, but distended now, marred now, not the clean, beautiful man he had been.

The husband arrived, and here was some consolation: the man loved Denise. When he took his leave, she accompanied him to the car, her husband staying in the house with the boys, and he took her in his arms, held her to him for many minutes without speaking, and when they separated she had mascara streaking across her cheeks from her tears, which he wiped away gently with his thumb. Take care of yourself, Frannie, she whispered, and he hugged her again, before letting her go, stroking her face. Take care of yourself, Denise.

28

I F the encounter with Denise had taught him anything it was that he had spent most of his adult life without seeing. He returned to London in time for Christmas. A year had passed since he had found Rita, and the memory of that first meeting played in his head as he retraced his steps. He had written a letter; it was neutral enough he hoped, that if opened would not implicate her. But the house was empty, dark. There were the same curtains in the windows and no signs of a change of ownership, but it remained empty for his next three attempts: they were away. Perhaps they had gone to India. Whatever, there was no sign of Rita; his letter remained unposted. It was the following late spring when he next returned to London and made the same expedition. This time, as he rang the doorbell he heard voices inside, and his heartbeat quickened.

Again, it was her mother who opened the door, this time wearing a sari, her hair neatly arranged in a bun.

'Mrs Kalungal, I'm not sure you remember me,' but her expression had already become guarded.

She nodded, then said, 'Wait here, please.'

She retreated, he heard voices, a deep baritone, and then she reappeared; behind her, a man. Not very tall, bald, with tortoise-shell glasses and his arm in a sling.

'My husband,' she said, and then stood to one side.

He offered his hand, and Rita's father took it, with his left hand; it was his right arm that was injured.

'Mr Kalungal,' he said, 'I'm Francois Martin.'

'Yes,' his voice was pleasant, 'I know who you are.' Of the painting of his daughter, of the visit to the cemetery in Brighton, of the week Rita had stayed in Lisbon, her father made no reference.

'I'm sorry to trouble you . . .' he glanced at the sling, and Rita's father followed his eyes.

'It's not serious. My shoulder. I had a fall at work.'

'I'm sorry to hear . . .'

Then they fell silent, and he tried to gather his thoughts.

'I was wondering,' he said finally, 'If I could see Rita?'

Her father regarded him silently. 'She's not here,' he said. 'She's in India.'

Her mother spoke rapidly, and her father nodded but did not reply, nor did he translate.

'She was in India when I last came as well . . .' smiling, trying to lighten his words.

'Yes,' her father said. 'She will be in India for some time.'

They stood side by side, her parents, a barrier. But he did feel what she had mentioned: that gentleness.

'She is staying with my brother,' her father said suddenly.

'I wonder,' he said, 'if I could have an address? So I can write to her?'

They regarded him silently. He glanced at the mother, who was now biting her lip, and he felt guilty at provoking such anxiety.

'You are the brother, are you not?' her father said finally.

'Yes,' he said, 'I'm Ben's brother.'

There was a pause, then her father spoke: 'We are sorry for your loss. But I think it's better that there is no contact between us.'

Us? He meant between the families, just as his own parents had decided to sever links with the Armstrongs. It was as if he was the only person who wanted to remind anyone of how these three families irrevocably shared a history with each other.

'That problem with the university,' her father continued, his choice of words was oblique, but his voice was kind, 'I think it is better for you even.'

Her father was correct, of course: what would be best was that he could forget and move on, not think of Rita for the next twenty years. But there was a nagging voice: not like Denise. I want the chance to make her real.

He nodded, smiled. 'Would you please give her this letter?' He passed over the envelope. 'And would you please let her know that I came to see her?'

'Of course,' and her mother muttered something. Her father hesitated and then he said, 'My wife wants you to know that Rita is well. We spoke to her just last night.'

'That's wonderful.' He was smiling, and he held his hand up in a wave. 'I won't keep you. I hope you recover quickly,' he gestured to her father's shoulder, and then he turned away and as he walked down the street he heard the door close, Rita's parents now out of sight.

It should have ended there, but it didn't. If he asked his parents, as he did, tentatively, at regular intervals, if they had heard from Rita, his mother always expressed some regret: she wished, at some time in the future, to meet Rita again. Not to interfere in her life but simply to talk to her. She had been a charming visitor when she had appeared on their doorstep. If his mother suspected his feelings, she said nothing.

One year he returned to her parents' street, to walk past the house and then on, through the gate at the end to enter the park. If she were returned from India, it was likely that she would bring her niece here to play. He would wait: no need to present himself to her parents and further compromise her in any way. There was a group of young men kicking a football, and as he walked along the path around the park the ball came rolling towards him. He stopped it with his foot and kicked it back. Thanks, mate, one called. They were of Rita's age; they could be her relatives. He had no idea if she had cousins who lived in London; he knew so little about her. What had Gildo said to him when he had learned that Rita was in India? They might get her married. Would these young men, now sitting on the grass, the ball to one side, have heard of any nuptials? He watched them out of the corner of his eye as they talked and laughed. One pulled his shirt over his head to cover his face, revealing a lean, dark, young man's body. Would this be the type that Rita would be offered to? Or someone older, more experienced, more philosophical about what had happened? He tortured himself for several circuits of the park. The young men left, and then so did he, following in their wake, past the house again, no sign of anyone inside.

Back in his flat, the painting he had made of her, from the photograph, before he had known her, remained in its position, in the stack on the floor. Once, in a clear-out, he contemplated burning it, cutting it, before sliding it back between its bedfellows. How he had painted it, those evenings he had spent sketching her first, then preparing the paints: these were vivid memories, as vivid as those he had of the days she had spent with him, sleeping in his bed. And often when he lay in the bed, he felt that he was seeing his environs differently, as if through her eyes: what she would have taken note of and might even now remember, wherever she was. And what she would tell of this to whomever she was with.

It was high summer now in Lisbon. He had just returned from a sojourn in the Algarve, visiting with Gildo and Jacinta, when he received a card with notice to collect a package from the post office in Graça. He assumed it was from his mother, who had taken to sending him books, reviews of his artwork. She seemed to need to write his address on an envelope, to reassure herself that one son remained on this earth.

The sun was hot on his head as he arrived at the collection office. There were two packages, it appeared. One was, as he had expected, from his mother. The other package also had a London postmark, but no postcode, the post officer grumbled; it was lucky they knew his whereabouts.

He did not return to his flat but took his packages to the outdoor café near the Miradouro by the church, where he saw a friend and joined him at his table, ordered a coffee. While his friend was talking to the owner of the café, he browsed through his post. His mother had sent a catalogue for a literary festival in South Africa, to which his father was invited to sit on a panel. The letter enclosed was a query from his mother, asking whether he would like to join them. It was an attractive prospect. He had always liked Cape Town; he could contact his alma mater and offer to give a series of workshops. Further, he could sense that his mother would appreciate his company; his parents would feel stronger when meeting old acquaintances with evidence of at least part of their former lives remaining intact. He listened with half an ear as his friend regaled him of an incident involving one of the many stray cats that prowled the streets, *os gatos de Lisboa*, while his mind revisited his old haunts as a student, the places where his embryonic art career was formed, where he had met Paula; much would have changed by now. He smiled distractedly as his friend neared his punchline, and opened the other package, withdrew a sheaf of typewritten papers, soft bound: a manuscript of some kind. As he sipped his coffee, he scanned the first page:

When I try to remember how it all transpired, my memories always play out in front of me through a filter, as if viewing the past through raindrops, broken shards of glass, a thin gauze, so that depending on why I am casting back, the two figures intersecting are distorted, lucid or faded. There is always a beat in my head.

Just as I tell a tale through my feet when I dance, I can count the steps of each encounter from the beginning: rising, arcing, then falling to its end. Each memory unfolds with its own rhythm, its own tempo, distinct from the other . . .

His heart was now in his mouth. He slipped his hand back inside the envelope and drew out a sheet of paper, this covered with the handwriting from the envelope, which he now recognised:

Dear Francois

I hope that this letter and the manuscript enclosed finds you well, and finds you – I don't know if you are still at this address. This is something I wrote to try to make sense of what happened four years ago now, between me and Ben. I'm sending it to you in case you ever wanted to try and understand how it all came about. When I was writing it, I realised that I wanted the story to end differently. I really hope that given the chance to have lived longer, Ben would have returned to Clare, the woman he loved for so much of his life. I might not have survived that happening. But the truth is I did survive; they didn't. They are together now, anyway, and I take some comfort from that.

After I left Lisbon and told my parents about Ben, I went back to India, and I stayed there for just over three years. But I have been back in London now for some time. I finished my degree a few months ago. I now have an internship at the British Library, and I also work at the library in Charing Cross. When you next speak to your parents, if you think they would like to receive them, please give my best wishes.

Rita

Francois? Francois? The voice of his friend was coming from somewhere near him; he had knocked his coffee over when he had leapt to his feet, his hands gripping the letter, spun around to look at the world around him, his eyes unseeing. Then slowly, he focused, understood. She had done it again: left him clues so he could find her.

29

I T was the moment when her mother had asked her if she wanted them to arrange something that she had understood everything. It was as if by offering one glimpse into a future, her mother had inadvertently shown another: moved aside a screen to a large airy space, the sunlight falling down in shafts, where she could see him on the other side, bending over something, his head turned away from her. When she had started writing about her moments with Ben, she found that she was holding a paper-chain of memories – some of Ben, some of Francois – and it was she who interlinked the two. For she could not imagine a life without one of them, as if a spell had been cast over her, so that she was unable to look beyond the two brothers: a realisation that felt ancient, as old as time. She wrote a farewell to Ben, a celebration of what he had been to her: a brief burst of light, like a comet. And as each encounter touched the page, evolving from beats of a dance to lines on paper, its place was taken by another. But this new story played out on Earth. Not the heavens, nor the nebulous universe of memory. She could spend days, months, years, trying to understand, and in that time anything could happen and everything could change. Her self-imposed banishment held that risk: she could not know that he would not reconcile with Lucie, or even meet someone else, marry, become a father. This was her penance, not a trio of prayers recited at speed: to live without any certainty that he would wait for her, to grow into a woman, to untangle herself from memories of his brother.

On returning to London, and on a break in the second week of her internship, she requested that Ben's book *Daughters of Africa* be brought to a reading room. She read the dedication, the acknowledgements, as she had done before; she had always believed that it was here where she would find Ben's voice. *For Clare; My gratitude to Patricia Zigomo-Walther.* Reading these words no longer pained her; they were a reminder of the work he had done, delving into people's lives with courage, leaving behind a small part of him with whomever he collaborated. She turned over, beyond the contents pages, the list of tables and figures, and started reading the introductory chapter. He wrote well; she was gripped. She had found his first book – the one Francois had lent her – harder to read; perhaps she had been seeking and, on failing, become unreceptive to his thoughts. Today, years later, when she was not looking, she found something.

What these practices shine a light on is how sibling relationships are intensely gendered, so that brothers share and inherit property: be that property land, a house or a wife. It was here, suddenly, where she could hear Ben, standing before her and others in a wood-panelled room, speaking with no notes, while on the slide behind him was projected her image: a young girl in front of a window, looking back over her shoulder. But just as strong as this image was another: Francois in his camp bed, shirtless, raised on one elbow, the taut muscle in his upper arm, his hair falling forward, holding the same book as this under the small lamp, his eyes poring over his brother's words. Had he seen her in these passages? She had wanted to turn back time, to that night when they had sat side by side on the castle wall. *If we answer honestly, we reveal our true nature.* She had felt so close to him, she could have, then, revealed her all to him, in a black night with the life inside her pricking at her skin, burning through her nerves. *Even if it was what I had wished for* – she could hear herself speaking to him – *I was never Ben's. To own,* to give away or leave behind. Sitting in the library, she had decided then what she would do. Over the years she had heard nothing of him and nothing from him, but when she had reached out, he had responded to her letter and the manuscript that accompanied it, in the exact manner she had hoped for.

So, she spent the afternoon looking at the clock; he had said he would arrive at half-past five, when she was finished for the day. The library was quiet. The young mothers and toddlers had all left now, and it was the quiet period before more people arrived on their way from work. At five, she was intending to pop into the small washroom for staff, where she could brush her hair and tidy herself. But as she pushed the returns trolley to its resting place, he stood up from one of the tables.

'Rita. I came early, I hope you don't mind.'

He was smiling at her surprise, and her heart dropped into her stomach. He bent forwards and kissed her on the cheek, and as if he were slicing through time she could suddenly feel the scrape of his jaw against hers. Then, as she was moving back, she felt his hand tighten on her arm, and he kissed her other cheek.

'We do it twice in Lisbon, remember?' he said. 'I know this is London, but you know what I mean.'

She laughed, and he laughed as well, spreading his arms.

'It's wonderful to see you,' he said.

They stood smiling at each other, and then he said, 'Don't let me stop you. I'll wait until you get off work.'

'It's just half an hour more.' Her voice sounded hoarse, and she cleared it. 'I'll be done soon.'

'Then I'll be waiting outside.'

He raised his hand in a small wave and left. For a few moments she remained still, rooted to the spot. The last time, she had stood with him as they looked out to the Tagus, down that river the armada would have sailed. And what she might tell Francois, or she might not, she had not yet decided, as in her mind was another river: sitting up high on its banks, the coconut trees a panorama before them, reflected again in the waters.

The minutes sped past. When she had finished her duties, she brushed her hair, peering at herself in the small mirror above the washbasin in the staff common room. She had spent far too long that morning thinking of what she should wear, settling finally for a favourite top over dark jeans, the long dangly earrings she had bought in Jewtown: a reminder of what she had learned of herself in those dusty, narrow streets. She came out of the building to see that he was indeed waiting outside, leaning against the wall, watching the passers-by. She paused a moment to steady her thoughts.

His hair was brushed back. He was wearing a dark, long-sleeved shirt: he had dressed for the occasion. She had a momentary confusion, a page from her manuscript, a man leaning against the wall, turning to look at her. It would forever be thus, she thought, but then she resisted: only if she made it so. For a moment she watched him, and then he turned and saw her, his face lighting up. As she walked towards him, she saw his eyes sweep over her briefly and felt herself catch her breath at how that made her feel. He straightened up, smiled at her, the dimple she remembered appearing in his cheek.

'It's a beautiful day,' she said.

'It is.'

He gestured towards the embankment. 'There's a nice place on the South Bank. You said you don't live far away from there, so I took the liberty of booking a table. Does that sound all right to you?'

He smiled, she smiled back, and they turned together towards the river. As they walked, they talked. She was renting a room in a house in Peckham. When she returned to London, she had wanted to try to strike out on her own. She was hoping she would get some paid work at the British Library, which was, however, looking unlikely, but for now she was enjoying being back in London. And yes, he was still living in Lisbon. He had spent nearly six months in Zimbabwe and then Mozambique that first year, and the following year he had not left Lisbon at all, a first for him since he had moved there. The result: his first solo exhibition for many years the following summer, in London. Two years ago, he had sold his share of Ben and Clare's flat back to Clare's sister, who was now renting it out as a holiday let. He had reinvested part of the money into the award his parents oversaw with Patricia Zigomo-Walther, and the rest in a small house in Cascais, along the coast from Lisbon, which he now used as his studio.

They fell silent for the last stretch. She tried to think of something to say, but they had exhausted the immediate practicalities. But then, as they neared the restaurant, he stopped and turned to her. 'Can I ask?' he said. 'When you went back, was it all right with your parents?'

He had that same soft look in his eyes as before. His concern for her, his gentleness: she could feel it, just as she had done those years ago.

'I didn't tell them I went to Lisbon or that I stayed with you,' she said. 'I didn't want to involve you in any way. But everything else, yes, I told them.'

He nodded, his eyes still holding hers.

'And it was a shock,' she continued. 'And it was hard for them to hear.' She paused. 'But it was good to go to India.'

'That's great,' he said, smiling. 'Great.'

Then he took her elbow and led her inside, up the stairs to the table that was booked for them, laid for two, looking out at the river.

Her face was more chiselled, which made her lips look fuller. Her hair was slightly shorter, so that it framed her cheekbones even more, brushing against her collarbone when she leaned forward. She was wearing a scoop-necked top made of some soft, floaty material which caressed her shape. Her limbs, her neck, were as slender as ever, but now combined with the new clarity in her expression were even more alluring. If he had ever doubted what he felt for her, well, his heart was pounding in his chest, and he had to hold on to the menu card so that he did not pull her to him, scare her with his longing to hold her. He did not find that time had passed; a filter been removed so that he saw her in a different light, with wiser eyes. Sitting opposite Rita, years after he had first found her, days after he had received her package, he was giddy with the elation he felt at seeing her again.

They ordered; the waiter left.

'The manuscript you sent,' he said. 'I read it from cover to cover.'

Her eyes glittered, but she said nothing.

'It was interesting, you know,' he said, 'to see your perspective of Ben.'

He hoped his voice did not betray how difficult it had been for him to read her words, be drowned in the images that flooded in, even as he had devoured what she revealed.

'I found,' she spoke slowly, 'that I had a photographic memory of what happened.'

He contemplated her words, then said, 'You're good at it. Writing.'

She smiled. 'I've always thought of myself as a dancer.' Then she flushed and laughed. 'It sounds pretentious, I know, but it was something new for me, to express myself through words. I kind of wrote everything down as if I were choreographing a dance . . .'

'Well,' he smiled back, 'I'm not sure if you remember what I told you about Mahler . . .'

'What is best in music is not to be found in the notes.'

He raised his glass to her. 'Here's to that photographic memory of yours.' And then he thought: would she remember all the moments she had spent with him, or was that only reserved for his brother? He took a few seconds to gather himself, resumed: 'I needed to find something that explained why I wanted to put colours on a canvas. And that something wasn't in the actual brush strokes. It was in the story that the picture told, even down to the order in which I paint the different parts.'

'I remember your love poem,' she said. 'To the island women. I'd love to see what you've been doing the last few years.' Then smiling: 'Your flat? With all that light and your paintings? I loved it.'

'Well, Rita,' he said. 'You must visit again.'

'I'd like that.' She lowered her eyes, did not meet his.

Visit again? Now that he had her in front of him, he wanted her never to leave his side. Her hands were tantalisingly close to his on the table; he did not touch them. He only took note that there was no ring on her finger, and no mention yet of a boyfriend, a suitor or a husband.

As their meals arrived, she told him more about her stay in India. She was sure her cousin had suffered from depression, but it was never diagnosed. She and Seline had grown even closer over the last few years: an added bonus to her sojourn in Kerala. Rita had become more proficient in the language. Her uncle had opened part of the house as a guesthouse; she swiped her phone and showed him some photos.

'You'll have to go and stay some time,' she said, and he smiled, nodded, definitely.

She asked about his return to Zimbabwe after so many years, and he told her about Patricia and her daughters, then his long overland journey through Mozambique. They could not distil four years into a dinner, no matter how much they lingered over the meal. So they spent the next couple of hours talking about the things near them: the food, the view of the river, the internship she had secured and the library where she worked. He described the house he now owned in Cascais, which he offered as a workspace for budding artists; he had fashioned three studios, not including his own. It was a short walk to the old wall of the city. As he described it, he could not help but imagine her standing on the balcony upstairs, looking out towards the sea. If he were asked, afterwards, what he could remember of the reunion, he would only be able to describe the shape of her lips, the brief feel of her fingers when she touched his arm, which happened twice. How he felt jealous of everyone she mentioned, of anyone who could know her without compunction, lay claim to her affections with impunity. After he paid the bill, he said he would see her home; the train was packed and they hung on to the straps, unable to talk in the crush.

His feet tried to slow them down, but before long they arrived on her street, and she pointed up: that window there, that was her room.

'It's not big,' she was saying, 'but it has an en suite. And it's super cheap because I dog-sit as well, which suits my landlady. She's away a lot.'

'It's a nice road,' he said.

The trees that lined the street, mature oaks and beeches, watched as he looked on her helplessly: this young woman, this girl, who had possessed his body and mind for the last years, as if a disruptive, winsome spirit. She might have sensed that he was thinking of the time that had elapsed, because she asked, her voice quiet, 'And how are your parents, Francois? Is it any easier for them, four years on?'

He considered the question.

'Probably not easier,' he said. 'But it could be something they have become resigned to. I'm not sure that's the right word. Anyway, they're keeping themselves busy. They're planning a trip to South Africa at the moment.' Then he paused. 'And they send their regards. They'll want to meet up with you if you want to.'

'That's nice.' Her voice was soft.

He smiled, 'And how are your parents? When I last saw them, your father was recovering from that shoulder injury.'

A silence descended.

'You saw my father?'

The air had turned cooler, and a breeze was ruffling her hair, blowing strands across her cheek. She was staring at him, aghast. There was a twist in his stomach as he spoke: 'I went to your parents' house a few times. I left messages, a letter. Did you not know?'

She remained still, her eyes on his, as the silence continued, then slowly shook her head. The atmosphere suddenly shifted. They had spent the whole evening talking of other things: incidental, peripheral things. It felt, suddenly, as it had those years ago, when she was in his flat, sleeping in his bed, and he had felt an extraordinary ease with the young girl he had known only for a few days, who had slotted effortlessly into his life, a feeling that whatever they said to each other was a step towards discovery: about her and, concurrently, himself.

'Well,' he said, after some moments, giving her a weak smile. 'I don't blame them. It was all a bit much. They might have had enough of the Martin brothers . . .'

And then they remained as they were, facing each other on the street, not speaking.

'But why did you go to see my parents?' she said finally.

He looked down at her. He could have made a flippant comment, laughed off the four years he had spent aching for her. But he had learned something – hadn't he? – when he had gone back to his childhood home: learned about how hard his brother had tried to be good, and how blind he, Francois, had been. He knew then that he would tell her about Denise, even though he had not told his parents; about how Ben had strived for redemption, disappointing himself even as everyone around him loved him. The girl needed to know that about his brother. And what did she need to know about him? There was now a hum in his head, the notes of a song, soaring high and low.

He said, 'Because I couldn't bear not knowing how you were or where you were. And even though I have no right at all, I wanted to see you again, Rita.'

She watched him speak, as if she were not only listening to his voice but reading his lips. For a long while she was silent. Again, he had that sensation, that she was not so young, with the way she held herself, the way she received his words with composure. She raised her eyes to his, spoke quietly.

'Why do you think you have no right?' Her voice too was not a whine, a demand; rather she sounded as if she understood everything already but only sought confirmation. None of this surprised him. She could certainly see, feel and intuit: this had been clear from what she had written.

He said, 'Because you're so young, Rita. And because you loved my brother.'

She absorbed his words, her face upturned to his. Someone was approaching, their footsteps sounded behind them, a dog sniffed at his ankles, and then they were alone again.

He found his voice. 'I wanted to see you today to make sure you were all right, but I also know that's not enough for me. It's all I can do to stop myself from touching you.'

Now there was only silence in his head. Mahler had abandoned him, refusing to be party to his inappropriate avowals. Best, he thought, if he could claw back some lightness, offer the girl in front of him a chance to shake his hand and then disengage herself from him. She had sent him a clue, true, but perhaps it was only in order for her to have one last reminder of his brother, before closing the door on the episode with finality.

'If only,' he said, grasping for levity, 'if only I were twenty years younger.'

She did not return his smile, and he allowed it to fade: too difficult to pretend now. Then she tilted her head slightly, so her hair fell against one cheek, as she held his eyes.

'I didn't just leave because of Ben,' she said. 'I left because of you, Francois. I needed time to become a person, not someone's story.'

She had that way, that wisdom, which, coupled with her artlessness, made her irresistible. Whether he would have done then what he did a few moments later if she had not stepped forward, he would not know. But, there was no need to know, because before he could say anything or do anything, she had raised her hand and put her fingers on his mouth, where it felt like they burned against him, and traced his lips, as he stood before her, unable to breathe. Then she drew them away and touched her fingers to her own lips.

He recognised the play from what she had written. When he had read that section, he had had to close his eyes and fight the longing in his chest, because he had wanted to be the recipient of her touch. She knew, he realised, that he would know. What was she saying to him now? He could spend years trying to understand what she meant, but instead he slipped his hand behind her neck and drew her close, kissed her on the mouth, which was as soft as he had imagined. A chaste, closed-lip kiss. She remained where she was, letting his mouth remain pressed against hers. Then he felt her arms slide around his neck, her mouth opened and their tongues met for a long time-stopping breath. When she drew away, he tried to still his heart, pressed his face into her hair, breathing her in.

He said, 'Rita . . .'

She whispered in his ear, 'I want you to come up with me.'

30

HER landlady's bedroom and sitting room were still, except for the sound of the television. The sound of tinned laughter erupted as they passed it, accompanied by the yelp of the dog. They crept up the stairs. She opened the door to her bedroom; he followed her in. It was a few metres square, the bed lay under the window, with the colourful coverlet she had brought back from India thrown over it. On the other side was the wardrobe and her desk, with laptop and lamp, above which were her shelves of books.

'It's cosy,' she said.

They had not moved on entering; they could not move. Their two sets of feet took up nearly all the floor space available. The striped rug she had also brought back from India was obscured with both of them standing on it. He pointed to the photographs she had taken and then blown up, framed and displayed: of the lane leading to the synagogue, the entrance to the antique store, and the Chinese fishing nets arcing up into the sky. 'They're good,' he said. 'But no photo of the lake and the earth bridge.' He smiled at her.

He remembered.

She shook her head: 'I didn't go there. They didn't even know I was back.'

She bent down and undid her sandals, and he followed her example, stepped out of his shoes, one by one, then laid them neatly lengthwise along the door. From where he stood, he inspected the books on her shelf.

'I don't have many,' she said. Then, she caved in: 'Perhaps this isn't such a good idea, there isn't room to swing a cat . . .'

He turned to her, smiling. 'This is an excellent idea.' Then he gestured around: 'I like seeing your things.'

He reached over and picked up a photo from the shelf, of Mira on her First Communion Day. 'She's grown,' he mumbled, then briefly touched her image: holding Mira's hand, the sun glinting off her sari. He ran his fingers along her books and then picked one out: an old dog-eared copy of *Jane Eyre*, showed it to her with a small smile. And then, further along, he picked out another, stared for a few moments at the cover: *War and Peace*. When he replaced it, he continued facing the shelves. She was not sure whether he was still looking, until he reached forward again and pulled out the copy of his father's novel, which Ben had given to her, which his parents had refused to take back from her. She had written about how she had held one end and Ben the other; Francois would be thinking of that now, and she could not breathe. But he said nothing, returned the book to the shelf and let his fingers touch some of the trinkets she had brought back from the antique shop. Then he looked up, pointed to the small en suite, 'May I?'

She nodded, and with one stride he was inside, squeezing around the door and closing it, and she heard the water running. She looked around frantically. She pushed some of the cushions on the bed to one side. She threw her jacket into the wardrobe, flung her bag on top, shut the door. He reappeared, filling the small room with his height and broad shoulders, something he seemed to be aware of because he sat down on the bed as if to free up some space, and she squeezed past his legs, feeling his fingers briefly brush against her as she moved past, slipped into the bathroom, closed the door, leaned against it.

Before they had left the banks of the great wide river, those years ago, Seline had said: this river is full of people who have drowned themselves because they couldn't have a life with the person they loved. She had turned and looked out at the water, had seen only the expanse of green-grey water, the reflection of the hills around them. It was a benign and beautiful vista, in contrast to what her cousin had said; but then Seline had continued: if we can choose, then how lucky we are . . . She did not imagine that her cousin was prescient, but that night, back in the old house in Mattancherry, her cousin's words had returned, and she had imagined herself walking into those waters, fully clothed. It was a vision that had not revisited her until now, this moment, standing in her small tiled bathroom. She could feel the river in her mouth, while next door Francois sat – alive, warm and near – after years of wondering whether she would or should see him again.

And what had she learned just a few minutes ago? That he had tried to find her, visiting her parents, walking in the park hoping to catch sight of her; she smiled to herself at that thought. What had he just said: that's not enough for me. What he needed to know: it was not enough for her either. She could hear nothing. He seemed to be sitting still, content to be surrounded by her things. He was waiting for her in her room, and she knew the move that was to follow whether in the next year, the next month, the next day, the next minute: the beat was already playing in her head. She undressed herself before she lost her nerve, pulled her bath-time sarong off its hook on the door and tucked it around her. And then she stepped back into the room.

His fingers were tapping on his knee, but he stopped mid-beat when he saw her, when she flicked off the light and let the sarong fall off her, onto the floor. He opened his mouth, to say something, but she moved forward, bent down and was suddenly kissing him, kissing him deeply, feeling his warmth, her body trembling against him. His hands were in her hair, and then she felt herself lifted off her feet so that she was on the bed, and he was on his side next to her, kicking off his jeans and pulling off his shirt.

It was impossible not to think of the first time with Ben. But Ben was nowhere in the room; he was in the pages of her manuscript, in a memory. There was no doubt that it was Francois touching her, and that he was everywhere: on her skin, in her bones and in her heart.

He had pushed aside the curtains because he said he wanted to see her, and the moon was complicit: huge and round and voluptuous, bathing them in a soft glow. She lay on her stomach, watching him stretched out beside her. He was tracing her spine with his palm, moving it down to the backs of her thighs and then up again: long, sweeping strokes. He was smiling, and in answer to the question in her eyes, he leaned forward and kissed one buttock and then the other – 'we do it twice in Lisbon, remember' – as she laughed, blushing, hiding her face in the pillow.

It was quiet now. He was gentle again, tender, after the torrent earlier. He had lost himself in her. And with that thought she remembered the insistence of his tongue, his hands pinning hers above her head, the strength of his body moving hard against hers: a memory which sent a tremor through her. She shifted slightly so his lips were now on her hip.

'They all say hello, you know,' he mumbled into her skin. 'Ricki and Moises and all those boys in Lisbon. They've asked after you every time I've seen them. I've always just said you were fine, hoping that was true.'

'How are Gildo and Jacinta?'

'Very well. They couldn't believe it when I told them I'd be seeing you. They send their love.'

She watched as he buried his head in her stomach, feeling his breath against her.

'Can I stay?' he muttered. 'I don't want to get you into trouble with your landlady.'

'Quite the opposite. She'd be ecstatic if she knew you were here.' She threw her head back theatrically: 'You're ravishing, Rita! You should be out! Out!'

304

He laughed. 'You *are* ravishing.' His teeth scraped against her shoulder. 'Delicious. I could have you for breakfast, lunch and dinner. I'm trying my hardest to hold back a bit, behave like a gentleman.'

The deference was gone, the restraint; she could not have imagined an exchange like this when he had arrived to meet her at the library. But now, suddenly, accoutrements had been stripped away, and they were lying naked as if reborn. And while unplanned, there was an intoxicating absoluteness in feeling the warmth of his body next to hers, in hearing his voice coming from deep in his throat, these words. She had felt the same, she remembered, that other time: that the moment had been fated. But the thought was only that; she did not repeat it, only let it dissolve on her tongue.

She watched as he laid his head on her shoulder, and she pushed his hair back from his forehead.

'You're the one who's delicious . . .'

'What, little old me?' He was grinning widely.

'You are.' She paused. 'And I know you're not short of admirers . . .'

'Well,' he reached forward and kissed her neck. 'As long as you admire me . . .'

She could feel his tongue now on her throat, his fingers brushing against her breast, his thumb circling the nipple. Her body was alive to his touch, but it was the absence of any denial that made her move slightly away. He sensed the change and stopped, lifted his head.

She tried to keep her voice casual, but failed, even to her own ears: 'So have you been on your own, all this time?'

The query hung between them. They were so close that their breath mingled, but she could feel herself moving backwards as if being pulled from behind.

'I've not met anyone,' he said finally, holding her eyes. 'But I've not been celibate, if that's what you're asking.'

And then, he spoke again, his eyes softening in that way she remembered so well, his voice quiet: 'Does that bother you?'

She turned away. 'A little.' Angry at the tears which arrived as she spoke, surprised at the hot wave that went through her. She glanced at him and saw the concern in his eyes. He would always expect, she realised, for her to match his ease with the ways of the world; and she would always lag behind, unable to catch up. She turned her face away; her throat was tight with anguish even though she had prepared herself for just this revelation. This, here, lying in her bed with him was, for her, momentous. And for him?

There was a long silence, when she could not look at him. She crossed an arm over her breasts, felt her skin grow cold under his touch. Now when he laid his head next to hers on the pillow, his hand on her hip felt tentative, as if asking permission. He was now as she had found him, all those years ago: careful with her, careful of not breaking her.

He spoke suddenly into the quiet, his voice low. 'It was always you I wished I was with, Rita, even imagined I was with. It wasn't healthy and it wasn't fair. It was a sort of madness.' Then, 'Does *that* bother you?'

'A little,' she whispered. 'It's a bit strange to know that.'

She looked at him; his eyes were still on hers.

'I'm not . . .' she searched for the right word, 'I'm a person, Francois. I'm not a photo or a painting.'

He regarded her silently and then laid a hand on her cheek, his thumb stroking her cheekbone. They were quiet for some time.

'You asked me that time – do you remember? – what I thought of you when I found the photograph.' He was speaking softly. 'I thought you were beautiful, anyone would. But then I found you, and you were even lovelier in person and inside here,' and he tapped her gently on her chest, his fingers lingering before returning to her hip. 'And in the same way, being here with you like this is more wonderful than I ever imagined. Because you're real to me, very real to me, Rita.'

She said nothing, and he turned slightly, drew his hand away and leaned back on the pillow, his arm over his head. He looked defeated suddenly, as if he was certain he had lost her, and his assumption pained her. Her heart quickened; she felt a sensation move through her, a realisation of something.

'I'm not going to copy your question,' he said, then gave her a weak smile before turning his head away again. 'I'm not sure I can bear to know.'

'Well,' she said, 'there hasn't been anyone.'

She regarded him through her eyelashes. She had an urge to stroke his cheek, feel the scratchiness of his jaw, then dig under his skin and lift out that thin film of sadness that he carried inside him, perhaps unaware of it himself. Just as she did, she thought: that's something we have in common.

'My parents wanted me to get married when I was in India,' she continued. 'To a pharmacist, like my sister-in-law. They didn't make a big deal. They just offered me that way out.'

He did not look at her, did not say anything. She watched as his chest rose and fell with his breathing.

'I didn't want that life,' she said, and then he turned, and his eyes on hers made her heart stop.

'Are you sure?' he asked.

'I've never been surer,' she said.

He reached over and traced her mouth with his finger. She felt her body melt into the bed, her head falling back onto the pillow just as he was raising himself on his elbow beside her.

She asked him, 'Will you ever be able to forget, that I knew Ben first?'

He smiled into her eyes, shook his head.

'But I don't think I have to,' he said. Then, quietly, 'What about you, Rita?'

She touched his lips and said, 'All I feel is you, in the here and now.'

He kissed her: he tasted sweet and troubled and full of desire. His hands ran lightly over her belly, his thumb slipping momentarily into her navel, then down below. His touch was feather-light this time, like brushstrokes in the air; she could barely feel him. He was bent over her, like he bent over his canvases, as if he was painting her image with his breath. A new image, not the young girl looking back, but who she was now, in this bed, with him. The warm rush rippled through her, she felt her body arching upwards and his mouth was on hers as if to catch the sound that came from her throat. Then he was pushing her legs further apart and was inside her again.

She closed her eyes, breathed in and out, as if expelling a spirit. He pulled her on top of him, so that her hair fell around them, pressed her to him and whispered, stay with me, Rita. Don't leave me again. His eyes were dark with longing. As he spoke, his hands slid around from the base of her spine so that they were at her hip bones, holding her close. And it came to her suddenly, from inside her, to her lips: I won't leave you. I'm yours to keep.

Acknowledgements

My deepest gratitude to my agent Stan, editor Alison Rae, Jan Rutherford, Kristian Kerr, Vikki Reilly, Edward Crossan, Jamie Harris and the rest of the team at Polygon, and copy-editor Ailsa – thank you all for your wisdom and encouragement. And to the Kalayil clan, the Peacock clan and all my wonderful friends whose enthusiasm and support mean so much to me.

My thanks to the scholars whose work on land reform and women's rights in sub-Saharan Africa informed and inspired me: Anne Whitehead, Dzodzi Tsikata, Maureen Kambarami, Lesley Gray and Michael Kevane.

The KAITE project in Zimbabwe, which supports small-scale, sustainable farming, and SOS Children's Villages are real-life initiatives that also inspired me and deserve recognition for the tremendous difference they make to people's lives.

Thank you to James: for filling my life with words and song.

And to my two precious daughters: be brave, be strong.